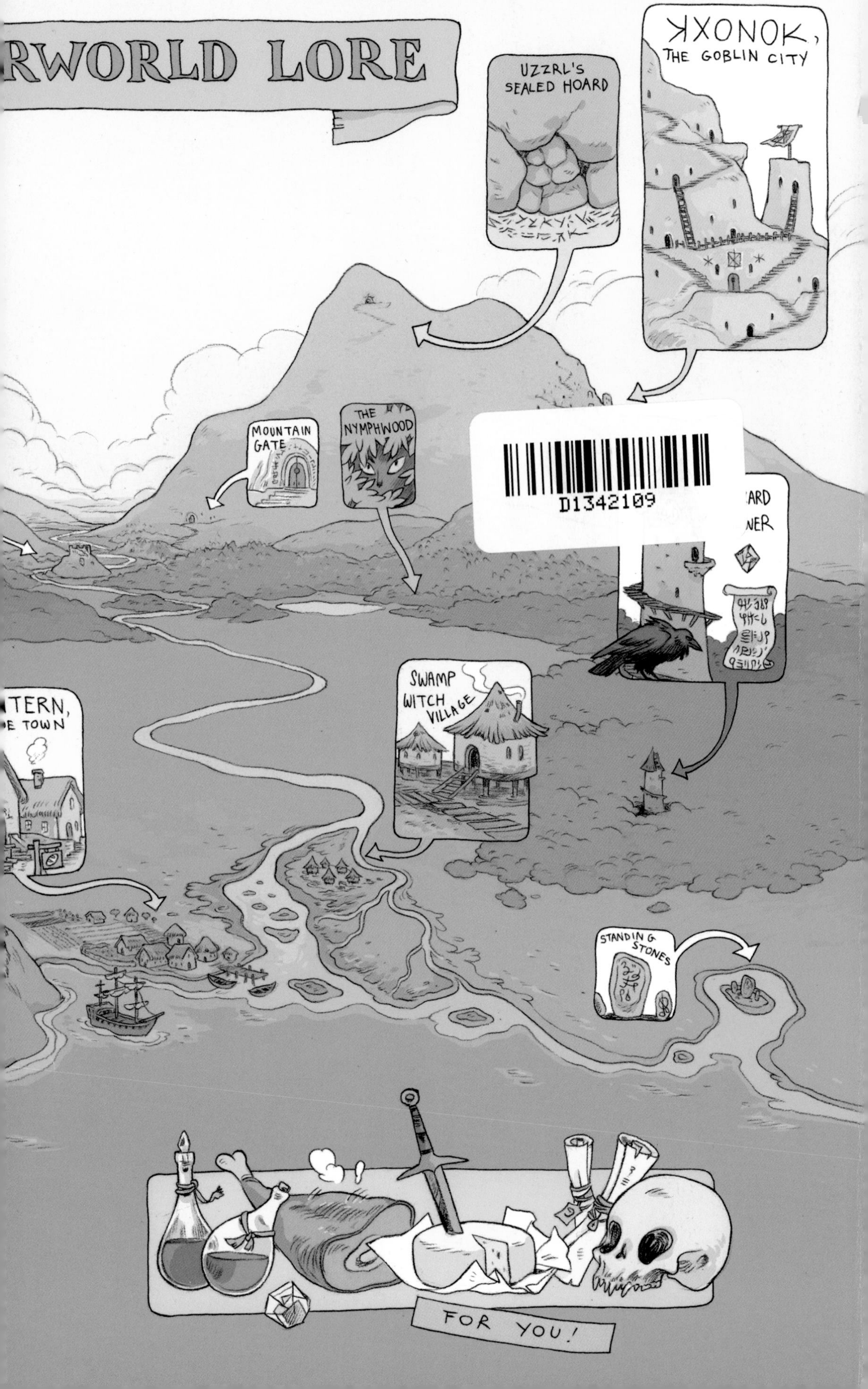
RWORLD LORE
UZZRL'S SEALED HOARD
KXONOK, THE GOBLIN CITY
MOUNTAIN GATE
THE NYMPHWOOD
ARD
NER
SWAMP WITCH VILLAGE
TERN,
E TOWN
STANDING STONES
FOR YOU!

Layout & Production by Tricia Ramos

IMAGE COMICS, INC. • **Robert Kirkman**: Chief Operating Officer • **Erik Larsen**: Chief Financial Officer • **Todd McFarlane**: President • **Marc Silvestri**: Chief Executive Officer • **Jim Valentino**: Vice President • **Eric Stephenson**: Publisher / Chief Creative Officer • **Corey Hart**: Director of Sales • **Jeff Boison**: Director of Publishing Planning & Book Trade Sales • **Chris Ross**: Director of Digital Sales • **Jeff Stang**: Director of Specialty Sales • **Kat Salazar**: Director of PR & Marketing • **Drew Gill**: Art Director • **Heather Doornink**: Production Director • **Nicole Lapalme**: Controller • **IMAGECOMICS.COM**

the Hchom BOOK

by
Marian Churchland

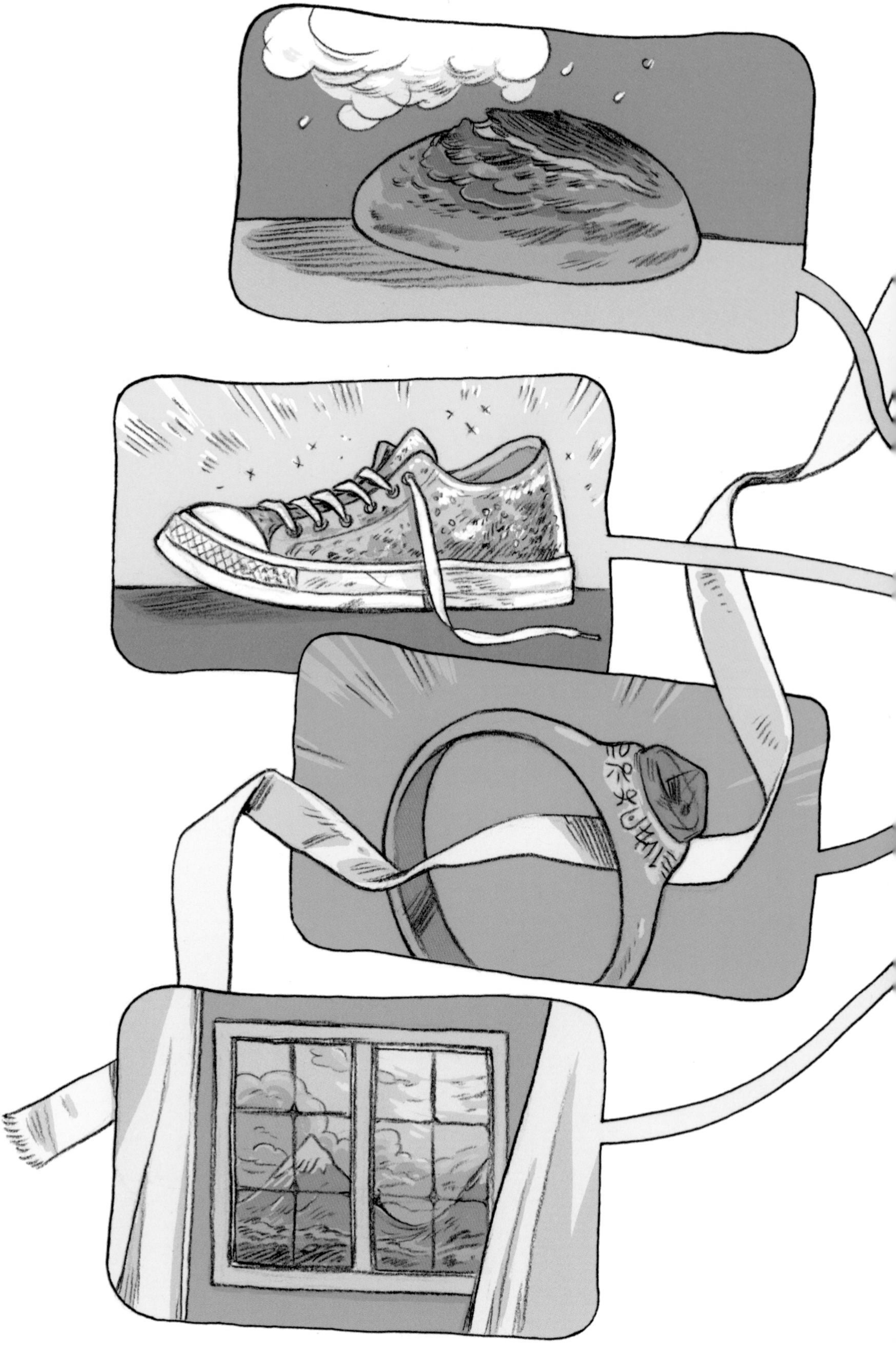

Contents

Introduction:
Concerning
Goblins

Before Hchom, I drew myself in a cartoonish but mostly literal way. I took my role as a portraitist seriously, and included all my features as I saw them, but I was also deeply, deeply self-conscious. I needed people to think I wasn't hideous, so I told a muted version of the truth, and as a result, communicated absolutely nothing.

I was a mess while I was working on this blog. For nearly its entire span, anxiety ruled my life, and all my energy went into maintaining the illusion that I was coping, that I was good. I'm sure it's no coincidence, then, that my first goblin drawing was for a post about a jacket that I'd named the "bad jacket". The goblin was patchy, stubbly, and perfectly hideous: a flip-off to my more artificial portraits. It acknowledged the part of me that is unashamedly ugly—that is grabby, selfish, hoarding, and gluttonous.

From that point on, the goblin functioned as a kind of drag persona, wearing all the things I was otherwise too timid to wear; admitting freely that it didn't want to share its cake with anyone; entering a cafe and buying five or six entire pastries, all for itself, with absolutely no sense of embarassment; spending $100 on a fist-sized sparkly rock because why not. It often made horrifyingly unwise decisions, but it made them confidently, and with no reference to anyone else. Unlike me, it knew exactly what it wanted.

I don't believe that grabbiness and selfishness and hoarding and gluttony have much true merit if any, but I do think that all of them, that want, slick and ugly, will always be there, swimming around in the depths, kicking up little currents and eddies that make their way to the surface and divide its calm. That monster is not moral, but its connection with life is direct and immediate. I see it when I look at these posts, when I think about what this website meant to me in a dark time. I see a thirst for life, an understanding that it is good, that I should want it.

I believe in respecting and befriending our monsters; that there is comfort to be found in that connection, as well as wisdom. Only something that has lived its life in darkness knows how to guide us through it, so here, in this unserious and cartoonish form, is a slice of both my darkness and my path through.

A brief note on the organization:

I haven't treated this book as an archive of the blog. I've edited posts for size, and contextual clarity, and occasionally for style, though I've kept the basic content intact. I've redrawn old art in a few cases, or given it a new coat of paint, and I've sorted everything into chapters (which are internally chronological). Hchom.com remains untouched.

Chapter 01:

The Hchom Larder

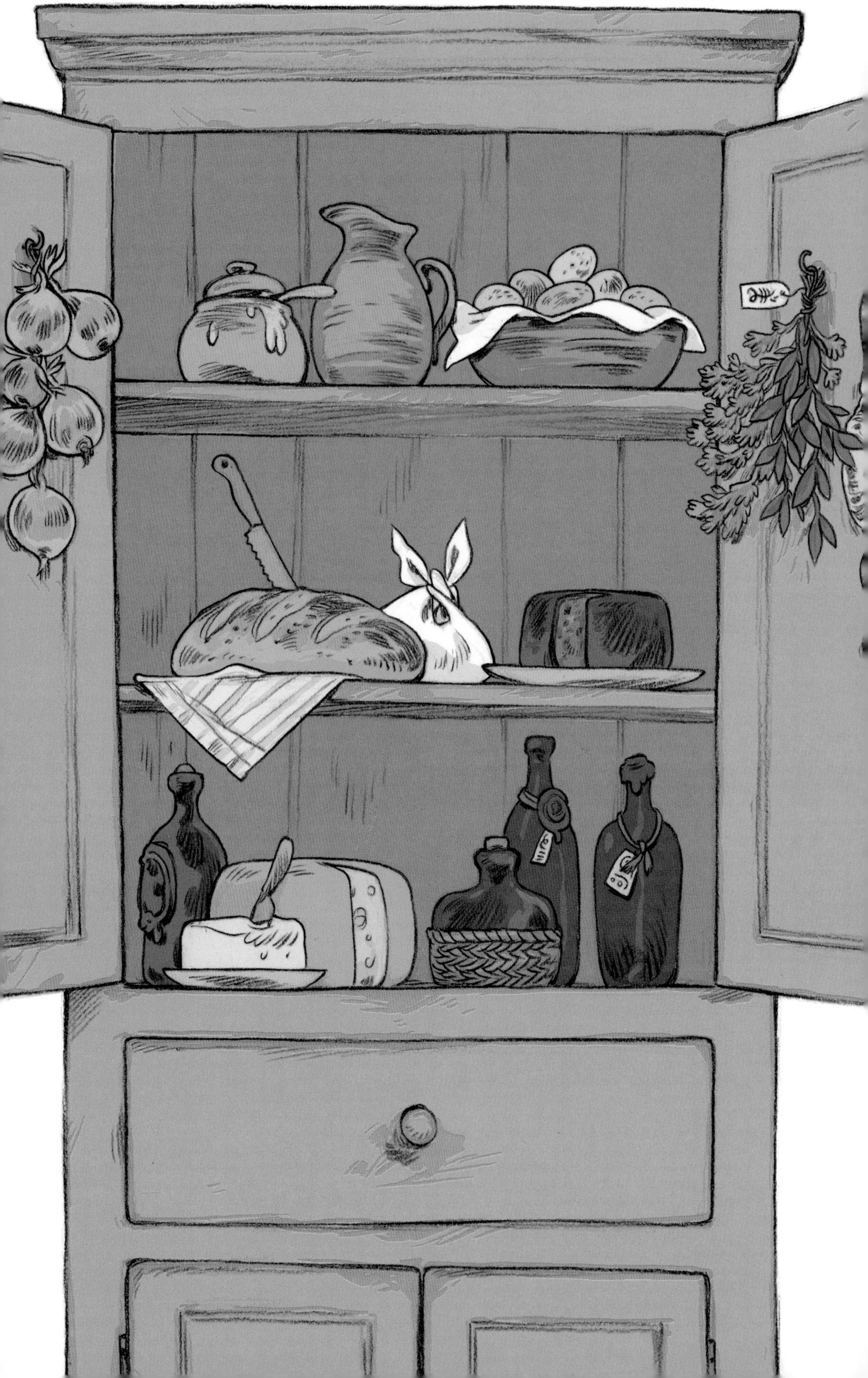

I believe in feasting on the eve of battle, by which I mean there's no knowing what lies ahead. It could be victory or it could be death, so you might as well approach it feast-first, and that's as natural a way to begin this book as I can think of.

My fantasy larder owes its existence to all the stories I've read—especially those from my childhood—that understand the importance of interrupting a period of anxiety and peril with a generous snack: like Bjorn's table in *The Hobbit*, Badger's hospitality in *The Wind in the Willows*, and even Bastian's carefully rationed sandwich and apple in *The Neverending Story*.

I've spent a lot of time imposing scarcity on myself, trying to be vigilant—if not stringent—about what I eat, how much slack I give myself, how I fill my hours and minutes. No doubt that's why I search for ways to protect my love of food, my occasional laziness, my willingness to kill time on nothing but time.

Many of us live with more anxiety and peril than we know what to do with. We could all stand to have that interrupted. So in the tradition of Bjorn and Badger, I'm opening my larder to you and sharing my plenty. If I ever welcome you to my home in real life, I'll do my best to secure us (each) a beautiful pie. In the meantime please view all of this, though fictional, as literally as you possibly can.

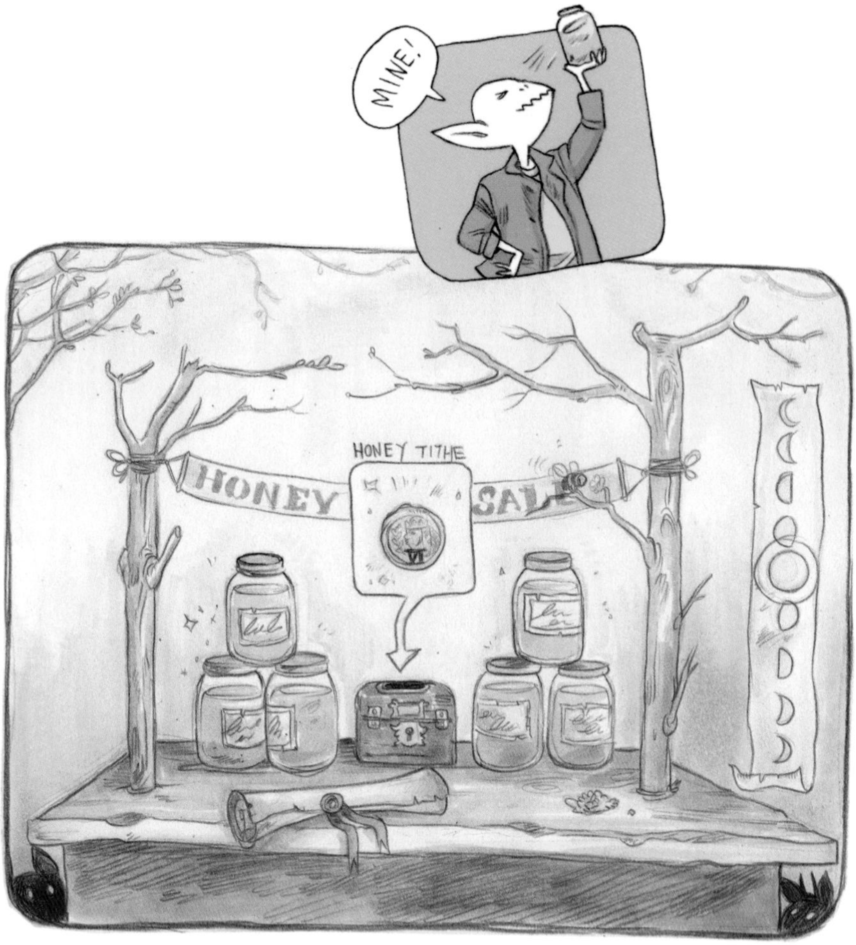
MINE!
HONEY TITHE
HONEY
SAL

Fantasy Honey

(02/16/2010) *The other day I was out walking, and I encountered this little stand selling honey (and it was the stand doing the selling, because it wasn't manned by anyone). It may have been the 13-degrees-and-sunshine-in-February vitamin D high, but I thought it was the most amazing thing I'd ever found. See above. At least that's what it looked like, as far as I was concerned. I imagine it appears when the moon is full, and only if the person searching for it is Pure of Heart. I promptly fed its slot a tidy $6, and ran off with my honey.*

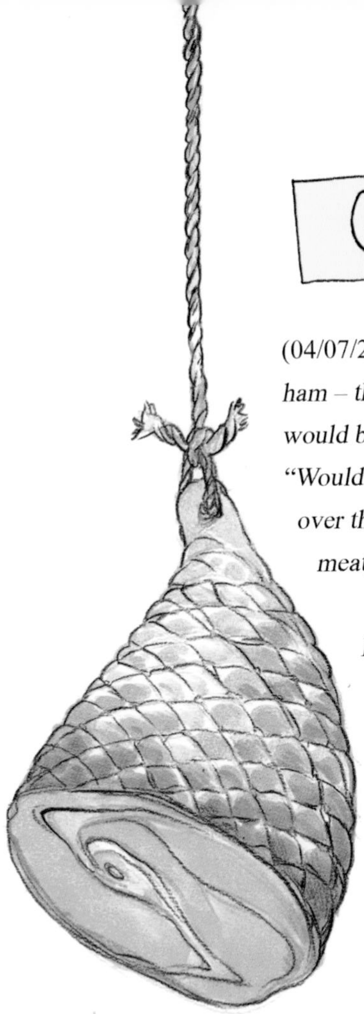

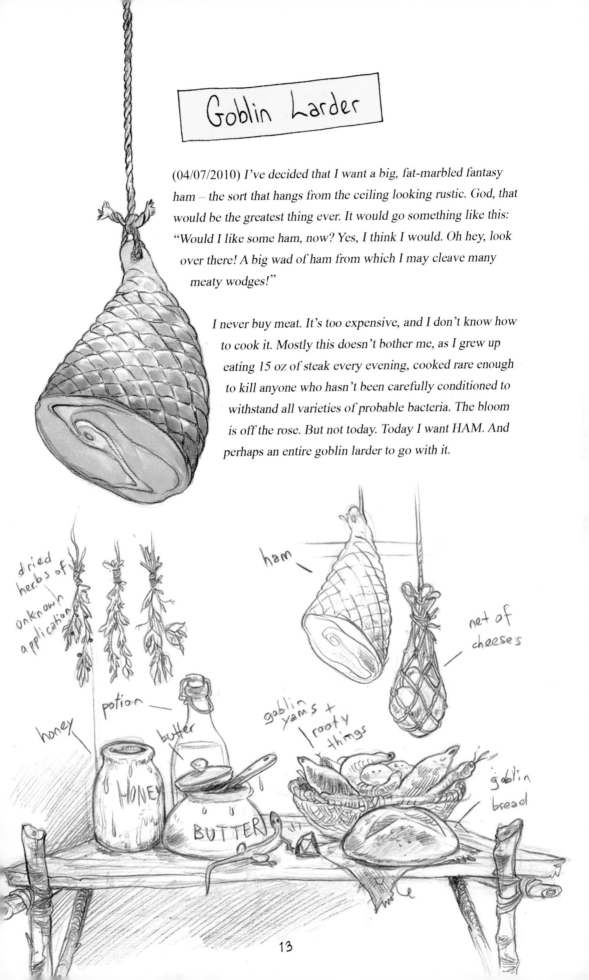

Goblin Larder

(04/07/2010) *I've decided that I want a big, fat-marbled fantasy ham – the sort that hangs from the ceiling looking rustic. God, that would be the greatest thing ever. It would go something like this: "Would I like some ham, now? Yes, I think I would. Oh hey, look over there! A big wad of ham from which I may cleave many meaty wodges!"*

I never buy meat. It's too expensive, and I don't know how to cook it. Mostly this doesn't bother me, as I grew up eating 15 oz of steak every evening, cooked rare enough to kill anyone who hasn't been carefully conditioned to withstand all varieties of probable bacteria. The bloom is off the rose. But not today. Today I want HAM. And perhaps an entire goblin larder to go with it.

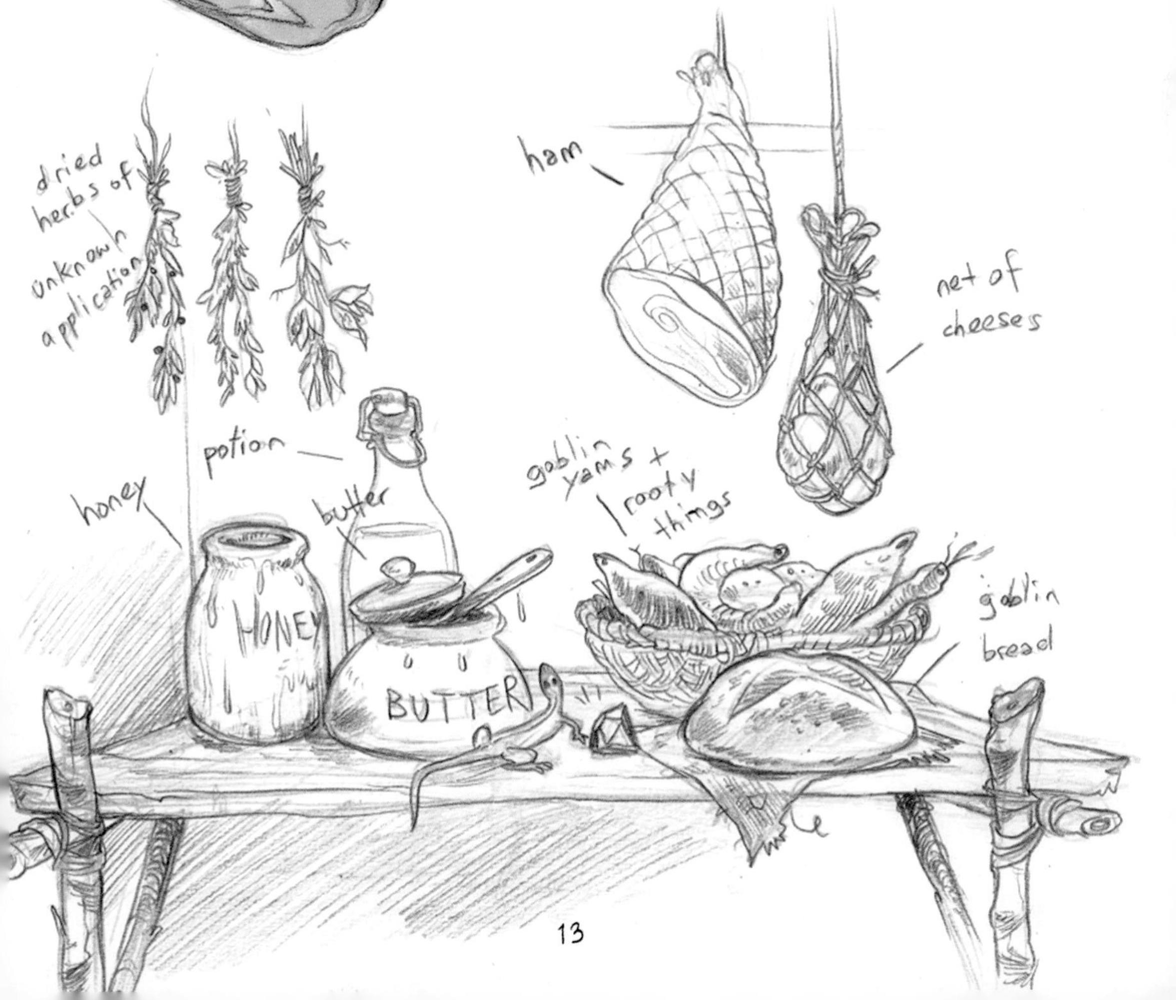

dried herbs of unknown application
ham
net of cheeses
potion
honey
butter
goblin yams + rooty things
goblin bread
HONEY
BUTTER

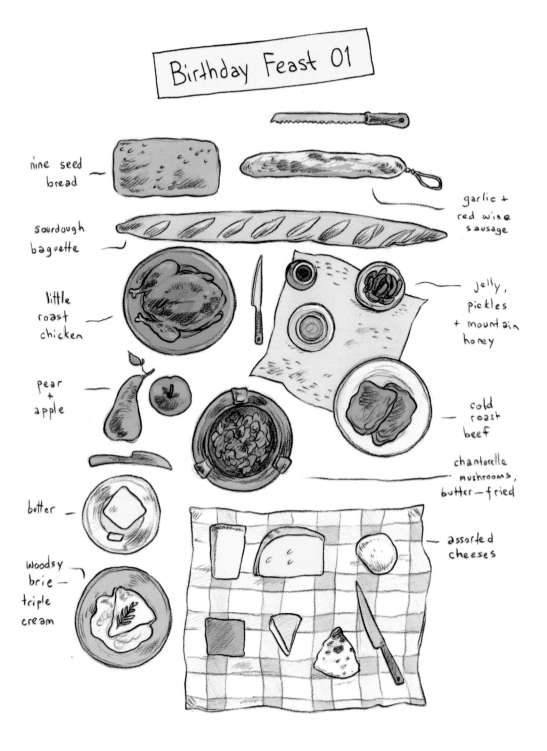

Birthday Feast 01

- nine seed bread
- sourdough baguette
- little roast chicken
- pear + apple
- butter
- woodsy brie — triple cream
- garlic + red wine sausage
- jelly, pickles + mountain honey
- cold roast beef
- chantarelle mushrooms, butter—fried
- assorted cheeses

(06/16/2010) Yesterday was my birthday. I spent most of the day collecting components for this, the finest feast ever. Sadly I was cameraless, but the drawing is fairly accurate. I want to do it all over again every day forever.

Birthday Feast 02

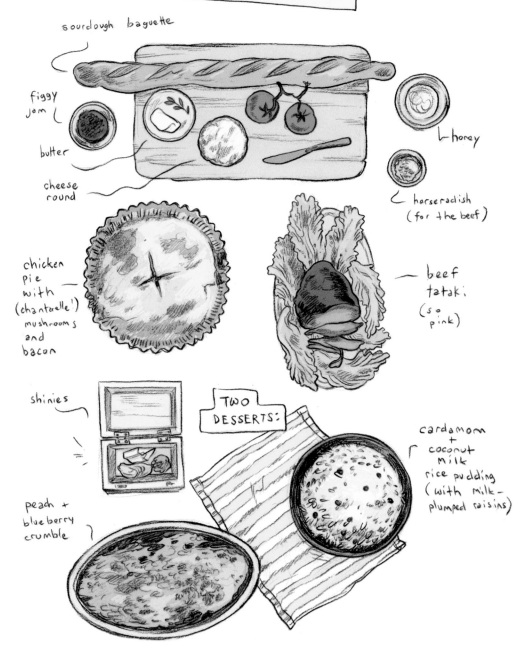

sourdough baguette

figgy jam

butter

cheese round

honey

horseradish (for the beef)

chicken pie with (chanterelle!) mushrooms and bacon

beef tataki (so pink)

shinies

TWO DESSERTS:

cardamom + coconut milk rice pudding (with milk-plumped raisins)

peach + blueberry crumble

(06/28/2010) *On Saturday, my friends Sachi and Kimi made me a birthday dinner, and look, it was totally out of my hands, OK? It was like a giant supercomputer from the future took my original birthday feast, processed all the information, did some calculations using advanced alien technology, and came up with a new, superior birthday feast. With TWO DESSERTS. Nobody knows my tastes better than these people. If I had to choose my last meal on earth, I would want them to cook it for me, and I would die a happy woman.*

Border (brand) Crumbles

- taste associations: like the cookies my Irish grandmother would sparingly feed me when I played Robin-Hood Lego at her house.

Hob Nobs

- reliability: very high
- needs more: butter
- needs less: not butter

COUNTRY CHOICE
ORGANIC

"Country Choice" vanilla sandwich biscuits

- tea dipping: Yes.
- would be improved by: jammy fruit centres.
- best feature: proper vanilla, not fake.

Classic "Fruit creme"

- usually a bit stale
- will still eat the whole box

Bird's Nest Cookies

pro: I make them, so they'll be good

con: I have to make them

Peanut Butter and Jam

- I've never actually tried these, but the concept seems sound.

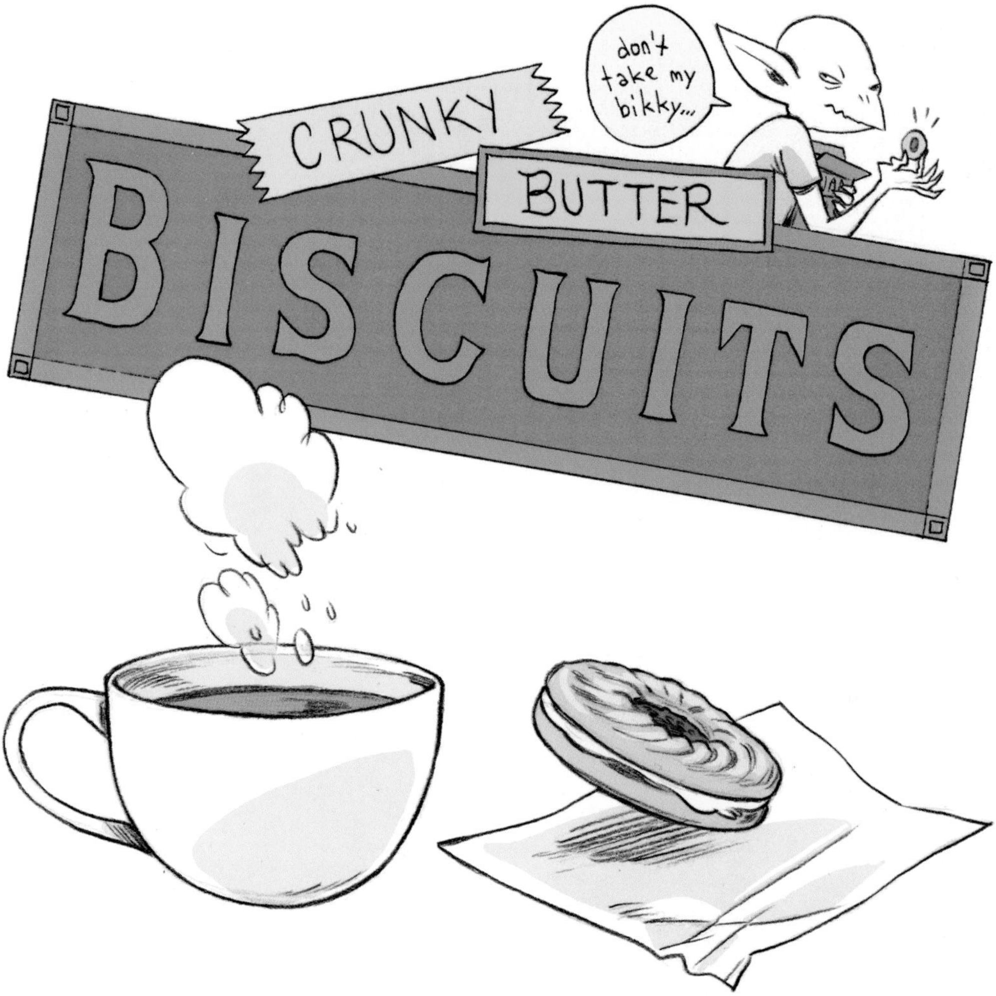
don't take my bikky...
CRUNKY
BUTTER
BISCUITS

I feel that biscuits deserve a lot of margin space, so I've given them a whole two-page spread. They are the quintessential break snack, as in, by eating one or two you can claim fifteen minutes for whatever sedentary time-wasting you like best.

My favourite biscuits tend to fall into the oaty category, but I'm also very fond of anything that sandwiches dense vanilla creme (and I mean it when I say dense, because I've noticed a recent trend for frothy light filling with no firmness, and come on, people, don't waste my time). When I can find a decent quality vanilla creme sandwich biscuit with a jammy fruit centre, I'm dead and in heaven.

Let me also note that while I'm usually a coffee person, I believe the stereotype applies, here: biscuits go with tea.

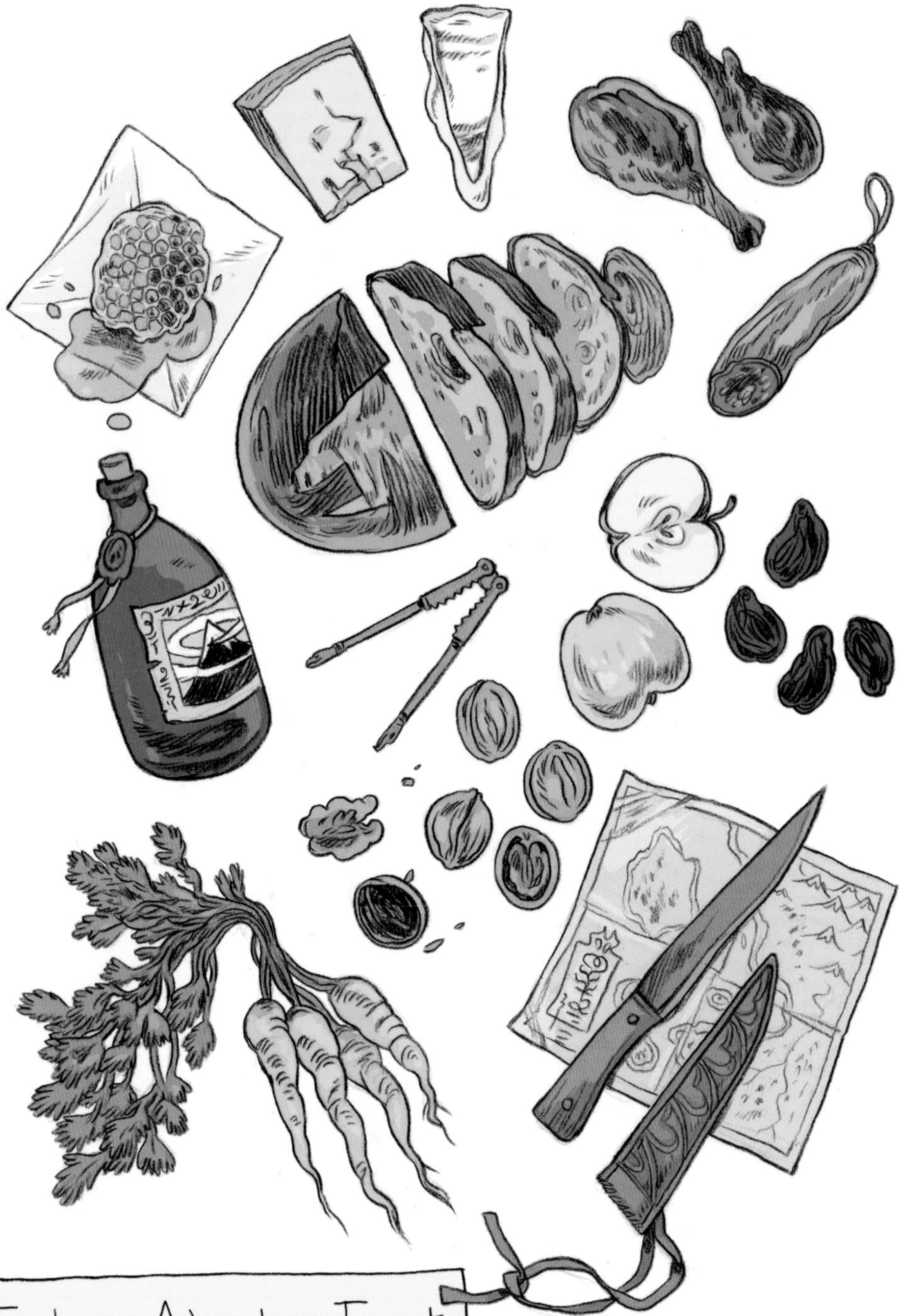

Fantasy Adventure Feast

My sister and I will often get together for a fantasy adventure feast. I don't have any strict guidelines, except that the food should be roughly convincing in whatever fantasy setting you like best, and it should be something theoretically packable. As in, if you carried it around with you all day in a rustic satchel it wouldn't be ruined (and if you want to ignore that last bit, then Fantasy Tavern Feast works just as well).

Five Breads

(06/09/2011) *Some while back, a commenter challenged me to list my four favourite breads. Now, after much hardship and personal sacrifice, I have chosen five (one more for the cheap seats).*

1. Whole Wheat from Baguette and Co.
They actually no longer make my real favourite, which was called "Ancient Grains Bread", dense and dark and perfect. But this is also excellent and versatile.

2. Pecan and Dried Fruit from Terra Breads
If I had to nominate an enduring favourite from the list, this might be it. It's like a Bran Brack, so thick with raisins and nuts it's nearly fruitcake. Best buttered toast ever.

3. Walnut from Terra Breads
This bread is my traditional choice for leftover roasted-bird sandwiches. It's my Old Reliable.

4. Multigrain from Beyond Bread
I'm also very fond of the Peasant Bread, here. Dense, hearty stuff. Good for fantasy adventures.

5. Porridge Loaf from Fife Bakery
This is a retroactive substitution, but I had to get it on the list because Fife bakery is incredible, and this bread in particular has a delicious, unusual crumb, really a lot like a bowl of porridge baked into a loaf.

THE CRUNKY SALAD

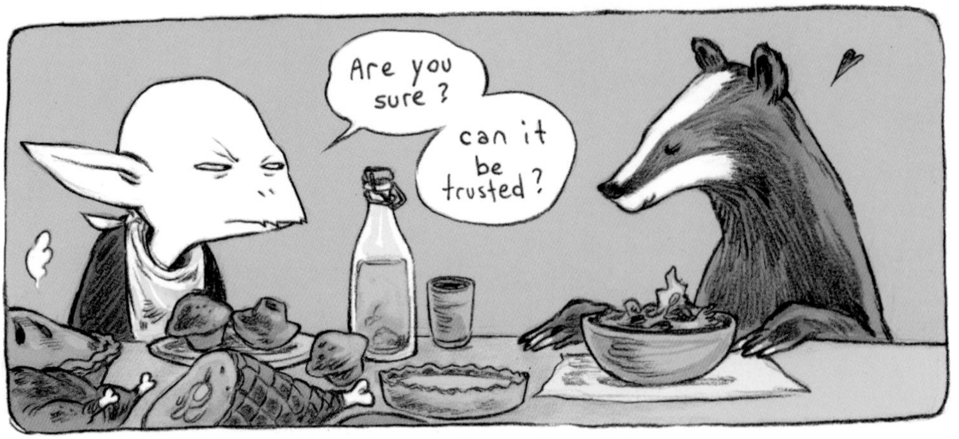

Are you sure ?
can it be trusted ?

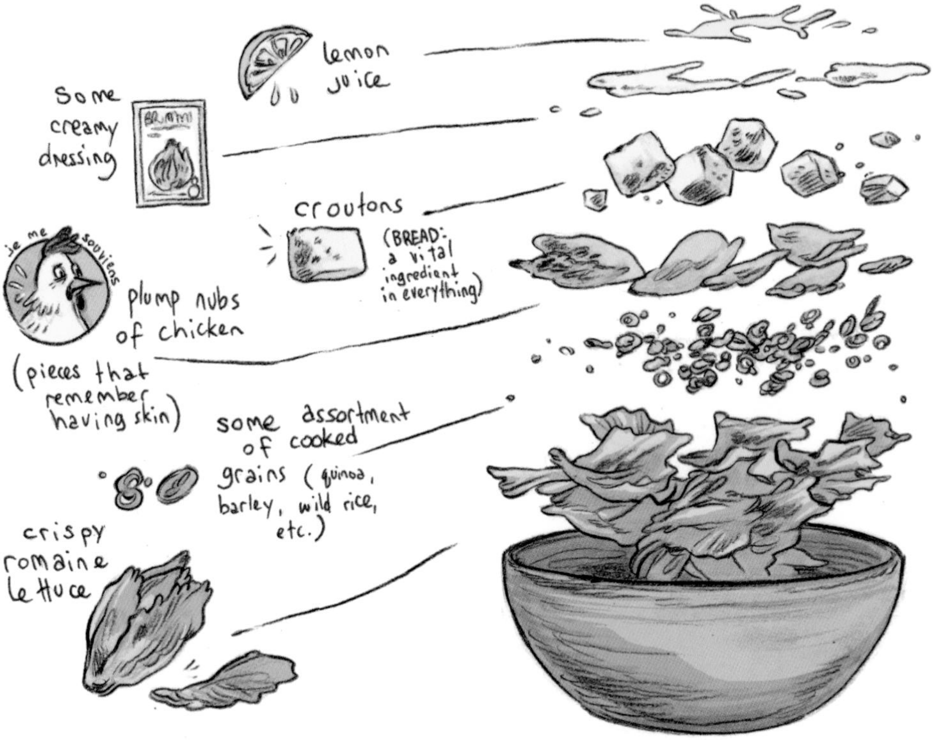

lemon juice
Some creamy dressing
croutons
(BREAD: a vital ingredient in everything)
je me souviens
plump nubs of chicken
(pieces that remember having skin)
some assortment of cooked grains (quinoa, barley, wild rice, etc.)
crispy romaine lettuce

(07/27/2011) *I used to believe that salads were something people inflicted on themselves as part of some unpleasant dieting ritual. How wrong I was! This is my "crunky salad", and what I've been eating nearly daily (at least at the beginning of every week, while the allowance is still holding up). Note that I often add a hard-boiled egg, making it, I guess, a kind of Oyako-salad.*

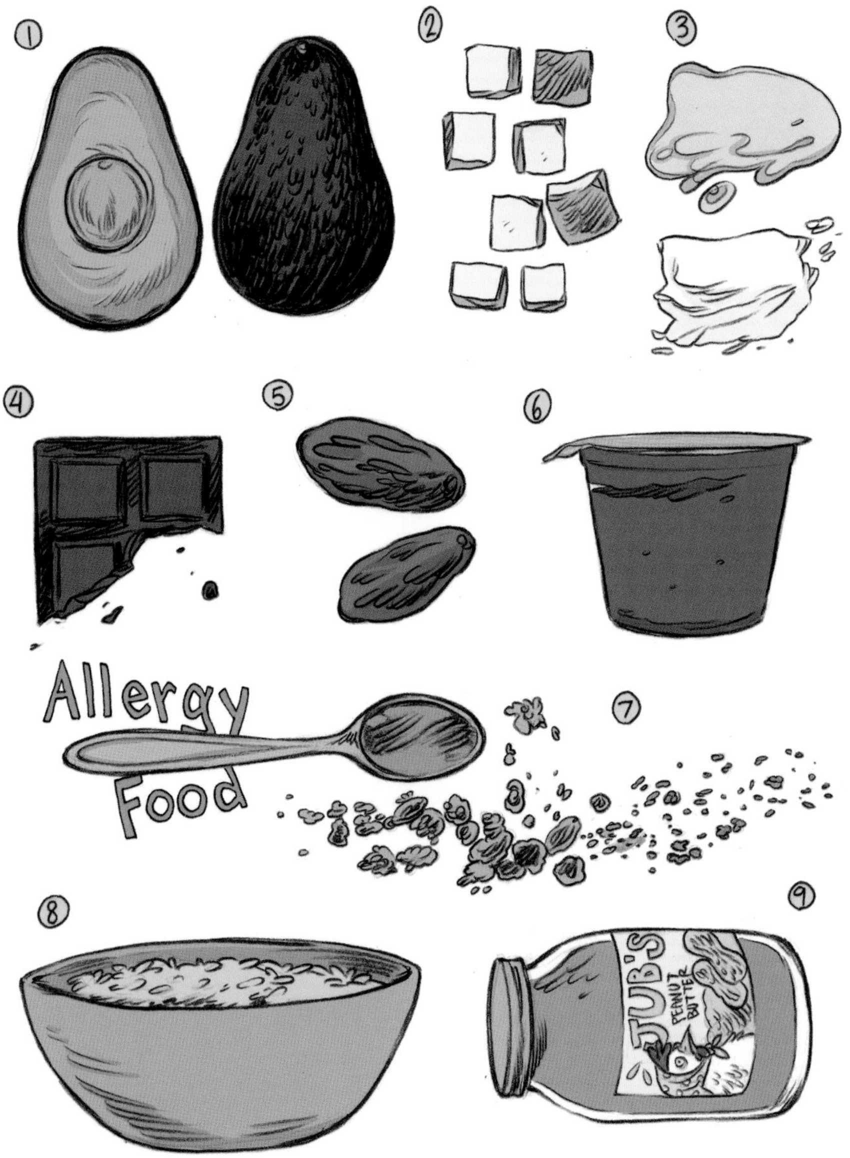

1
2
3
4
5
6
Allergy Food
7
8
9
JUB'S
PEANUT BUTTER

I was a mess for a while there. At one point, when things were really plummeting, I wanted something to blame and at the same time something to distract me from my real problems, so I decided I had food allergies. This was a very trendy thing to discover about yourself, and I wasn't entirely without cause for suspicion: my sister spent the first half of her life unable to eat almost anything that wasn't rice and goat dairy, and my cousin has celiac. Still, in my case it was pyschosomatic at best. I touch on this briefly in my chapter introduction: it's hard not to default to scarcity as a way to feel like you're in control.

For six months or so, I ate a very restricted diet, and here I tried to illustrate its appeal. The soy puddings were an atrocity, in retrospect, but the rest of it was actually pretty good.

Goblin Tea

(07/09/2014) When I was a teenager, my high school best friend and her mum used to take me along to attend Afternoon Tea at this little tea house in our neighborhood. Oh man, this place! It was about as froufy and lacy as you could possibly imagine, and I was constantly anxious about the gawkiness of my elbows, and the un-crossedness of my ankles; but the food was great, and they particularly excelled at those triple tiers of tiny scones and pastries. I don't need to tell you that the only thing better than one very nice pastry is nine or ten of them arranged for my enjoyment, so greed won out easily enough against my (butch teenager trapped in teahouse) discomfort—even to the point where I was constantly pressing to return.

I think about that place all the time, even fifteen or so years later. So here is my proposed Goblin Tea.

Layer 1: Sandwiches. I have no particular interest in those traditional crustless tea sandwiches, so instead I want thin slices of baguette with some kind of meat and cheese and arugula. Also, I want mini croissants, and there's no end to what might be in them because croissants make everything taste better.

Layer 2: Scones. All I want are plain scones and raisin or currant scones. But like, THE BEST scones—no playing fast and loose. Also jam and butter.

Layer 3: Desserts. Guys, it was so hard to narrow this down to three. But as of my current mood, I want little lemon bars, and tiny flaky fruit tarts, and little choux pastry puffs with maybe a small measure of vanilla custard in them (but I have a weird preference for eating them totally plain).

Videogame

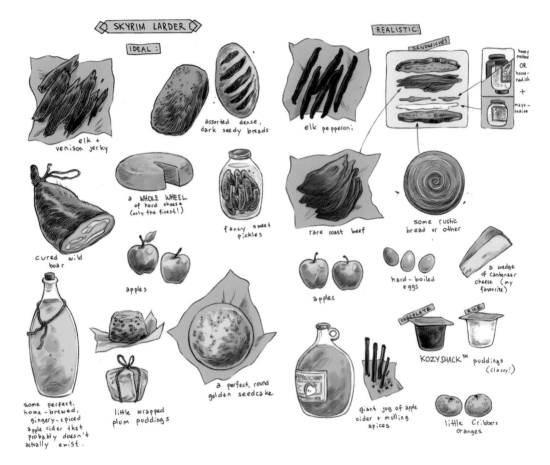

SKYRIM LARDER

IDEAL :

elk + venison jerky

assorted dense, dark seedy breads

a WHOLE WHEEL of hard chese (only the finest!)

fancy sweet pickles

cured wild boar

apples

some perfect, home-brewed, gingery-spiced apple cider that probably doesn't actually exist.

little wrapped plum puddings

a perfect, round golden seedcake

REALISTIC:

SANDWICHES

honey mustard OR horse-radish + mayo-naise

elk pepperoni

rare roast beef

some rustic bread or other

apples

hard-boiled eggs

a wedge of Cantenaar cheese (my favourite)

CHOCOLATE   RICE

KOZY SHACK™ puddings (classy!)

giant jug of apple cider + mulling spices

little Cribbers oranges

(11/05/2011) *I'm planning my SKYRIM WEEK larder—both imaginary and realistic. On the 10th of November, to kill time and suppress anxiety before the midnight launch, I mean to make a serious pilgrimage and collect enough tasty things to allay starvation while I play the game for roughly a week straight uninterrupted.*

The ideal larder would be, you know, ideal. Even though I couldn't actually consume all of that food before it went bad. But the realistic variation is nothing to damn well sneeze at. A comic artist's budget means a nearly meatless existence (at least for me), but I have this $20 gift certificate to Oyama Sausage—a gift from my BFF—which I've been saving for a rainy Skyrim. I've been thinking about those roast beef sandwiches for weeks.

Larder

GEROLSTEINER
SPARKLING
ROOT BEER
Lemon

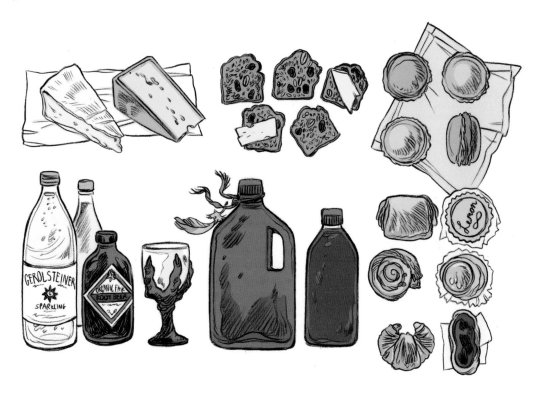

(11/16/2014) *Since* Dragon Age *is half set in a Frenchish fictional country, I feel compelled to make French snacks and pastries my loose theme. There are worse compulsions to be faced with, I'm sure.*

So what do we have here. Cheese, of course. Cheese seems to be an ongoing feature in every fantasy game ever, and Bioware games in particular, so cheese there must be. Alongside that I'll be getting these Raincoast Crisps, which have been the ubiquitous local fancy cracker for the last fifteen years or so. As an aside: when I was in my early twenties, I thought the key to looking like a proper adult was to show up at events and parties bringing these crackers (and cheese) as an offering.

Next, I'd like all sorts of little buttery pastries. I don't even have to elaborate, because you guys already know what I'm about. Tiny ones would be ideal—then I could get tons—but I'll probably have to make do with two or three in a normal size. Also, I had to think of something else to draw, and macarons seemed appropriate? I mean, I wouldn't kick them out of bed. Actually, macarons: pretty much welcome in my bed at any time.

Last of all we have our beverages. In reality, once I'm totally engrossed in a new game, the contents of my larder start to feel rather distant and uninteresting. So I need to provide myself with a broad assortment of things I can drink: various fizzies, and silly trendy juices that become rapidly less socially acceptable when I pour them into my, ahem, taloned goblet (look at it, it's glorious). And of course, as I said, there will be endless cups of tea. And sweet, sweet coffee.

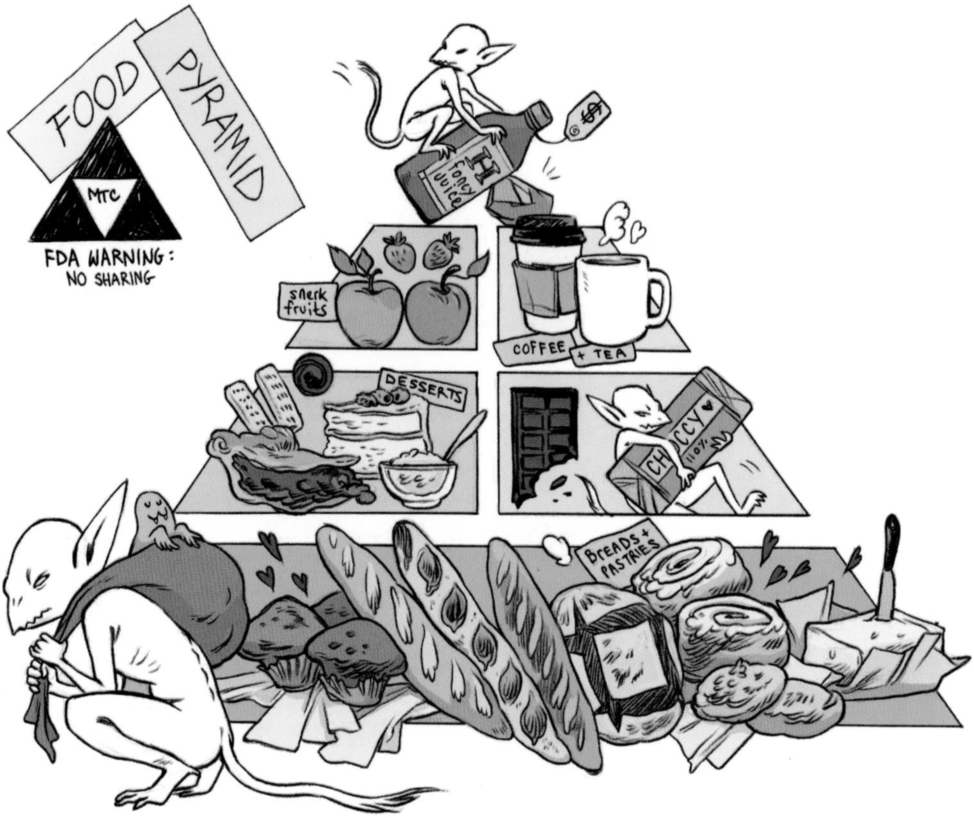
FOOD
PYRAMID
MTC
FDA WARNING:
NO SHARING
fancy juice
snerk fruits
COFFEE
+ TEA
DESSERTS
CHOCCY
110%
BREADS + PASTRIES

(09/05/2014) *What we have here, of course, is my own version of the government-approved food pyramid of the 80s and 90s. For anybody not familiar, the base represents the food you're supposed to eat in the largest quantities, ascending to the foods you're supposed to eat in the smallest quantities. I'll spare you guys my rant about how flawed I think the original was (and is), but individual and ever-changing food pyramids are a different thing entirely.*

What does mine contain? WELL. The bottom level is obviously all breads and muffins and scones and stuff, followed one tier up by various desserts (the distinction between these two might be a little fuzzy, but nevermind). Then fine choccy, of course, then fruit, and by fruit I mean mostly apples. Then coffee and tea (which probably should have been lower down, if I'm being honest). Then last of all, the top tier changes month by month depending on what silly thing I'm fixating on. At the moment it's those stupid, trendy (expensive, argh) green juices that I used to mock, but now crave constantly.

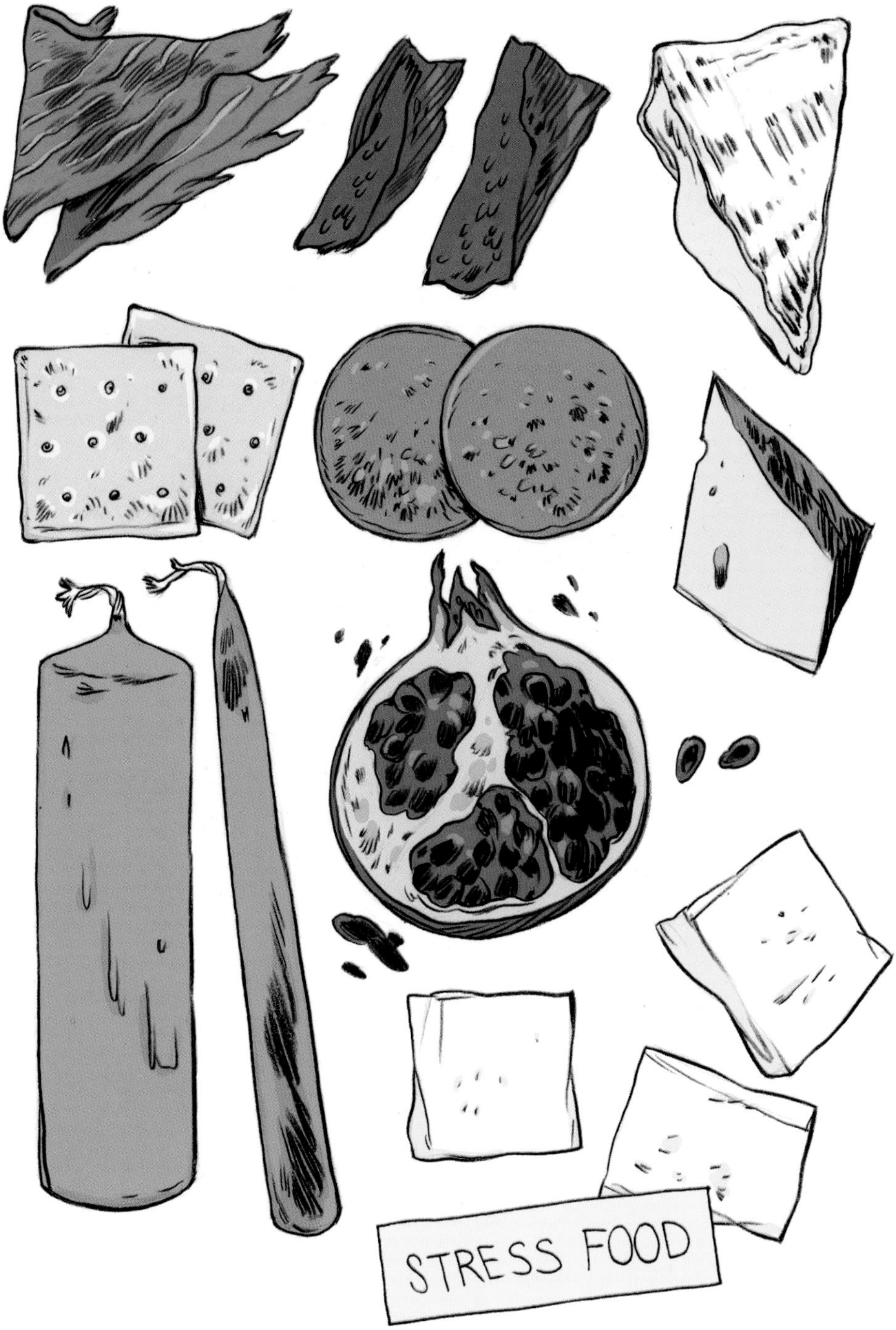
STRESS FOOD

(12/22/2015) *Looking at this list, I'm convinced that that my immediate response to any stressful situation should be to crash an upper-crust wine and cheese dinner party. Well. Noted for future reference, I guess.*

I know the candles don't count as food, but on the other hand you probably could consume a high-quality beeswax candle without necessarily dying?

Secret of Mana
SQUARE SOFT

(02/06/2017) *When we were really young, my sister invented a snack we called the "toaster sandwich". It was pretty much what you'd expect a kid to come up with: toasted bread sandwiching a messy combination of peanut butter and jam and honey.*

Now listen, I was total balls as older siblings go. I don't expect to surprise a single human being when I tell you that I was a weird broody child, and I wanted everyone to leave me alone so I could draw animals and read about Narnia. Spending time with my bouncy, affectionate sister was not on the itinerary. This toaster sandwich thing, however, was an exception. It was our bonding ritual. I would play videogames—Secret of Mana *or* Zelda *or whatever—and my sister would watch, and sometimes she'd make us a snack, and even in my infant broodiness, I had to admit, those toaster sandwiches were exceptional.*

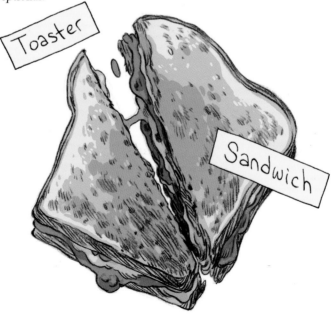

Toaster
Sandwich

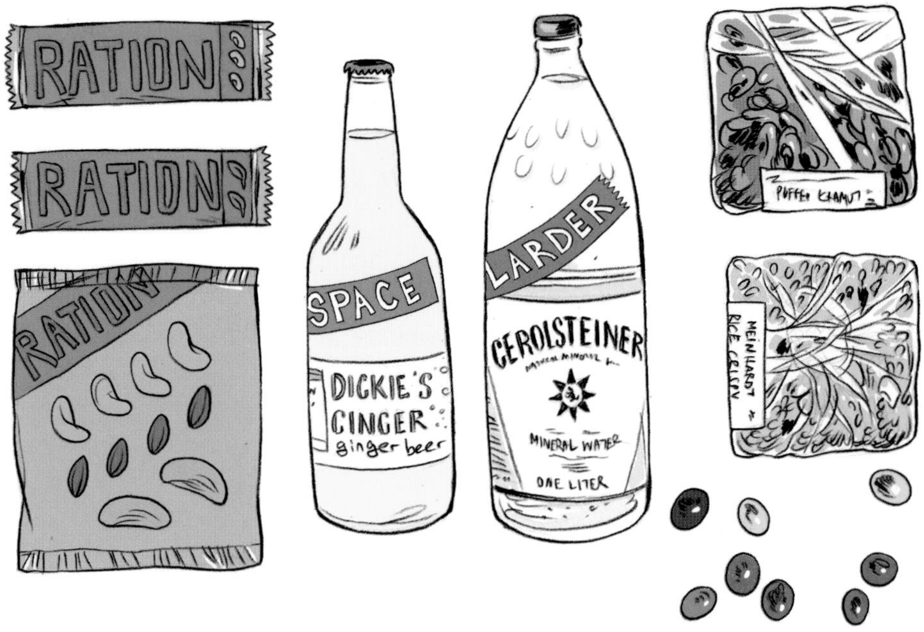
RATION
RATION
RATION
SPACE
DICKIE'S
GINGER
ginger beer
LARDER
GEROLSTEINER
MINERAL WATER
ONE LITER
PUFFED KAMUT
MEINHARDT
RICE CRISPY

(03/15/2017) *OK, let me first say that fantasy food is so much easier than space food. All you have to do is get some rustic bread, and some cheese, and a nice blotchy apple, and there you are: fit for adventure. So the space larder is a little muddled, by comparison.*

1. I think, for the sake of authenticity, I have to get a couple of protein bars which I can then pretend are space rations. Since they aren't the sort of thing I'd normally eat, I can almost make them seem appealing based on their novelty. They're like chocolate bars, right? But with a… uniform sandy texture?

2. What else is spacey? And ration-y? All I could really think of were mixed nuts, maybe just because I want them.

3. I've done a lot of whining about wanting the perfect ginger ale, and somehow fate has never punished me for it. In fact, I've recently found something pretty close to perfect, made by a local company, Dickie's. So this is my excuse to stock up, since my normal budgeting involves never paying for beverages (other than coffee and tea, of course; I tell myself that this balances out my other bad spending habits, even though it can't possibly).

4. Fizzy water, too: another special occasion purchase.

5. How do I describe these? They're this puffed kamut square thing… like, if rice crispy squares were made with Sugar Crisp cereal, but marginally healthier? Anyway, a local Vancouver grocery store, Capers, used to make them, and thankfully they still do, although they've since been enveloped by the soft maw of Whole Foods.

6. Also, normal rice crispy squares. Puffy cereal held together by sugar, just in general.

7. Last of all, I must have some peanut M&M's. Which aren't even unreasonable, you know, because after I made this list I did an image search for astronaut food, and there they were, amongst all the shiny, vacuumed packages. Official candy of space.

Love Food, etc.

I associate certain foods with feelings or states—don't we all? I think the classic is "heartbreak", and everyone knows the stereotype of being broken up with and eating an entire tub of ice cream. There's a lot of crossover, so the categories have to be loose, but here's my attempt to break it down:

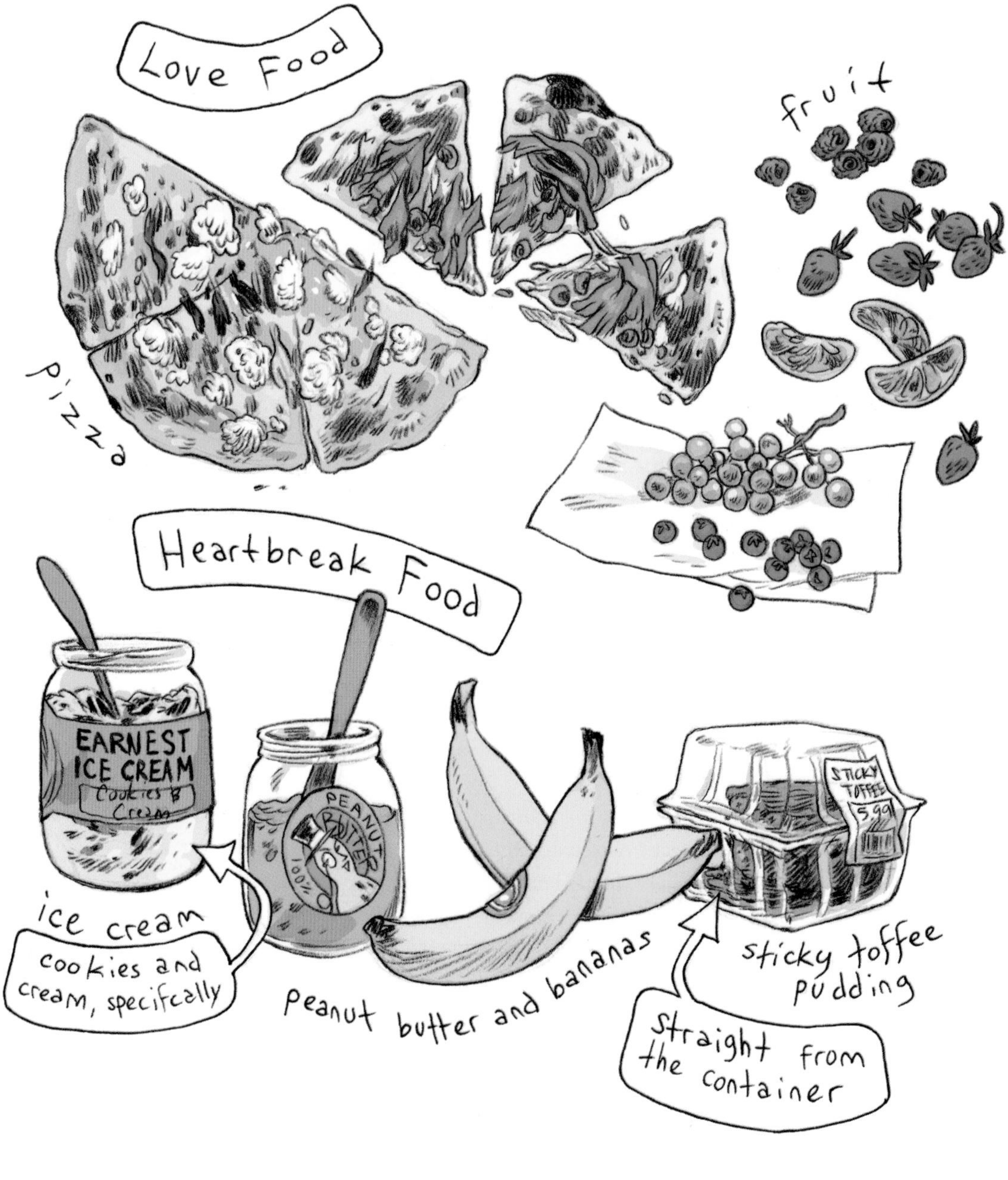

Love Food
fruit
pizza
Heartbreak Food
EARNEST ICE CREAM
Cookies & Cream
PEANUT BUTTER
STICKY TOFFEE
5.99
ice cream
cookies and cream, specifcally
peanut butter and bananas
sticky toffee pudding
straight from the container

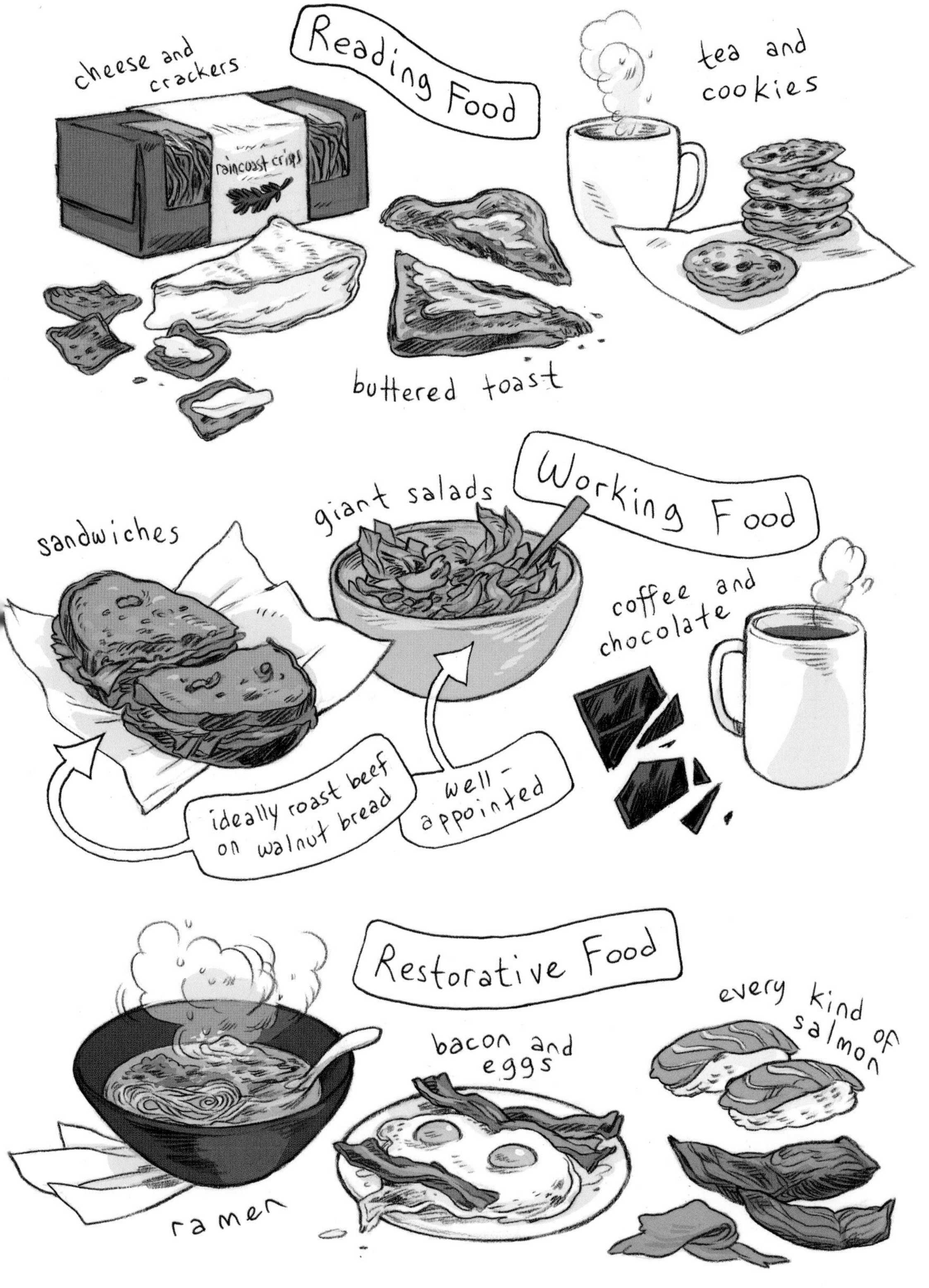
Reading Food
cheese and crackers
raincoast crisps
tea and cookies
buttered toast
Working Food
sandwiches
giant salads
coffee and chocolate
ideally roast beef on walnut bread
well-appointed
Restorative Food
every kind of salmon
bacon and eggs
ramen

RECIPES

These recipes aren't original or impressive, but it seems right to include them. I've tinkered with them endlessly over the years (in some cases having long forgotten the original recipe) and they're all well established in the regular Hchom larder.

COCONUT Rice Pud

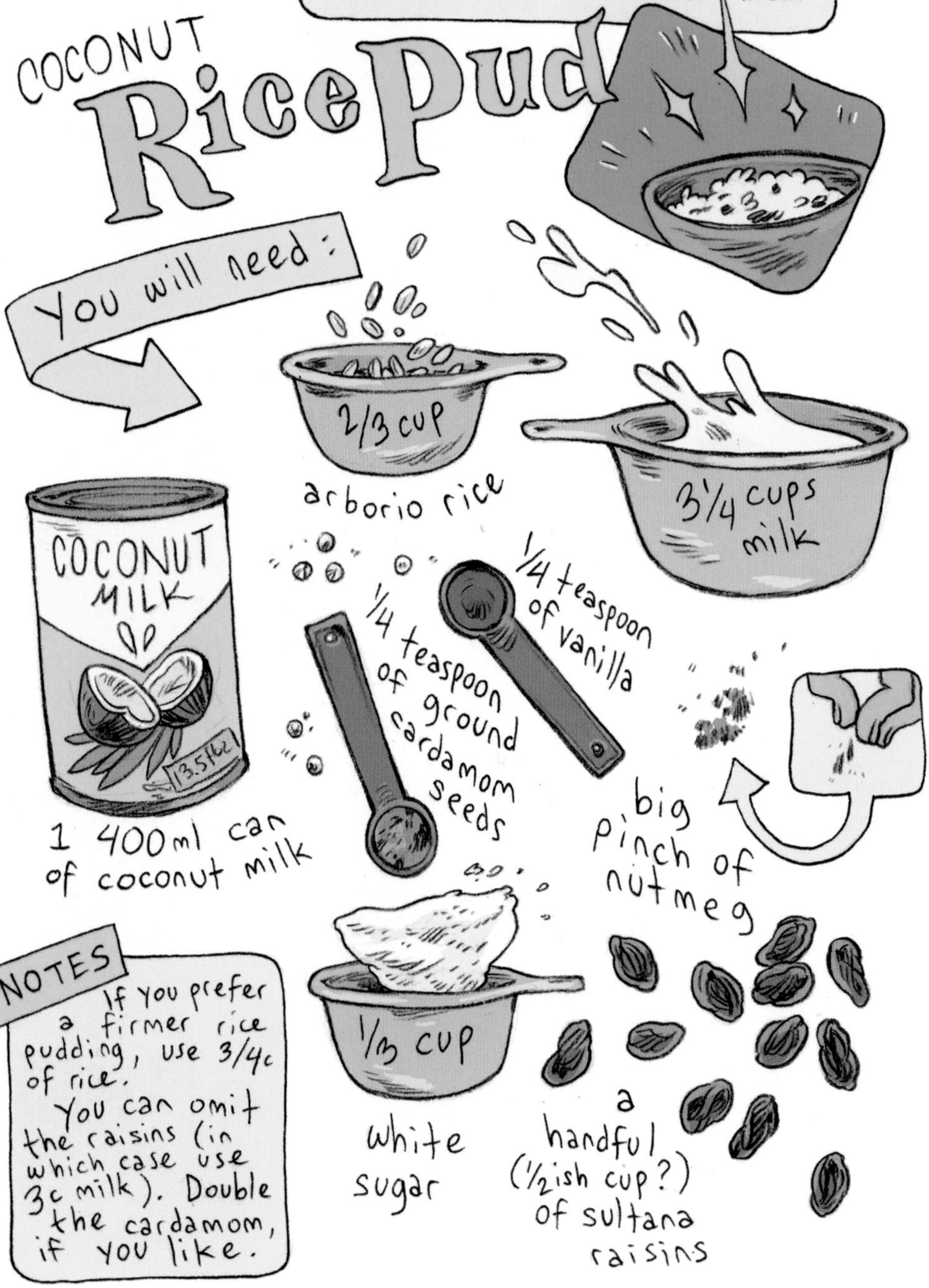

You will need:
2/3 cup
arborio rice
3 1/4 cups
milk
COCONUT
MILK
13.5 floz
1 400ml can
of coconut milk
1/4 teaspoon
of ground
cardamom
seeds
1/4 teaspoon
of vanilla
big
pinch of
nutmeg
1/3 cup
white
sugar
a
handful
(1/2ish cup?)
of sultana
raisins

NOTES

If you prefer a firmer rice pudding, use 3/4c of rice.

You can omit the raisins (in which case use 3c milk). Double the cardamom, if you like.

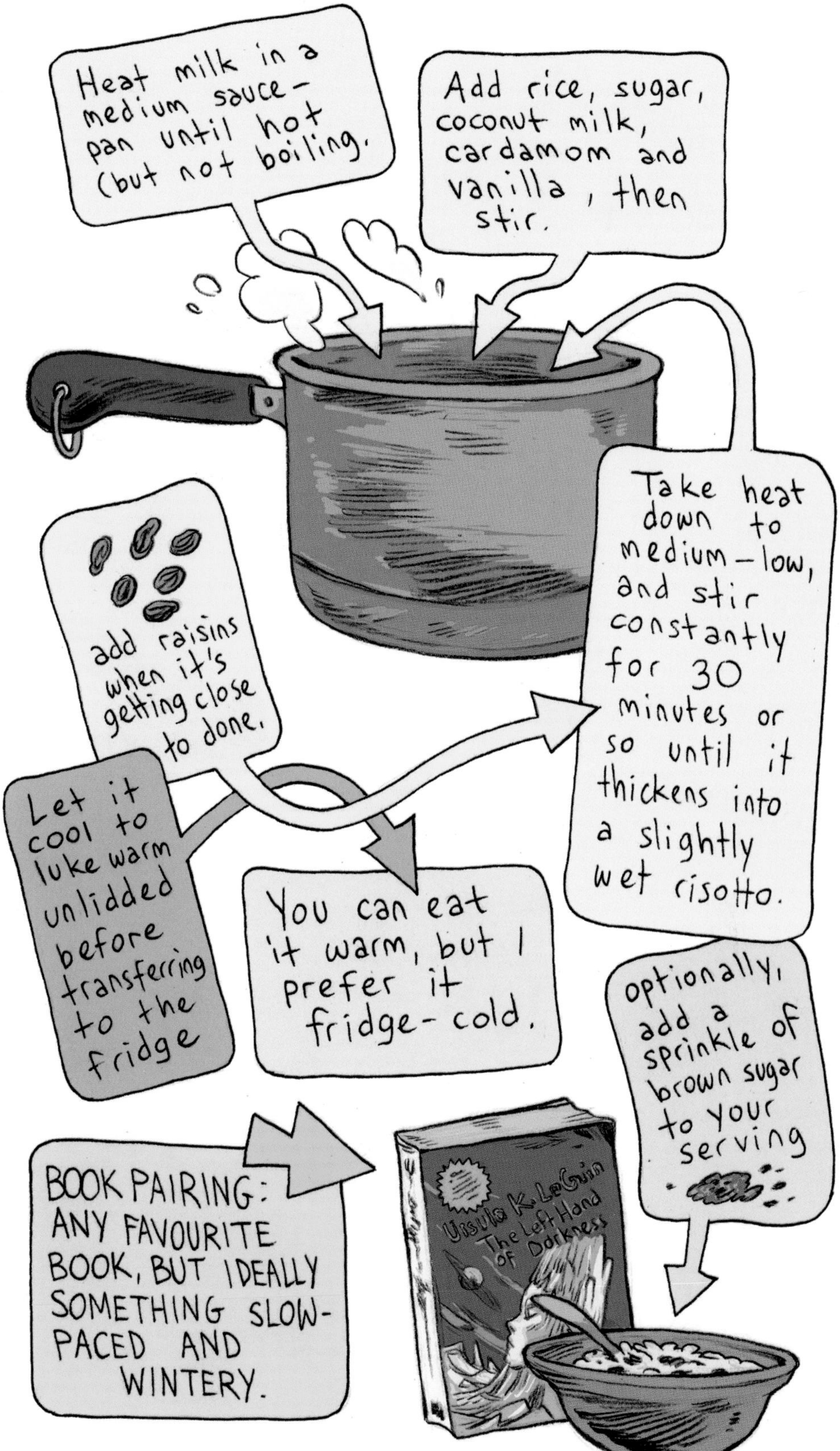
Heat milk in a medium sauce-pan until hot (but not boiling.
Add rice, sugar, coconut milk, cardamom and vanilla, then stir.
Take heat down to medium-low, and stir constantly for 30 minutes or so until it thickens into a slightly wet risotto.
add raisins when it's getting close to done.
Let it cool to luke warm unlidded before transferring to the fridge
You can eat it warm, but I prefer it fridge-cold.
optionally, add a sprinkle of brown sugar to your serving
BOOK PAIRING: ANY FAVOURITE BOOK, BUT IDEALLY SOMETHING SLOW-PACED AND WINTERY.
Ursula K. LeGuin
The Left Hand of Darkness

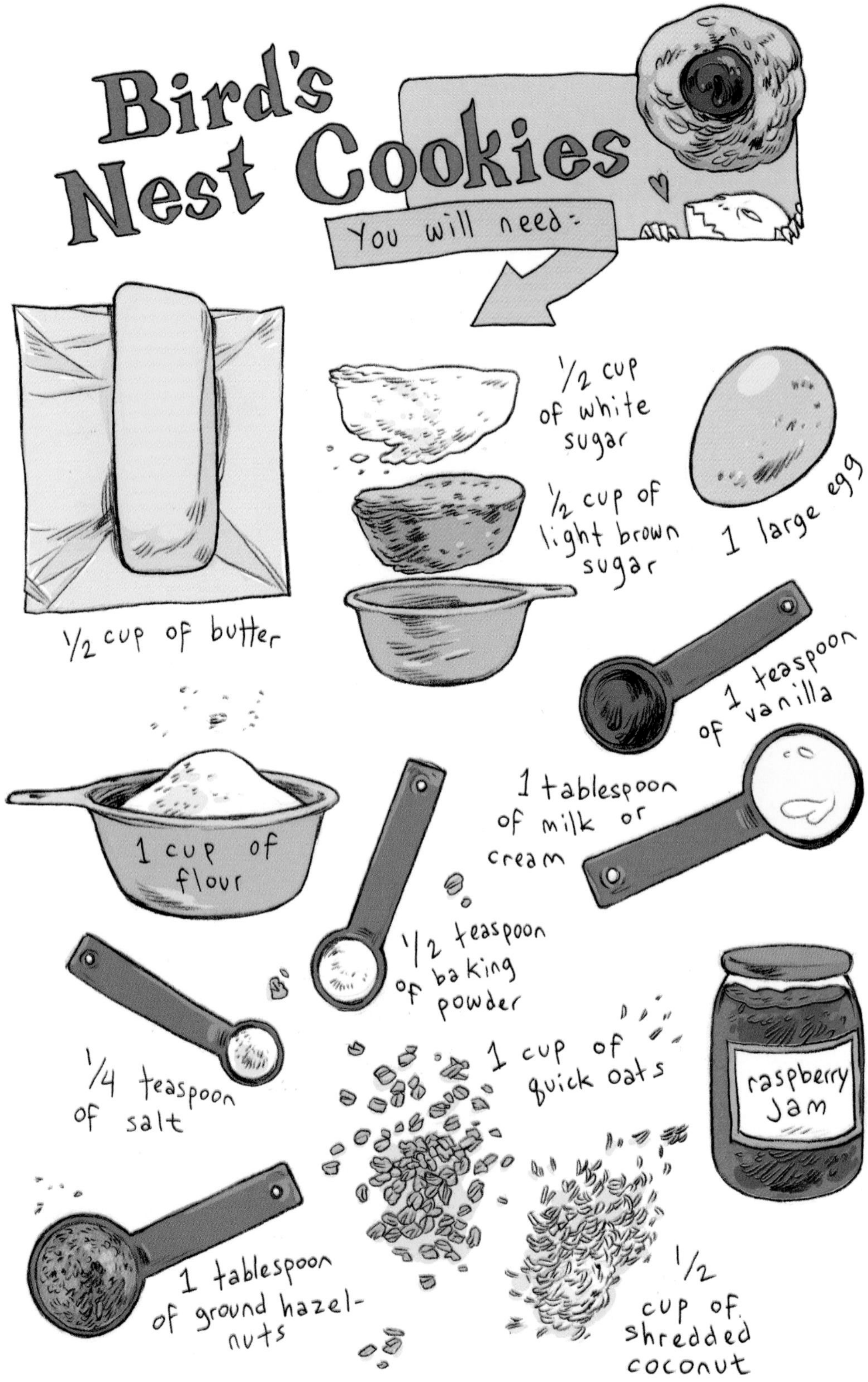
Bird's Nest Cookies
You will need:
1/2 cup of butter
1/2 cup of white sugar
1/2 cup of light brown sugar
1 large egg
1 teaspoon of vanilla
1 tablespoon of milk or cream
1 cup of flour
1/2 teaspoon of baking powder
1/4 teaspoon of salt
1 cup of quick oats
raspberry jam
1 tablespoon of ground hazel-nuts
1/2 cup of shredded coconut

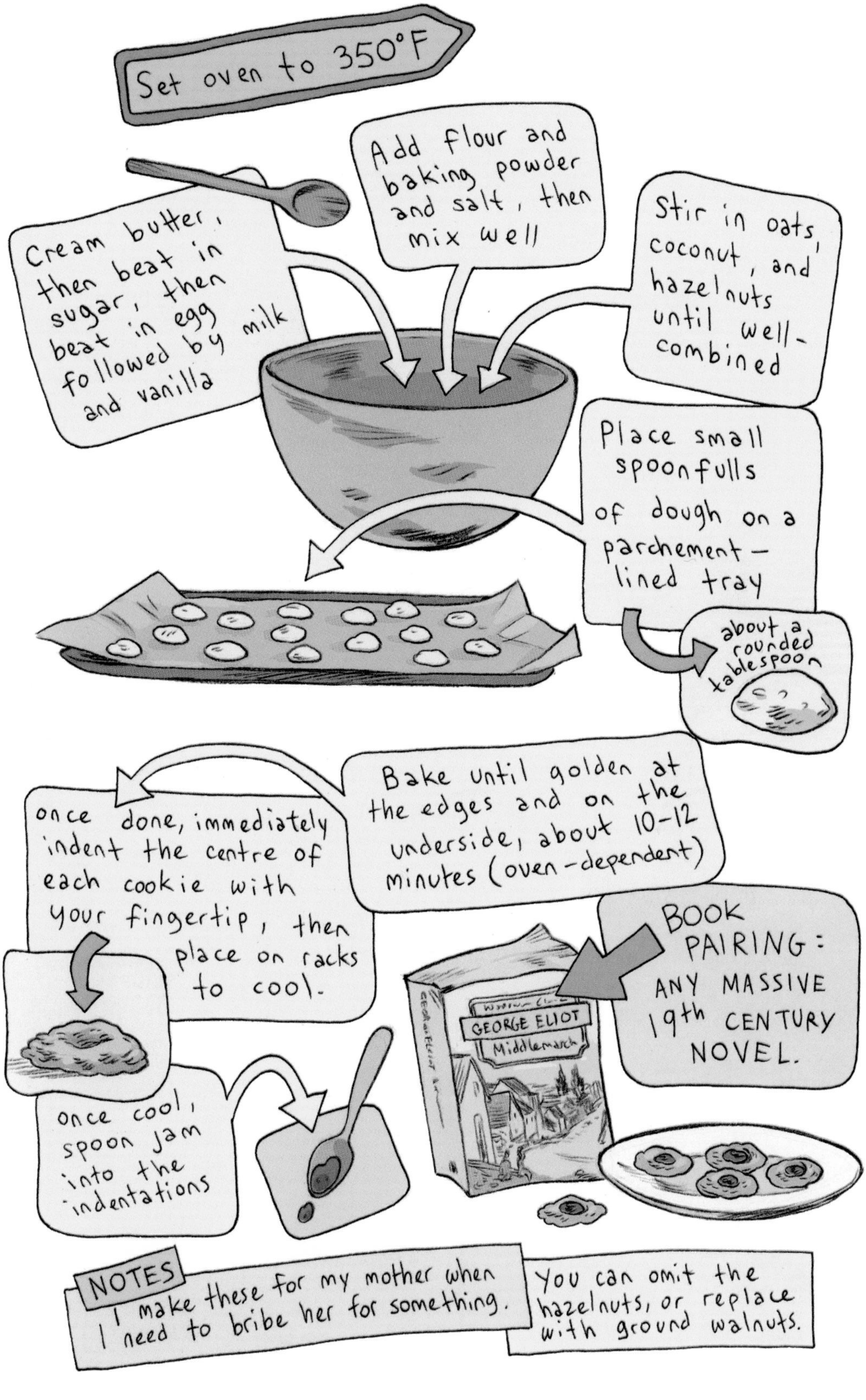

Set oven to 350°F
Cream butter, then beat in sugar, then beat in egg followed by milk and vanilla
Add flour and baking powder and salt, then mix well
Stir in oats, coconut, and hazelnuts until well-combined
Place small spoonfulls of dough on a parchement-lined tray
about a rounded tablespoon
Bake until golden at the edges and on the underside, about 10-12 minutes (oven-dependent)
once done, immediately indent the centre of each cookie with your fingertip, then place on racks to cool.
once cool, spoon jam into the indentations
BOOK PAIRING: ANY MASSIVE 19th CENTURY NOVEL.
GEORGE ELIOT
Middlemarch
NOTES
I make these for my mother when I need to bribe her for something.
You can omit the hazelnuts, or replace with ground walnuts.

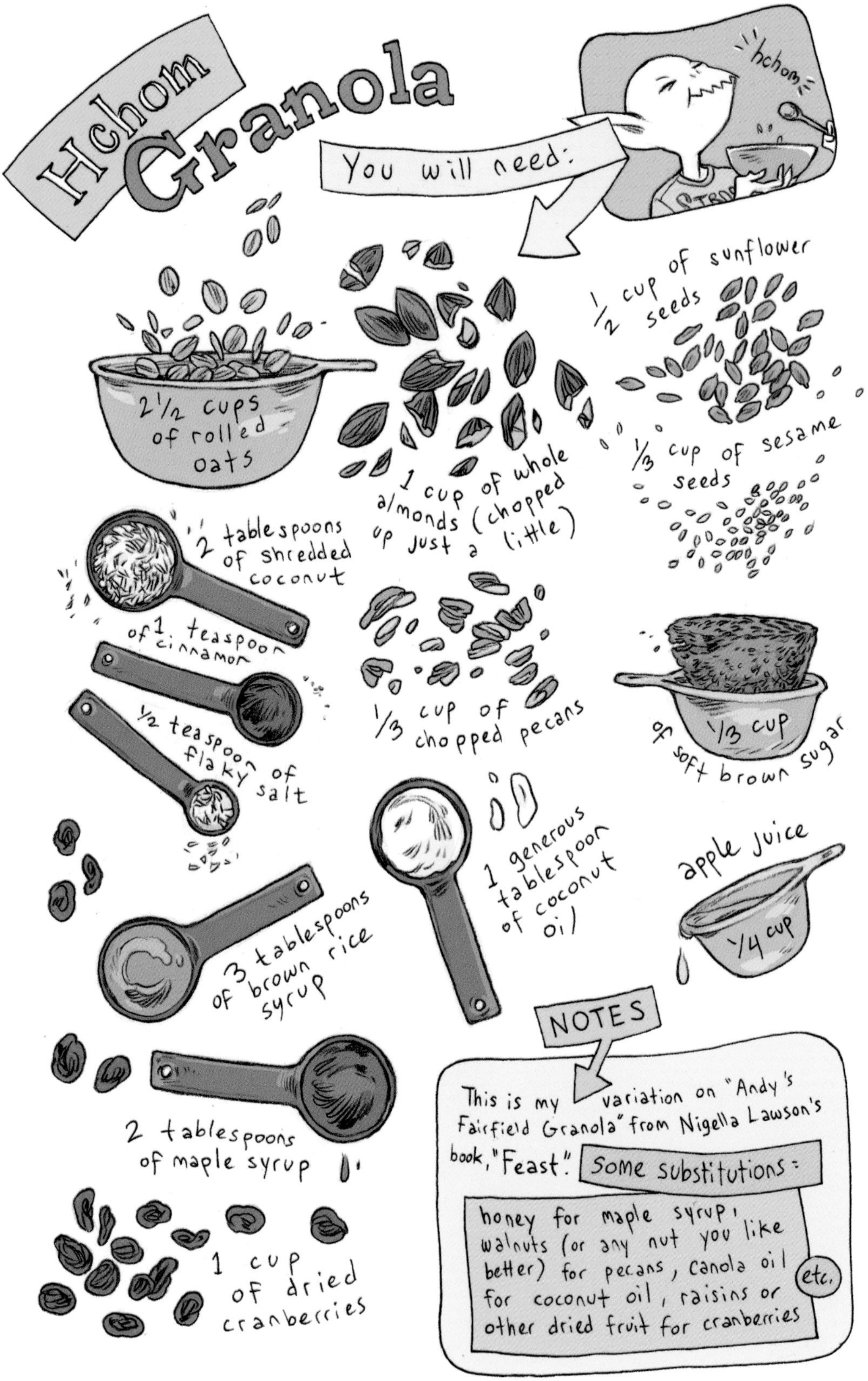

Hchom Granola
hchom
You will need:
2½ cups of rolled oats
1 cup of whole almonds (chopped up just a little)
½ cup of sunflower seeds
⅓ cup of sesame seeds
2 tablespoons of shredded coconut
1 teaspoon of cinnamon
½ teaspoon of flaky salt
⅓ cup of chopped pecans
⅓ cup of soft brown sugar
1 generous tablespoon of coconut oil
apple juice
¼ cup
3 tablespoons of brown rice syrup
2 tablespoons of maple syrup
1 cup of dried cranberries
NOTES
This is my variation on "Andy's Fairfield Granola" from Nigella Lawson's book, "Feast."
Some substitutions:
honey for maple syrup, walnuts (or any nut you like better) for pecans, canola oil for coconut oil, raisins or other dried fruit for cranberries
etc.

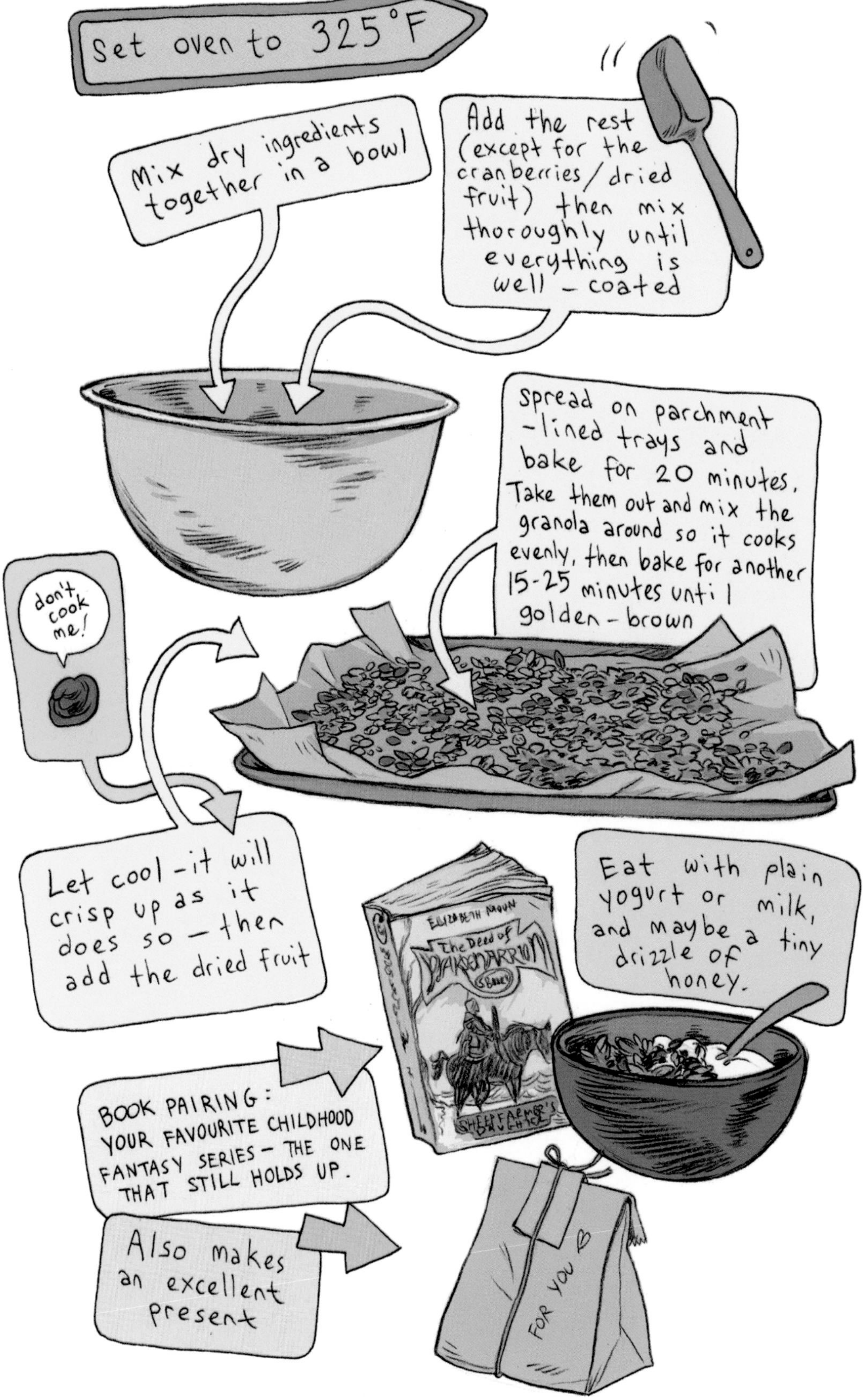
Set oven to 325°F
Mix dry ingredients together in a bowl
Add the rest (except for the cranberries/dried fruit) then mix thoroughly until everything is well-coated
Spread on parchment-lined trays and bake for 20 minutes. Take them out and mix the granola around so it cooks evenly, then bake for another 15-25 minutes until golden-brown
don't cook me!
Let cool-it will crisp up as it does so-then add the dried fruit
Eat with plain yogurt or milk, and maybe a tiny drizzle of honey.
BOOK PAIRING: YOUR FAVOURITE CHILDHOOD FANTASY SERIES- THE ONE THAT STILL HOLDS UP.
ELIZABETH MOON
The Deed of Paksenarrion
SHEEPFARMER'S DAUGHTER
Also makes an excellent present
FOR YOU

Chapter 02:

The Hchom Closet

Clothes are about identity, aren't they? At various times in my life, I've worn them passively or actively. I've worn them to rebel against convention, or to project a more likeable self. I've worn them passionately, but more often I've worn them with resignation, stuck in a role.

I should have no problem doing what I want, I don't fear ridicule! But that "want" is full of contradictions. Part of me wants to dress exactly like a boy, in full suits or jeans and old t-shirts, while another part of me wants to dress like a mad drag witch trailing a froth of tulle and sequins and ichor. Some deeper, nameless part doesn't know what it wants, and is afraid to find out. Ridicule is easy. It's myself that I'm afraid of.

I doubt I'll ever completely solve that fear, but giving air to it has helped. As I wrote in the introduction, my goblin is bold where I am reluctant; it can host multiple personas, and by dressing it I was able to bring a little of that ease, and then a little more, into my own habits. I was able to loosen some of my self-containment and simply express.

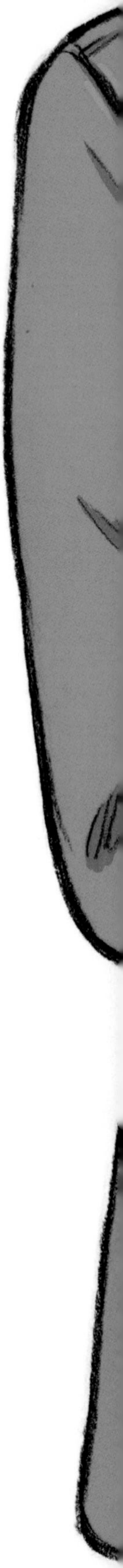

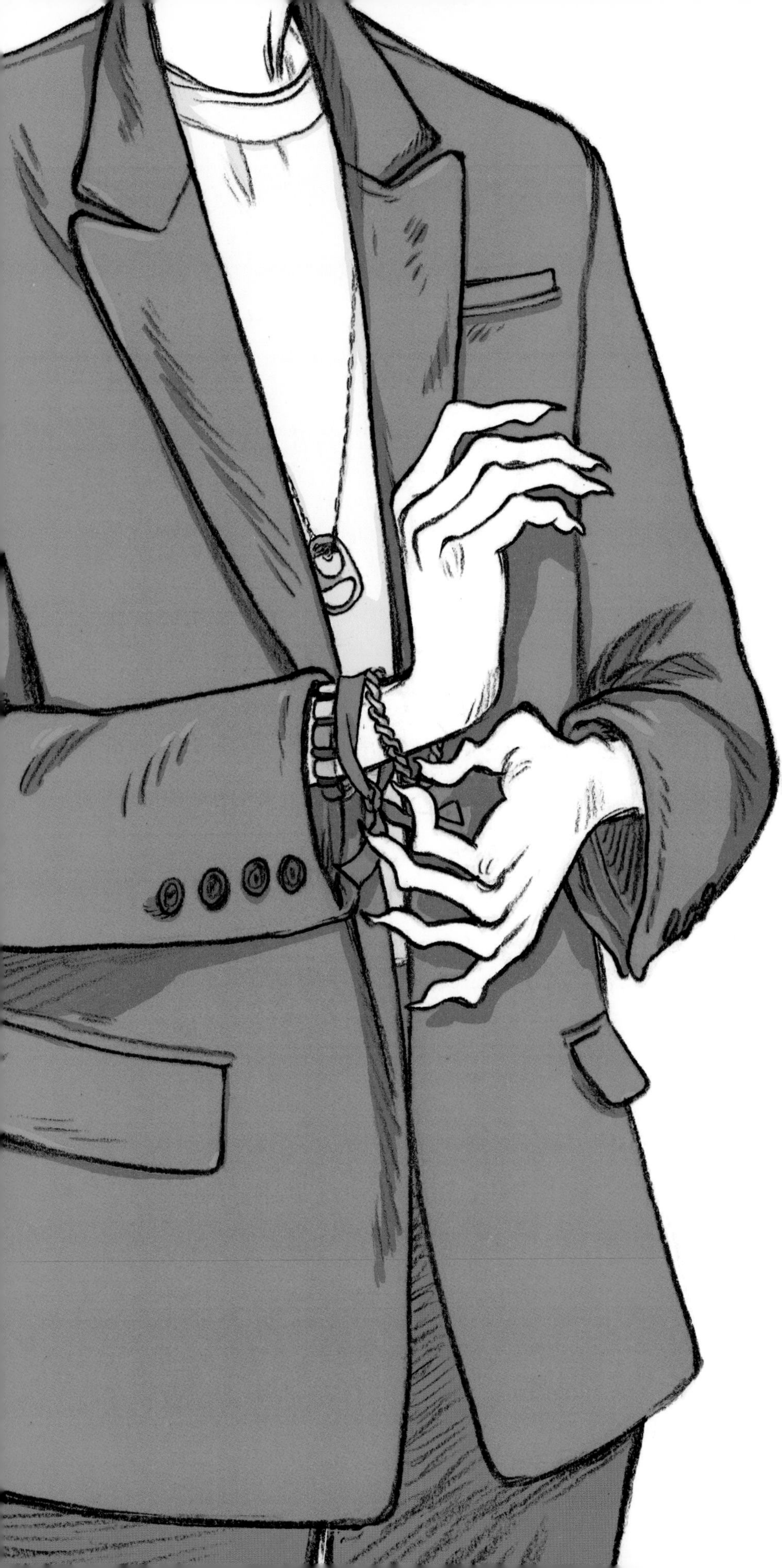

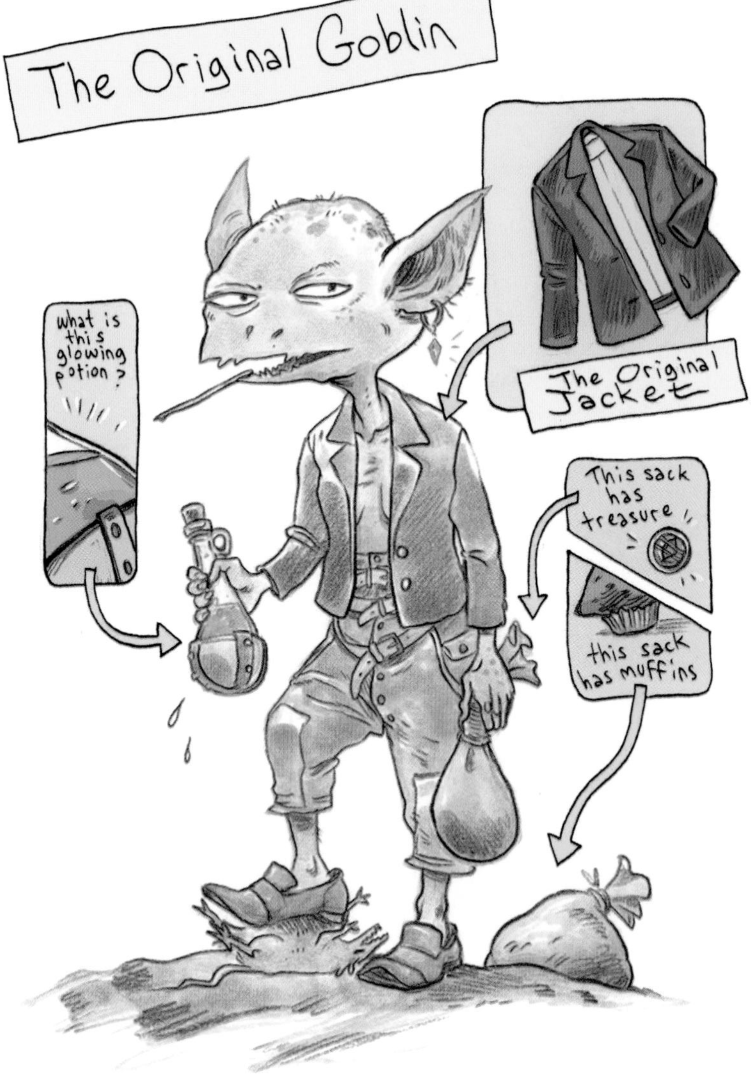
The Original Goblin
what is this glowing potion?
The Original Jacket
This sack has treasure
this sack has muffins

Equip Items

(03/13/2010)

1 – Shoes: Zeha oxfords

2 – Socks/Stockings: Mostly none, but black wool men's dress socks from November to February

3 – Trousers: Narrow (but [if possible] slightly roomy) black jeans.

4 – Dress/Skirt: I don't own any of either, but we've discussed the possibility of a onesie dress.

5 – Jacket/Coat: Ok, this is a bit unfair, because the coat I drew above isn't one I actually have. Or rather, not in the colour and fabric I'd most like. Anyway, if life had any meaning at all, I'd own a navy wool Siren Suit jacket by Borne, this designer out of New York that only existed for a few years (as far as I know). This is the best jacket ever. Really. I don't want to be one of these people who makes insane, hyperbolic statements about items of clothing, but I would SACRIFICE FIVE THOUSAND KITTENS to have one. I mean, writing books and making art is all well and good, but my real ambition in life is to find this designer, and implore her, weeping, with fists full of cash, to make me another one, please, just one more.

6 – Underwear: Cotton Jockey bottoms (cheap), and nice French bras (expensive – I'm a weird size, and it's a bitch finding ones that fit well).

7 – T-shirt: Well-worn men's white cotton t-shirts, altered on the side-seams (ineptly, by hand) for a nice, loose-narrow fit.

8 – Sunglasses: Whatever cheap (soon to be sat on and crushed) pair I've bought on the spur of the moment at the start of summer.

9 – Accessories: Lark handmade leather wallet. Though really, if I'm being honest with myself I should say a muffin.

10 – Absolute basic for an evening: A nice woolly onesie, obviously.

Impossible Jacket 01

Horn spoon

pocket full of gems and silks and things

Sneaky sneak-shoes

(05/10/2010) *As usual, I'm burdened with absurd and impossible wants. There are certain things that I want all the time with professional efficiency. Like pie. I want pie so much right now, with such well-oiled zeal, that I barely even have to think about it. It's not that I necessarily want to eat pie this very second; it's just always better to have some pie on hand, ready for when I do.*

Jackets are another thing I always want. They are the most transformative item of clothing, maybe: they are like armour, and actually, this one also is armour. I want it—did I mention?

This isn't even one of those fantasyish things that I'd feel foolish walking around in. I think it would look awesome, and very nearly normal with a t-shirt and jeans.

Impossible Jacket 02

ALIEN RIFLE
SCOPE. LIKES
FLAN.

SPACE
SILVER

WEIRD
FANCY
SPACE
SKIN-ARMOUR

SPACE
ROCK

(05/12/2010) I guess this jacket isn't actually all that impossible. Only for me, financially. I'm not even positive that I like motorcycle jackets, but this one appeals to me with its quilted bits and less-pointy-than-usual collar. Plus, it's made by this old, heritage company in England that does recreations of its vintage stock, cut to your measurements, and it's customizable, so for once it would not be too short for me. No fake distressing, or anything like that. Kind of fashionless. Plus, conveniently, I think it has a bit of a space sniper look to it. But then, I would.

This particular jacket is called the "Super Monza", meaning that I would have to call mine the Super Monza Fighter II Turbo.

Impossible Jacket 03

(06/01/2010) Now this jacket is seriously impossible, as far as acquisition goes. It's made by Luxirare, and you can see it on her website. I find Luxirare to be fascinating. The stuff she makes (food and clothing) is almost always totally perpendicular to my own tastes, which is no impediment to my liking it. Sometimes I like it a lot, and sometimes I don't. Often I have a strong negative reaction to it, and that's interesting too.

Anyway, this jacket certainly doesn't match my usual aesthetic (androgynous and plain in the extreme), but I think it's very pleasant and wearable, even in its weirdness. Or especially in its weirdness.

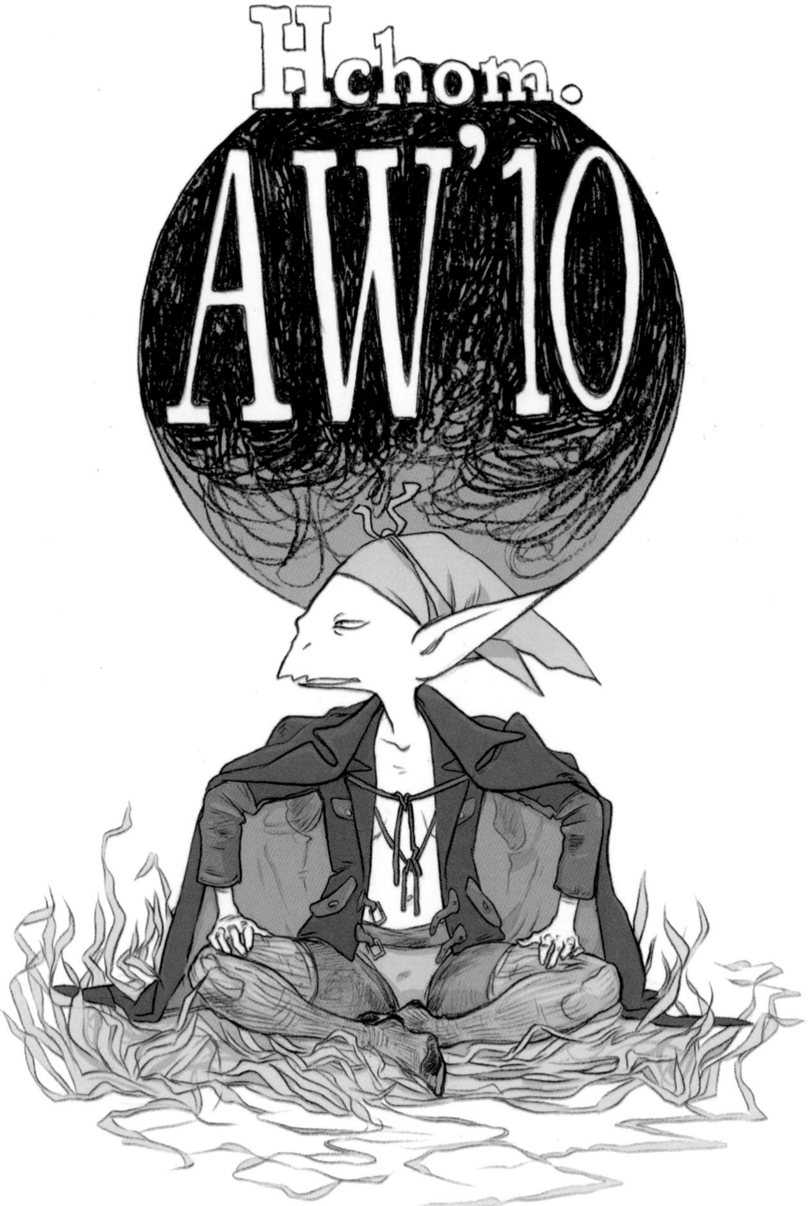
Hchom.
AW'10

(06/09/2010) *I've always wanted to make a fashion line. When I was a kid I would design whole collections of clothing for Yoshi (the green dinosaur from* Super Mario Brothers*). Or rather, Female Yoshi: "Yoshina", as I'd named her.*

My main idea, here, was to only include things that I absolutely knew I would wear, which makes it all fairly conservative. Mainly this is stuff that I wish other people would just get right (or that other people do get right with a steep charge). At some point in the future I'd like to do a whole set where the guiding priniciple is "there's no way I'd walk the streets in that". It would be all haubergeons and space suits.

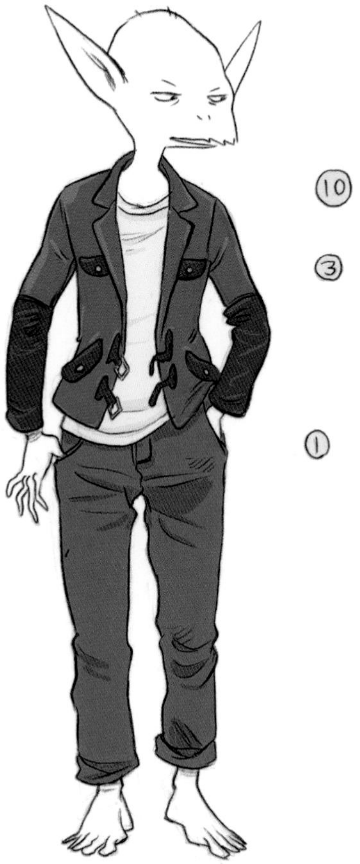
10
3
1
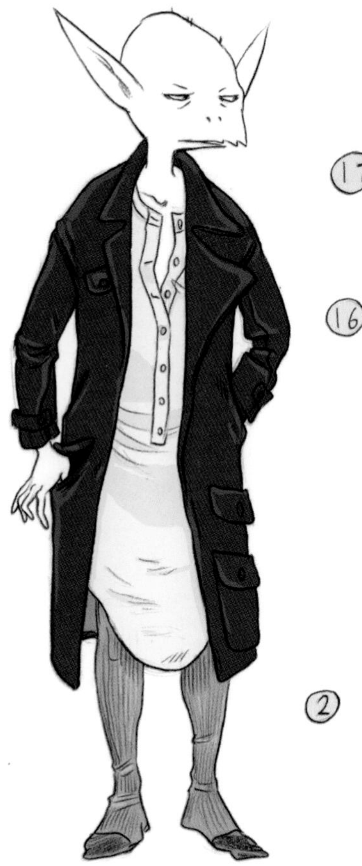
17
16
2
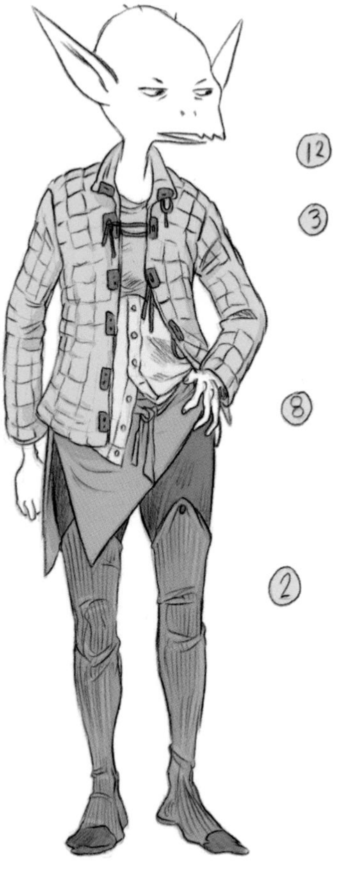
12
3
8
2
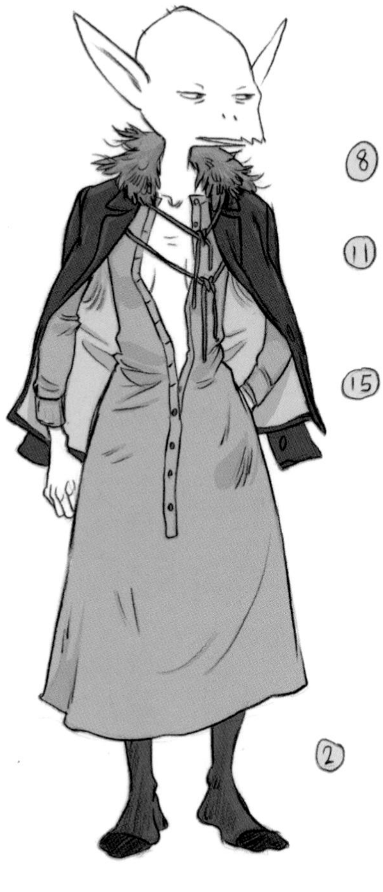
8
11
15
2

6

9

22

13

4

14

①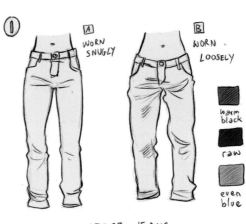

A WORN SNUGLY

B WORN LOOSELY

warm black

raw

even blue

PERFECT JEANS

②

socks

under socks

silky black

ribbed grey

ribbed taupe

SOCK LEGS

③

white

heather grey

cream

PERFECT T-SHIRT

④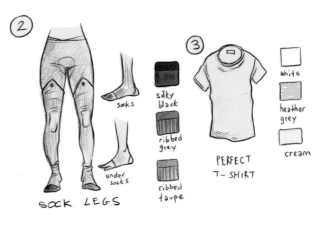

white

heather grey

cream

FFCCOO

FIN TANK

⑤

grey

FFCCOO

FIN APRON

⑥

cream/grey

blue pinstripe/warm black

TRANSFORMER SHIRT 1

⑦

grey/cream

warm black/blue pinstripe

TRANSFORMER SHIRT 2

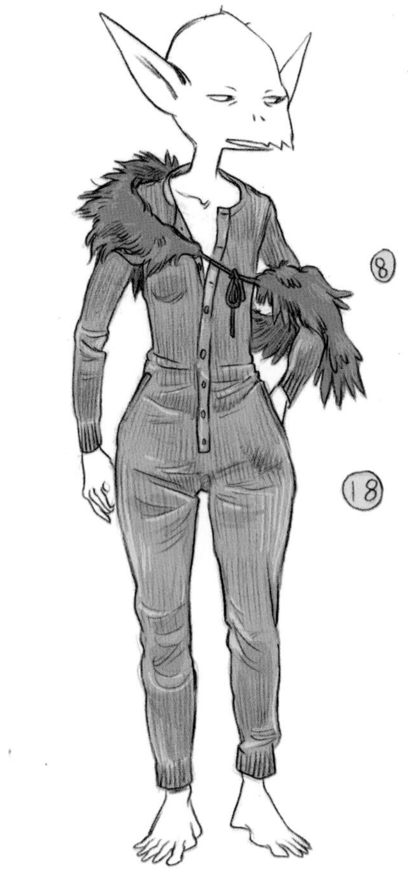
8
18

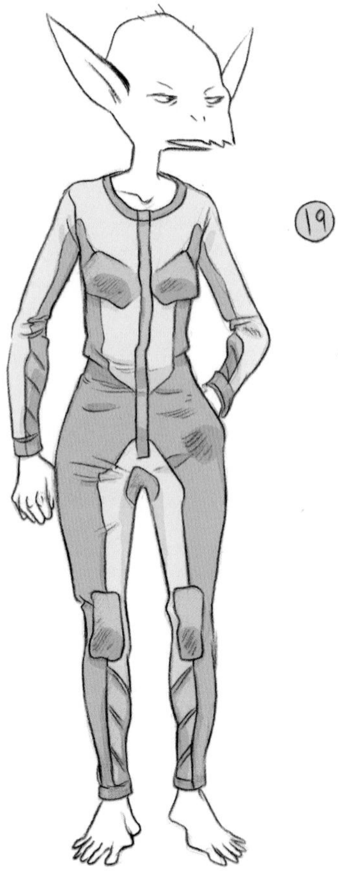
19

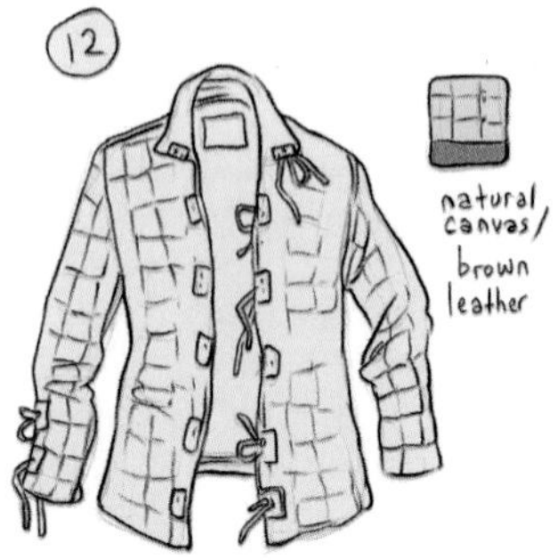
12
natural/
canvas/
brown
leather

CRUSADES JACKET

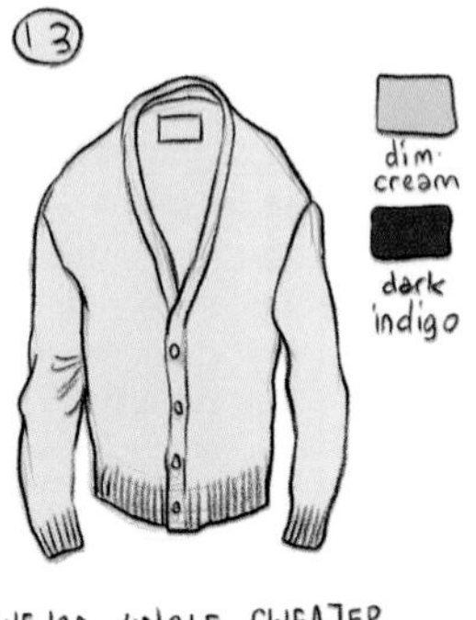
13
dim
cream
dark
indigo

WEIRD UNCLE SWEATER

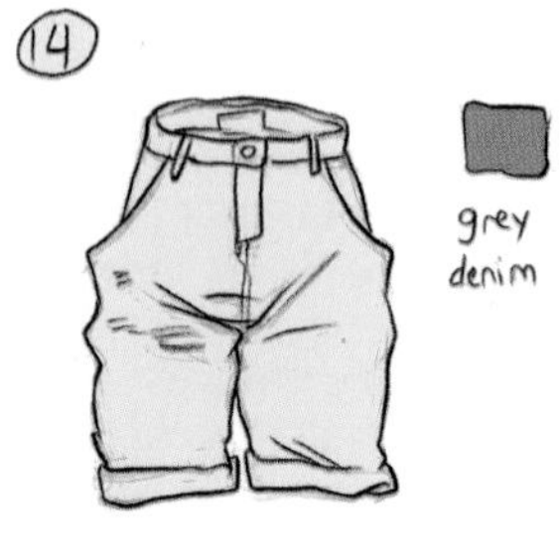
14
grey
denim

CRAZY AUNT SHORTS

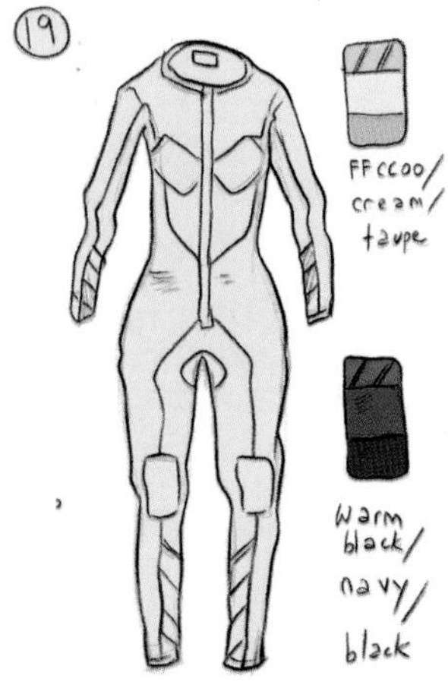
19
FFCC00/
cream/
taupe
warm
black/
navy/
black

SPACE ONESIE

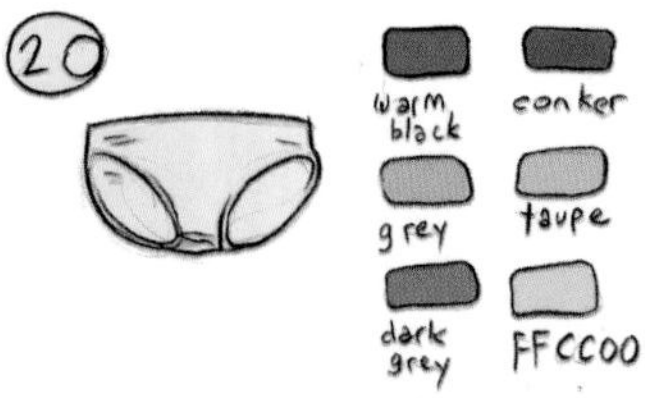
20
warm
black
conker
grey
taupe
dark
grey
FFCC00

ETERNAL UNDERWEAR

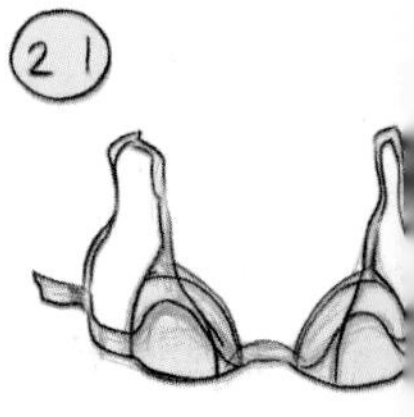
21

SUP BRA

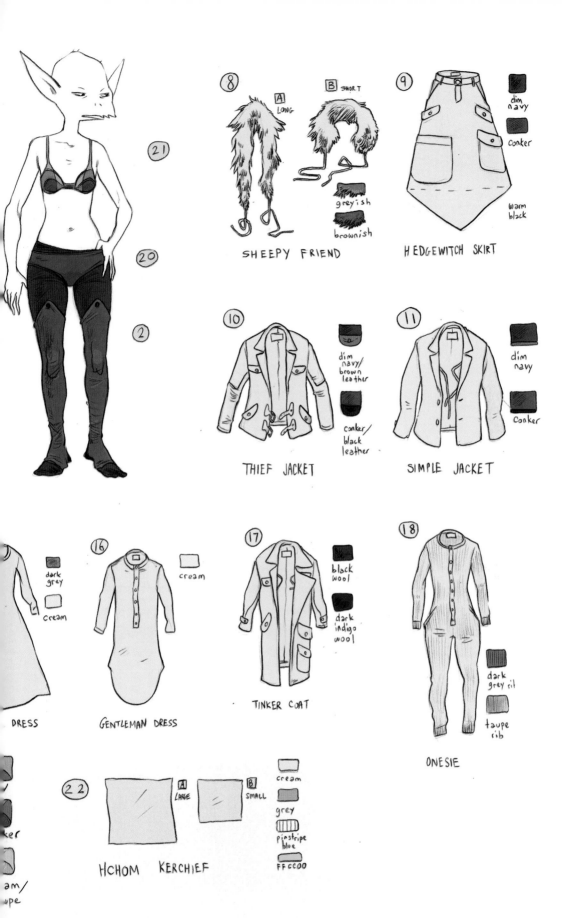

21

20

2

⑧ SHEEPY FRIEND

Ⓐ LONG

Ⓑ SHORT

greyish

brownish

⑨ HEDGEWITCH SKIRT

dim navy

conker

warm black

⑩ THIEF JACKET

dim navy/ brown leather

conker/ black leather

⑪ SIMPLE JACKET

dim navy

conker

DRESS

dark grey

cream

⑯ GENTLEMAN DRESS

cream

⑰ TINKER COAT

black wool

dark indigo wool

⑱ ONESIE

dark grey rib

taupe rib

ker

am/ upe

㉒ HCHOM KERCHIEF

Ⓐ LARGE

Ⓑ SMALL

cream

grey

pinstripe blue

FFCC00

Impossible Jackets

I'm a jacket addict, and that's no exaggeration. I've bought jackets I knew I couldn't afford, and then hidden them for months because I was too ashamed to tell anyone. I've gone hungry for jackets. I punctuate important parts of my life with jacket purchases: I need birthday jackets, and school jackets, and surely I deserve a breakup jacket, and then maybe a jacket to celebrate getting a bus pass. Amazingly, for every jacket I aquire, there are five more I wanted and couldn't have. These are what I call "impossible jackets."

Impossible jackets are distinct from my wants, because I acknowledge that I'll never own them. They're either too expensive, or too exclusive, or no longer available. In some cases, they simply don't exist, so I draw them instead. Here are some examples.

Impossible Jacket 04

"Possible" Jacket
still impossible

53

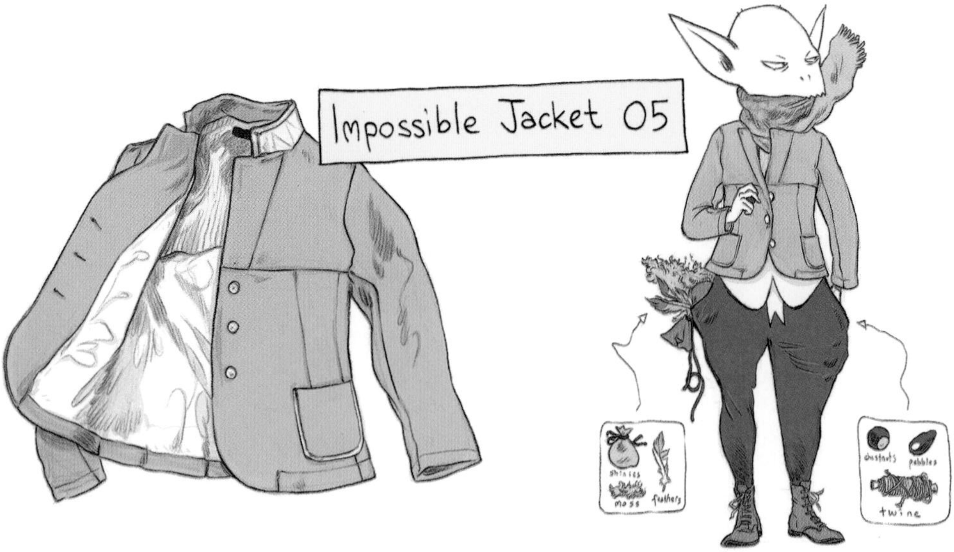
Impossible Jacket 05
shinies
moss
feathers
chestnuts
pebbles
twine

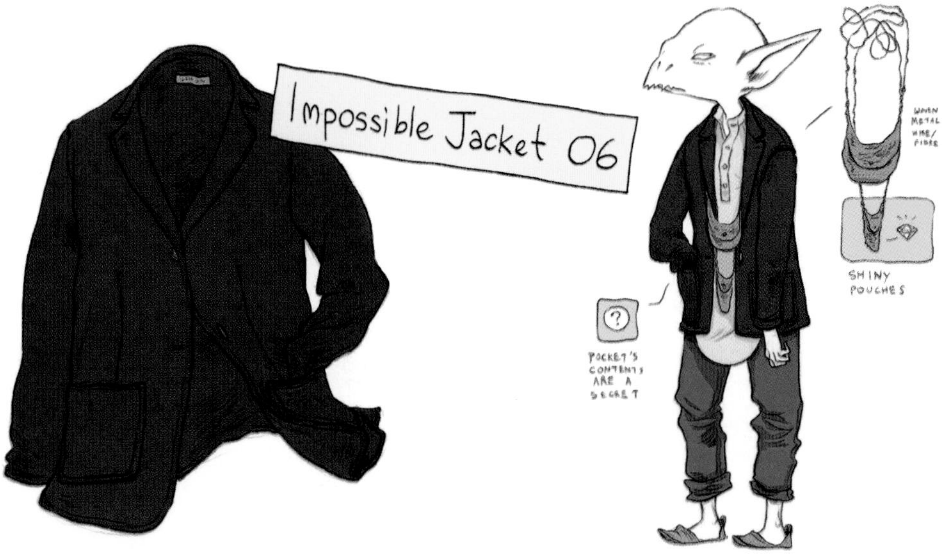
Impossible Jacket 06
WOVEN METAL WIRE/ FIBRE
SHINY POUCHES
?
POCKET'S CONTENTS ARE A SECRET

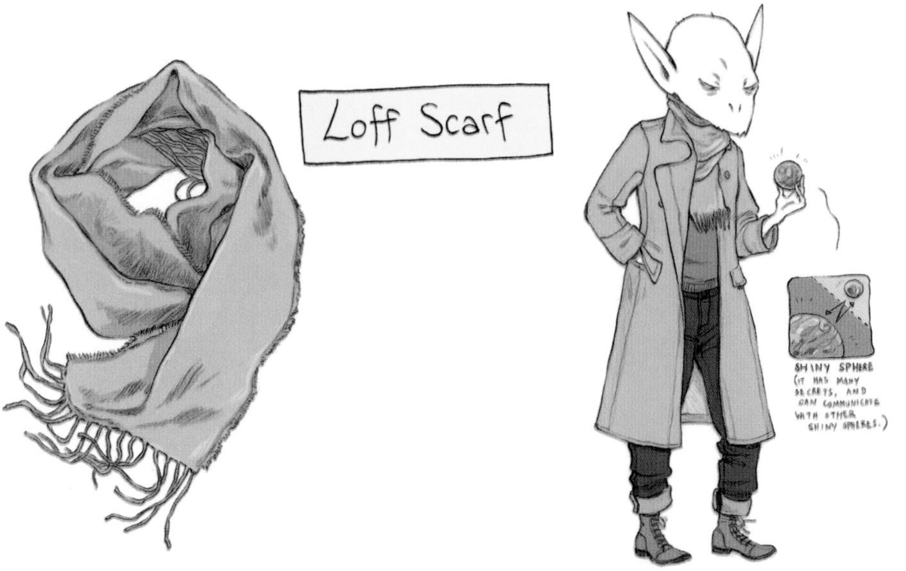
Loff Scarf
SHINY SPHERE
(IT HAS MANY SECRETS, AND CAN COMMUNICATE WITH OTHER SHINY SPHERES.)

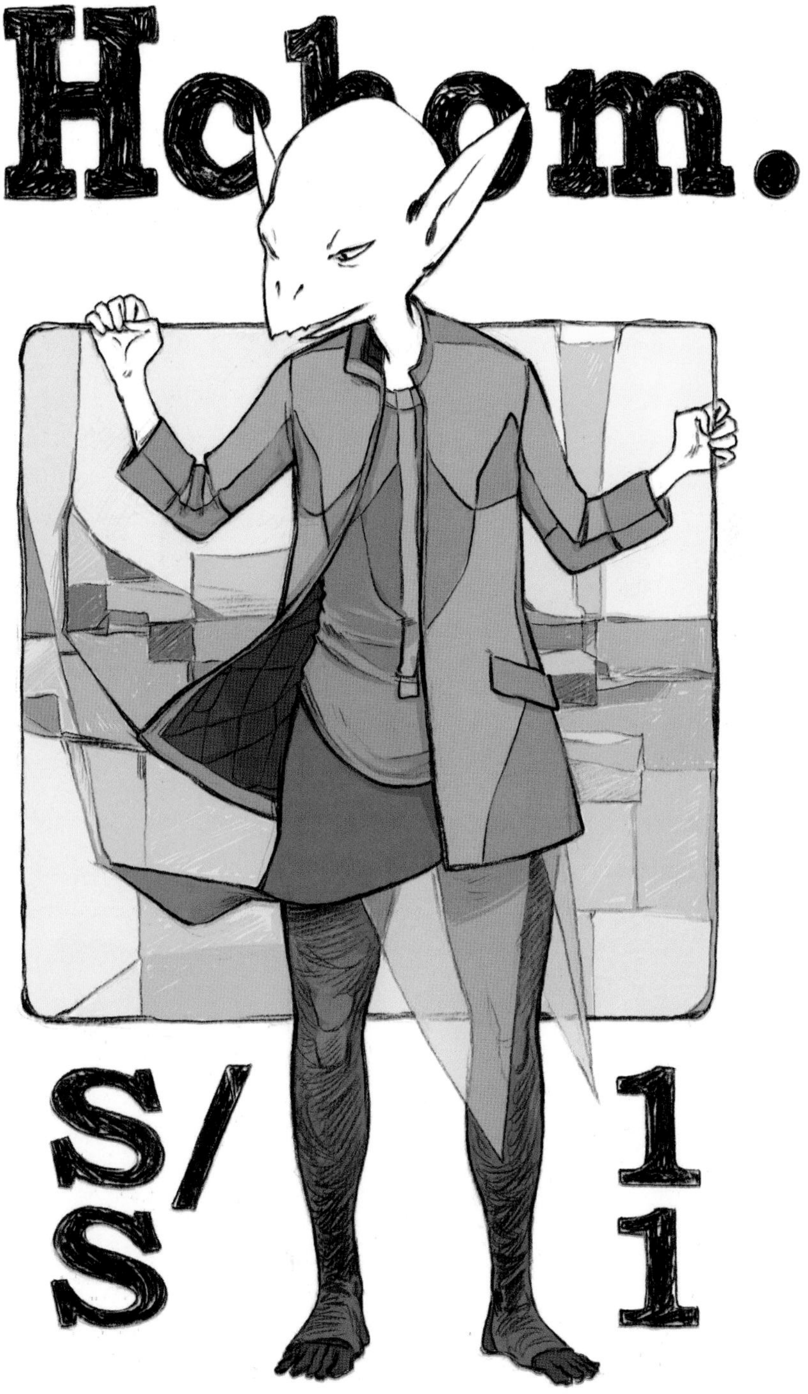
Hobom.
S/S
11

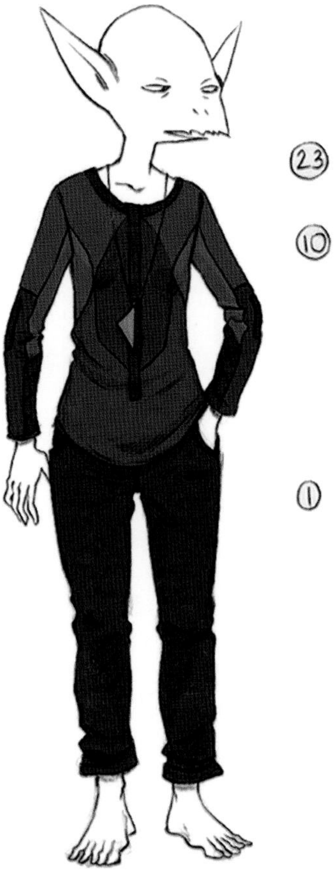
23
10
1

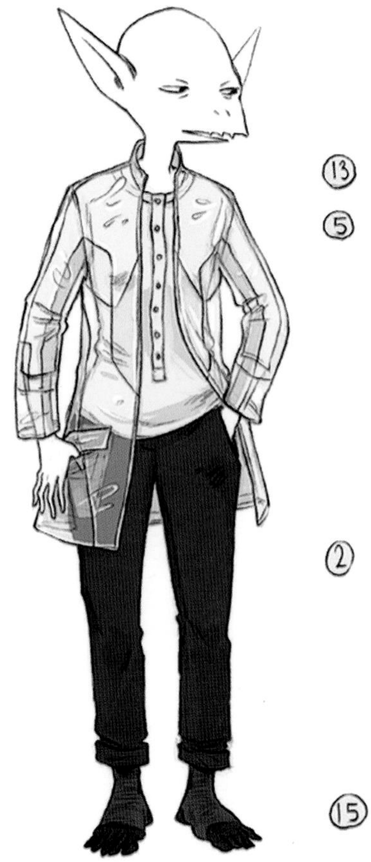
13
5
2
15

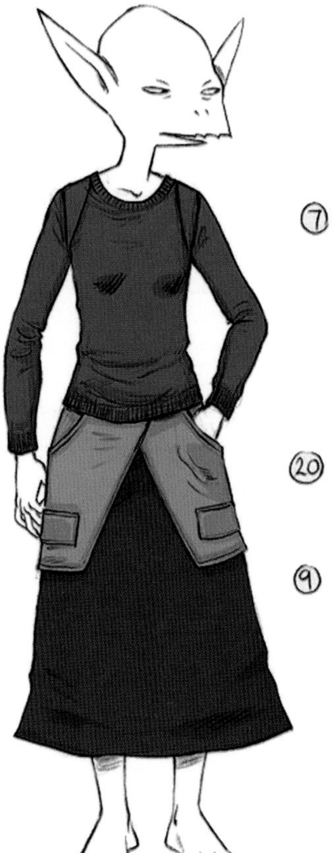
7
20
9

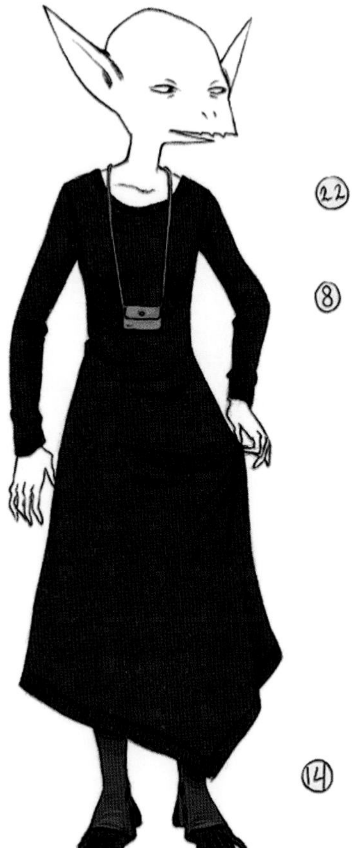
22
8
14

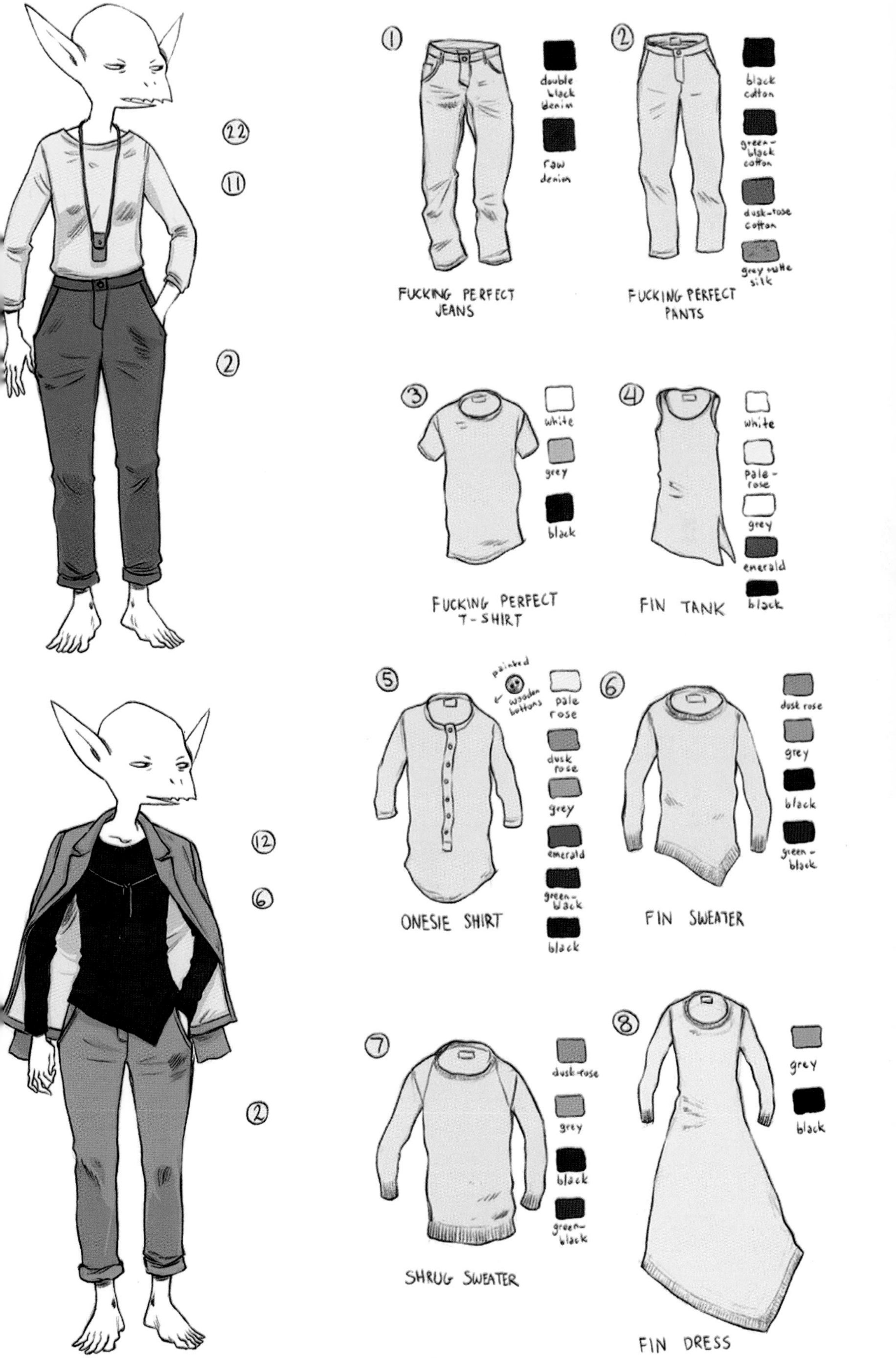
22
11
2
12
6
2
1
double black denim
raw denim
FUCKING PERFECT JEANS
2
black cotton
green-black cotton
dusk-rose cotton
grey matte silk
FUCKING PERFECT PANTS
3
white
grey
black
FUCKING PERFECT T-SHIRT
4
white
pale-rose
grey
emerald
black
FIN TANK
5
painted wooden buttons
pale rose
dusk rose
grey
emerald
green-black
black
ONESIE SHIRT
6
dusk rose
grey
black
green-black
FIN SWEATER
7
dusk-rose
grey
black
green-black
SHRUG SWEATER
8
grey
black
FIN DRESS

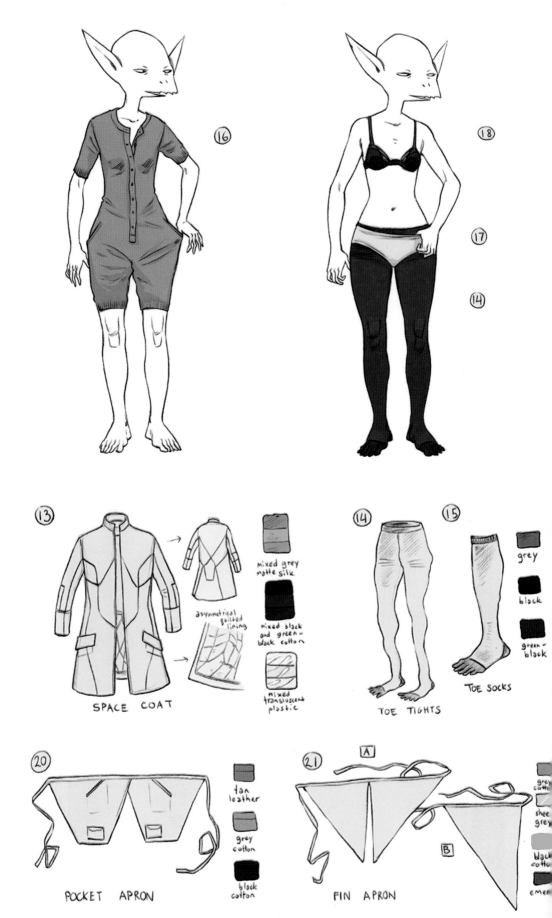

16

18

17

14

13   SPACE COAT

mixed grey
matte silk

mixed black
and green-
black cotton

mixed
transluscent
plastic

asymmetrical
quilted
lining

14   TOE TIGHTS

15   TOE SOCKS

grey

black

green-
black

20   POCKET APRON

tan
leather

grey
cotton

black
cotton

21   FIN APRON

A

B

grey
cotton

sheer
grey

black
cotton

emer

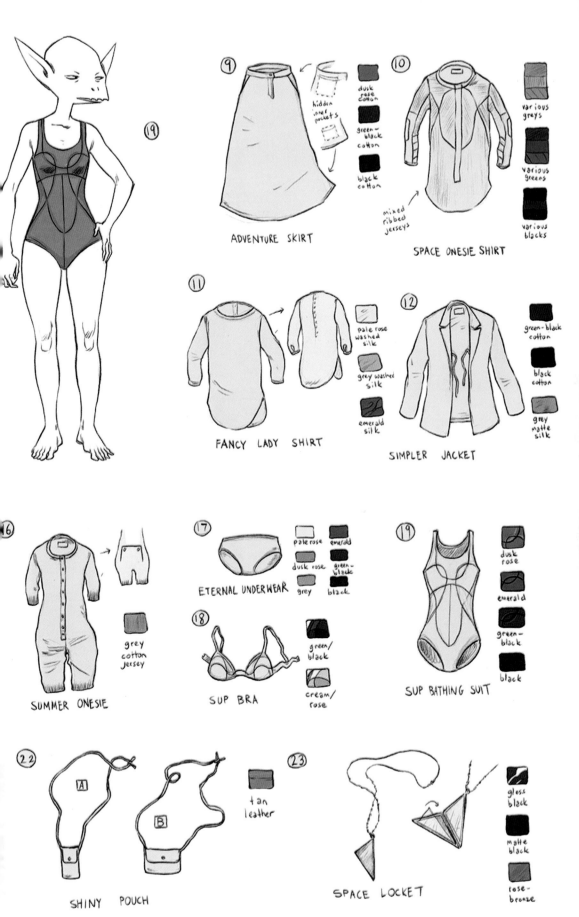

(9) ADVENTURE SKIRT

hidden inner pockets

dusk rose cotton

green-black cotton

black cotton

(10) SPACE ONESIE SHIRT

mixed ribbed jerseys

various greys

various greens

various blacks

(11) FANCY LADY SHIRT

pale rose washed silk

grey washed silk

emerald silk

(12) SIMPLER JACKET

green-black cotton

black cotton

grey matte silk

(16) SUMMER ONESIE

grey cotton jersey

(17) ETERNAL UNDERWEAR

pale rose   emerald

dusk rose   green-black

grey   black

(18) SUP BRA

green/black

cream/rose

(19) SUP BATHING SUIT

dusk rose

emerald

green-black

black

(22) SHINY POUCH

A

B

tan leather

(23) SPACE LOCKET

gloss black

matte black

rose-bronze

(19)

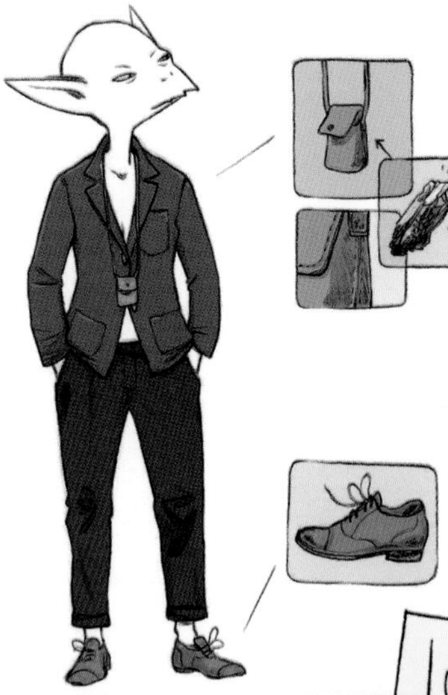

(06/24/2011) *I have a fancy wedding to attend in August, and this is the kind of androgynous gentlewoman look that, ideally, I would like to show up in. All I really need are very expensive pants. Isn't that a human right?*

Also, I wish this shiny-holding leather pouch actually existed. I have an ongoing daydream that I'll someday meet the amazing local leatherworker, Tannis Hegan, and convince her to take a commission.

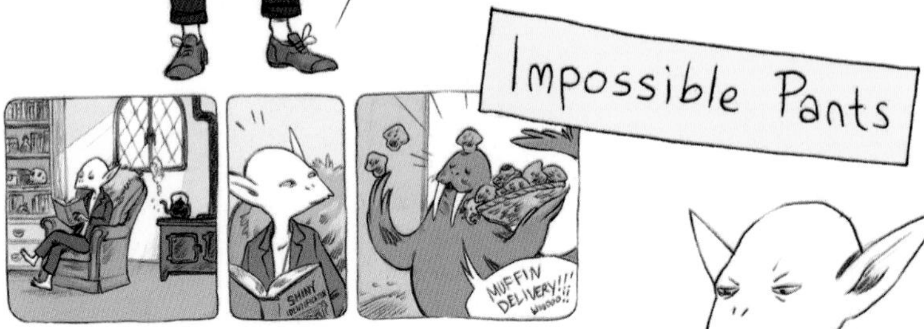
Impossible Pants
MUFFIN DELIVERY!!!

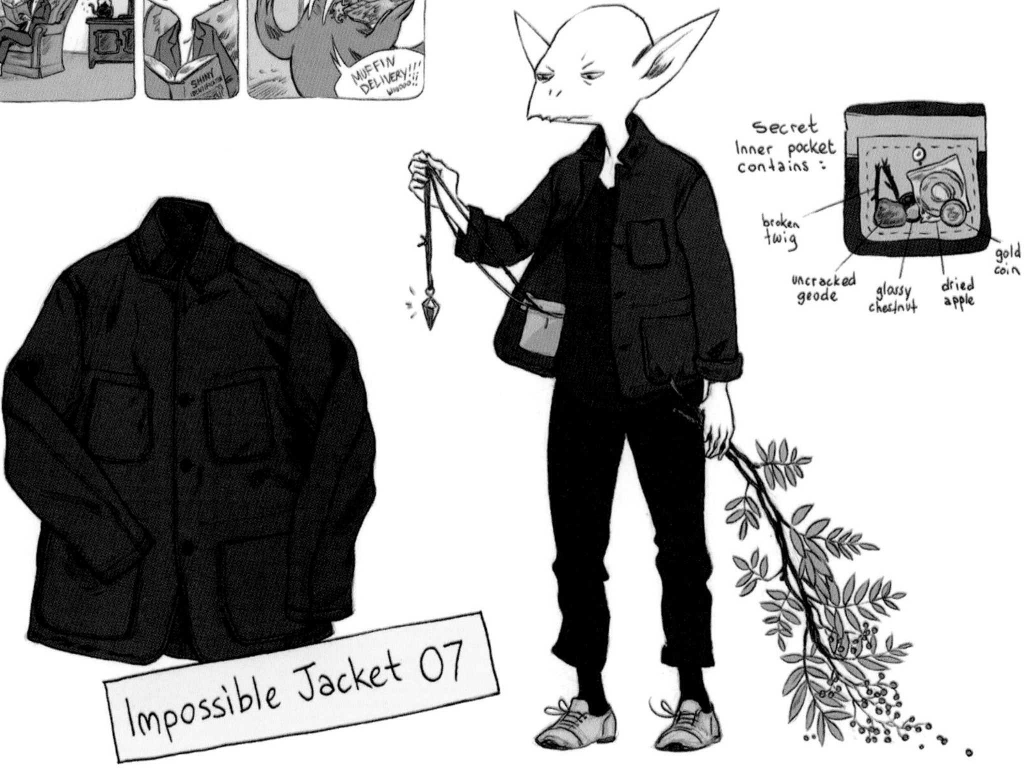
Secret Inner pocket contains:
broken twig
uncracked geode
glossy chestnut
dried apple
gold coin
Impossible Jacket 07

(09/06/2011) *This is a Bedford Jacket. It's made by Engineered Garments, which is a brand I love—and a menswear brand, all the better. I have a winter coat by them, altered to fit, and it's the best coat ever. So what I want now, since what we have is never good enough (and really, the coat is getting a bit threadbare at the cuffs), is a version of this Bedford jacket in a heavy wool flannel and a nice dark navy, if you please.*

Also, while I'm free and easy with the demands, I'd like some bright yellow gentlemen shoes. For my Urban-Dandy-Tom-Bombadil cosplay project, you understand.

Hchom.

A/W 1 1

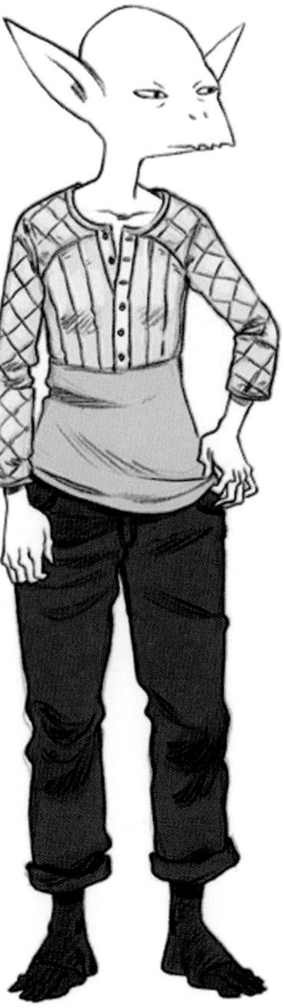

12
1 A
3

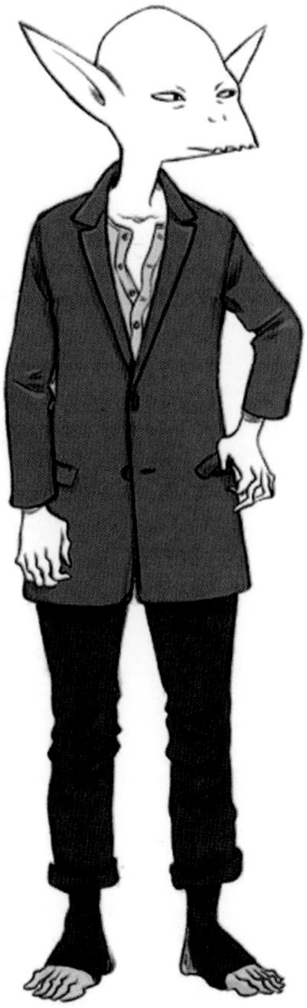

13
6
1 B
3

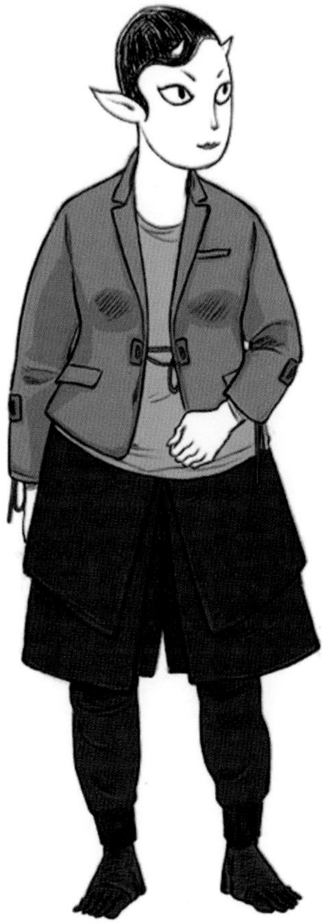

15
4
19
8
3

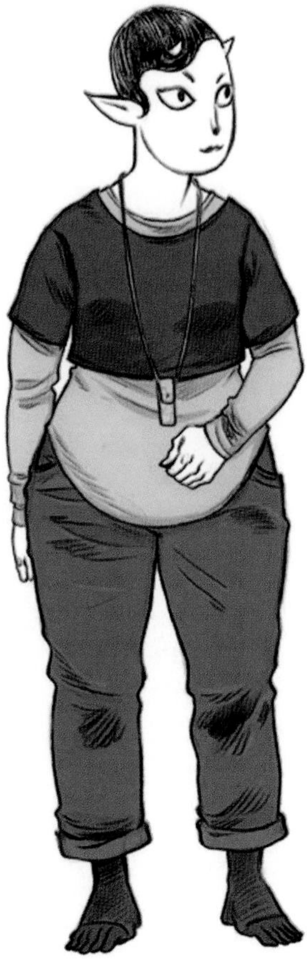

21 B
17
5
1 A
3

10

3

14

11

1 B

3

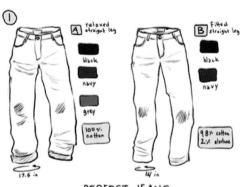

① A relaxed straight leg / B fitted straight leg

black
navy
grey
100% cotton

black
navy
98% cotton 2% elastane

17.5 in   14 in

PERFECT JEANS

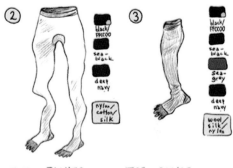

② black/FFCC00 / sea-black / deep navy / nylon/cotton/silk

③ black/FFCC00 / sea-black / sea-grey / deep navy / wool/silk/nylon

TOE TIGHTS   TOE SOCKS

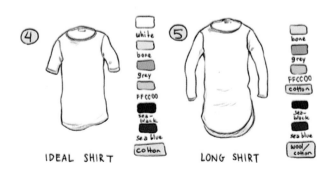

④ white / bone / grey / FFCC00 / sea-black / sea blue / cotton

⑤ bone / grey / FFCC00 cotton / sea-black / sea blue / wool/cotton

IDEAL SHIRT   LONG SHIRT

⑥ bone / grey / FFCC00 cotton / sea-black / sea blue / wool/cotton

⑦ bone / grey cotton / black / sea blue / dark garnet / wool/cotton

LONG HENLEY   LONG DRESS

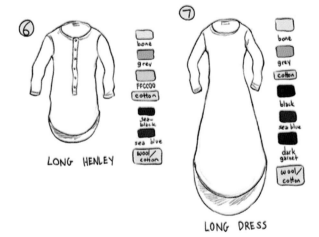

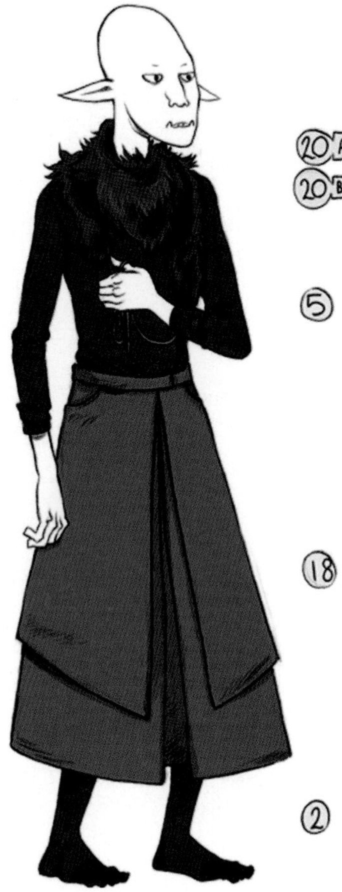
20 A
20 B
5
18
2

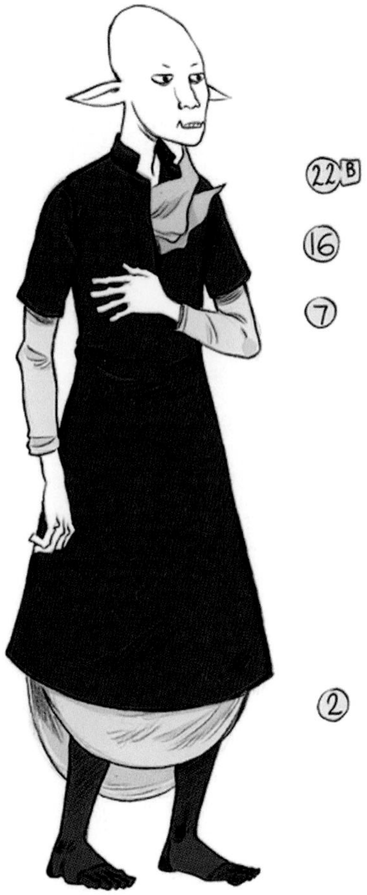
22 B
16
7
2

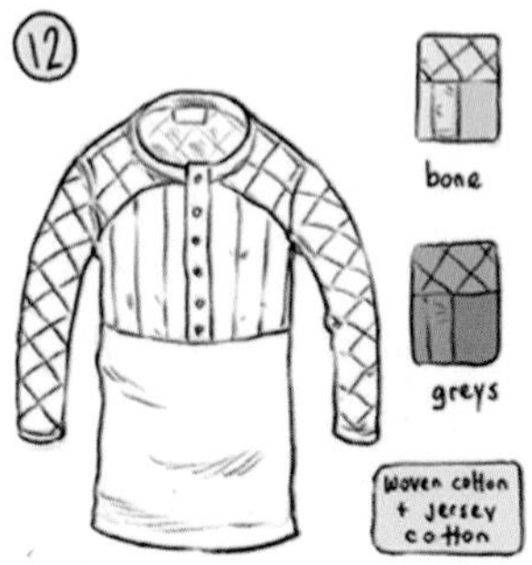
12
bone
greys
woven cotton + jersey cotton

CRUSADES SHIRT

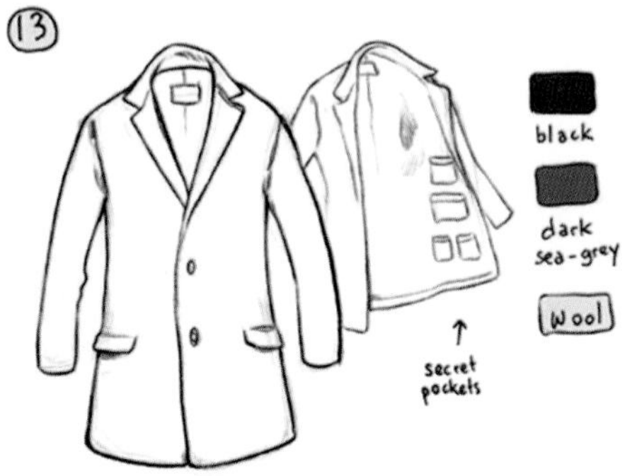
13
black
dark sea-grey
wool
secret pockets

SECRETS COAT

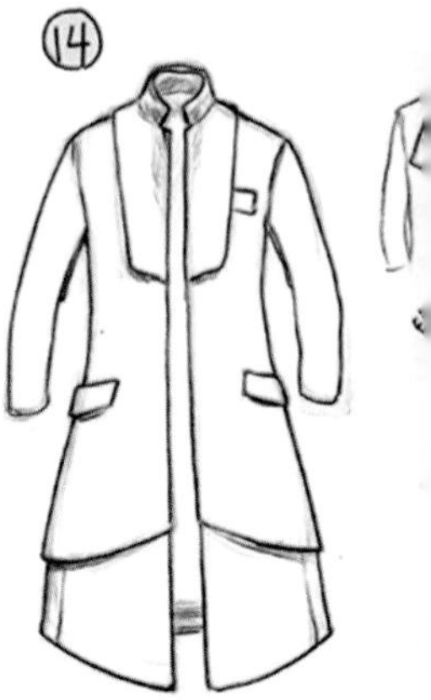
14

FLAP COAT

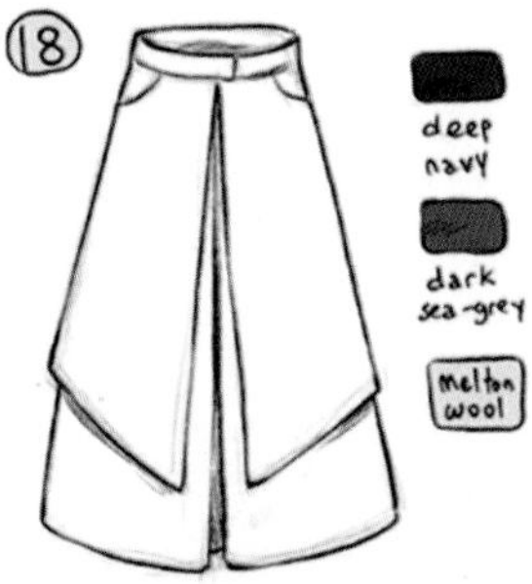
18
deep navy
dark sea-grey
melton wool

FLAP SKIRT

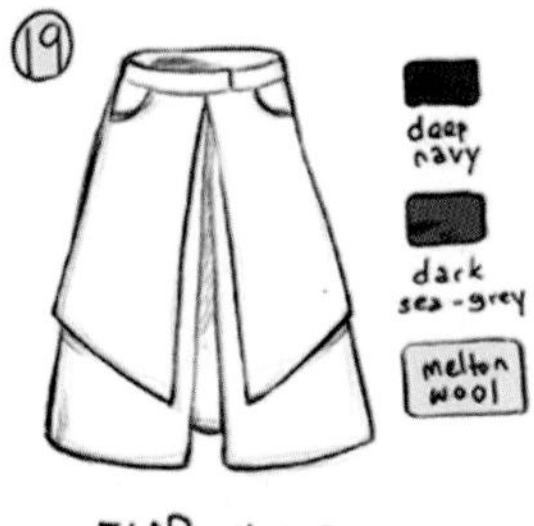
19
deep navy
dark sea-grey
melton wool

FLAP SHORTS

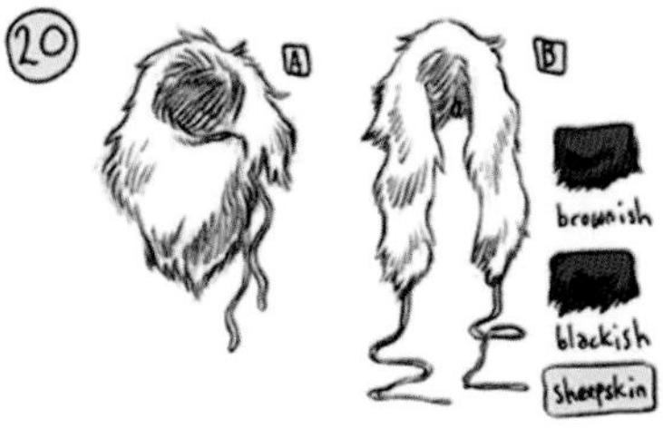
20
A
B
brownish
blackish
sheepskin

SHEEPY FRIEND

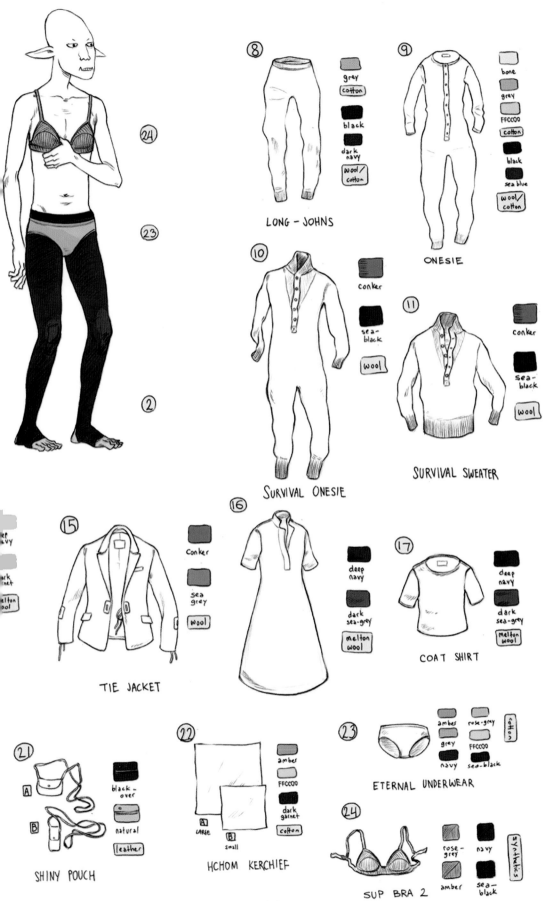

24

23

2

⑧ grey
cotton

black

dark navy

wool/cotton

LONG - JOHNS

⑨ bone

grey

FFCC00

cotton

black

sea blue

wool/cotton

ONESIE

⑩ conker

sea-black

wool

SURVIVAL ONESIE

⑪ conker

sea-black

wool

SURVIVAL SWEATER

⑮ conker

sea grey

wool

TIE JACKET

⑯ deep navy

dark sea-grey

melton wool

⑰ deep navy

dark sea-grey

melton wool

COAT SHIRT

㉑ A

B

black-over

natural

leather

SHINY POUCH

㉒ ambes

FFCC00

dark garnet

cotton

A LARGE

B small

HCHOM KERCHIEF

㉓ ambes   rose-grey

grey   FFCC00   cotton

navy   sea-black

ETERNAL UNDERWEAR

㉔ rose-grey   navy   synthetics

amber   sea-black

SUP BRA 2

65

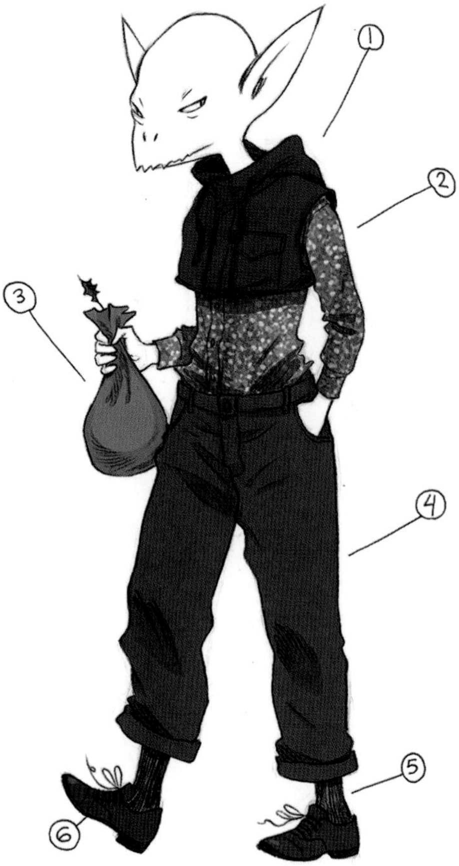
1
2
3
4
5
6

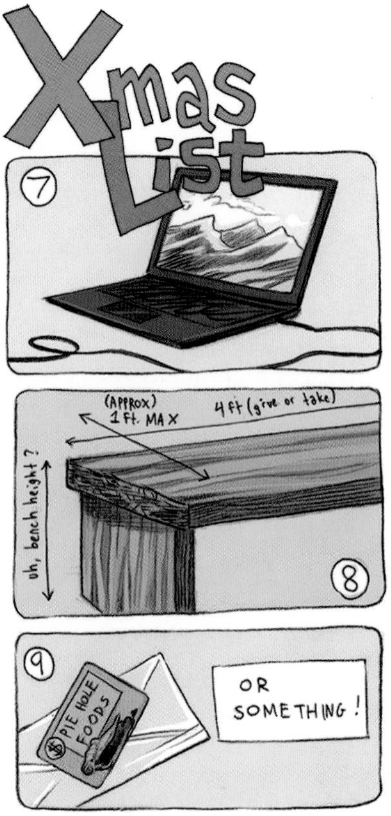
Xmas List
7
(APPROX)
1 Ft. MAX
4 ft (give or take)
uh, bench height?
8
9
PIE HOLE FOODS
OR SOMETHING!

(11/28/2011) *1. This is likely an impossible request, but I want it more than anything: the Engineered Garments FWK shoulder hoodie (in navy or black, if you please, but I wouldn't turn down grey). I should have ordered this from Nepenthes back in the fall, but a bunch of things got in the way. It's probably a good thing that they don't ship to Canada, or I'd be constantly abusing the privilege (it's not really a good thing, guys, that's just me trying to soothe myself). Anyway, Hchom and Christmas lists both get a quota of impossible items, yes? This is the impossiblest.*

2. I'm trying to think what FWK (best brand ever—all I want to wear right now) piece I can ask for as consolation. I have a curious attraction to this liberty print shirt.

3. This bag has a pudding in it, just saying. Possibly also a kitten and a pony, and a large quantity of very expensive, single-origin dark chocolate.

4. Though I don't really need them, I could always use a backup pair of oversized Levi's 501s. Perversely (or not, as you prefer), I like the cheaply made $30 ones better than the fancy vintage/heritage versions.

5. Socks, just for something to attach a number to. And because I'm down to four pairs, three with holes in the heel.

6. These shoes are too pricey to ask for, but I want them and therefore I'm listing them. Plus, look, they completed the ensemble.

7. I was thinking about asking for one of those tiny, cheap computers, as a secondary laptop, then I decided that was silly, and of course I don't need one (but I put it up anyway, because it was already drawn and scanned). So yes, ignore this. Most useless Christmas list ever! Moving on…

8. I'd like Dad to make me a bench out of parallam (my dad invented this wood), for my hallway.

9. Gift certificates that provide me with tasty things are always good.

Impossible Pants 02

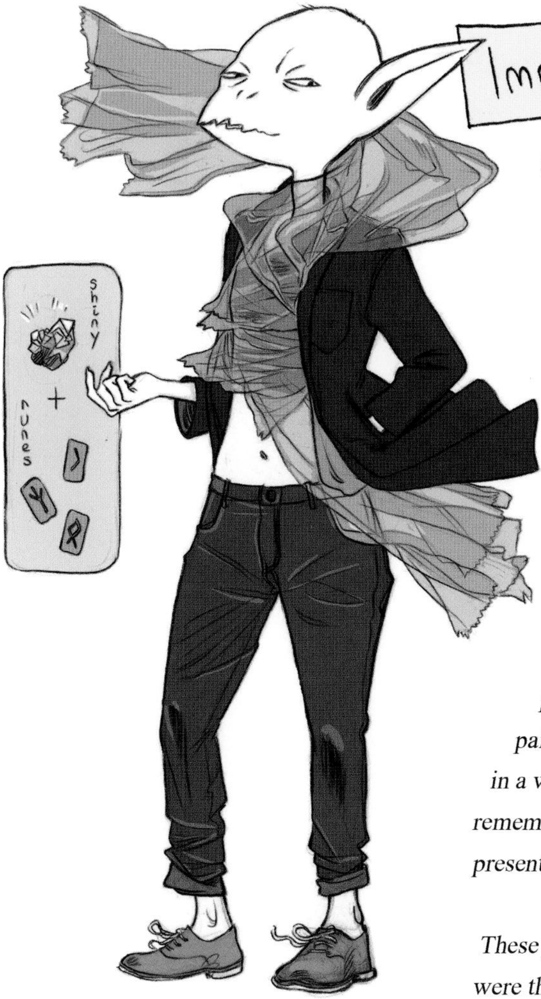
shiny
+
runes

(02/20/2013) I expect all of us (or those of us who can spend time being wistful about absurd stuff like this) remember a particular pair of pants that were THE ONE. I should hesitate to write "the one pair to rule them all", but I won't. Because perfect pants call for tired-out Lord Of The Rings references, and you only live once.

Anyway, moving on unedited, my personal perfect pants were these: a pair of Acne jeans in a style called "Hug", in a wash called—I can't believe I remember this—"So What" (you might presently be asking yourself, "so what?").

These jeans, I assure you, were perfect. They were the sort of crisp (no stretch) close-loose cut that only works if they fit you with total precision. Total precision! Which, for jeans? Impossible. But these did fit like that, in my case. Then eventually the knees gave out and ripped, first one then the other, so I cut them up into shorts. INTO SHORTS. LIKE A FOOL.

And I have thought about these pants so often over the past four years, it must prove what my doctor tells me every time he takes my blood pressure, which is that I don't have enough stress in my life (although I promise you, doctor, that cannot be the issue). But here is where all my plans for this post fall apart, because when I was searching the internet for a picture of these specific jeans in this specific wash, I actually found them—one last pair of them, though they are at least five years old, in exactly my size and inseam—on a Danish website, hugely reduced in price, practically tossed out in the street for anyone to pick up and take home. So with limited help from Google translate, and a very dubious idea of my ever actually receiving them (they may yet be impossible), I ventured an order.

Impossible Jacket 08

(03/15/2013) *I've already written about this jacket, but it deserves a post of its own. And for me it is, perhaps, THE impossible jacket.*

It's made by a label called BORNE—long-defunct but forever amazing. This one in particular is the Siren Suit Jacket, but you must accept my authority here: this designer had some kind of deal with the devil going, and every single jacket she made was flawless. FLAWLESS.

And I YEARN for them. Let me quote myself from an old post: "my real ambition in life is to find this designer, and implore her, weeping, with fists full of cash, to make me another one, please, just one more." And it's still true. If I could travel through time (like a terminator), there are a lot of things that I could fix—things that ought to take priority. But no. I would return to the winter of 2006, sell one of my plump young organs, and buy two of every jacket in this line.

GRIMOIRE

spells

trapped
spirits

plant
cuttings

(poisonous?)
xx

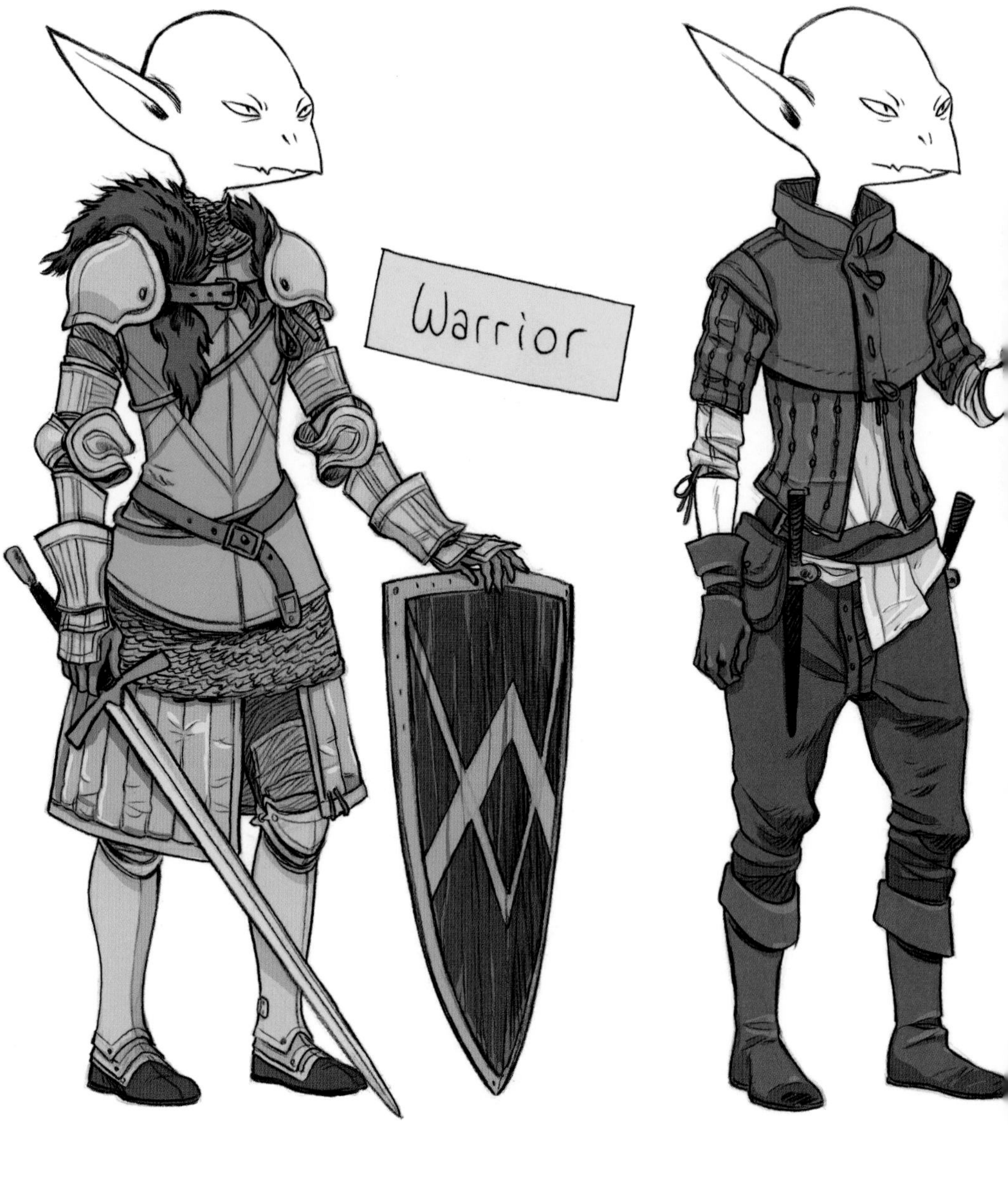
Warrior

(09/23/2013) *I've been doing an odd thing, over the last year or two: I've started to create mage characters in videogames, and not just as an afterthought on some bored fourth play-through, but for actual preference. This might sound like an "odd thing" only in the sense of "why the hell is this worth mentioning", but if you are like me and prefer to express your complex personhood via well-ruled-out fantasy conventions, then you will understand that a change of class is like a change of identity.*

Since I must compact things into nice, tidy theories, I've noticed that this class-switching happens roughly once a decade. When I was a teenager, I invariably went for the warrior-type. In my twenties,

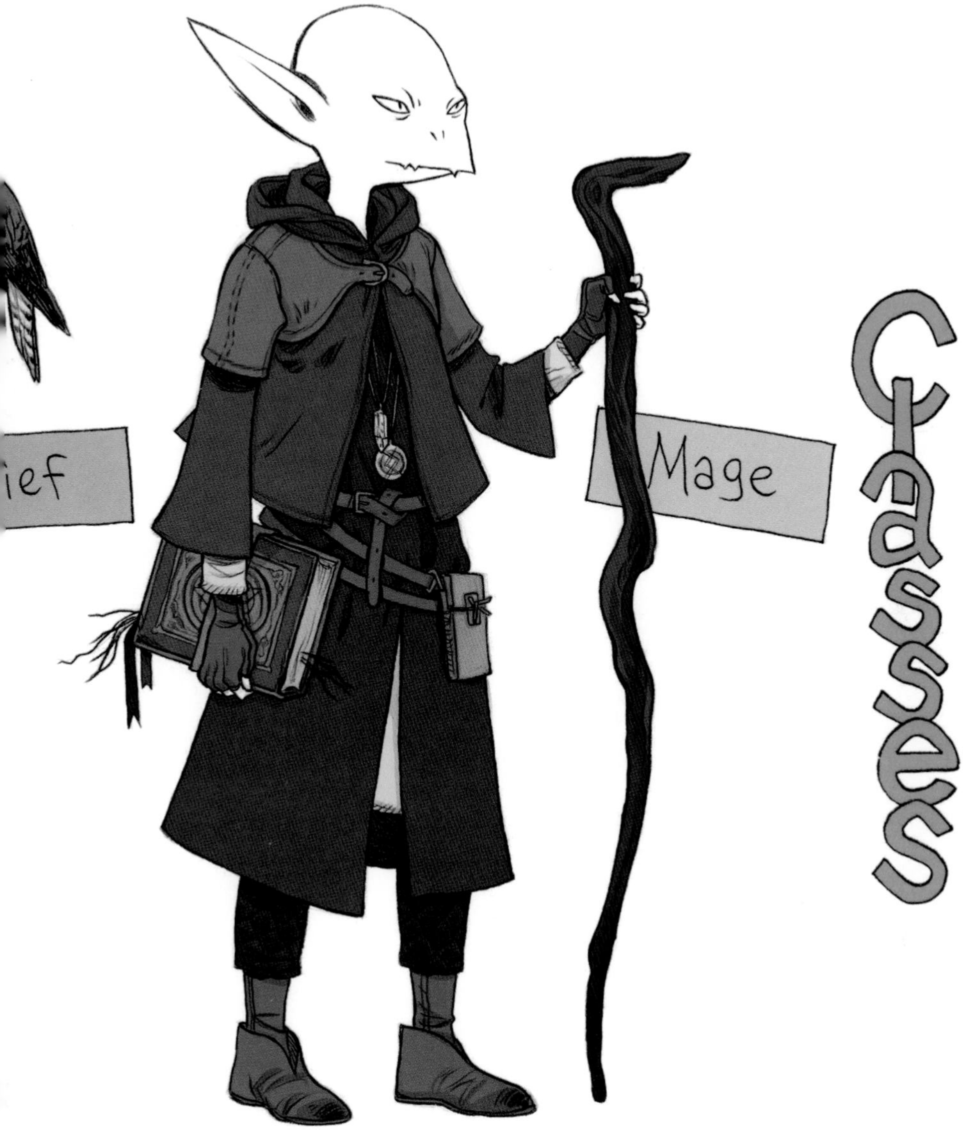
ief
Mage
Classes

it was always a thief. I'm embarrassed to say that during these eras I viewed mages as the default girl-class, as if that was a terrible, shameful thing to be avoided at all costs. So now my sudden interest feels almost subversive. Like, ooh, a mage, can I get away with it? Will nobody stop this brazen act of rebellion? Will I be able to find robes that don't look like a prom dress?

Maybe my theory will hold another decade, and I'll take it full circle. I like to imagine myself at 40, going a little overboard with the shield-bash. Or maybe at that point we transcend the basic classes, and get into rangers and paladins and other shady stuff. We'll see. In the meantime, here are some character-class-exemplifying goblins.

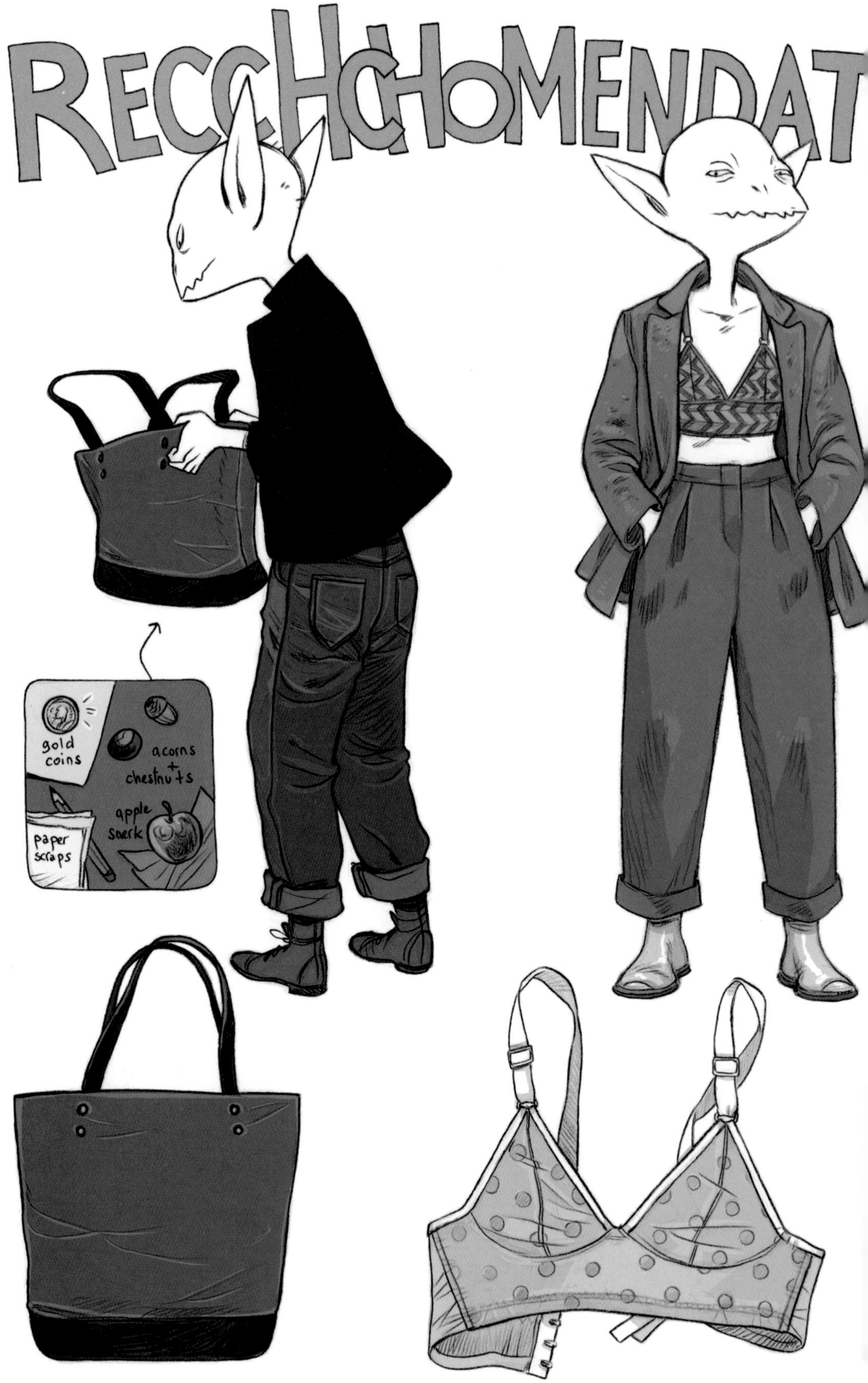
RECCHHOMENDAT
gold coins
acorns + chestnuts
apple snerk
paper scraps

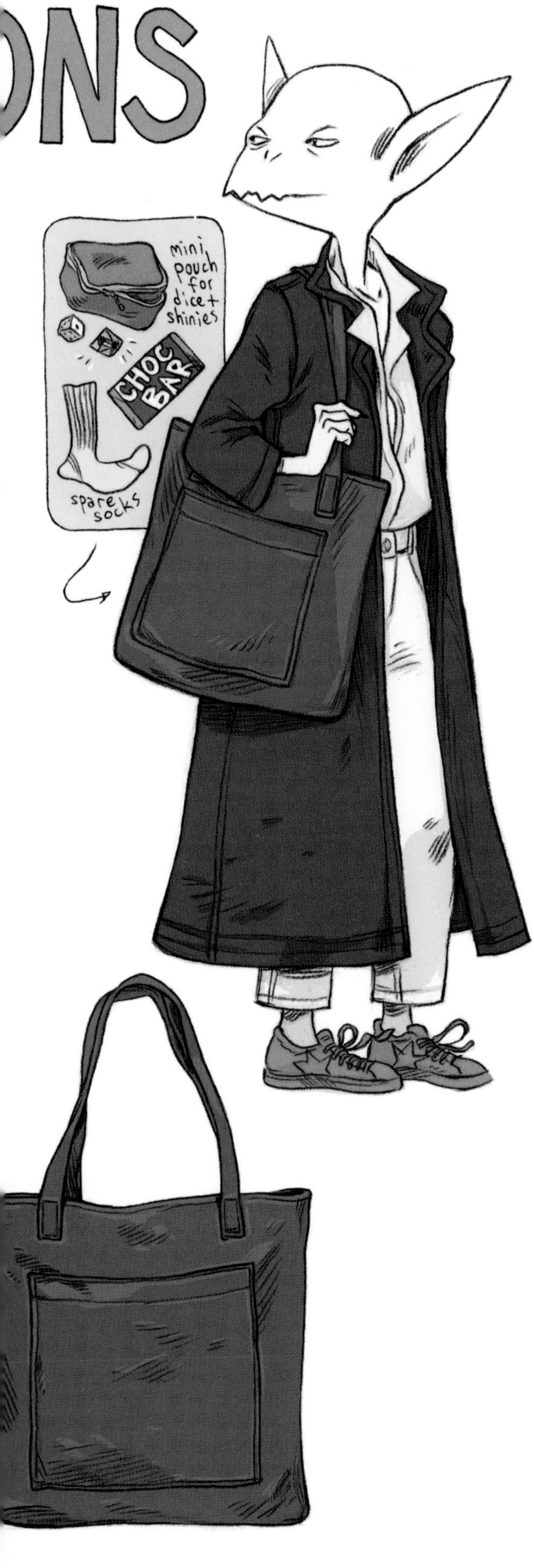
ONS
mini pouch for dice + shinies
CHOC BAR
spare socks

1. Southern Field Industries Bags from Saitama Japan: glossy leather and waxy canvas and many pleasing structural details.

2. Fortnight Lingerie from Canada: elegant, and surprisingly durable; available in beautiful materials and colours.

3. Erin Templeton Bags from Canada: simple and perfect; made here in Vancouver, often from recycled leather. The pouches and zip wallets come in every bright colour, and I want them all.

(06/27/2014) Once, in a bygone age, I bought new jackets like they were no big deal. New jacket? Pshaw. Three jackets a year, at least, and time let me play and be golden in the mercy of his means. But a new jacket means more to me, now, and I have to consider very carefully how it's going to fit into my wardrobe, and what I'm going to wear it with, and so on.

So here is my new black jean jacket, three ways:

1. Personal everyday uniform of black jeans, white/grey/black men's t-shirt, and sneakers. I like to think that this outfit is a blank canvas for the excellence of a jacket.

3.

Jean Jacket

2. All baggy everything. I've been trying really hard to master this style and discover just the right balance of proportions, but I suspect that the key to it looking really awesome is actually just not caring.

3. Strange nerd-mage with embarrassing fantasy accoutrements? Truly, I wish I owned this absurd full body hood-tunic. I like to think that a slightly braver Marian could dip her toes into the wide waters of androgynous skirts and dresses. Future hopes and dreams.

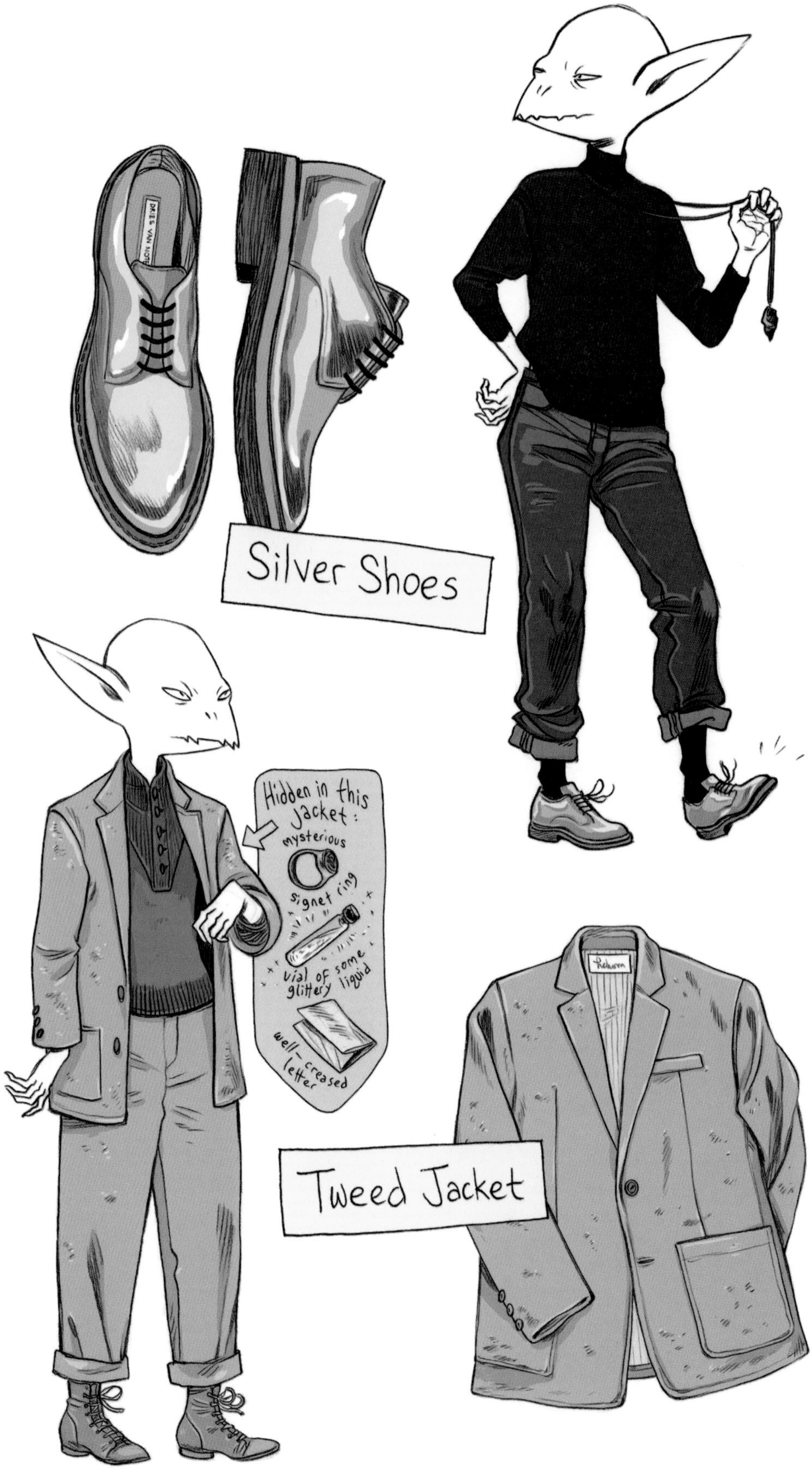
Silver Shoes
Hidden in this jacket:
mysterious signet ring
vial of some glittery liquid
well-creased letter
Tweed Jacket

Chapter 03:

The Hchom Hoard

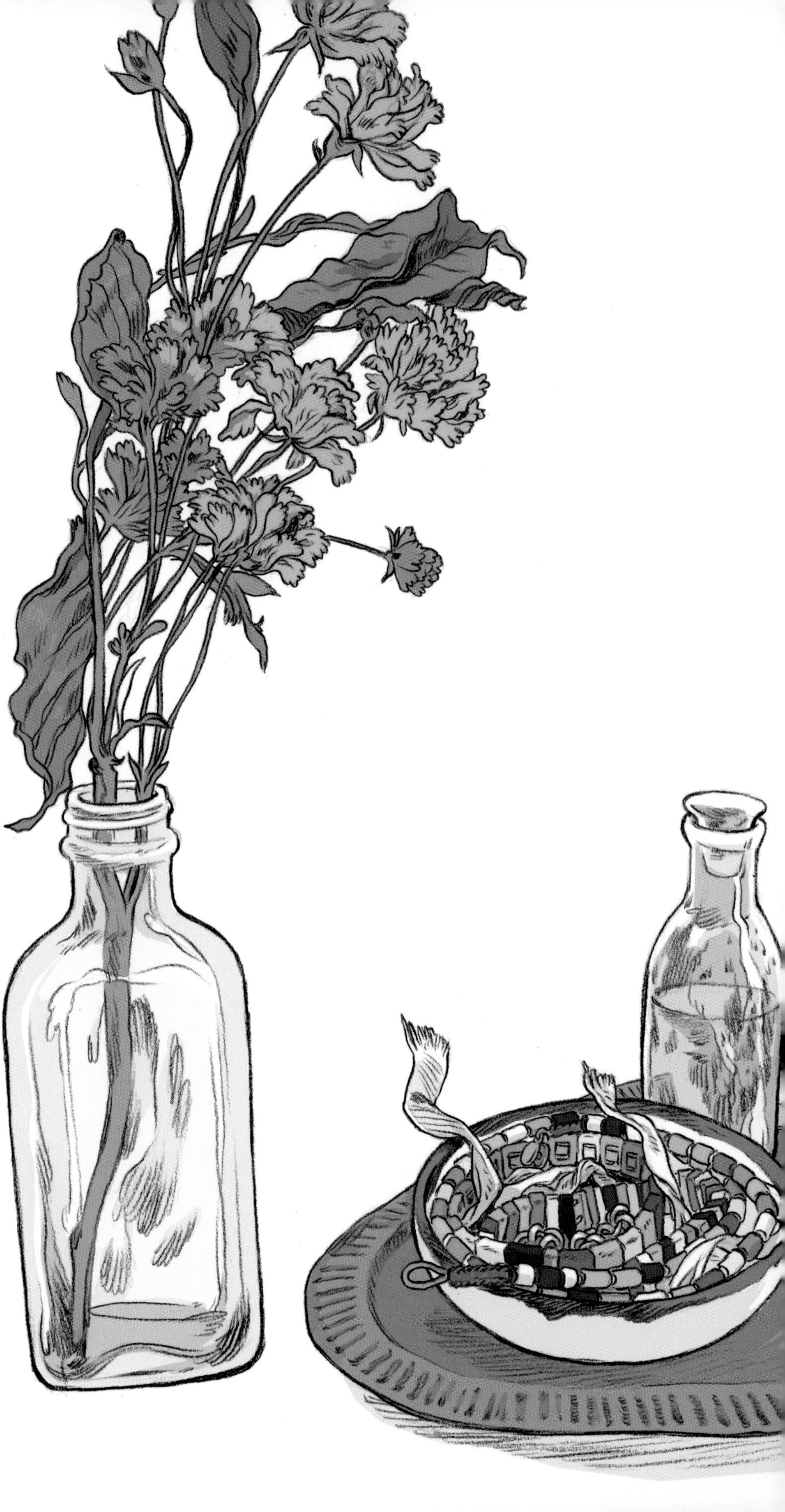

Now here we get to the real meat of this book, the hoard! My want is bottomless; I could plumb it forever and still go on wanting. And yet, my lifestyle is relatively minimal. I don't own a lot of stuff—I take less satisfaction from ownership than I do from desire—and honouring a want by drawing it or writing about it is often enough to release me from that particular geas.

I asked my sister to give me ideas for this chapter, and she said something I didn't expect: she said that my hoards remind her of how I used to make shrines when we were kids. Without worshipping anything in particular, I would build little shrines in the forest and leave offerings there. In fact, I still have one that I maintain, and the last offering I left, just a week ago, was a tiny, transluscent pink egg I found abandoned on the ground.

Maybe there's something shrine-like, too, about the way I catalogue my wants, and the way I arrange them on the page. Is this starting to sound like a stretch? I know it's not spiritual, but the form and repetition have a ritual quality, as if there's something I'm trying to conjure, or appease. A different life, or a different self, or something less definite, where wanting replaces knowing.

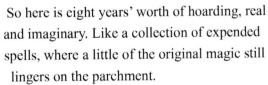

So here is eight years' worth of hoarding, real and imaginary. Like a collection of expended spells, where a little of the original magic still lingers on the parchment.

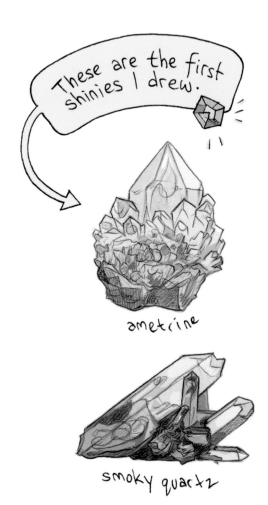

These are the first shinies I drew.

ametrine

smoky quartz

H.B.M.

Happy Birthday Marian

A birthday is a day of sanctioned wanting. On mine, I perform what I imagine is the standard ritual: I make a ceremony of deciding what I'd like for breakfast and dinner and dessert, what unreasonable thing I might buy for myself, etc. I've gone overboard a few times; entitlement quickly turns to misery, but all in all, it works just fine. What I like even better than the birthday itself, however, is the anticipation. Every child knows that the best presents are the ones you have yet to recieve.

2010
TES V
?
!!
?

(06/05/2010) *1. TES V: I'm hoping they announce the next Elder Scrolls game at E3, as a present just for me. 2. Of course, that means I'll need a new laptop. 3. I'm fixated on this skirt, and I don't know why. It's very expensive (and also a skirt). 4. While I'm asking for impossible things, why not my own cabin? That would be nice. 5. If I have a cabin, I suppose I'll need a car. 6. I'd like to have a shiny with a gift-granting creature trapped inside it. I think about what I'd do if faced with three wishes on an almost daily basis, and even after decades of angsting over the question, I still don't know how I'd handle it. Maybe that's the appeal. 7. Sunny weather. 8. Almond croissants. One for breakfast, and six more to make pudding with later on. 9. Fine larder meats. 10. And a trip to the shiny store, of course. How could I not?*

SNEAK
SHOES

SNEAK + 5
-1 HP/ STEP for
10,000 steps.

300G 4.0

(06/25/2010) *This June, I decided that my birthday was going to be all about facing my fears, and making tentative forays into solid girl territory, so these are like a training-wheels version of lady shoes. I don't have much of a shoe fixation, not even secretly beneath my seventeen impenetrable anti-girl firewalls—I reserve that sort of fervor for jackets—but I liked these, because I thought they looked sneaky. Which is another protective mechanism of mine, by the way. If I see something feminine and I want it, I know I can't just naturally act on that feeling. I'm no fool. So I invent an entryway for it. I make it an inventory item, with helpful stats, and then I can want it without shame. Plus, these were an easy one, because I'm partial to anything handmade, and really, they're just old man shoes that have been re-shaped a little… well, I have to start somewhere.*

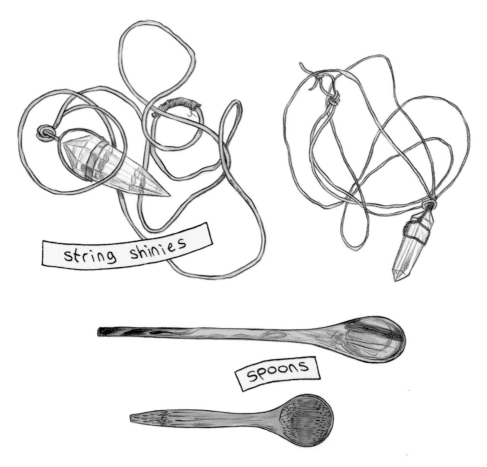

string shinies

spoons

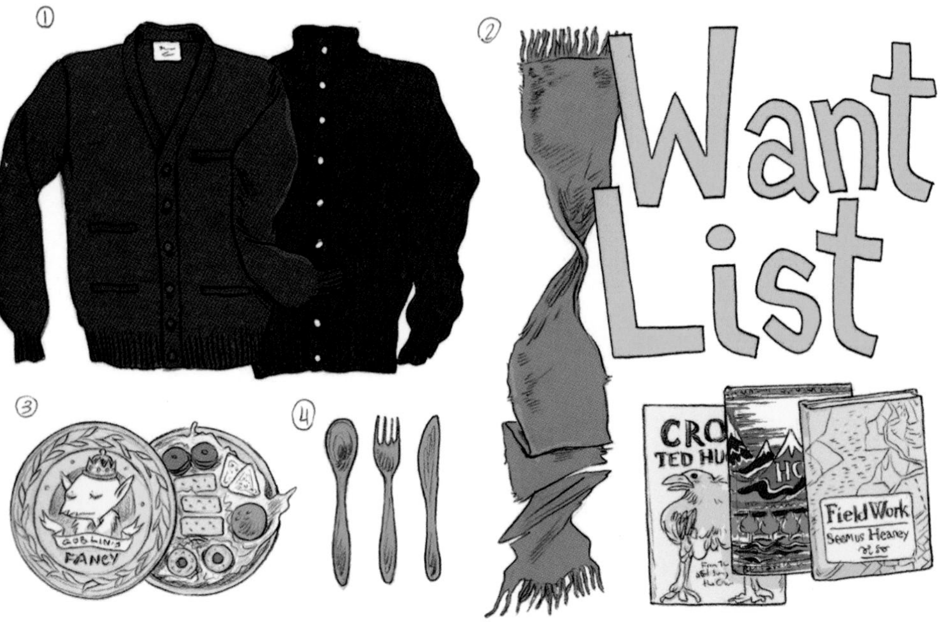
Want List
1
2
3
4
GOBLIN'S FANCY
CRO
TED HU
Field Work
Seamus Heaney

(10/13/2010) *1. MEN'S SWEATERS. Are superior to women's sweaters, I think. I like this one (pockets), and this one (Danish?).*

2. I've had a link to these Irish scarves (under Donegal Tweed > Scarves) in my "want" folder since I was about 18. That's 10 years of wanting!

3. Biscuits. Well. These biscuits obviously don't exist., but I have a specific yearning for a perfect tin of assorted biscuits. There has to be one out there somewhere.

4. Ok, wooden cutlery? I know, it's ridiculous, but I WANT it.

5. And though I don't get Hchom, mixed up with, like, Elevated Things, and Stuff, I'd like first edition copies of these books. I figure they don't count, because I want them mainly as Treasure.

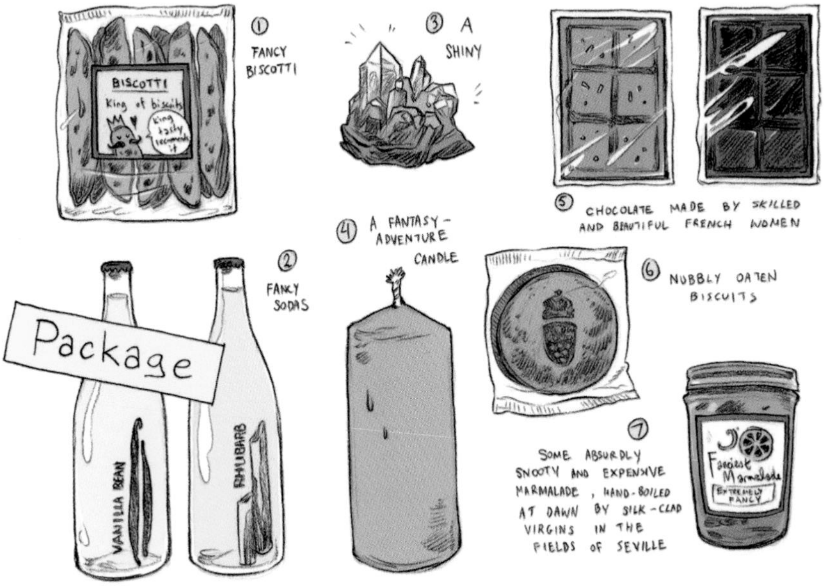
1 FANCY BISCOTTI
BISCOTTI
King of biscuits
3 A SHINY
5 CHOCOLATE MADE BY SKILLED AND BEAUTIFUL FRENCH WOMEN
4 A FANTASY-ADVENTURE CANDLE
2 FANCY SODAS
Package
VANILLA BEAN
RHUBARB
6 NUBBLY OATEN BISCUITS
7 SOME ABSURDLY SNOOTY AND EXPENSIVE MARMALADE, HAND-BOILED AT DAWN BY SILK-CLAD VIRGINS IN THE FIELDS OF SEVILLE
EXTREMELY FANCY

(04/08/2011) *I'd really like a package. The above assortment: many fine little things that would pair well with some hefty, familiar fantasy novel from my childhood. I'd demand that my sister make it for me, but that would be a jerk move just right now as she's flying to Prague in a week for a forestry conference. Prague! Damn that girl.* (Note: she made it for me anyway.)

Month of Wants

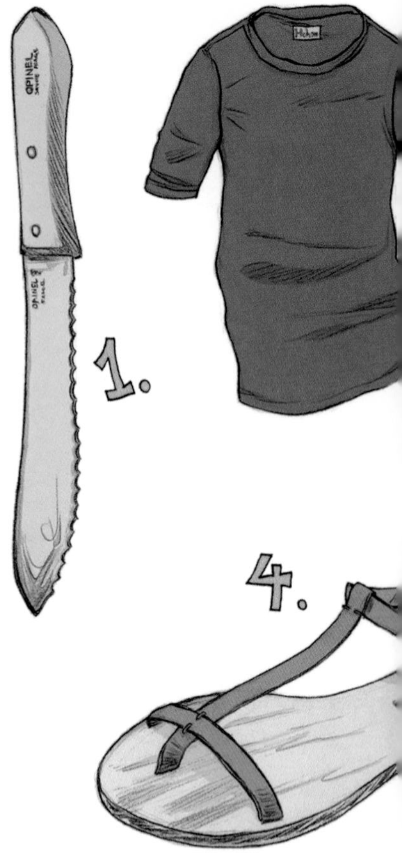
1.
4.

1. (04/12/2011) *Well, here's an unimpressive beginning. I wish I could say that this was a thrice-cursed demon-hunter's dagger, but no. It's just a bread knife.*

I eat a lot of bread, you see. A good loaf of bread will carry you through the week, no problem. It won't let you go hungry. It will tenderly sing you to sleep at night. And using a bad bread knife is like repaying a friend by hacking it into crumbling, uneven slabs that fall apart when you pick them up. Nobody would fault me for buying a new one, but right now that is sixty dollars I cannot spare.

2. (04/16/2011) *I would like some really excellent T-shirts. The kind you encounter about once a decade, and you wear them until they're falling off your back, all the while wishing you'd bought ten more.*

The shirt on the left is my Ultimate Marian Shirt. It doesn't exist as far as I know, but I want one in every increment of grey. The UMS of my imagination has longer sleeves than your average T-shirt, and a narrow body, very elongated.

The second shirt is just old-fashioned men's long underwear. It's no UMS, but I wouldn't mind having one.

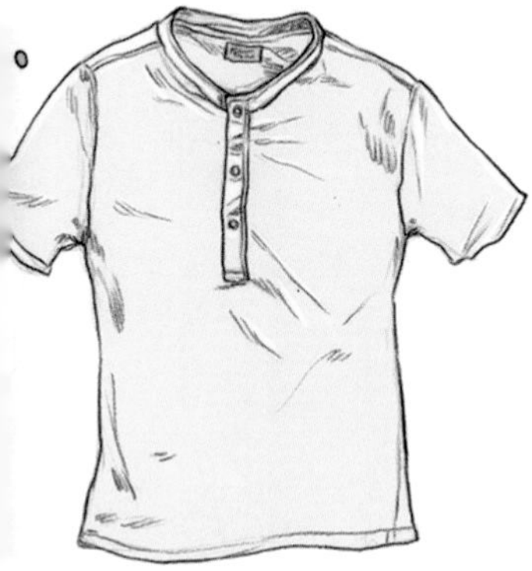

3.

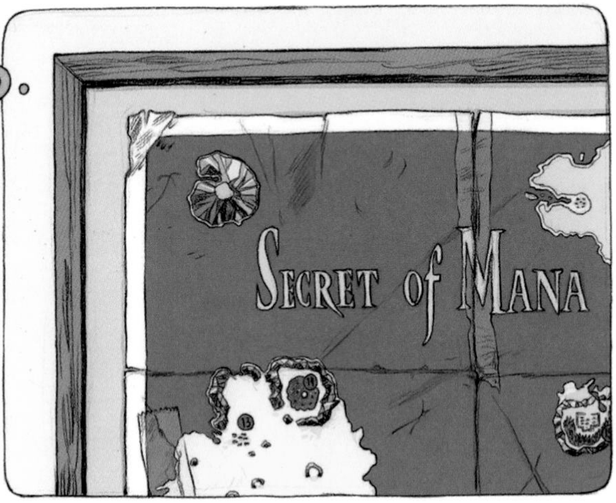
SECRET of MANA

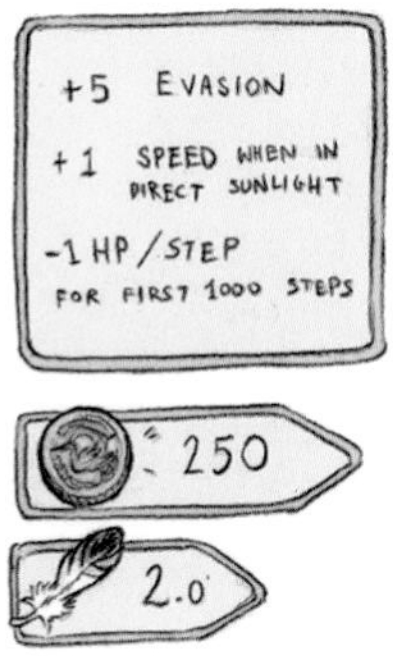
+5 EVASION
+1 SPEED WHEN IN DIRECT SUNLIGHT
-1 HP/STEP FOR FIRST 1000 STEPS
: 250
2.0

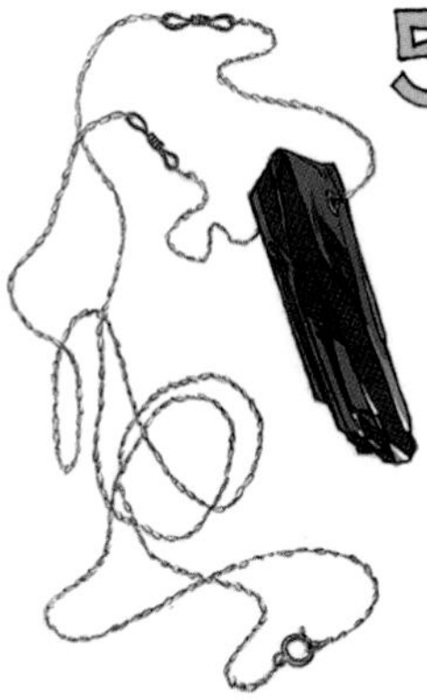

5.

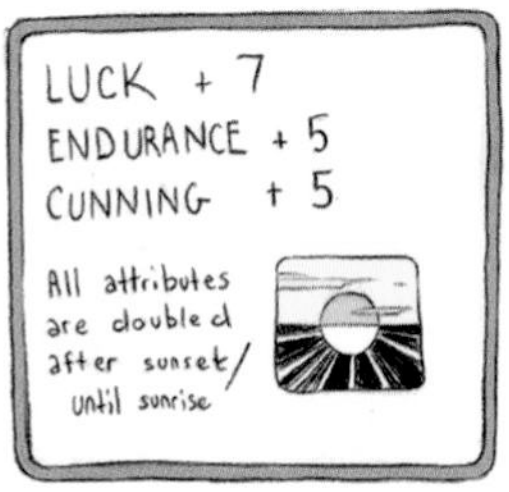
LUCK + 7
ENDURANCE + 5
CUNNING + 5
All attributes are doubled after sunset/ until sunrise

3. (04/22/2011) *I have a fine collection of old videogame maps:* Secret of Mana, Final Fantasy VI, Zelda A Link to the Past, etc. *They are nerd gold, well besmeared from hard use, ripped up and taped back together again. I've been wanting to frame them for something like the last fifteen years, but even half-decent frames are so expensive that I've never been able to do it.*

This is an ongoing want, though. A patient want. Many want-lists into the future, it will still be there, wanting away quietly.

4. (04/24/2011) *For the first time in several years, I won't have a deadline during the summer. Consequently, I'm romanticising the living piss out of it. Also, perhaps you didn't know, but a person can't function properly unless they get adequate sunshine on their ankles.*

What I need in order to enjoy my freedom and not die from lack of sunlight are these N.D.C. sandals. Because if I have to spend one more summer with my feet boiling in my closed shoes, well, I will not be pleased.

5. (04/30/2011) *I very rarely wear or buy jewelery, but I often walk past jewelry displays, and fantasize about prying all the stones off the settings. You know, for my hoard.*

A good shiny amulet could change my mind, however. Look at this one, made of black tourmaline: serious minimalistic wizard-thief gear.

H.B.M.

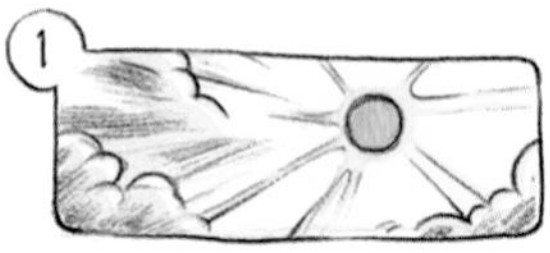

SUNNY WEATHER
For adventures
(it rained last year...)

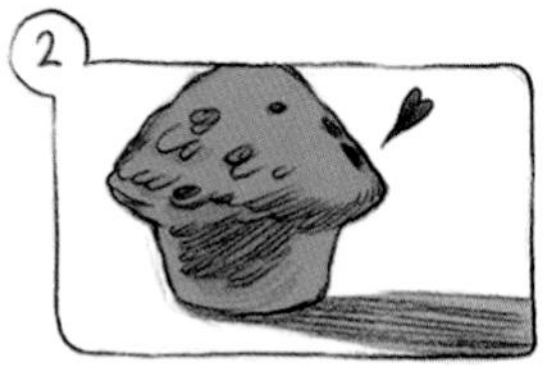

BIRTHDAY MUFFIN
WOOOOOO!!!

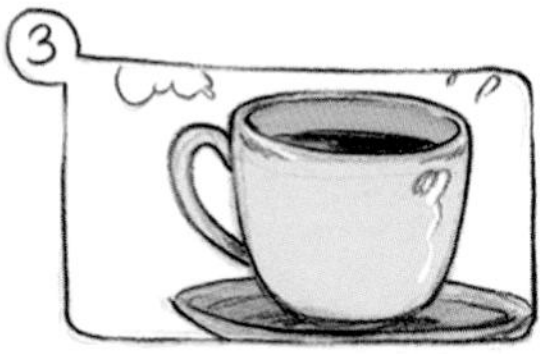

BIRTHDAY COFFEE
WOOOOOOO!!!

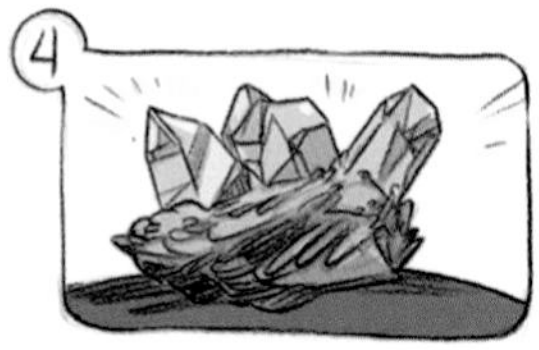

BIRTHDAY SHINY
(traditional)

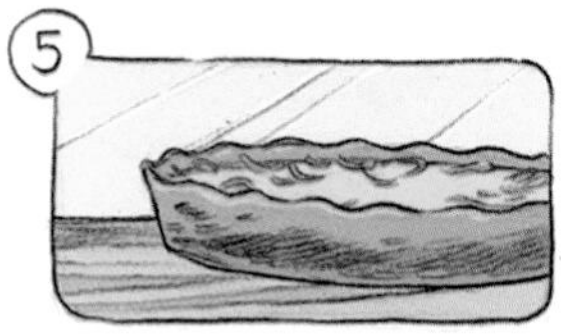

AN ENTIRE
LEMON - ORANGE FLAN
from Sweet Obsession
(traditional? Maybe?
starting now?)

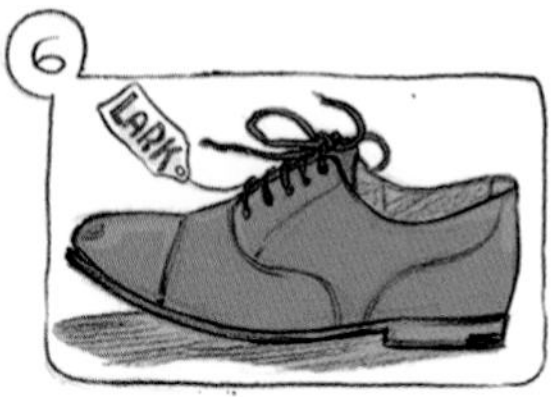
LARK.

NEW, FANCY
GENTLEMAN SHOES
Because my beloved old ones, now twice-resoled, are looking pretty beat-up.

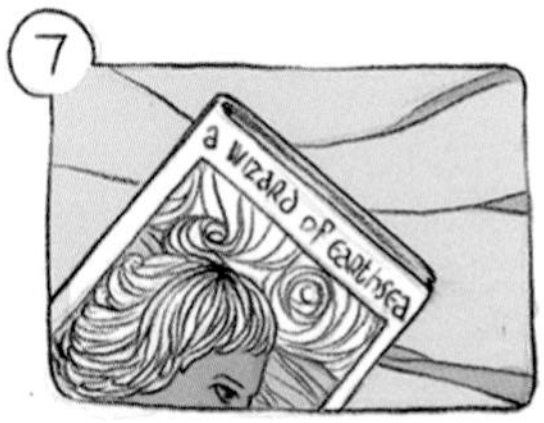
a wizard of earthsea

A FIRST EDITION
COPY OF A
WIZARD OF
EARTHSEA
Because Loff.

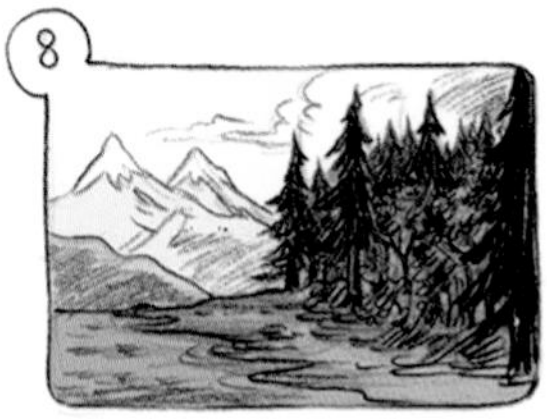

100 ACRES OF FOREST,
ISLANDBOUND, OCEANFRONT,
TAX - FREE
(with two cabins [one for Brandon])

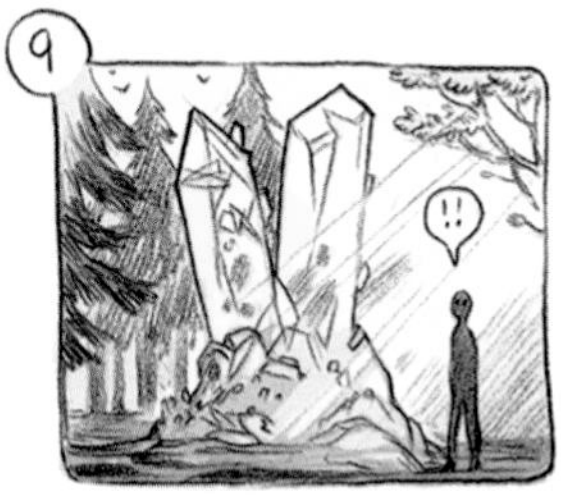
!!

A HUGE, GIANT
SHINY
It can go in
the centre of
my forest

2011

Xmas List 02

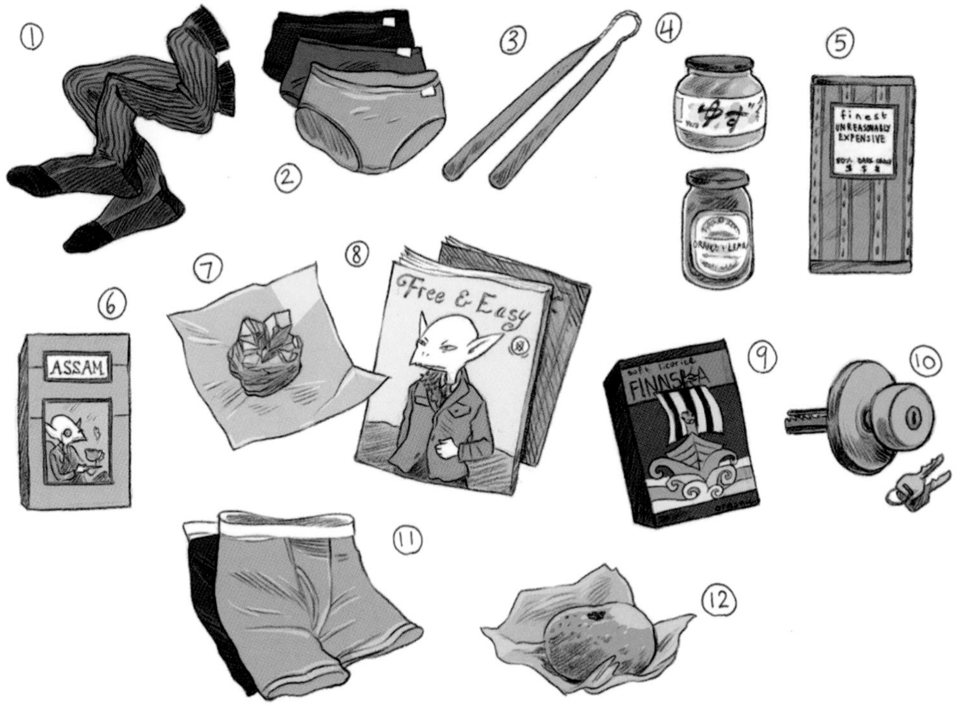
1
2
3
4
5
finest
UNREASONABLY EXPENSIVE
6
ASSAM
7
8
Free & Easy
9
FINNSKA
10
11
12

(11/29/2011) *I think stockings are the best part of christmas. Certainly they are in my family—the finest care package of the year. There are a few specific traditions I didn't list here. For instance, we always get a bag of Lego to put together before breakfast (to keep us occupied, so my parents can have time to wake up).*

1. Socks—never has the need been greater! My ideal sock would be knee-high, built to stay up, black, and very thin.
2. Underwear. I like getting socks and underwear for Christmas. And not even fancy underwear, which I don't like; only the plainest and most boring full-coverage cotton briefs, which I've worn since I was a teenager. I'll never change my ways. You'll have to pry them from my cold, dead… well, anyway.
3. Beeswax candles are always good (for fantasy ambiance, etc.). The huge towers are the best, but I drew tapers because those are cheaper.
4. The fanciest marmalade. There's no such thing as too much.
5. The fanciest dark chocolate, same deal.
6. Tea is good. Note: it does not have to be the fanciest.
7. A shiny!
8. A Japanese men's fashion magazine.
9. Finnska licorice. There may be better licorice somewhere out there, but I have yet to find it.
10. A lock, for practicing my lockpicking! Just a regular five-tumbler doorknob lock, which is usually the most basic one there is.
11. Men's boxer-briefs. These are the best pyjama bottoms, I find, because they fit perfectly under a onesie.
12. Orange in the toe!

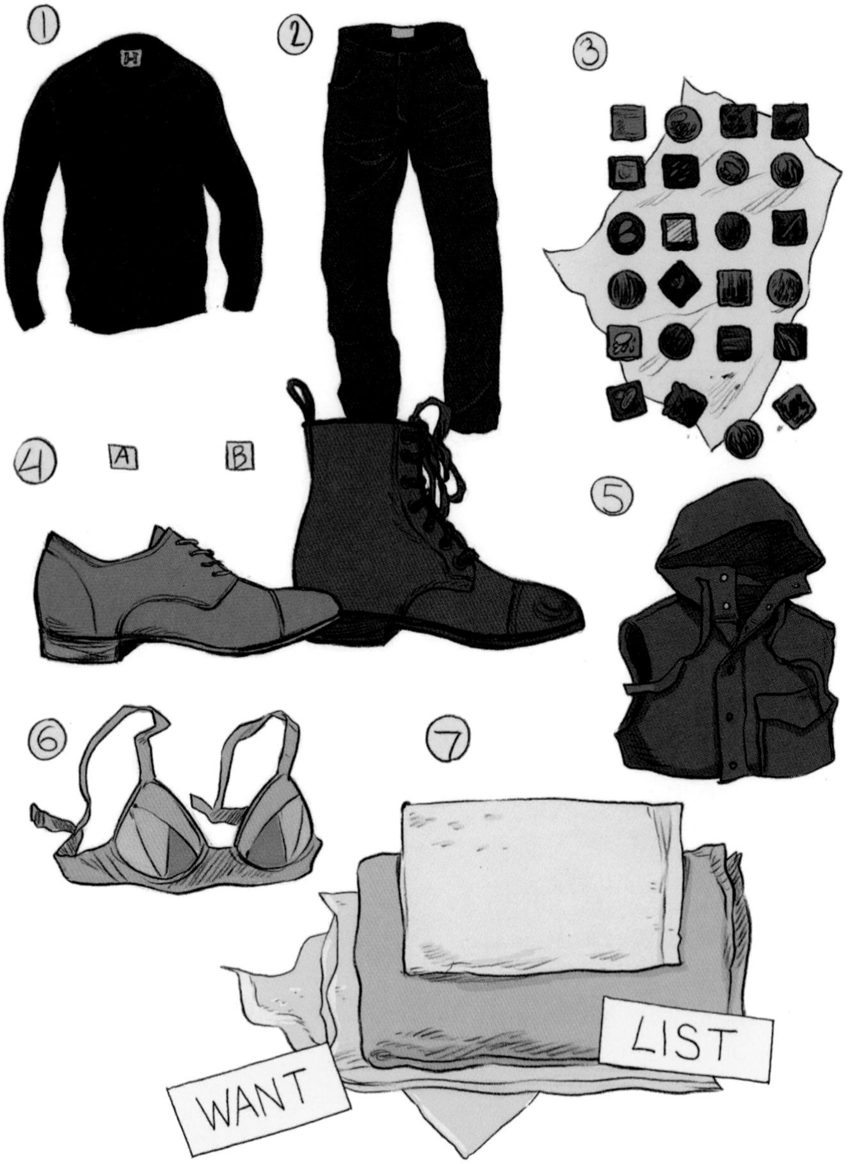

1
2
3
4
A
B
5
6
7
WANT
LIST

(03/03/2012) *This might be the most practical want list ever made (by me), but my current wants just happen to mainly consist of things that I need. Albeit, very nice versions of those things.*

1. This is a plain, semi-fitted wool crew-neck sweater. I want one in that shade of navy which is so dark it appears black until the light catches its impossible undertones of rich blue. 2. On lady-pants days, my official jean of choice is the Acne Hex. I could wish them just a centimeter wider in the leg opening, but the rise is perfect, and all-in-all I find them to be ideal for my purposes. 3. Ok guys, so there's this newish chocolate place in Vancouver called Beta 5, and they have this thing where you sign up to have packages delivered to you every month. How happy would you be? 4. Shoes are really more of a need than a want, at this point. 5. I know I've already mentioned the FWK Engineered Garments Shoulder Hoodie. But you can expect it to be on every want list of mine forever, because I think it's the raddest and most made-for-Marian thing I've ever seen. Want want want want. 6. Can I have some nice, sharp bras, without any lace or padding or "customised lift" or whatever? 7. A new set of bedding would be just the thing. I don't balk at the dull wants.

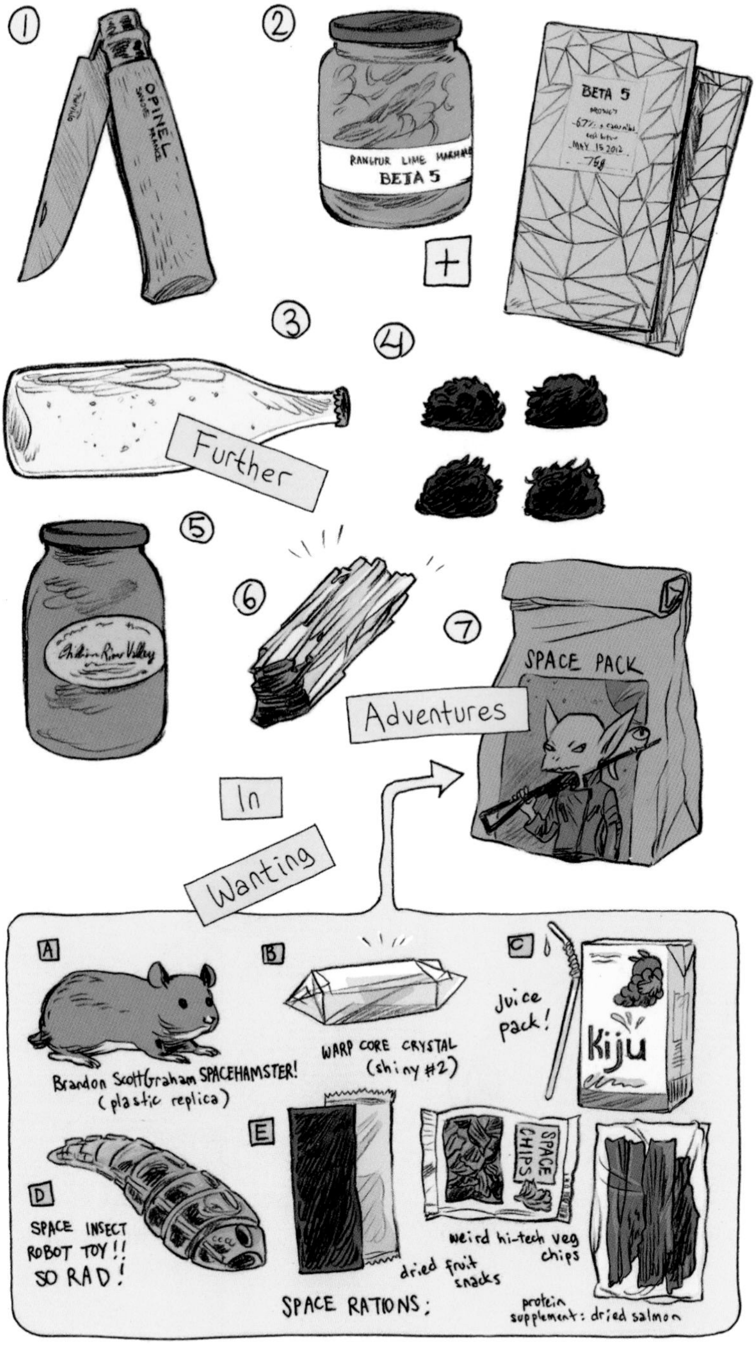
1
OPINEL
2
BETA 5
BETA 5
+
3
4
Further
5
6
7
SPACE PACK
Adventures
In
Wanting
A
Brandon Scott Graham SPACEHAMSTER!
(plastic replica)
B
WARP CORE CRYSTAL
(shiny #2)
C
Juice pack!
Kiju
D
SPACE INSECT ROBOT TOY!! SO RAD!
E
SPACE CHIPS
weird hi-tech veg chips
dried fruit snacks
SPACE RATIONS:
protein supplement: dried salmon

(03/22/2012) *1. When I was a kid, I spent a lot of time collecting sticks, and whittling the ends into sharp points so I could name them after the swords in bad fantasy books and old Squaresoft RPGs. Atma-weapon! Masamune! So I'd like another pocketknife. 2. I'm aware I talked about Beta 5 in the last Want List, but everyone knows that wants just fester if left unfulfilled. 3. Some fancy fizzy thing. 4. Vast, vast quantities of chocolate macaroons. 5. My famed hoard of many honeys is down to one jar. That's like when the Carebears' care-o-meter (or whatever it was called) drops nearly to zero, and Carealot starts crumbling to pieces. 6. Desperate times call for NEW SHINIES. 7. It's been way too long since I've received a Loot Bag—like the kind they gave out at children's birthday parties. And if I'm going to be specific, I want a SPACE-themed Loot Bag.*

H.B.M. 2012

Sunny weather for adventures.

①

Traditional birthday muffin and coffee

②

Traditional birthday shiny

③

A nice old, weathered shiny box

④

New sunglasses (I sat on my old pair)

⑤

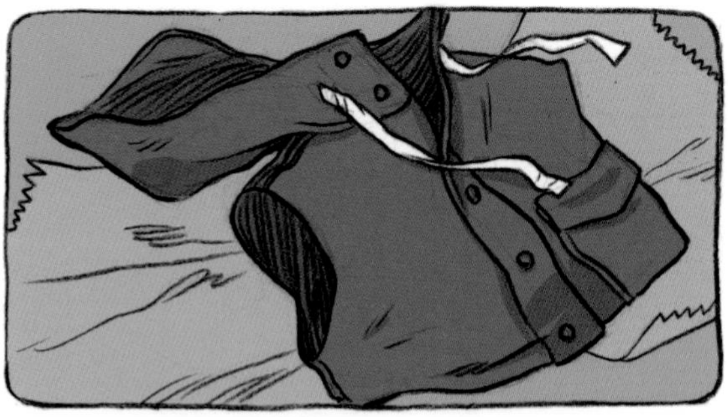

① FWK shoulder hoody, now and forever, the Once and Future Want

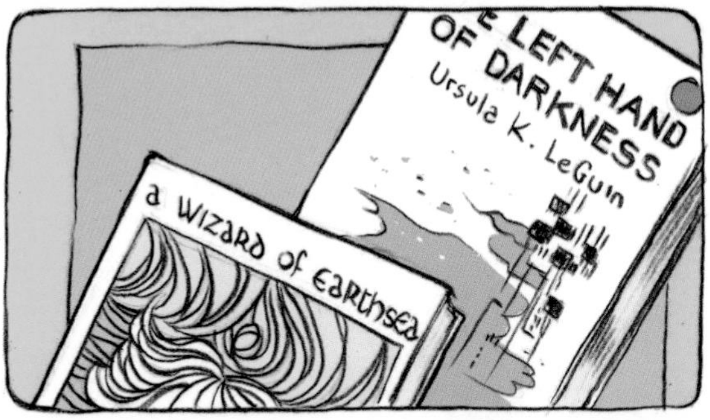

E LEFT HAND OF DARKNESS
Ursula K. LeGuin
a WIZARD OF EARTHSEA

② First printing copies of Ursula LeGuin books

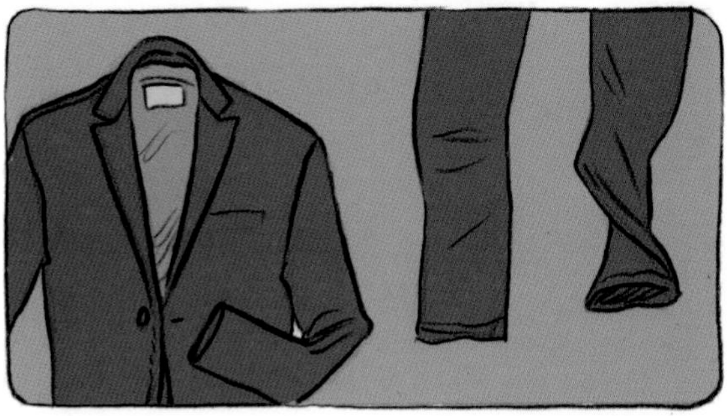

③ A master-tailored suit

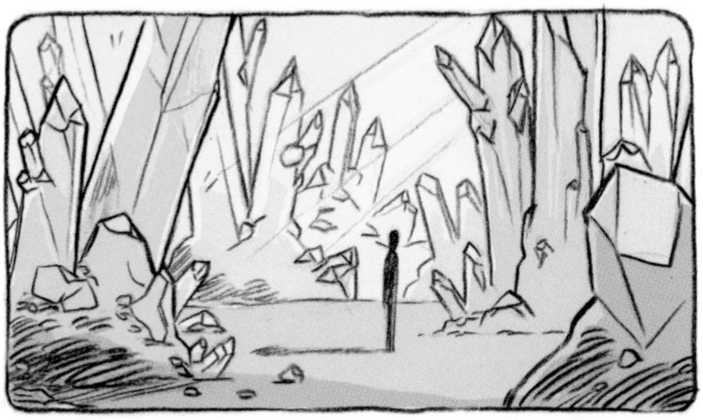

④ A shiny forest.

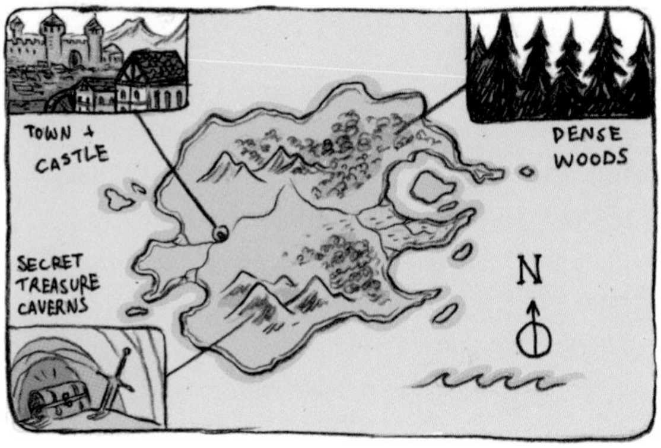

TOWN + CASTLE
DENSE WOODS
SECRET TREASURE CAVERNS
N

⑤ A fantasy adventure island

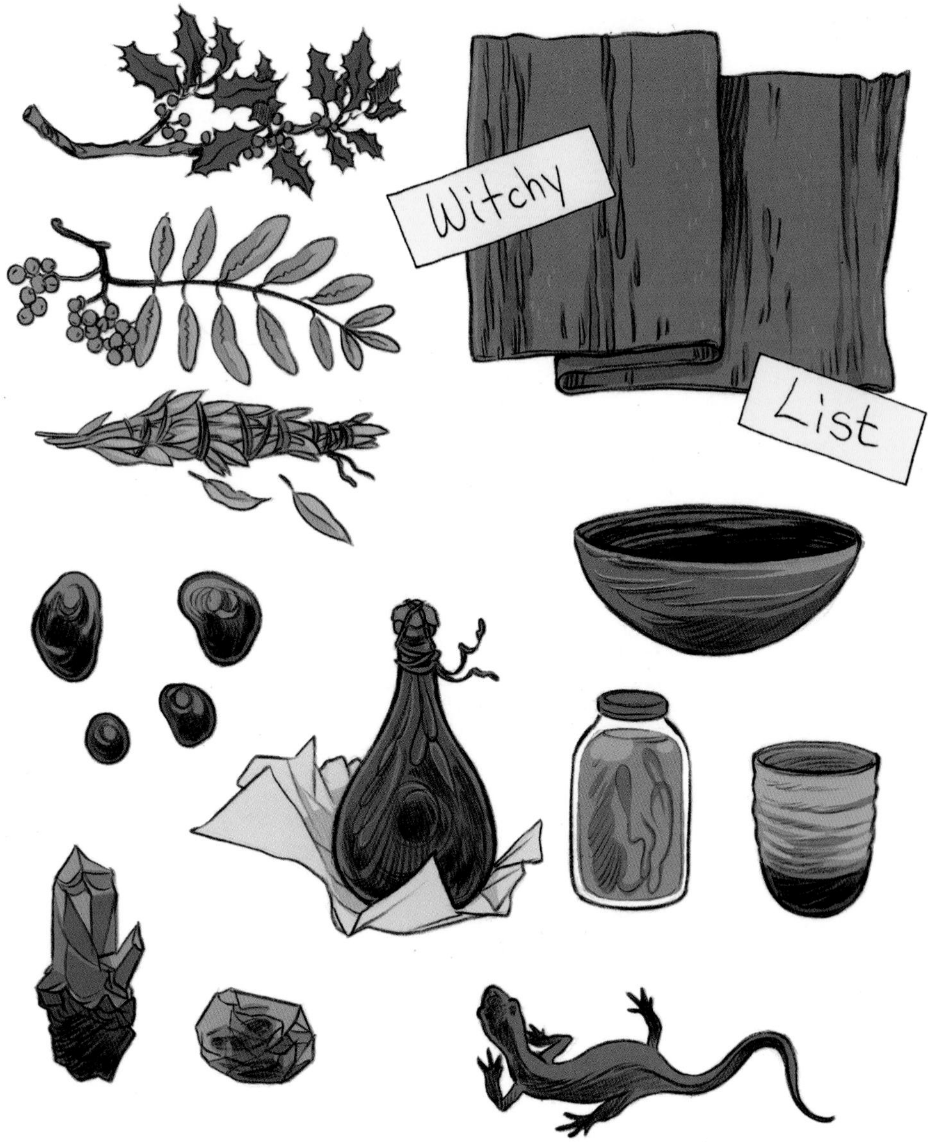
Witchy
List

(12/10/2012) *Right now, fresh from my eternal loop of rotating teenage boy-or-girl phases, I'm into witchy stuff, and I'm yearning to style myself towards some combination of Mortiana, the white-haired, bloody-egg-cracking, womb-clutching woman in* Robin Hood: Prince of Thieves, *and my eternal lifestyle icon, Aughra from* The Dark Crystal. *Left to right, top to bottom:*

1. Tree sprigs and herbish bundles, for no particular purpose. 2. Rough-woven woolen things that might work as little rugs, or wall hangings? Wall hangings are pretty witchy, I think. 3. Smooth, black river stones. 4. My sister and I were recently discussing the comparative secrets of certain shiny things, and she wrote that one shiny had "I like a boy" secrets, while the other had "I know how to make a potion that will kill a man on a night with no moon" secrets. My sister is so smart, and also I want that potion. 5. Darkest autumn honeys—full of all the year's secrets, speaking of which. 6. Dark-glazed and raw-clay ceramics. Though really that's just me trying to couch my mundane domestic whatnots within other, cooler themes. 7. Shinies, opaque with iron. 8. Newt friend.

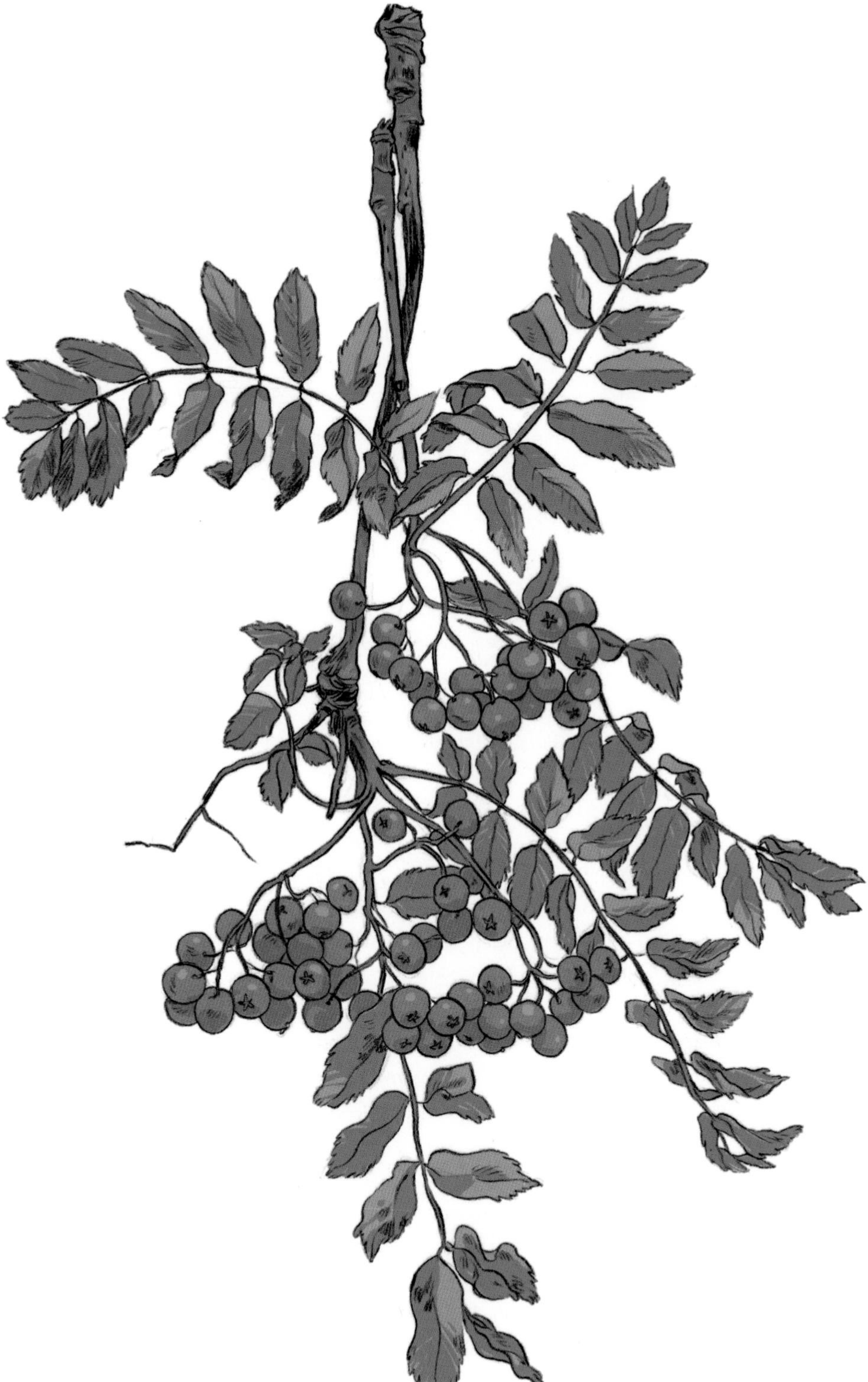

H.B.M. 2013

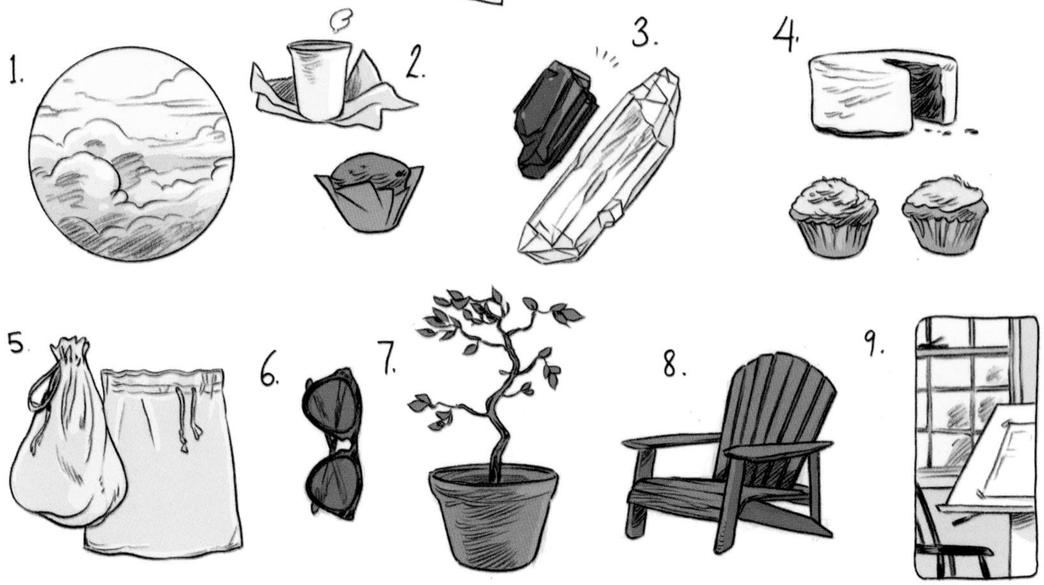
1.
2.
3.
4.
5.
6.
7.
8.
9.

(06/04/2013) *1. I'll be on a plane for most of my birthday this year, so I'll have to replace my usual request for clear weather with one for good travel conditions: not missing any of my flight connections, and not finding myself seated beside rude (or alternately, really nice, chatty) people.*

2. Tradition demands a birthday coffee and a birthday muffin. I can even get into bitter airplane coffee, in the spirit of adventure.

3. Shiiiiiniiiieeeeesssssssss!!!!!

4. In a perfect world (one that revolves around my petty demands): I want to come home to a carrot cake from my favourite bakery. Best carrot cake in existence (note: my dad and my sister did indeed greet me at the airport with this cake! I still feel surprised and grateful and sheepish about it).

5. Here's an oddly practical request, as if to make up for demanding that cakes magically materialize in my apartment. I really need laundry bags; so much so, it's become an obsessive want.

6. I still don't have a pair of sunglasses.

7. I have only recently discovered that, by prudent application of water, I'm actually able to keep plants from dying (mostly). So now I want lots of them, filling up my new balcony.

8. And on the subject of balconies, I also need a chair. Just the most basic, classic wooden kind—with the flat armrests that also work as perches for your beverage. It's an added bonus if somebody else has already used it and weathered the wood to a nice, dull grey.

9. This last one is mostly just wistfulness. I was hoping to find a studio space in town. A cheap, well-lit, private studio within walking distance would be better than a whole shiny forest, for serious.

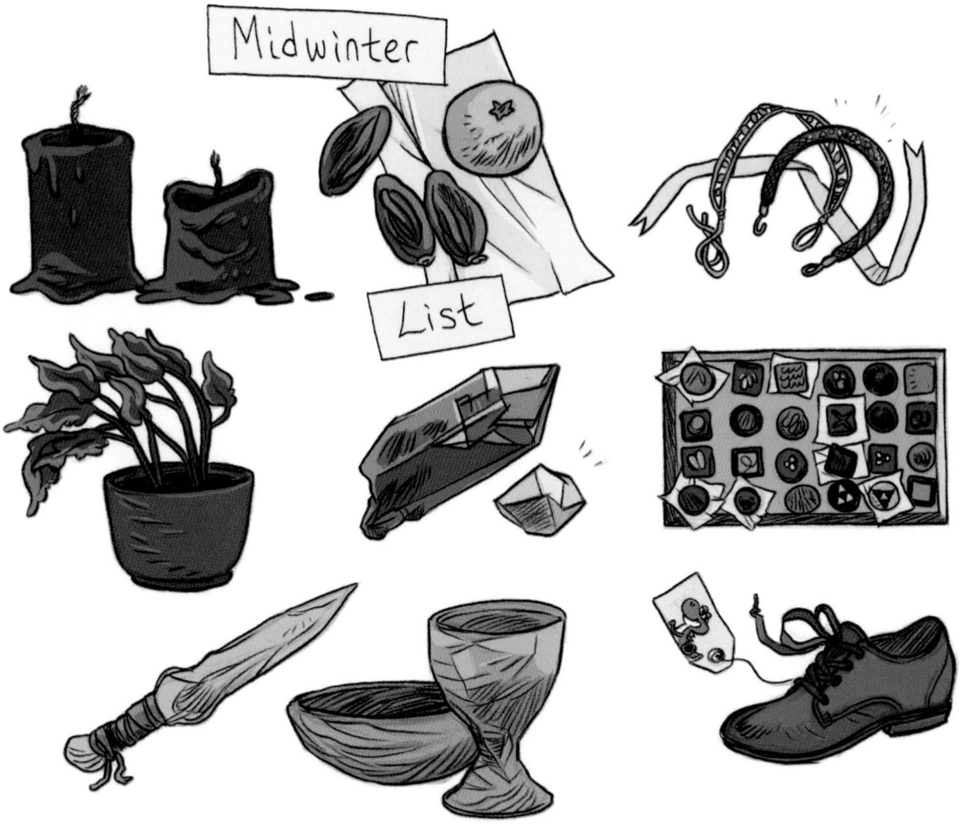
Midwinter
List

(12/22/2013) *1. Witchy dark candles. They still have to be beeswax, though. Always beeswax forever. Spend all your money on things that you will burn.*

2. Dates and oranges.

3. I've been wearing stuff on my wrists, lately. In lieu of having any real bracelets, I've been tying on bits of ribbon from packages, but I'd like a broader range. Realistically just leather ones and stuff, but I also want one of these crystal-filled nylon tubes.

4. I'm slowly becoming one of those people who has lots of fussy plants. Not yet "lots", in my case, but that's what I'm aiming for.

5. Huge piece of black quartz.

6. Entire box of chocolates all to myself. This never goes well, because I end up eating the whole thing in one sitting, then feeling really sick. But I still want them.

7. Bone knife? I don't want this in any real sense, but I wanted to draw it.

8. I've always felt that my day-to-day life was lacking in rough-carved wooden bowls and goblets.

9. I've been putting these shoes on want lists for at least two years now, but I still need them, so on we go. I'm not sure why I drew Yoshi on the tag, it seemed hilarious in the moment.

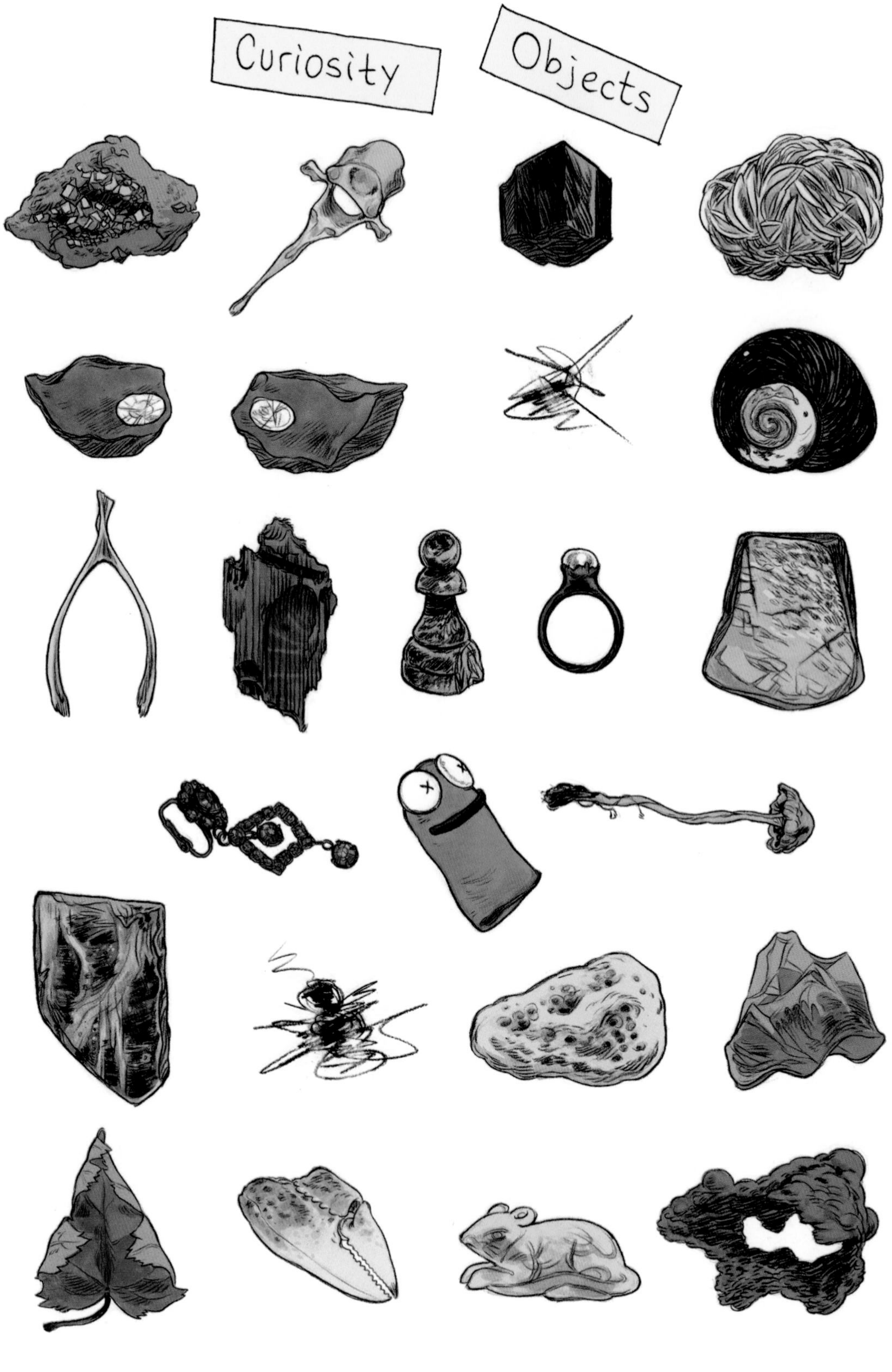
Curiosity
Objects

(05/15/2014) *This illustration (the original line art) was part of the* Cabinet *show, at Gallery 33, in Amsterdam. From left to right,*

1. Chunk of Pyrite that sits on my mantel (it's not really a mantel, just a chunk of wood I put above my desk, but mantel sounds authoritative)

2. Fox vertebra I found on a farm in Ontario

3. Chunk of black tourmaline (orcish mischief)

4. Gypsum rose

5 & 6. A rock that my friend found in a glacier in Iceland, cracked open to reveal a secret, hidden shiny

7. Curious scribble

8. Seashell from Saturna Island

9. Wishbone from a chicken

10. Worm-eaten driftwood

11. Dirty wooden chess pawn that I found in an alleyway

12. Pearl and copper ring from my sister (not for wearing, just for hoarding)

13. Unusual piece of ammonite fossil that looks like dragon skin

14. Costume jewelry earring that belonged to my maternal grandmother (very, very shiny)

15. The original mysterious creature known as my friend

16. Shrivelled old mushroom that I pulled out of a fairy circle in my nearby park

17. Sunstone/moonstone from the Ural Mountains in Russia

18. Another scribble—who knows, it just seemed to need them.

19. Agate that my sister brought me from one of her adventures

20. Slag glass from the Ohio River

21. Dried leaf from some trundle last fall—not sure why I kept it

22. Crab claw

23. Tiny jade rat that my sister brought me back from Singapore

H.B.M. 2014

(05/30/2014) *Lo and behold, my birthday is in just over two weeks. So here's my—what is it —fourth annual Hchom birthday list? Who can keep track, they all look more or less the same.*

1. I'll be away from home again this year, dogsitting my aunt and uncle's two enormous golden retrievers. With borrowed dogs come borrowed cars (ancient proverb), so maybe clear weather isn't necessary. On the other hand it's traditional, so I'd better ask for it anyway.

2. Coffee and muffins of reasonable quality are crucial to the success of any birthday. This year my birthday is on Father's Day, so the cafes will likely be swamped, but I have no problem battling the patriarchy to secure my share of pastries.

3. When was the last time I made a want list without a shiny? I'm not sure if it's ever happened, or ever will.

4. So there's this newish pie place of excellent repute within walking distance of my apartment, and I haven't tried it yet. That's what I would do, if I could—I'd order an entire pie; maybe, like, a raspberry rhubarb? But since I can't, and good pies are hard to find, I'd accept a nice, fluffy cake. I'd accept it pretty graciously, and with a surprising minimum of petulance.

5. Every list must have at least one really boring item. So, I need some white T-shirts. T-shirts! The simplest thing! Why are they so troublesome?

6. I've been wanting some shiny shoes for a while now—I've been watching silver oxfords come and go, without seeing any that I could afford (or that had the right sort of shape), and now I also reckon I could use some sparkly Converse. At some point I'll grow desperate enough to try making them for myself.

7. My current gaming laptop is getting a little long in the tooth, and if I had some kind of unexpected windfall—like, if previously unknown Aunt Martha died and left me her moderate savings—I'd get myself a really fancy new computer.

8. Ok, this one doesn't count, because I actually found myself a black jean jacket on sale earlier today and decided to order it. Also, it's sort of a letdown after a gaming laptop. Oh well, it fills the space.

9. My sister is getting married this July, and in an ideal world I'd wear a full, tailored suit to her wedding. Someday it will happen, though, and I will look SO HANDSOME.

10. We need at least one deeply unreasonable thing, so I'd like to have a magical Howl's Moving Castle-style doorway in my apartment. At first I put it at the back of my closet, but then I thought about how all my sweaters and jackets would get scuffed with constant elbowing, so now it's beside my bed. I'm imagining a little sort of postcard slot, into which you insert an image of your destination. Here we have some forest ruins, a crystal temple, and a fantasy village with fantasy bakeries.

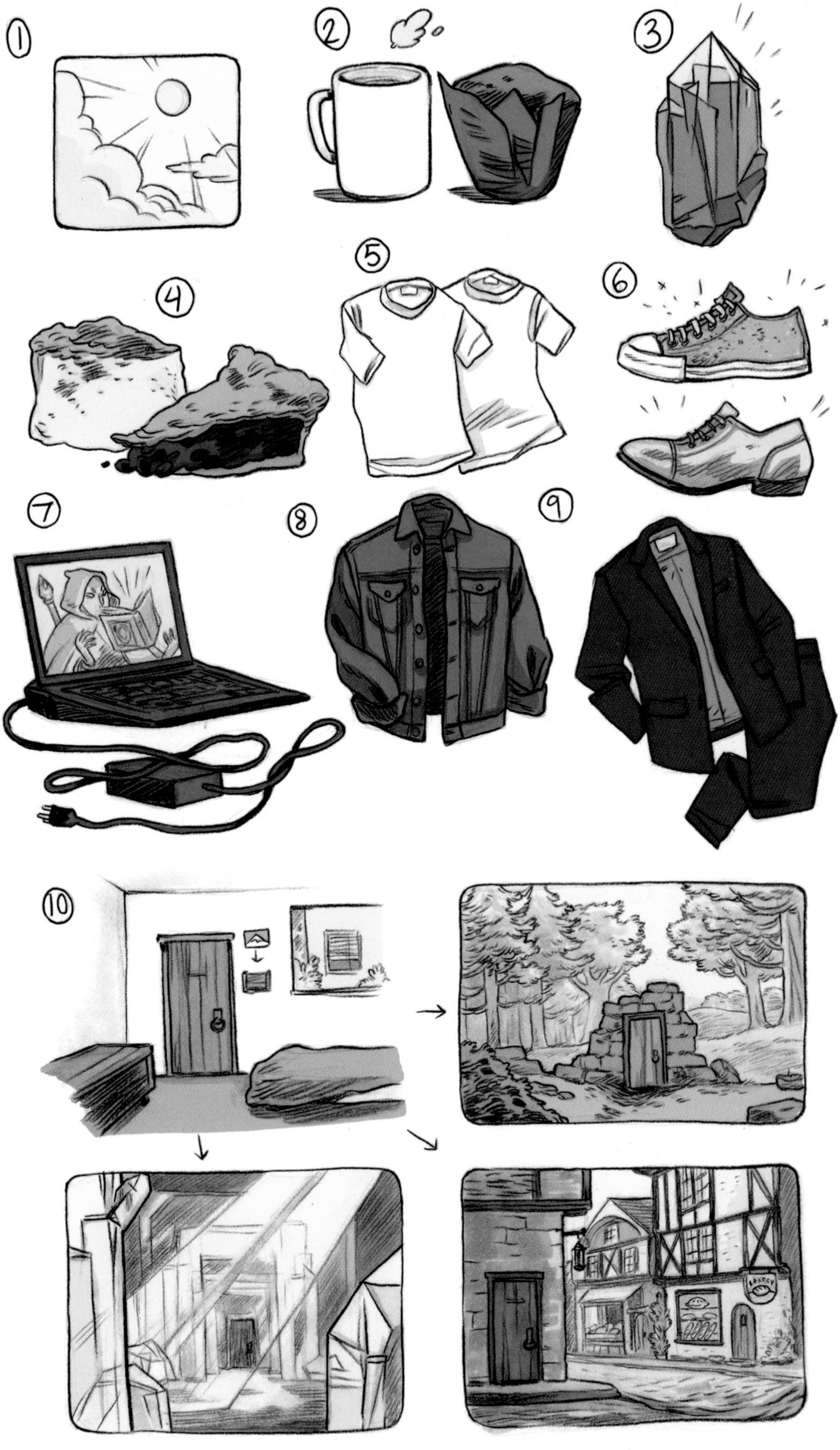
1
2
3
4
5
6
7
8
9
10

H.B.M. 2015

(05/21/2015) So we've all been around this block a few times together, and do I even need to run through the first four items? Yes, well, I probably do.

1. Good weather. By which I mean good walking weather: not too sunny or humid, but also not raining. If I'm going to be really specific, then I want huge scudding clouds with occasional (dramatic!) god rays.

2. The birthday muffin and the birthday coffee. Brandon mocked me for this, pointing out that I buy these things almost every day, and he's not wrong. But on my birthday I get to feel extra entitled, and entitlement makes all muffins and all coffees taste better.

3. The birthday shiny. My current shiny of interest is beryl (aquamarine or emerald) and I'd like a good raw hunk of it, thank you very much and don't mind if I do.

4. Long did I debate between cake and pie! But I seem to be in a cake frame of mind just as I make this list, so I'm demanding an entire fluffy, sugary cake, possibly with a bowl of raspberries alongside.

5. A couple people have recommended Callisto Jewellery (based in BC!) for her fantasy adventureish pendants, and I'd really like to add one to my increasing hoard (the hoard forever hungers). Ideally I'd commission something with my ongoing beryl theme in mind, but I like the pearl pendants as well.

6. A… phone? I was just writing elsewhere that I've never had a phone. Why would I want to own something that made me more socially assailable? And in particular, why would I want to carry it with me everywhere? But I'm slowly coming around to it—major selling points being the camera, and the easy access to vintage games.

7. I always need shoes for walking. I wear through shoes like you wouldn't even believe.

8. An aviator jacket! Ideally this one by my beloved Engineered Garments. There's a void in my wardrobe—a dark vacuum—and only this jacket can fill it.

9. I have this space on my wall that needs a huge painting, so ideally I'd harangue poor Brandon into taking a big, white-painted piece of plywood, and rendering me a mountain landscape. Notice how, though I complain about my own deadlines, I'm perfectly happy to saddle other people with these time-consuming, work-interrupting, totally selfish demands.

10. For the (traditionally extra unreasonable) last request, I wanted to expand on the fantasy adventure island concept from a few years back, but I didn't have time to map it all out, so here's a sliver of horizon to summon the general feeling. We're supposed to have a hot summer, this year, and the only way I can deal with temperatures above 25 Celsius is by fantasizing about forests and oceans.

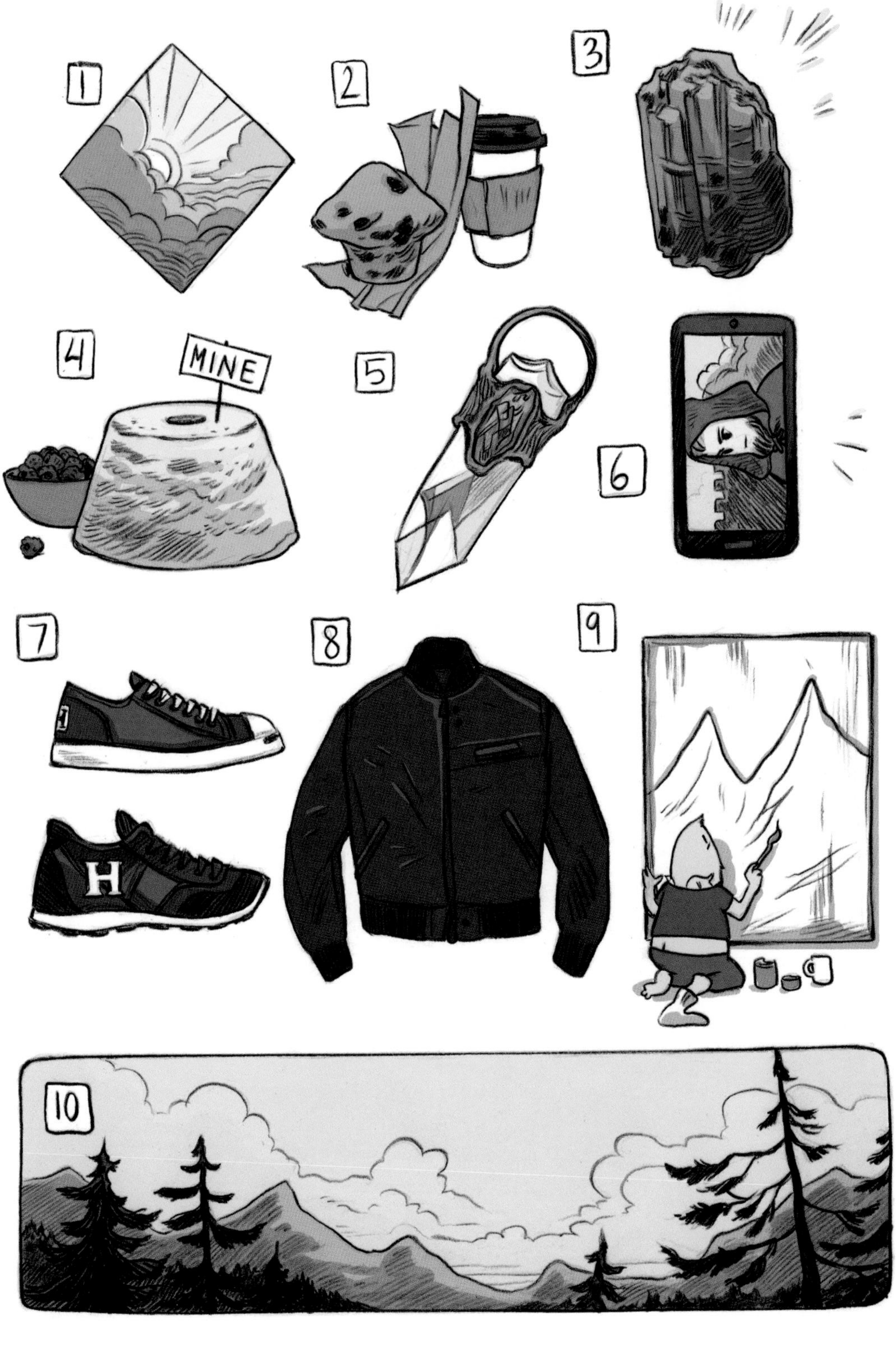
1
2
3
4
MINE
5
6
7
H
8
9
10

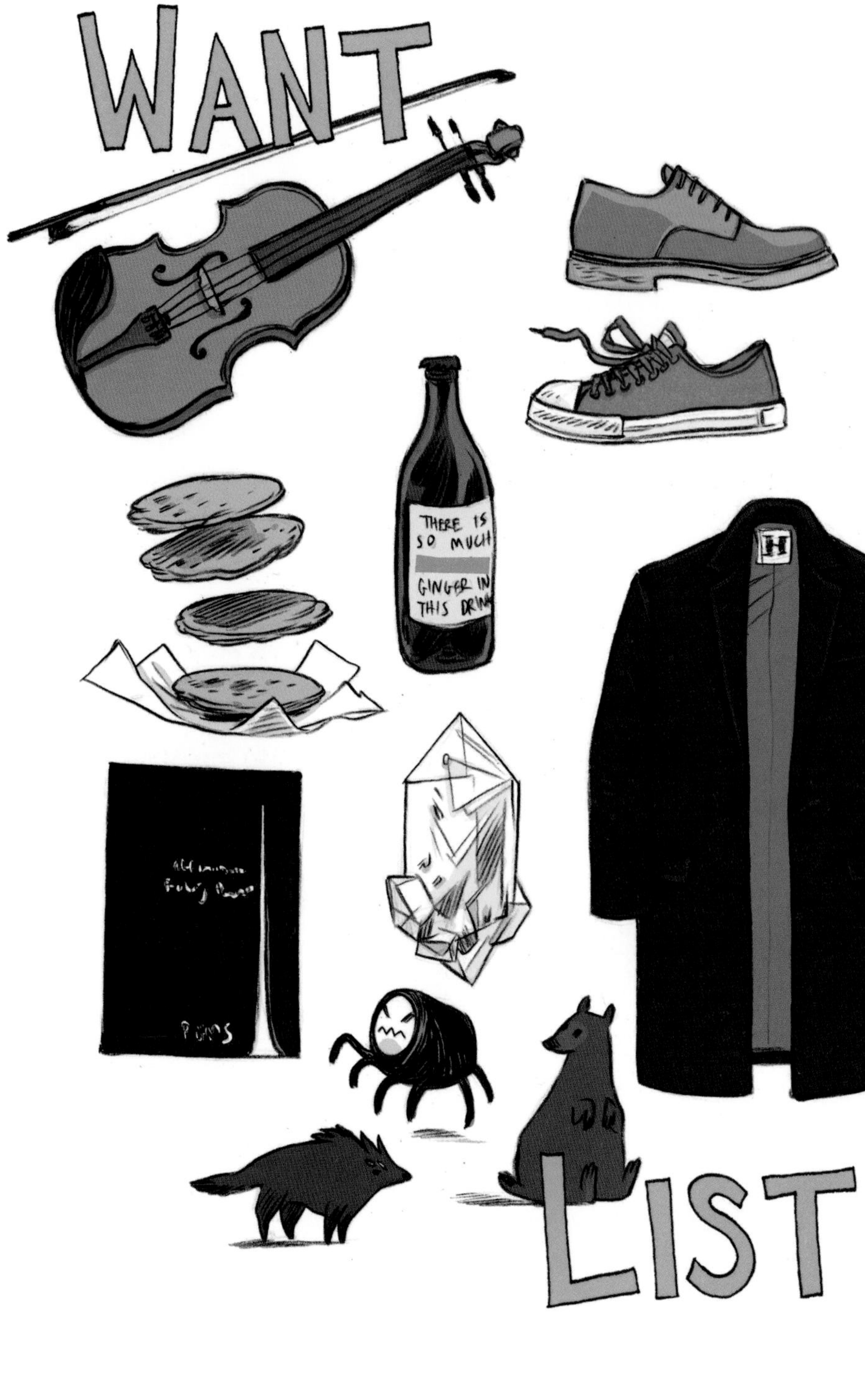
WANT
THERE IS
SO MUCH
GINGER IN
THIS DRIN
H
LIST

(10/22/2015) *My current wants have naturally coalesced into a want list, so here it is.*

1. First of all—and maybe one or two of you can actually give me your advice—I've decided that I want to learn how to play the viola. But even if I manage to get my hands on an instrument, there's still no way I can pay for lessons, which leaves me teaching myself.

In my far-flung fantasies, I'm a latent virtuoso! Ha ha... In my more reasonable but still pretty unreasonable fantasies, I pluck my way along until I'm a kind of hedge-violist who can play some Chrono Trigger songs almost well.

Realistic best-case scenario, my neighbours hate me for the next several years, but are kind enough not to call building management. Realistic worst-case scenario, it's a decorative hunk of wood forever representing my shame and failure, and my family never listens to my gift requests ever again.

2. You know what doesn't require me to develop new skills, though? Shoes. I always need shoes. My feet are made of razors (current working theory). I'd like some bright red sneakers, and I still wish I could get those Dries Van Noten Derbies. They don't even have to be shiny silver. I'm not picky.

3. I want oatcakes. But better oatcakes than you can get from a box, at least in my boxed oatcake experience (which is extensive).

4. And I really want some kind of, I don't know, triple strength ginger ale. I have a high resistance to everything in the ginger/horseradish/wasabi family (are they actually a family?), so normal ginger ale just tastes like sugar water.

5. I guess the coat comes next. I didn't arrange my list very well. Anyway, I haven't bought a winter coat in nearly a decade, so it seems like a reasonable thing to want. I'd go with a men's overcoat, one size too large, in the same navy-black as every other piece of outerwear I own.

6. Alice Oswald has a new poetry collection coming out late next summer, and I'm so excited. Jumping up and down and batting at dust motes excited. That's almost an entire year away, however, so wants being wants, I'd like to have a copy right here, right now.

7. And a shiny, of course. There are rules about this. Quartz crystals with various inclusions (hematite, chlorite, etc.) are the shinies of the moment.

8. Tiny animals. Brandon and I used to get little plastic ones for each other, but we exhausted all the really good options, and now I've gone further into the dark to find people who make custom creatures out of porcelain. There's no end to the weird nerdy shit I could commission from these unsuspecting strangers.

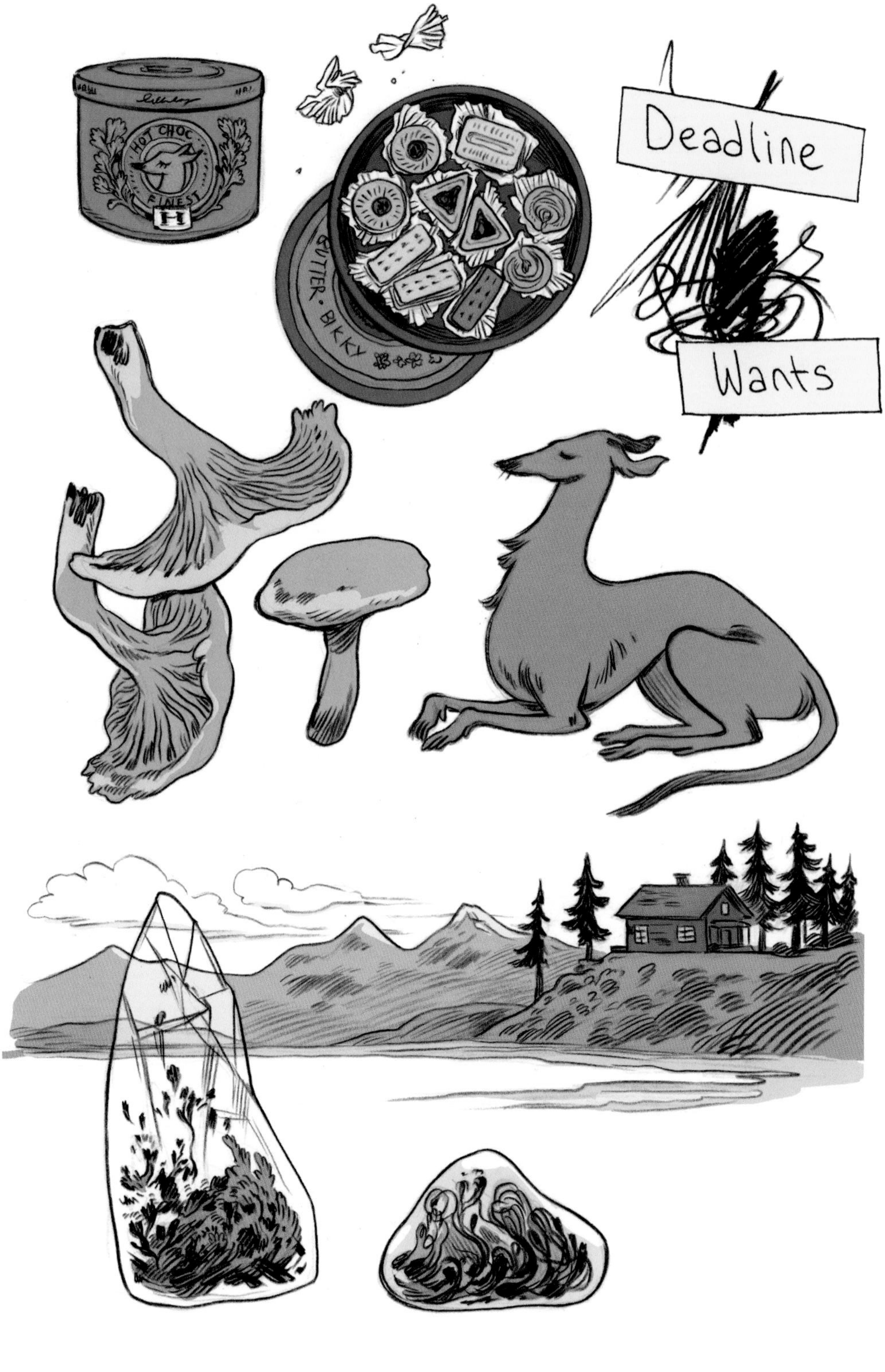
HOT CHOC
FINEST
H
BUTTER · BIKKY
Deadline
Wants

(10/15/2016) *Am I still milking this (routine and utterly unremarkable) deadline? Of course I am. Here's my current list of wants:*

1. I'm on a hot chocolate kick. I actually prefer the add water to powder stuff over the real thing, but that doesn't stop me from wanting a really fancy version of that powder, packaged in some impractical (but attractive!) vintage tin.

2. Speaking of which, remember those round tins of stacked biscuits? I've mentioned them on a previous want list, and they're probably still a regular thing on other continents, but you never see them here anymore. I doubt they're any better than your average boxed cookie, but they carry all the glamour of extinction, so I can't help but want them anyway.
Plus, it doesn't hurt that my grandmother used to offer them to me when I'd visit her house to play Lego, and she'd only let me have one or two at a time. She was teaching me good manners, and moderation... for shame, Marian. Lessons wasted.

3. When I make these want lists, I'm often left with one blank spot. Normally I mull over it for a while, and fill it with something ever so slightly less wanted, but that always feels wrong, and worse yet, it's a stone in my shoe forever afterwards. So from now on I'm just going to make scribbles instead. Which feels psychologically apt, right? Sort of? The vacant heart of wanting!

4. Chanterelles are really expensive this year, for some reason—too expensive for me to afford, which is surely a form of damnation. Now I'm the wraith who haunts the mushroom section of the grocery store, waiting for the price to go down, occasionally extending a pale claw in yearning, hissing and wailing when any creature of warm flesh approaches...

5. I so, so badly want a dog! I can't have one for several reasons—most crucially, because my building doesn't allow them—but I daydream about it constantly. I can't even check the greyhound rescue site, because I get fully attached to every single dog they post, and then my sulking is proportionate to my wanting.

6. As luck would have it, my parents are going on a trip and leaving their house (which is on Bowen Island) empty just as I finish my deadline, so now I have this incredible motivator. I can't be even half a day late, because that would steal from my limited fund of island time. This is the currency with which my soul may be purchased, in case you were wondering.

7. Shinies, of course. Today, lodolite and moss agate, because they have little forests inside them.

December Wants

(11/29/2016) *Here's a quick December want list, since it's the month of sanctioned wanting. And before someone thinks I'm a selfish monster, my personal theory is that having a robust and healthy want mechanism actually makes you better at giving things to people.*

1. I don't love lotions, but I have recently developed an appreciation for body oils as a ritual extension of my many baths.

2. I was telling my sister the other day, I'm very excited to be a butchish old lady with a huge secret collection of stones and jewellery and spangled gowns, and the thing I'm currently wanting for this future hoard is a proper opera-length string of sea pearls. Real vintage ones, you know, with lots of lustre.

3. I will sometimes wear (rather than merely hoard) bracelets. These silver bangles look very nice.

4. Shinies. We're all old hands at this by now.

5. How long will I harp on about wanting a full suit? Forever, of course, because wanting only begets further wanting. Someday I'll finally purchase one, and by then I'll already be thinking about tomorrow's suit; but right now I'd like something long-bodied and slightly oversized, in good grey tweed.

6. I always need socks for the same reason I always need shoes: because I rapidly destroy them.

7. My favourite type of cake (well, maybe tied with carrot cake) is proper dark fruit cake. But it's hard to find (or make) the good stuff, because… OK, I just wrote and erased (you're welcome) an entire paragraph about the quality and availability of candied fruit peel. Suffice it to say: it's hard. And I want it.

8. How many times have I drawn these same Oxfords on a want list? Sometimes I change the colours, but I don't think it fools anyone.

Tea Tray

(01/23/2017) *So this one is just ridiculous. Why do I want a tea tray? My apartment is small, and it takes me all of three seconds to carry any article of food from one side of it to the other. But look, as soon as you put something on a tray—especially any sort of tea or breakfast or, let's say, biscuit snack—its appeal suddenly doubles. Am I wrong? I don't think I'm wrong. I just want to take advantage of the math, you know; I can't be blamed for that.*

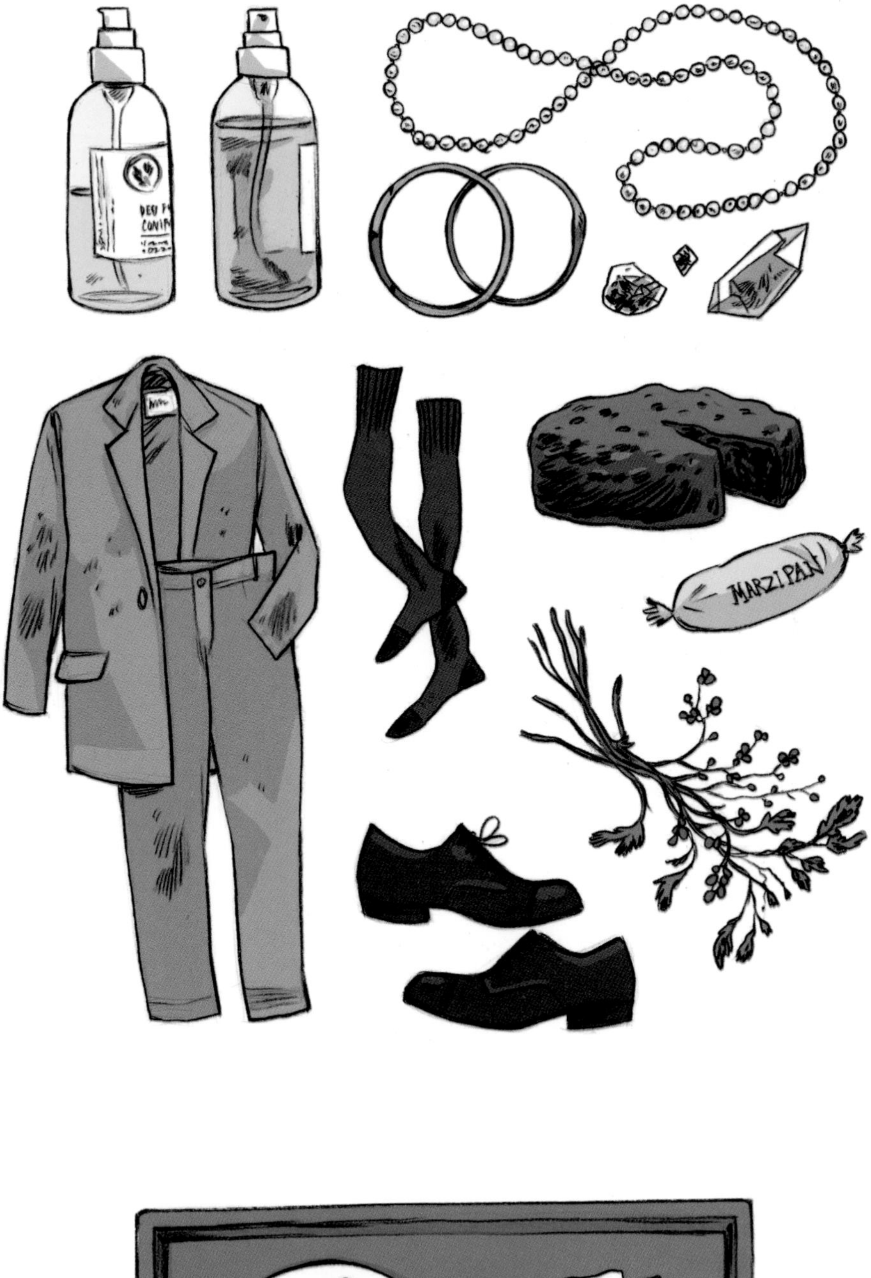
MARZIPAN

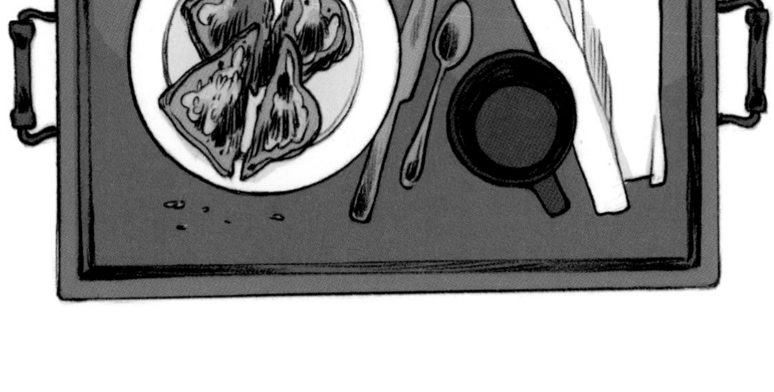

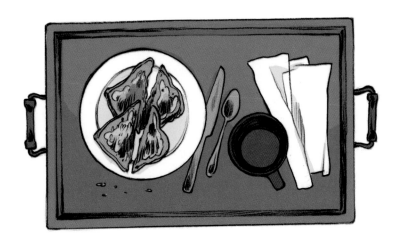

(01/27/2017) *I have a story that I like to tell myself, about how I'm going to be this woodsy, butch old hermit living with a vast hoard of treasure, and a subsection of that hoard will include spangled gowns, and elaborate, largely unwearable jewellery, and all the shiny lady things that you (by which I mean I) would never expect me to care about.*

I'm learning to be cautious of absolutes. Though I've spent a lifetime trying to resist the pressure to appear correctly feminine, disowning that stuff entirely doesn't seem to do me much good either. I'd like to learn how to approach it, as it occasionally appeals, without it feeling like a return to bondage. This is where the hoard is a sort of saviour, you see. The hoard's hunger is impartial; its appetites are irrational; its contents require no justification because they needn't answer to any practical duty; and most crucially, you can let those objects be external receptacles for the parts of yourself you can't comfortably (or consistently) contain. Not to sound like an evil soul-eating wizard or anything, but I think it works pretty well.

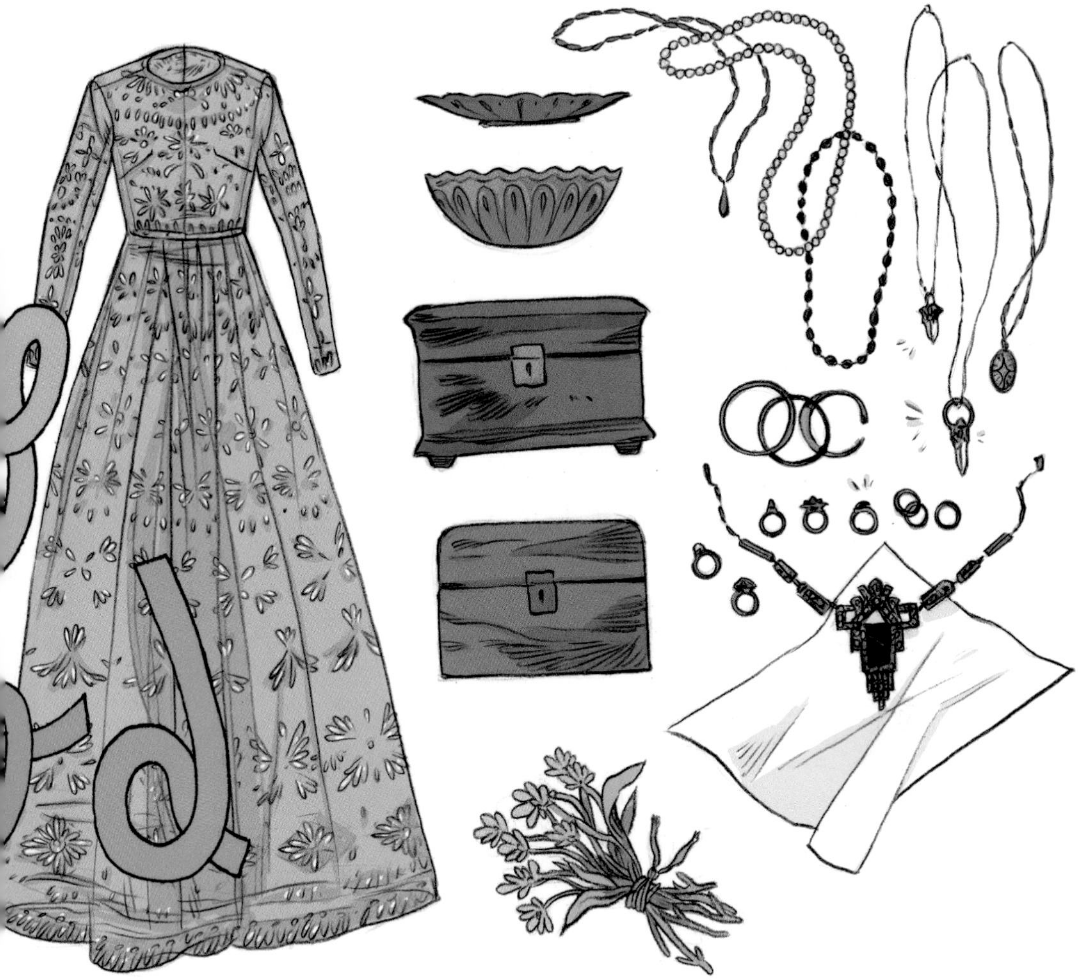

By the way, there's no reason for me to be an old lady in this story, except that I hope to have some real expendable income by time I get there. I don't intend to have children, and probably none of my future dogs will ever need to go to college, so it's not impossible that by the time I'm 85, I could: 1. afford a beaded Valentino gown, and 2. have the guts to zip it on whenever I damn well please and LARP around the forest like a drunken teenager. Also, I plan to be pretty foxy at that age, I'm just saying.

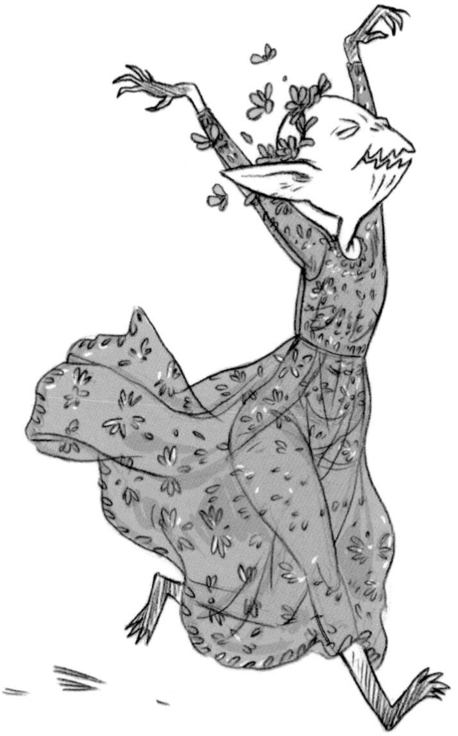

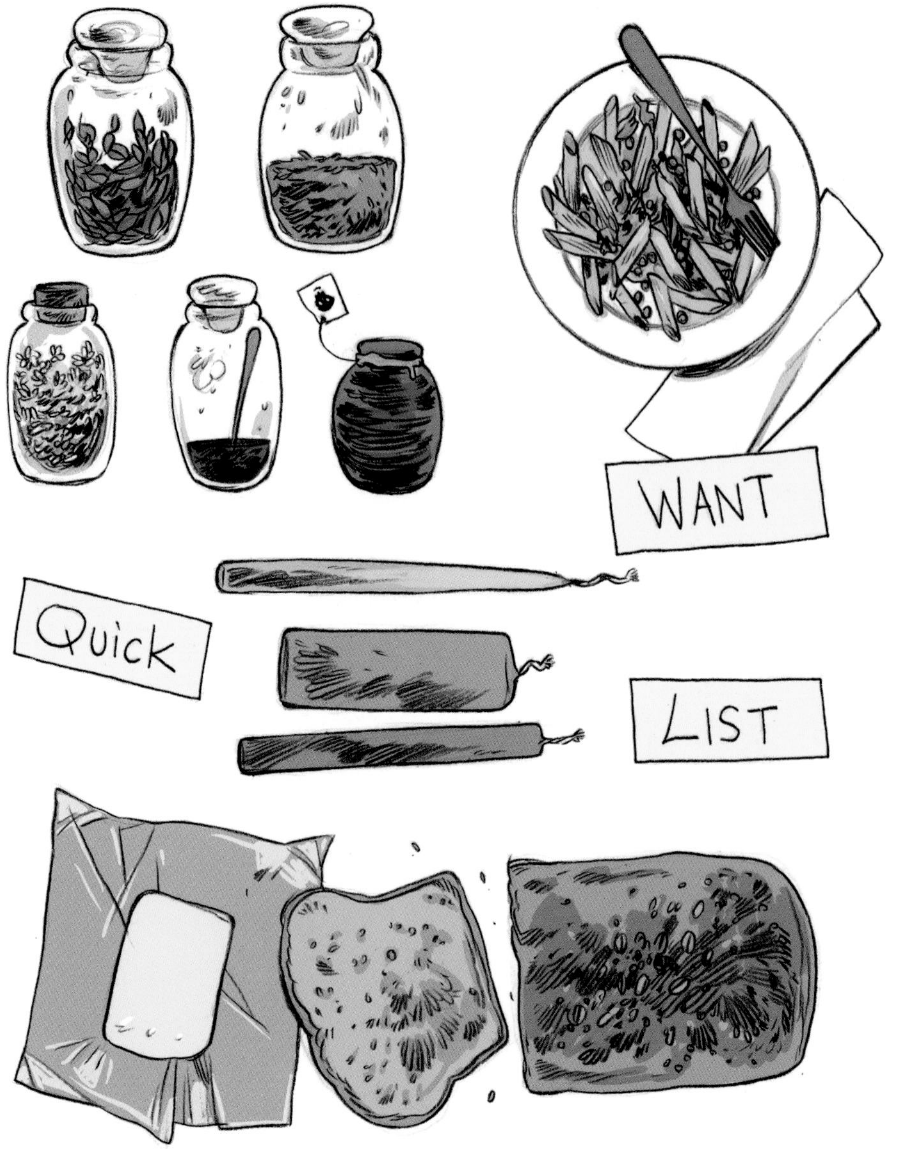
WANT
QUICK
LIST

(01/30/2017) *1. I'm reading a fantasy series in which the characters always seem to be preparing pots of herbal or medicinal tea, or having people bring them cups, etc. Naturally I want all of those teas for myself, even though they'd just sit in my larder and go stale while I continued using my plain, cheap teabags.*

2. Lately I've had an overwhelming craving for this cold pasta that they used to sell (ages and ages ago) at one of the older fancy Vancouver grocery stores. A moderately skilled person might recreate it, but I just want one serving, and I think I'd end up spending $50 on ingredients only to bungle the whole batch. I'm trying to tell myself that this is about the time and the place rather than the food, but it's not working very well and also might be a lie.

3. Beeswax candles: so expensive. So good to light on fire.

4. I want fresh seedy bread and cold butter. That, at least, should be easy enough. With any luck I'll be bringing a plump loaf home within a few hours of this post.

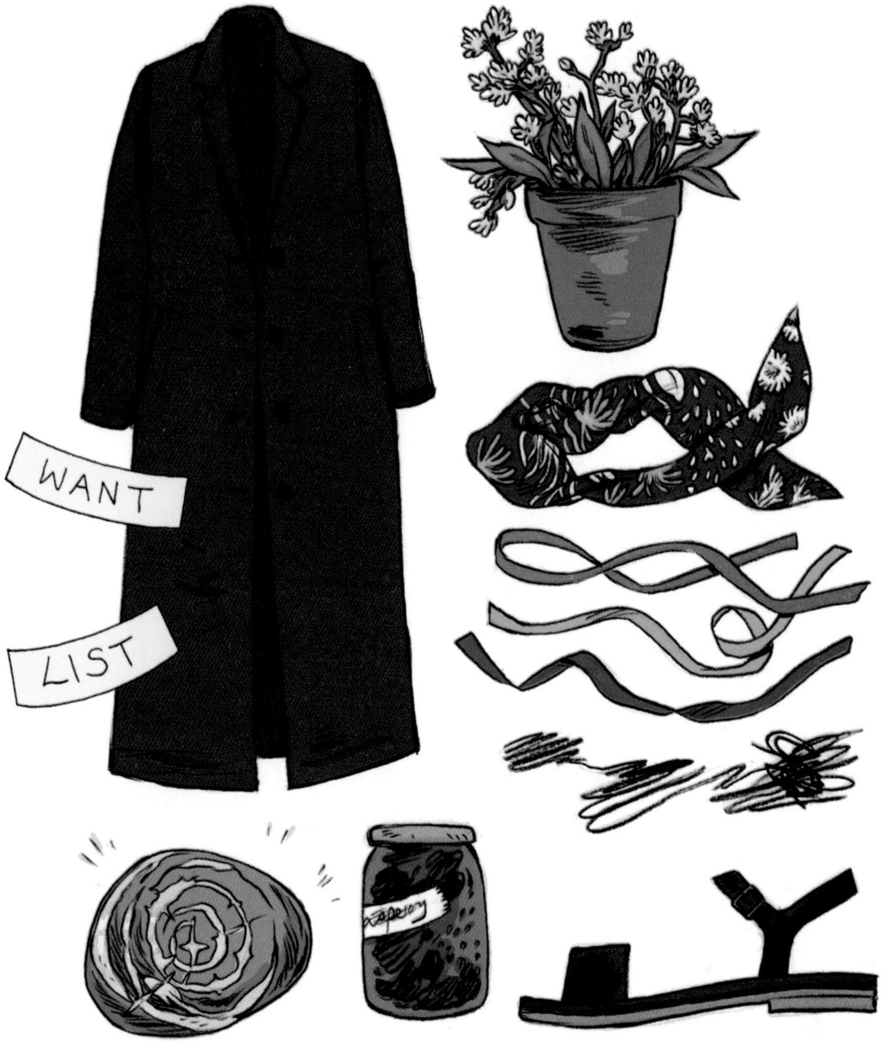
WANT
LIST
raspberry

(03/06/2017) *1. There appears to be a long coat trend underway, and I need to get in while the getting is good.*
2. Winter has been dragging on and on, at least by Vancouver standards. It's actually snowing! In March! I had to scrape it off my car with a cardboard coffee sleeve. I find myself really yearning for the cherry trees to come out already, and probably that's why I also find myself wishing I had some sort of blooming houseplant.
3. I could use some bright things in general. I doubt I'd ever wear a silk scarf, but I like to look at them. And I like to collect ribbons, mostly for the usual magpie hoarding purposes, but I'll also tie them around my wrists as makeshift bracelets.
4. Void scribble!
5. Posting about opals only redoubled my yearning for them, especially for those fossil ones.
6. I need raspberry jam. I mean, no big deal, I'll go buy some tomorrow, but what I really want is the jam you might encounter randomly, on a blistering summer day, in some half-abandoned roadside stall (the sort that has an unmanned slotted box for payment).
7. While my head is stuck in summer, I'll add that I'm overdue for some sandals.

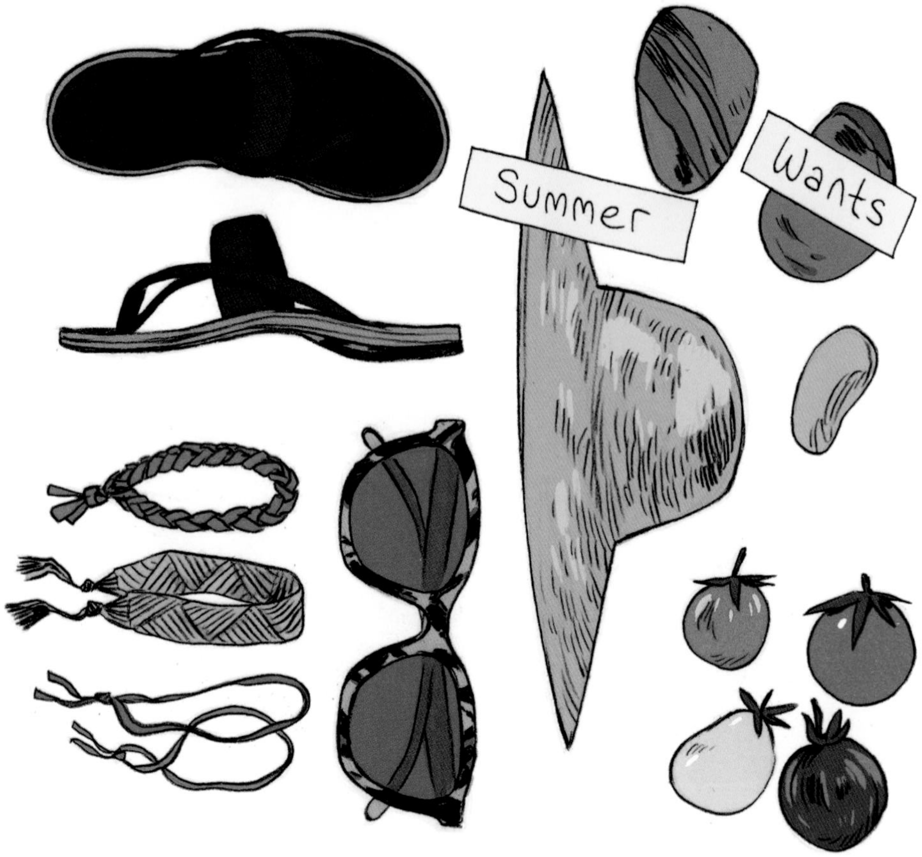
Summer
Wants

(04/03/2017) *I like summer best when it's still months away, and I can convince myself that I'll actually enjoy it and make good use of it. Here, therefore, is my summer want list.*

1. Sandals. I've needed a new pair for a while, since the ones I've worn for years (featured somewhere in the dark archives of the blog) have become too fragile for long walks. I'm very choosy about these things, as well you know, so it's taken me ages to find a replacement, but here they are, made by KikaNY. Look at them! They are perfect. They're also brutally expensive, once conversion rates and border taxes are factored in, but I don't care. I'll sell my organs to the devil, or whatever. Something. I'll make it happen.

2. I have a constant yearning for assorted colourful bracelets which I know I'll almost never wear. But they're very summery.

3. There was a brief time when I didn't need sunglasses, because my dad let me borrow his awesome old pair. But I lost them on a camping trip last year (SORRY DAD), so now I'm back to square one.

4. Another thing I've both needed and wanted for several years, building up to a point of desperation, is a hat. Mostly because I hate the sun and it burns us, but also because I sincerely want to look like a medieval farmer. But I have precise requirements, right? The hat must be completely unisex. The hat must be timeless. If the hat didn't make an appearance in an illuminated book of hours, then I refuse to wear it.

5. Whenever I go to a beach, I have to pick up a bunch of pebbles, each one of which looks beautiful in situ. Then I take them home with me; the result being that I have a shelf piled with indistinguishable grey rocks. But I like them anyway, and I want more.

6. Last of all, tomatoes. My people—my sister and my bff—hate tomatoes, which makes me feel a strange mixture of guilt and smugness when I stuff them down in vast quantities.

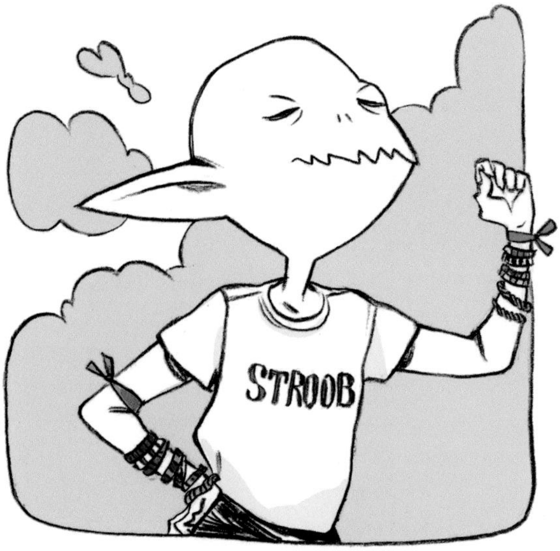
STROOB

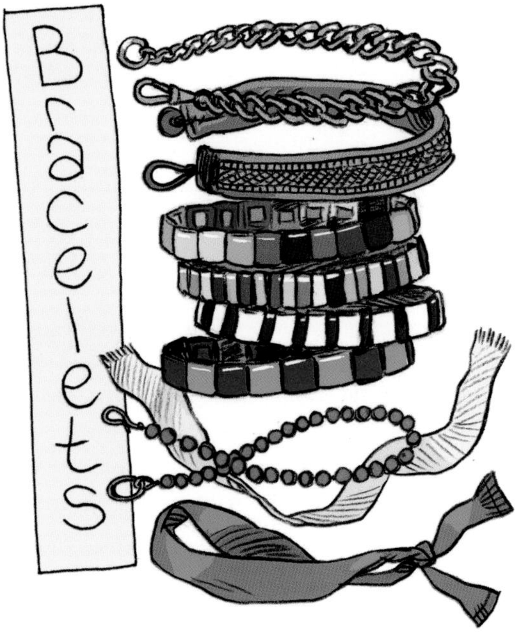
Bracelets

(06/07/2017) *1. At the top of this stack is what I call "the bracelet that will solve all my problems". It's made by a local designer, Anna de Courcy, and whenever I see a particularly well-dressed Vancouver-person, chances are high that they'll be wearing one of these (vintage watch-chain) bracelets; at which point I will stare at said person—creepily, with open longing—and interrupt whatever they're doing in order to announce my admiration and jealousy.*

2. Next, is a sort of generic, beaded leather cuff thing. I've been seeing them around, and would like to find one for myself.

3. I believe that these Roxanne Assoulin bracelets might also have problem-solving powers, especially if I could wear, like, seven or so at once—to stack the benefits, as it were. They look like chiclet gum, don't they? Chiclet gum of the gods.

4. Last winter I read at least three books in which various characters wore bright red coral jewellery, and it gave me a powerful need to own some for myself. Maybe I can convince my sister to split a string of beads with me, so I can make us a matching set…

5. Failing everything else, I'll always take bits of ribbon as a cheap stand-in.

(05/31/2017) *First of all, let me say, I've been feeling very materialistic and wantish, lately. I want new clothing to no particular purpose, and shiny useless trinkets, and anything colourful that's dangled in front of me. I'm like a child, but with less inherent good judgement.*

My birthday list is therefore rather pared down, paradoxical as that may sound. This is a list that demands purity, or at least a higher standard of wanting. That's how I feel about it this year, anyway, and grabbier lists can come later.

Starting with the left column, top to bottom:

1. The traditional birthday breakfast is coffee and a muffin, and oof, let me tell you, I've had some fine muffins lately. Still, I'm going to switch it up, and go for the cookies. Cookies so heavy with chocolate, that they're nearly black; that's where my heart is leading me, right now.

2. Next, the traditional shiny. Back in March or so, my sister took me to a local gem show, and one booth had these beautiful, densely included quartz crystals (mined from Vancouver Island, as I recall). I'm still annoyed that I didn't buy one.

3. This year, on my birthday, I'm travelling to Toronto to visit my close friends. I'm excited about it for all sorts of reasons, but ranking extra high is the fact that most of our plans involve sitting around at home, and drinking tea, and playing Zelda. Literally the best possible present.

4. And since I'm away for several days, leaving my plants untended and unwatered, I'm hoping it will pour with rain.

5. What do we have, here? A second shiny? Yes, well, I'm at the point in my shiny collecting trajectory where I have a profusion of cheaper, smaller stones, and enough medium-to-large ones that my apartment is starting to look like a low-rent museum of geology. What I really need to think about, now, are rare or precious stones. So here's an uncut sapphire—a nice, clear, gemmy one—don't mind if I do.

6. Dessert is another list tradition, and lately the internet has been flashing me pictures of beautiful, scarcely iced cakes. Is this a current fad in the cake world? Because I'm into it; cakes always have way too much icing for my personal needs and wants. So what I'm imagining, here, is a triple-stacked light sponge sandwiched with strawberry or raspberry jam, and iced just-so.

7. Beneath the roiling surface of my petty wanting, I know that what I really want is to go hang out with some oceans and forests. I've been doing a fair amount of it lately, you could argue. Nonetheless, I need more, and I mean to get as much of it as I can before the summer ends.

H.B.M. 2017

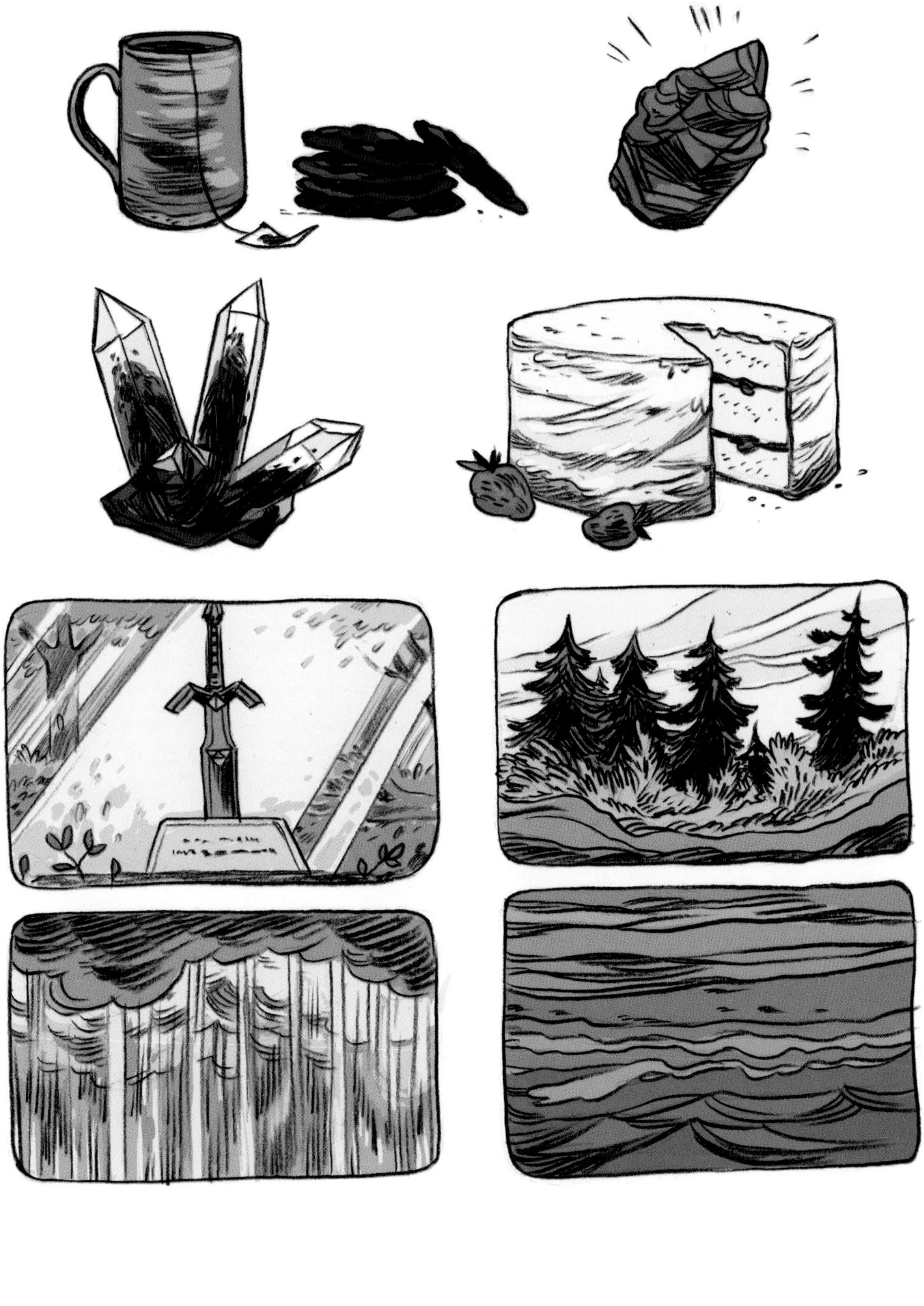

Shiny Collection

smoky quartz

The only things I truly collect and hoard in large quantities (other than books) are rocks and minerals. I love to trap someone in my apartment and make them look through all seven of my shiny boxes, ensuring they don't skip over anything and forcing them to stop and admire certain specimens in particular.

People often ask me to provide a full catalogue of my shinies—it's the request I get most frequently—and I've finally decided to give it a shot. I couldn't include everything, but here's a good, hefty slice. These are all the shinies I'd make you look at, if you were here.

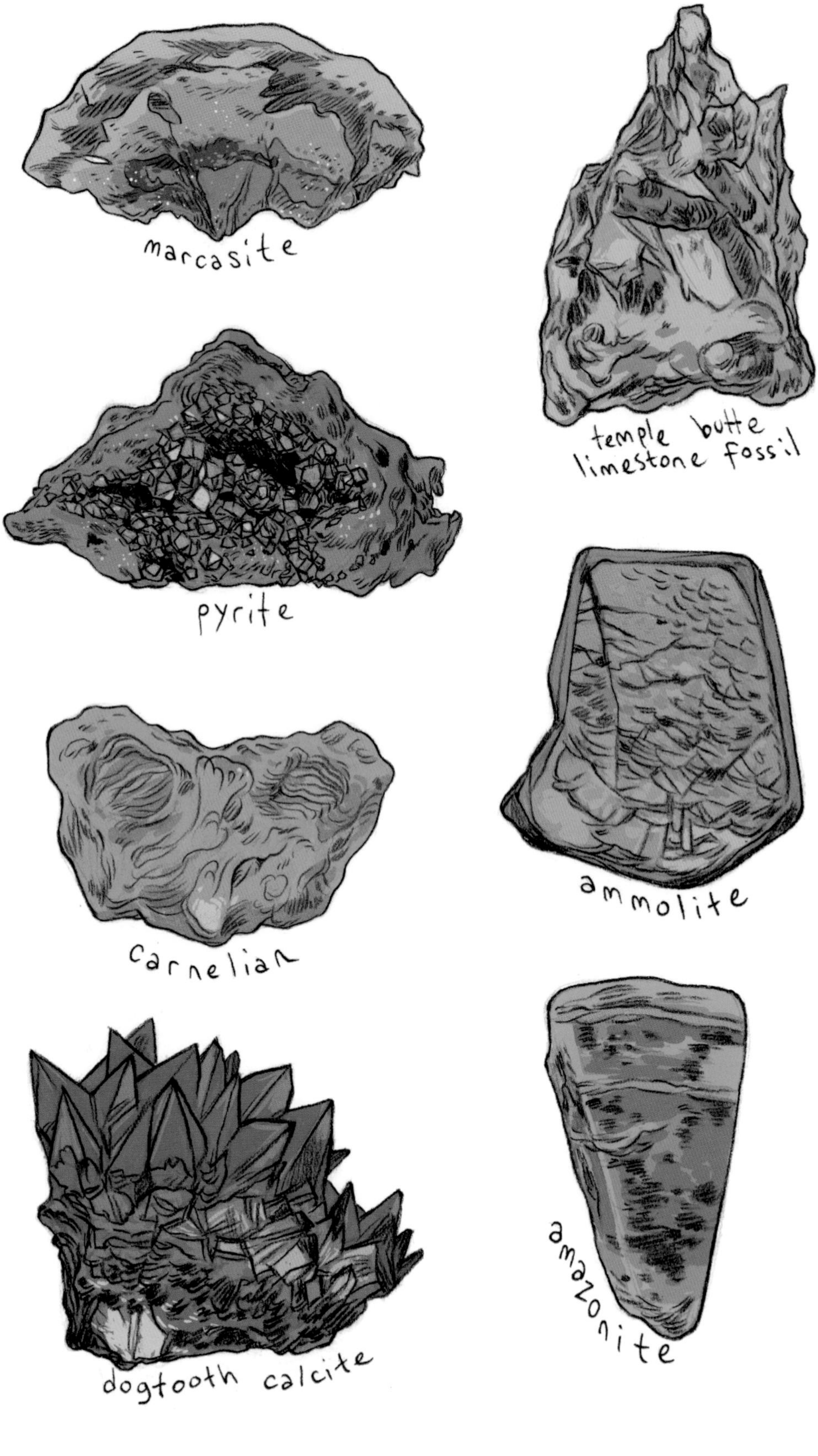
marcasite
temple butte
limestone fossil
pyrite
ammolite
carnelian
amazonite
dogtooth calcite

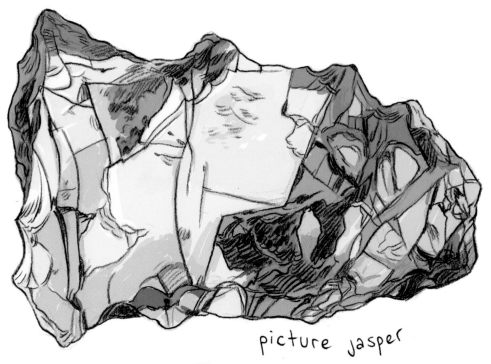

picture jasper

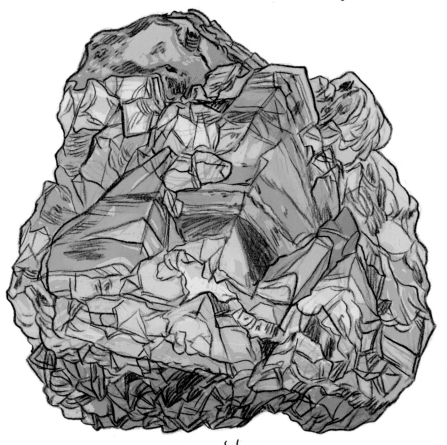

fluorite

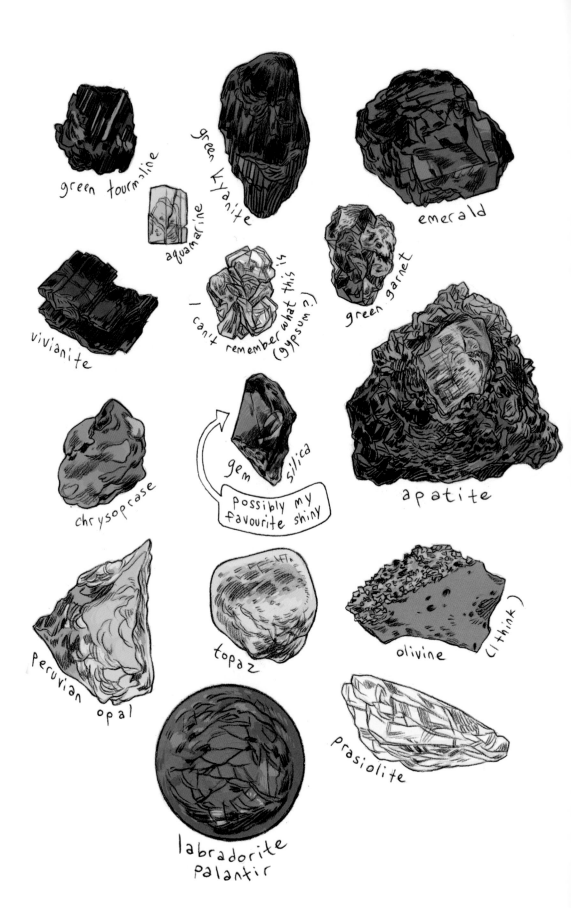

green tourmaline

green kyanite

aquamarine

emerald

vivianite

I can't remember what this is (gypsum?)

green garnet

chrysoprase

gem silica

possibly my favourite shiny

apatite

Peruvian opal

topaz

olivine (I think)

labradorite palantir

prasiolite

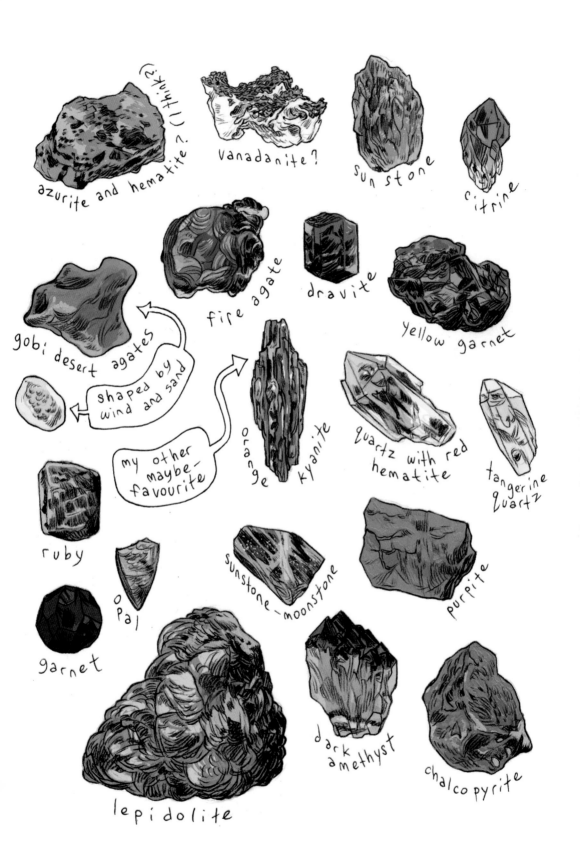

azurite and hematite?. (I think?)

vanadanite?

sunstone

citrine

fire agate

dravite

yellow garnet

gobi desert agates

shaped by wind and sand

orange kyanite

quartz with red hematite

tangerine quartz

my other maybe-favourite

ruby

opal

sunstone-moonstone

pyrite

garnet

lepidolite

dark amethyst

chalco pyrite

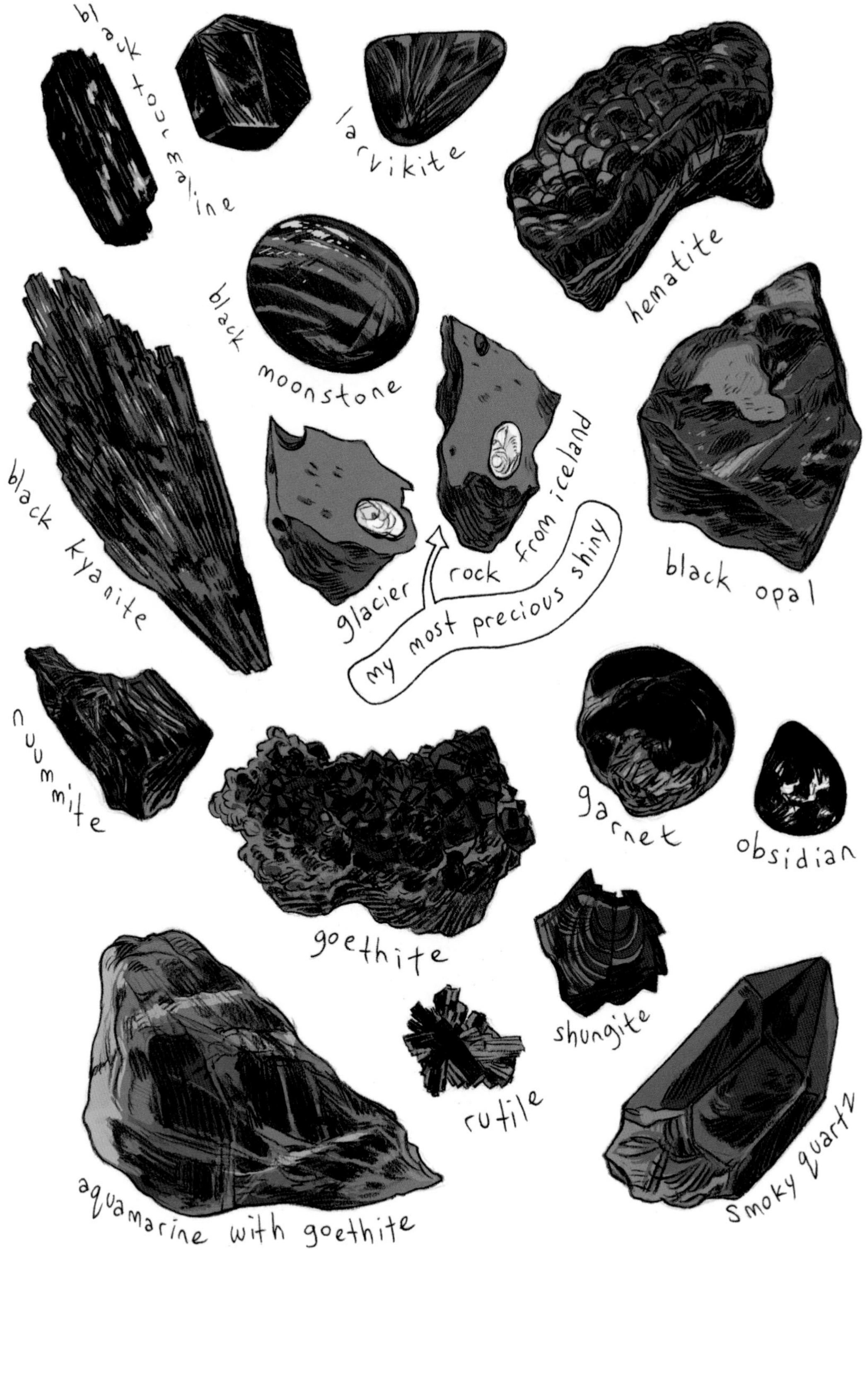
black tourmaline
larvikite
hematite
black moonstone
black kyanite
glacier rock from iceland
my most precious shiny
black opal
nuummite
goethite
garnet
obsidian
shungite
rutile
aquamarine with goethite
smoky quartz

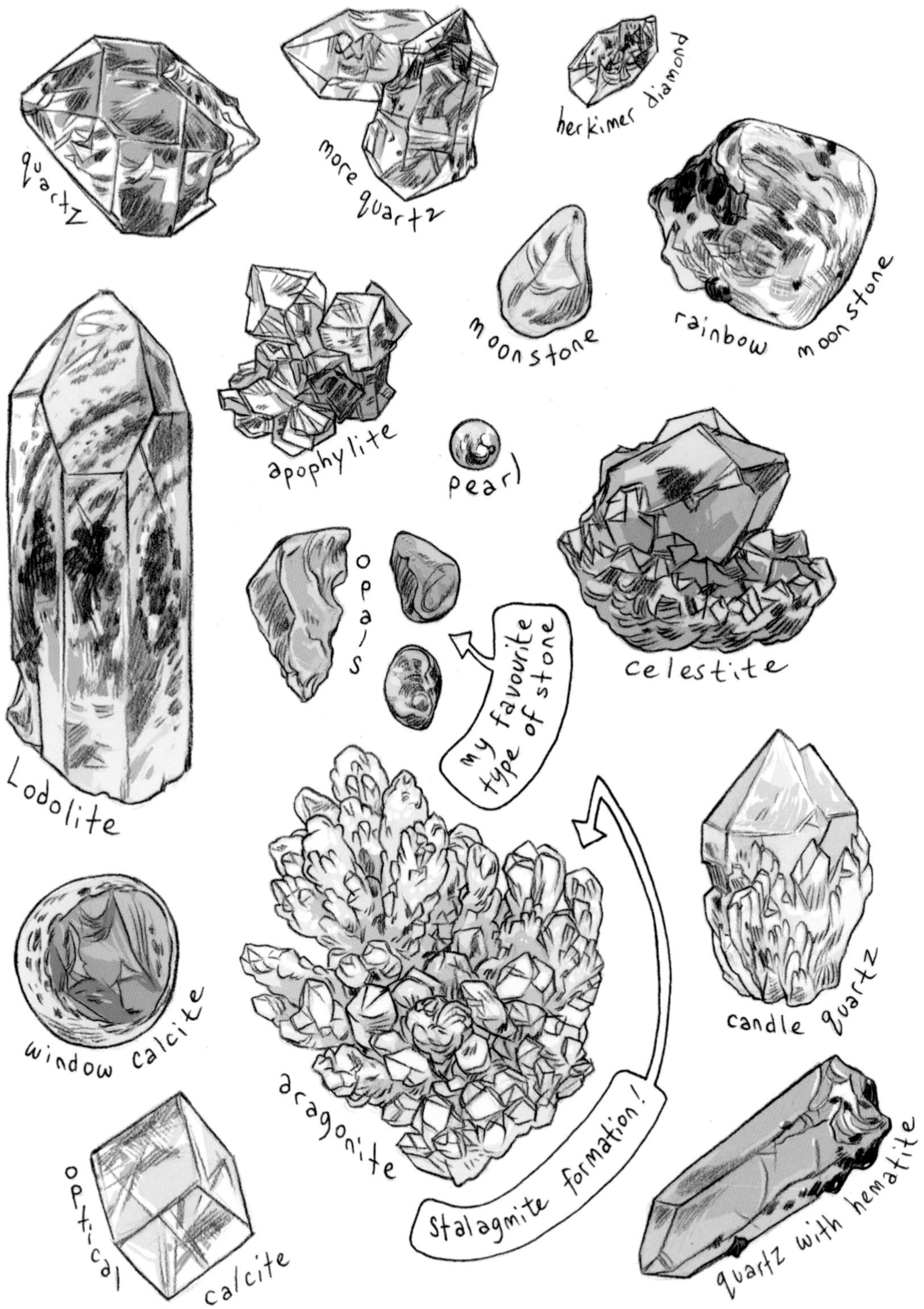
quartz
more quartz
herkimer diamond
moonstone
rainbow moonstone
apophylite
pearl
Lodolite
celestite
opals
my favourite type of stone
stalagmite formation!
candle quartz
window calcite
aragonite
optical calcite
quartz with hematite

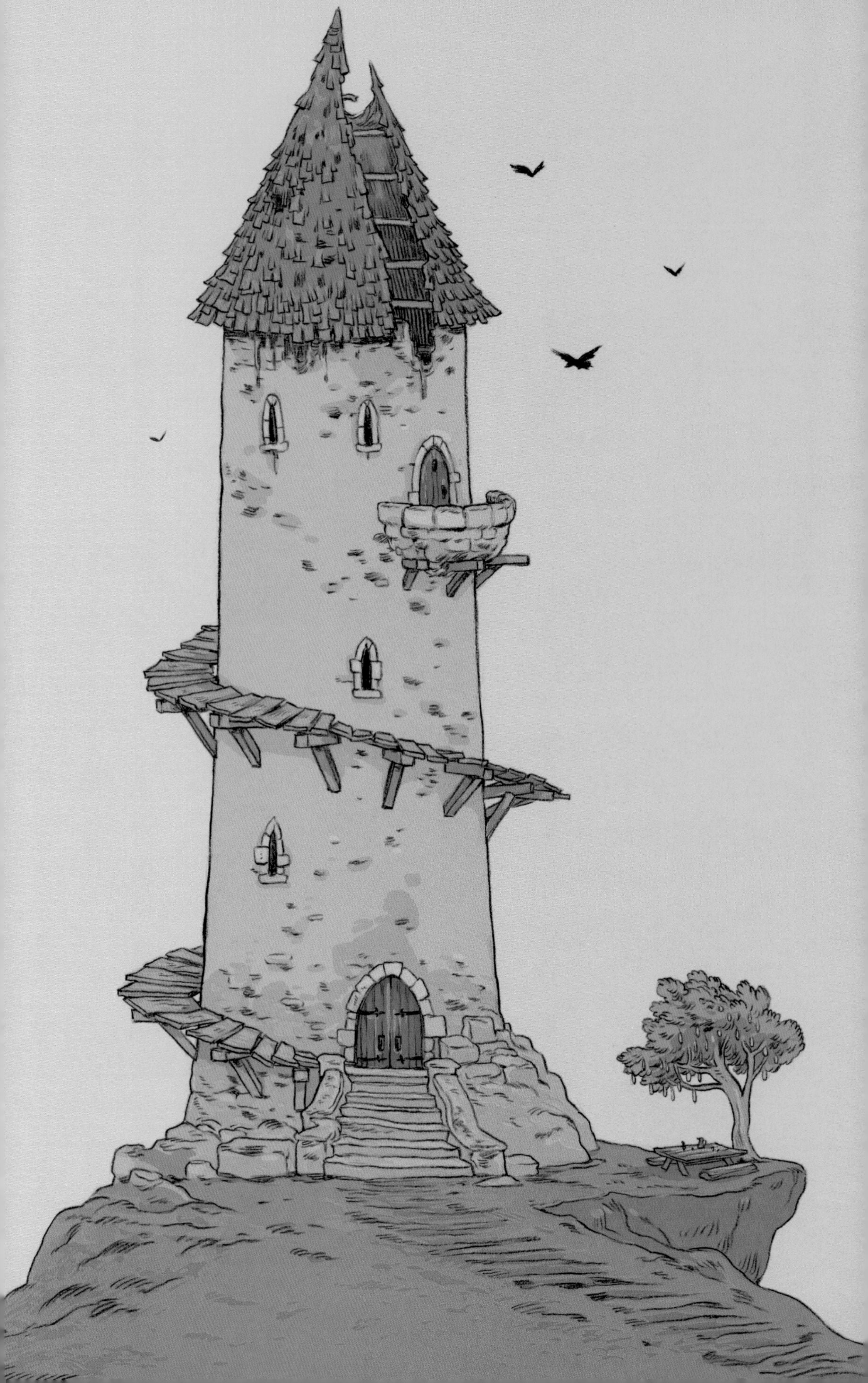

Chapter 04:

The Hchom House

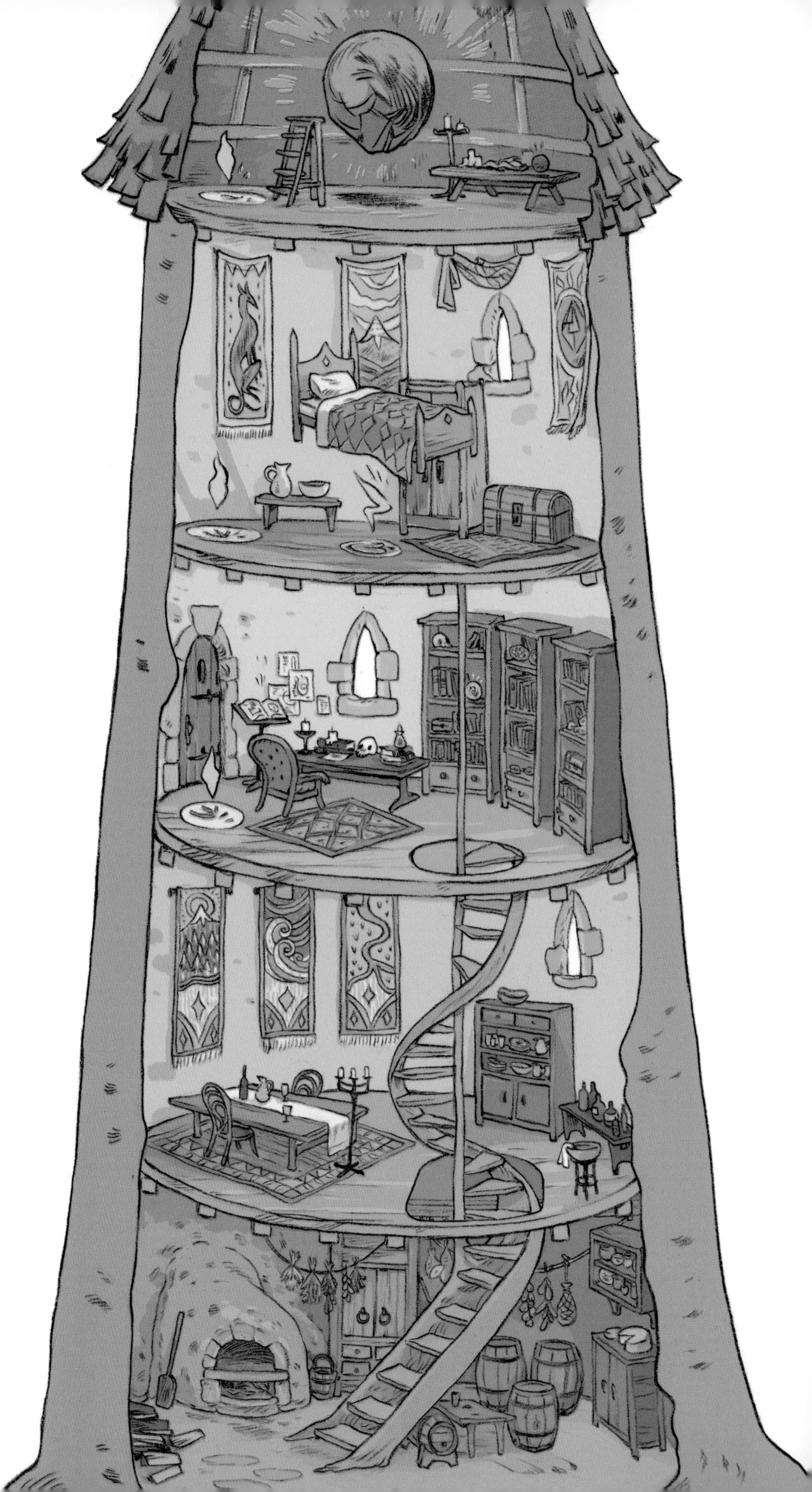

As a teenager, I was fixated on my future first apartment. I created what I thought were realistic layouts, right down to the colour and square footage of my tastefully threadbare vintage carpets. My imaginary boyfriend (usually some videogame magazine editor) would visit me there, but he wouldn't live with me, because I knew I wanted that space all to myself.

My real first apartment didn't live up to the fantasy. How could it have? A fantasy is not a plan: plans are grounded and steady, while fantasy is light-footed, always racing ahead and dodging around corners. A good plan will follow a fantasy, and a good fantasy will never let itself be caught. That apartment was a daydream, but a productive one; it told me something about how I wanted to live.

Although I've called this the "House" chapter, I've also included posts that fall into a distinctly out of house category, posts about adventure in wilderness spaces. These are mutually supportive subjects, I think. The adventure is anchored by the home. The home is not confining, but it is utterly sound: it will be there when you return. Though life turns out to be filled with closed rooms and dead ends, this is a fantasy worth pursuing—this buoyant balance—even in the form of wizard towers and underground cutaways. Space, it turns out, is my very deepest want.

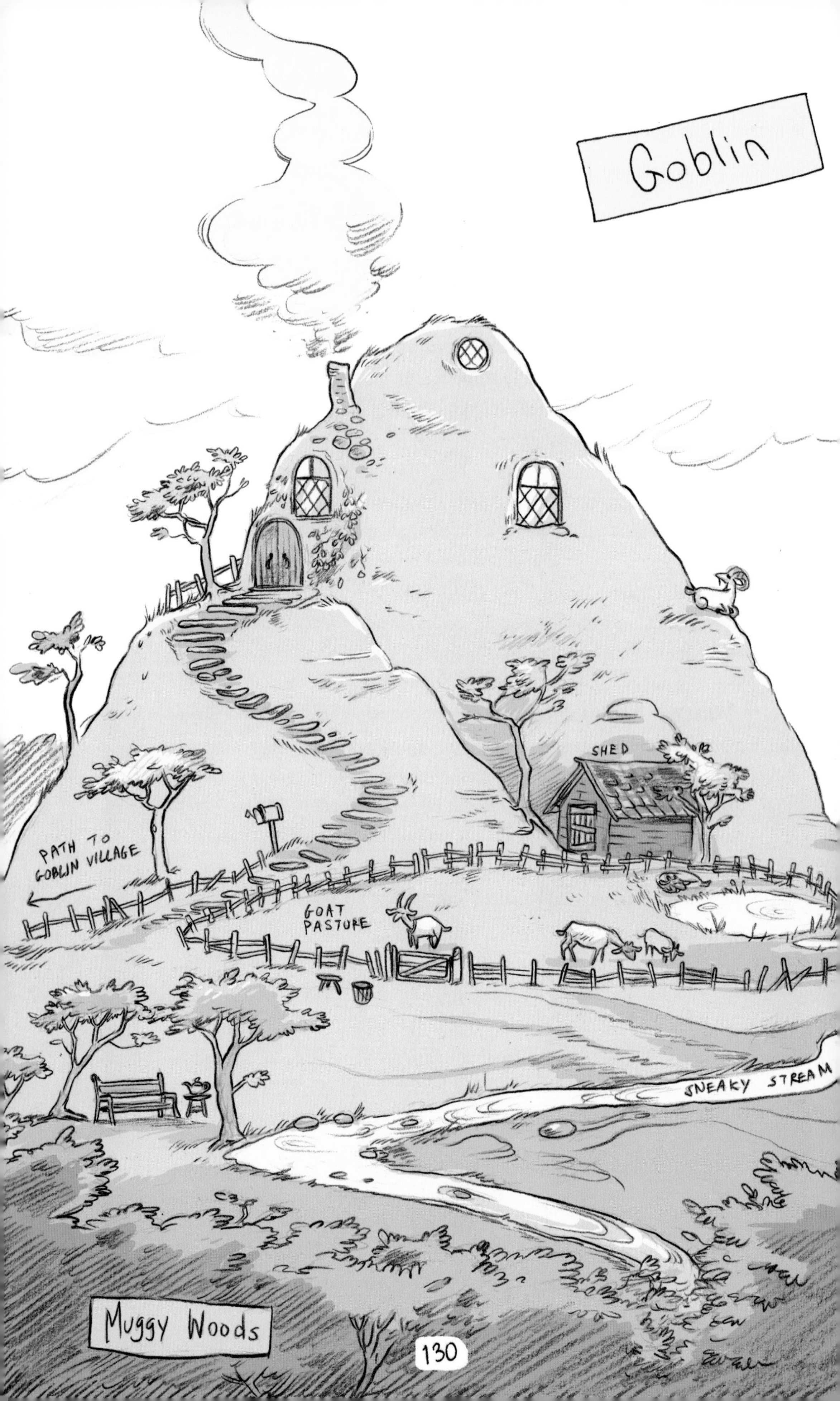
Goblin
SHED
PATH TO GOBLIN VILLAGE
GOAT PASTURE
SNEAKY STREAM
Muggy Woods

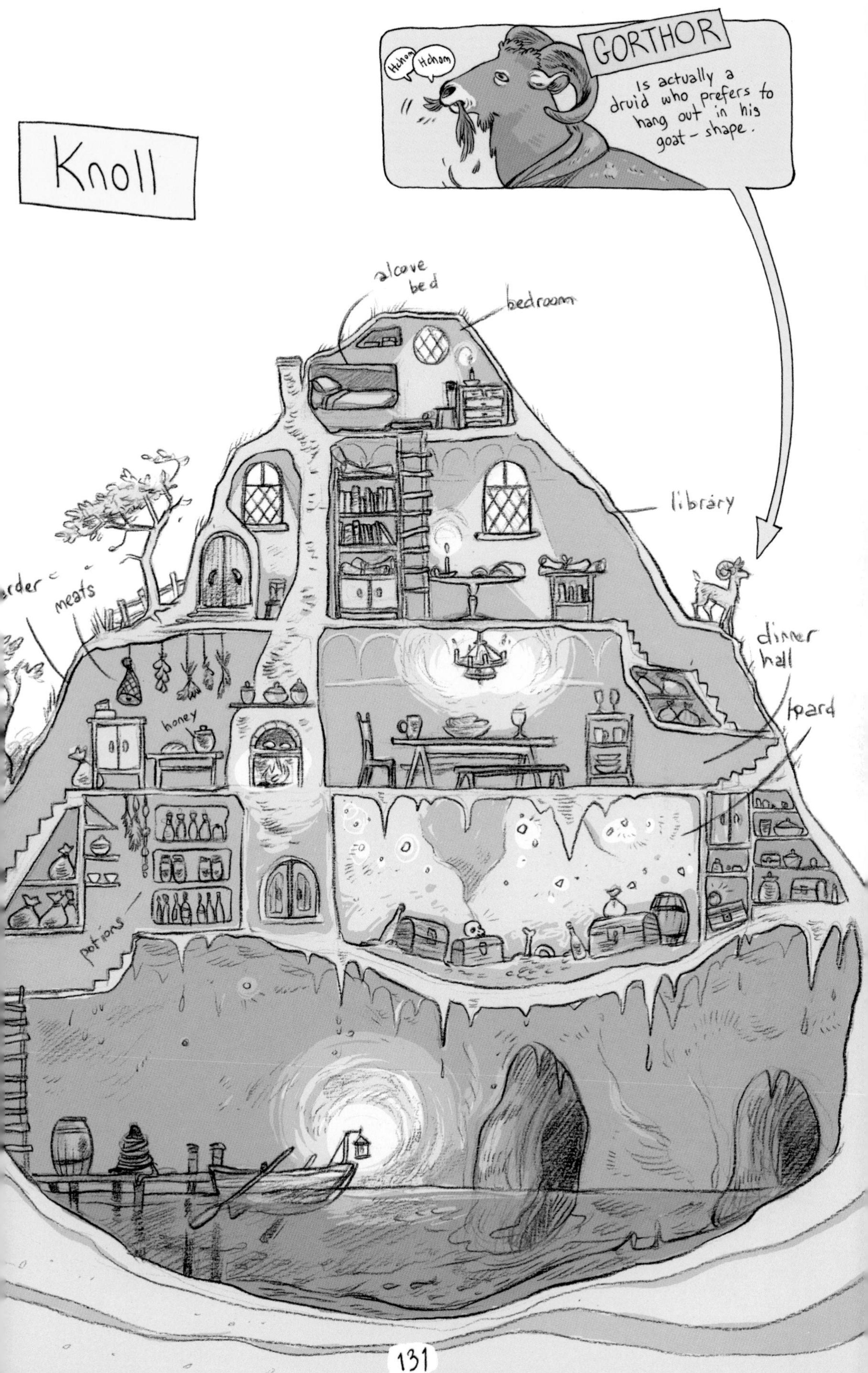
Knoll
Hchom
Hchom
GORTHOR
Is actually a druid who prefers to hang out in his goat-shape.
alcove bed
bedroom
library
dinner hall
hoard
meats
honey
potions

Mouser

(11/24/2010) *Wouldn't a cosy spaceship be the best thing ever? Hot damn, yes it would. Space ports, though, would have to be all muffin shops and fine croissanteries (for space muffins and space croissants).*

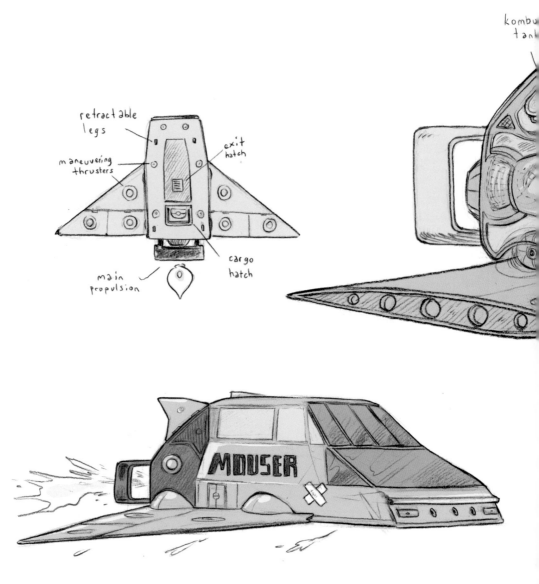

retractable legs

maneuvering thrusters

exit hatch

cargo hatch

main propulsion

kombu tank

MOUSER

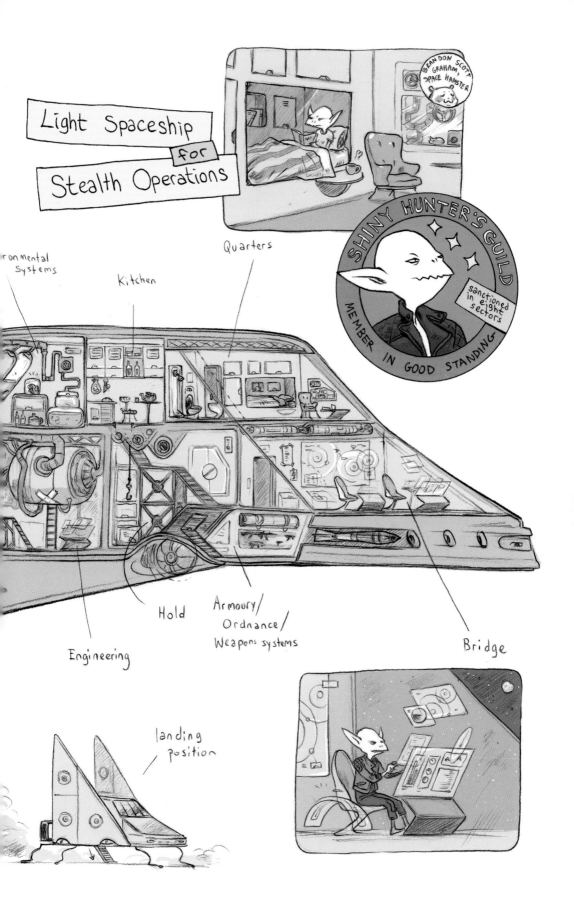

Light Spaceship for Stealth Operations

BRANDON SCOTT GRAHAM, SPACE HAMSTER

SHINY HUNTER'S GUILD
MEMBER IN GOOD STANDING
sanctioned in eight sectors

Environmental Systems

Kitchen

Quarters

Hold

Engineering

Armoury/ Ordnance/ Weapons systems

Bridge

landing position

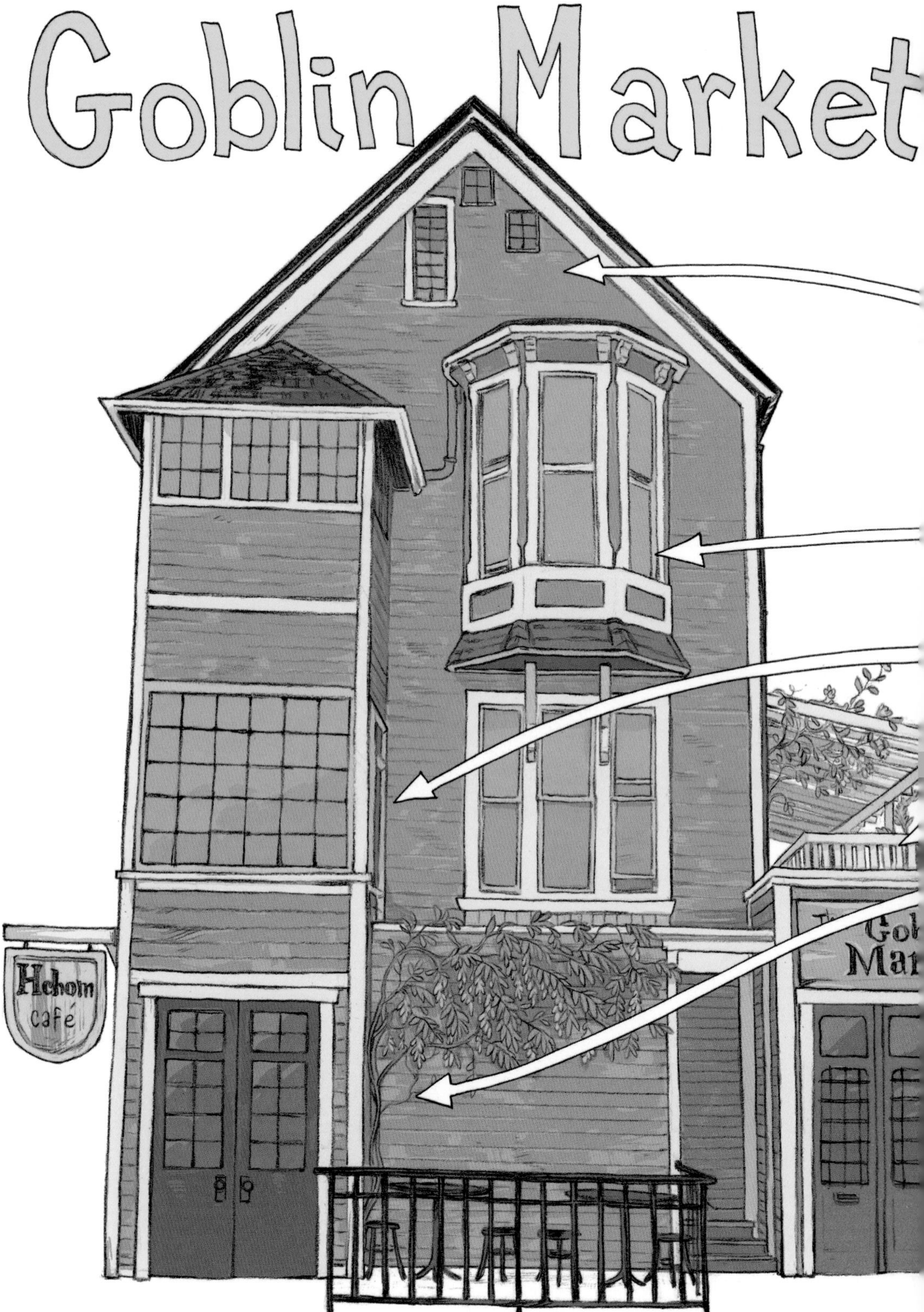
Goblin Market
Hchom
café

I used to live across from this heritage house at Main and 8th Ave. The house was charming in part because it had survived so long surrounded by apartment buildings and retail fronts and the lengthening shadow of skyscaper condos, but also in part for its own odd, patchwork character. I had an ongoing fantasy in which I owned it and ran both a cafe and an "adventurer's market" out of its ground-floor business spaces.

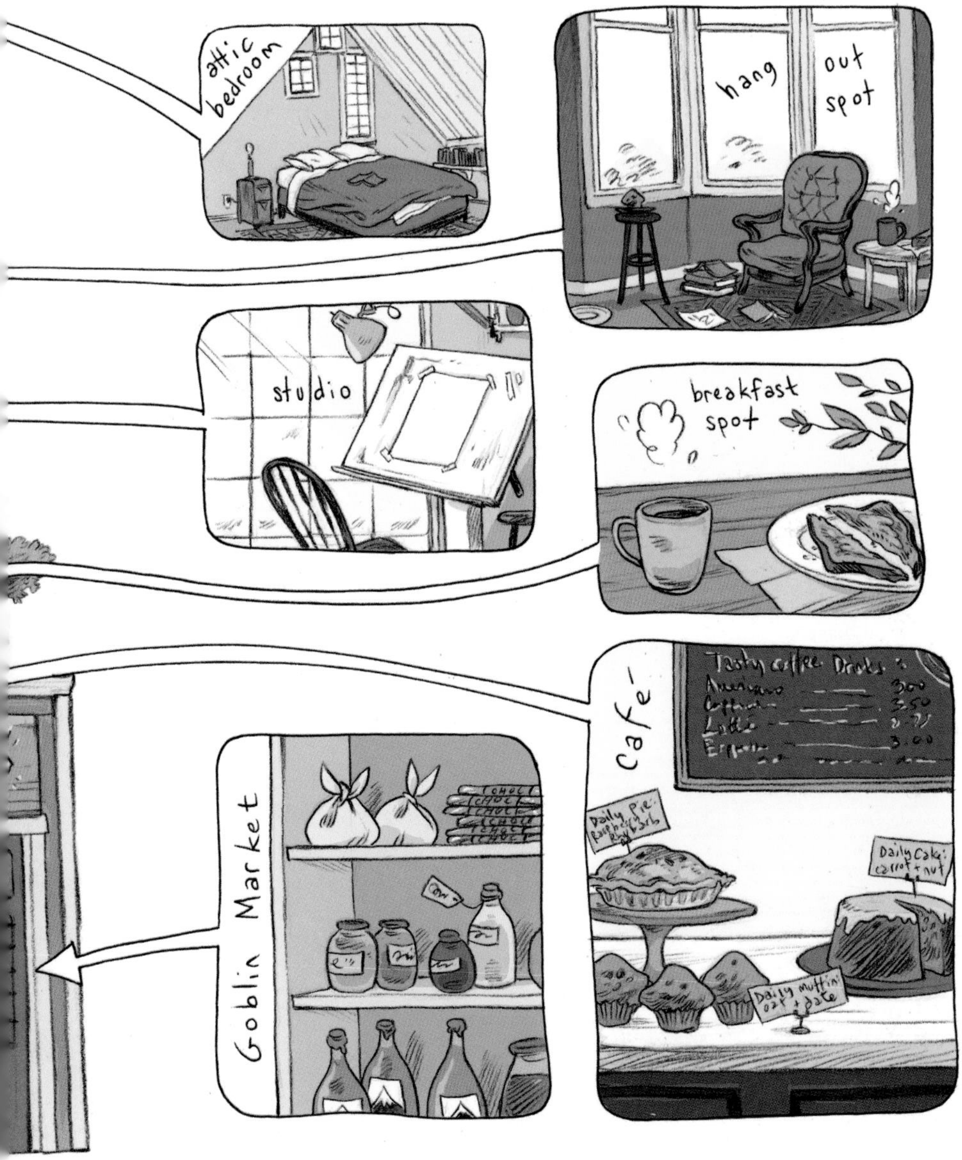
attic bedroom
hang out spot
studio
breakfast spot
Café
Tasty coffee Drinks
Daily Pie: Raspberry Rhubarb
Daily Cake: carrot + nut
Daily muffin: oat + date
Goblin Market

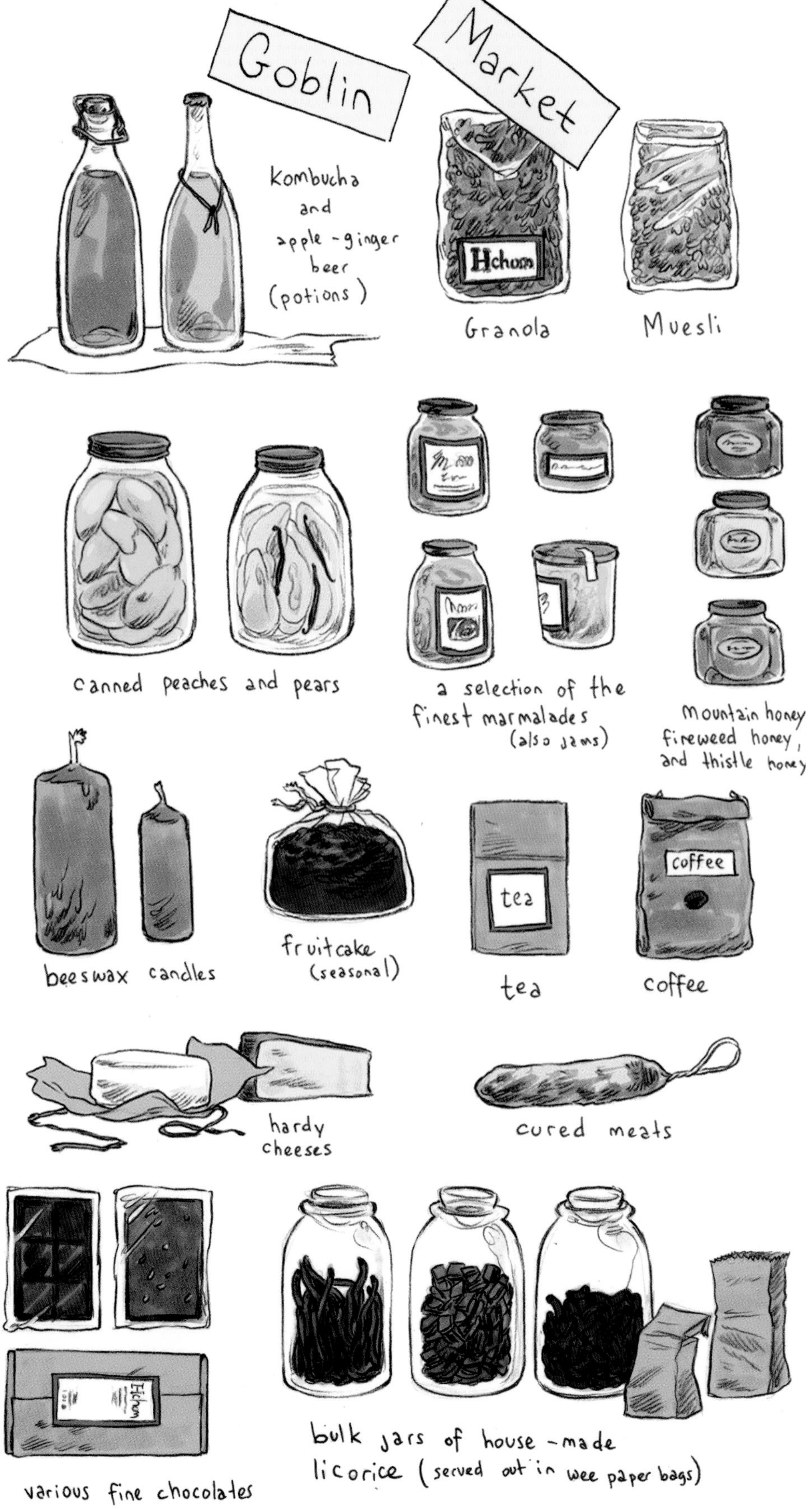
Goblin Market
Kombucha and apple-ginger beer (potions)
Hchom
Granola
Muesli
canned peaches and pears
a selection of the finest marmalades (also jams)
Mountain honey fireweed honey, and thistle honey
beeswax candles
fruitcake (seasonal)
tea
tea
coffee
coffee
hardy cheeses
cured meats
Elchom
various fine chocolates
bulk jars of house-made licorice (served out in wee paper bags)

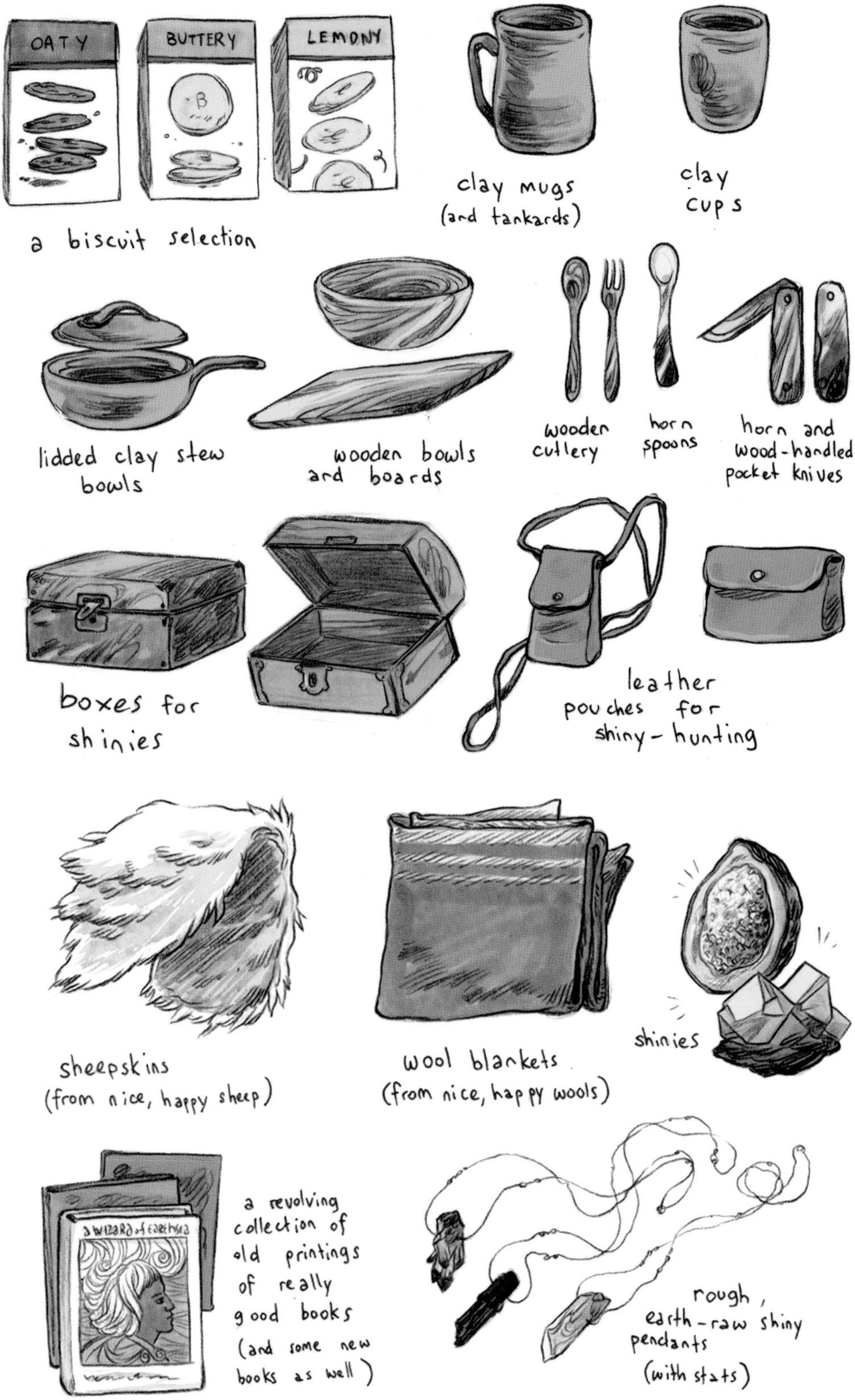
OATY
BUTTERY
LEMONY
B
a biscuit selection
clay mugs
(and tankards)
clay
cups
lidded clay stew
bowls
wooden bowls
and boards
wooden
cutlery
horn
spoons
horn and
wood-handled
pocket knives
boxes for
shinies
leather
pouches for
shiny-hunting
sheepskins
(from nice, happy sheep)
wool blankets
(from nice, happy wools)
shinies
A WIZARD of EARTHSEA
a revolving
collection of
old printings
of really
good books
(and some new
books as well)
rough,
earth-raw shiny
pendants
(with stats)

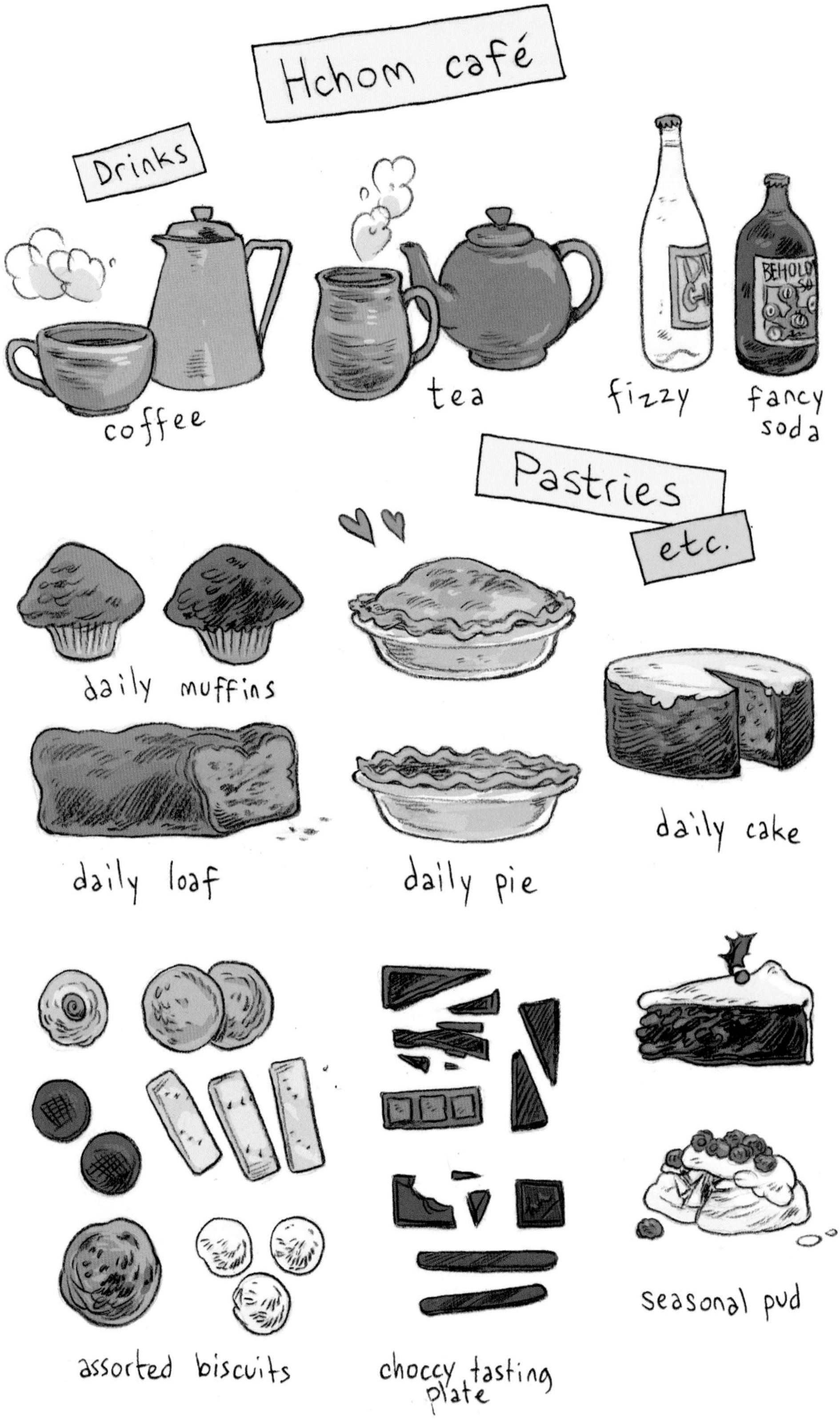
Hchom café
Drinks
coffee
tea
fizzy
fancy soda
Pastries
etc.
daily muffins
daily loaf
daily pie
daily cake
assorted biscuits
choccy tasting plate
seasonal pud

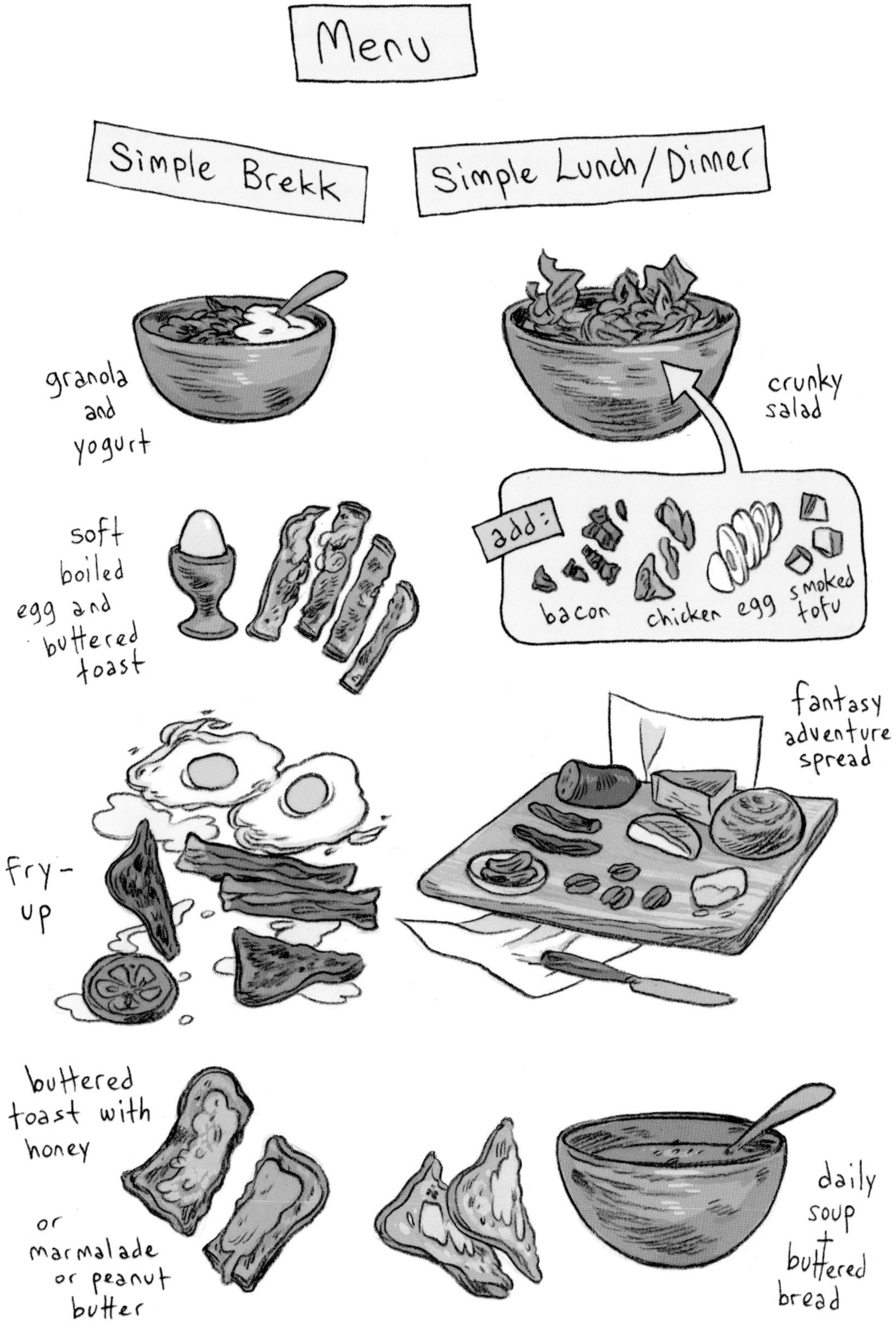
Menu
Simple Brekk
Simple Lunch/Dinner
granola and yogurt
crunky salad
add:
bacon
chicken
egg
smoked tofu
soft boiled egg and buttered toast
fantasy adventure spread
fry-up
buttered toast with honey
or marmalade or peanut butter
daily soup + buttered bread

(09/19/2011) *I've been waiting for autumn to begin, as usual, since early July. This year I tried to embrace the full summery-ness of things, but I couldn't really manage it. Autumn is when the adventures begin; when the shinies, deep in their caverns, are waiting to be pried loose and carried home.*

And being the material creature that I am, the season has its attendant needs and wants. Let me, ahem, highlight a few from the list to your right…

1. This Danish fisherman's sweater is one that I've been yearning for since almost a year ago. Plus, a commenter has vouched for it as being the best sweater ever. When I think about what the taxes and border fees would amount to, I cringe. Cringe, and… maybe get it anyway, thereby bankrupting myself forever? Better to die destitute and happy (and warm)?

2. Toe socks. They have turned me completely around on socks (which I've never liked wearing) and now I want a full compliment of them.

3. The leather toolkit was in fact modeled after a handmade leather toiletry kit. Sure, it's totally over-the-top as something to put your toothpaste in (maybe the toothpaste costs $200 as well), but as a goblin toolkit? Totally reasonable. If I had a nice big sheet of leather, I'd try to make one for myself.

4. A giant jug of apple cider. You know the huge glass ones at the store? Inevitably pricey, but promising to be tastier than anything you've ever had before? At least, that is what they seem to be promising whenever I see them. Maybe I'll get one when Skyrim comes out, and take swigs from it during the loading screens.

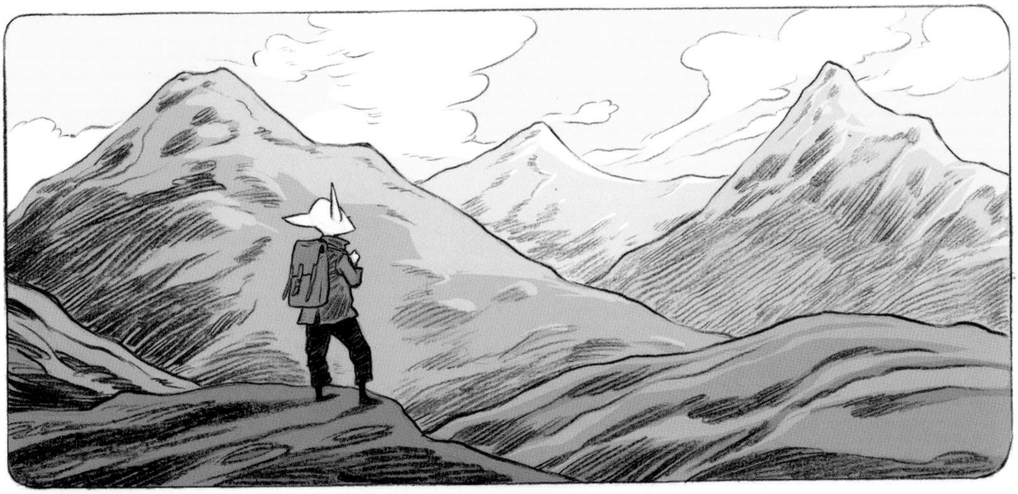

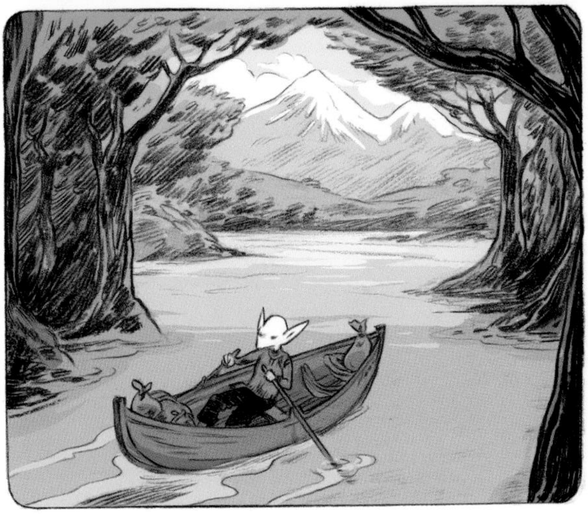

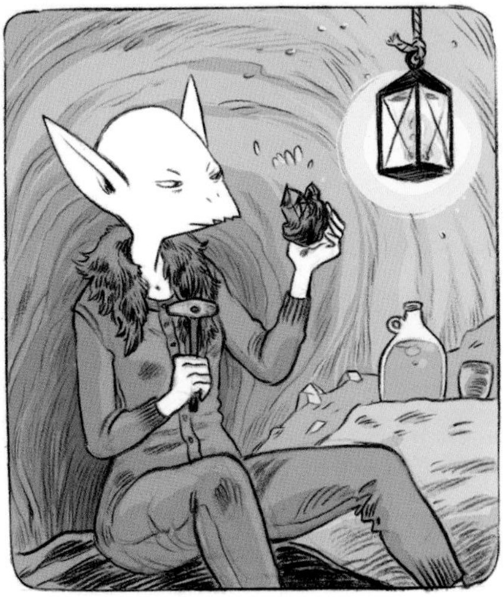

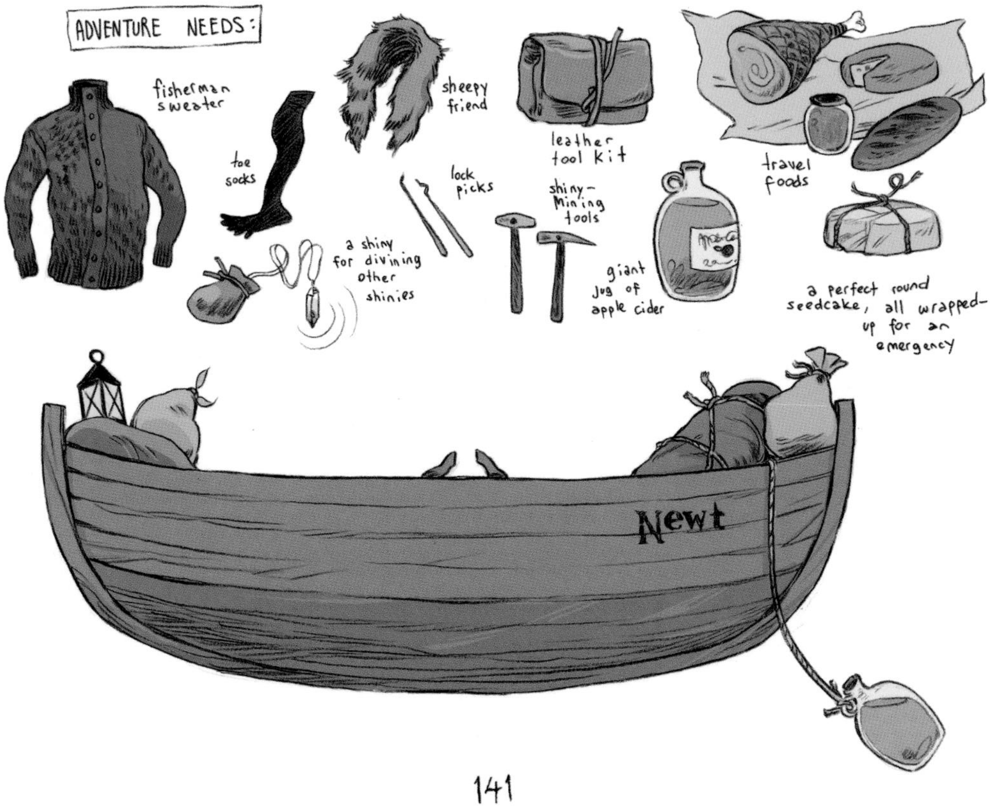

ADVENTURE NEEDS:
fisherman sweater
toe socks
sheepy friend
leather tool kit
travel foods
lock picks
shiny-mining tools
a shiny for divining other shinies
giant jug of apple cider
a perfect round seedcake, all wrapped-up for an emergency
Newt

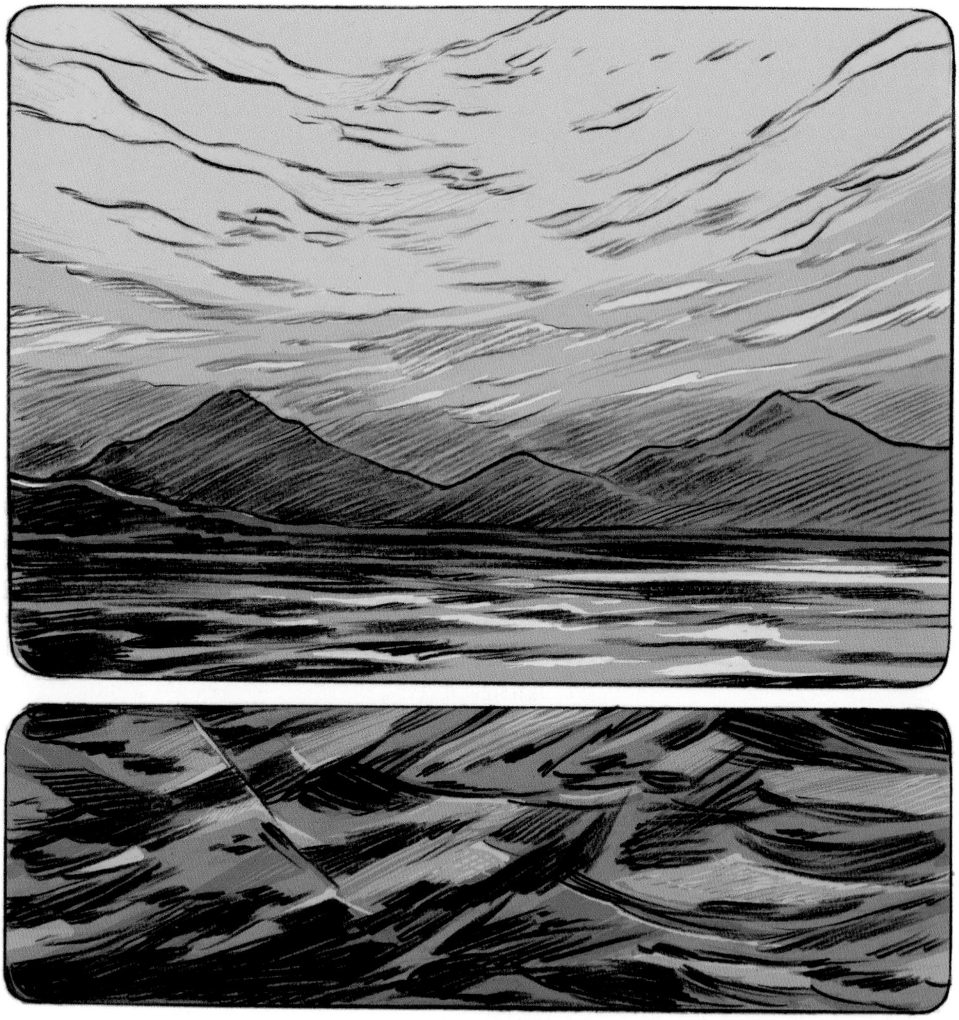

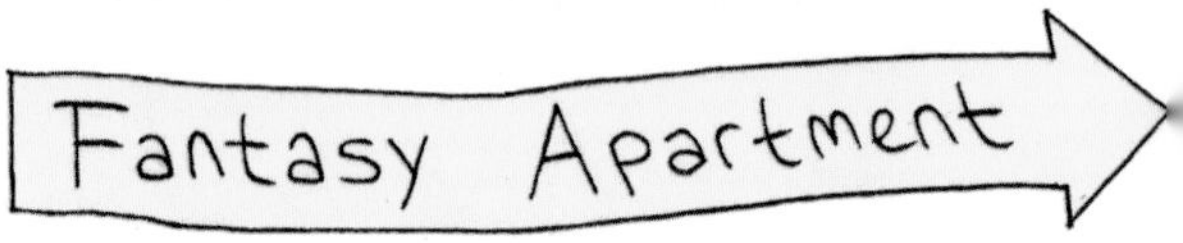
Fantasy Apartment

(05/16/2012) *Normally my fantasy living space would be something a little less staid and reasonable, but there's nothing like sudden nest-insecurity to make a nice, one-bedroom unit of moderate size seem like the most appealing thing on earth.*

So dear Vancouver, can we make this happen? Plus, I must say, I've never had hardwood floors before, and I think it's time. The bathtub carved out of solid quartz crystal would be a nice touch, but I'm ready to discard that expectation if necessary.

Look, Vancouver, I'm the best tenant ever. I'm obsessively tidy, and I write rent cheques a year in advance, and I only practice my shrill wind instruments, like, once or twice a month. You want me! You want me to want you! Do we have an understanding? Two apartments, same building, nice location, decent rent, good flooring. GO.

Where is my hoooooooome?

FANTASY APARTMENT

(But seriously, pretty reasonable.)

Old teak drawer unit. It belongs to my parents, but I COVET IT and WANT IT. Perfect for art supplies.

BALCONY!
← optimistic shrubbery (likely to die)
(hardwood floors? please pleaseplease?)
← wall-mounted bookshelves
WINDOW
WINDOW
WINDOW
(don't much care about kitchens)
KITCHEN
DOOR
CLOSET
BOOKS
BEDROOM
BATHROOM
CLOSET

← more optimistic greenery
↑ paper/art storage

Custom bookshelf for comic page + art book storage. Hi dad, want to help me make this sometime?

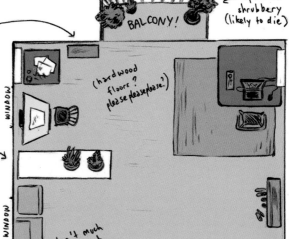

Wouldn't mind a new bed (plain, short headboard + footboard. More teak! Always teak forever!) [walnut would be OK too.]

Bathtub carved from quartz (how could anyone not want this...)

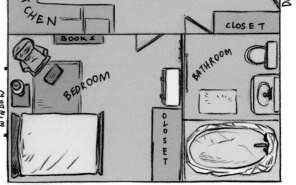

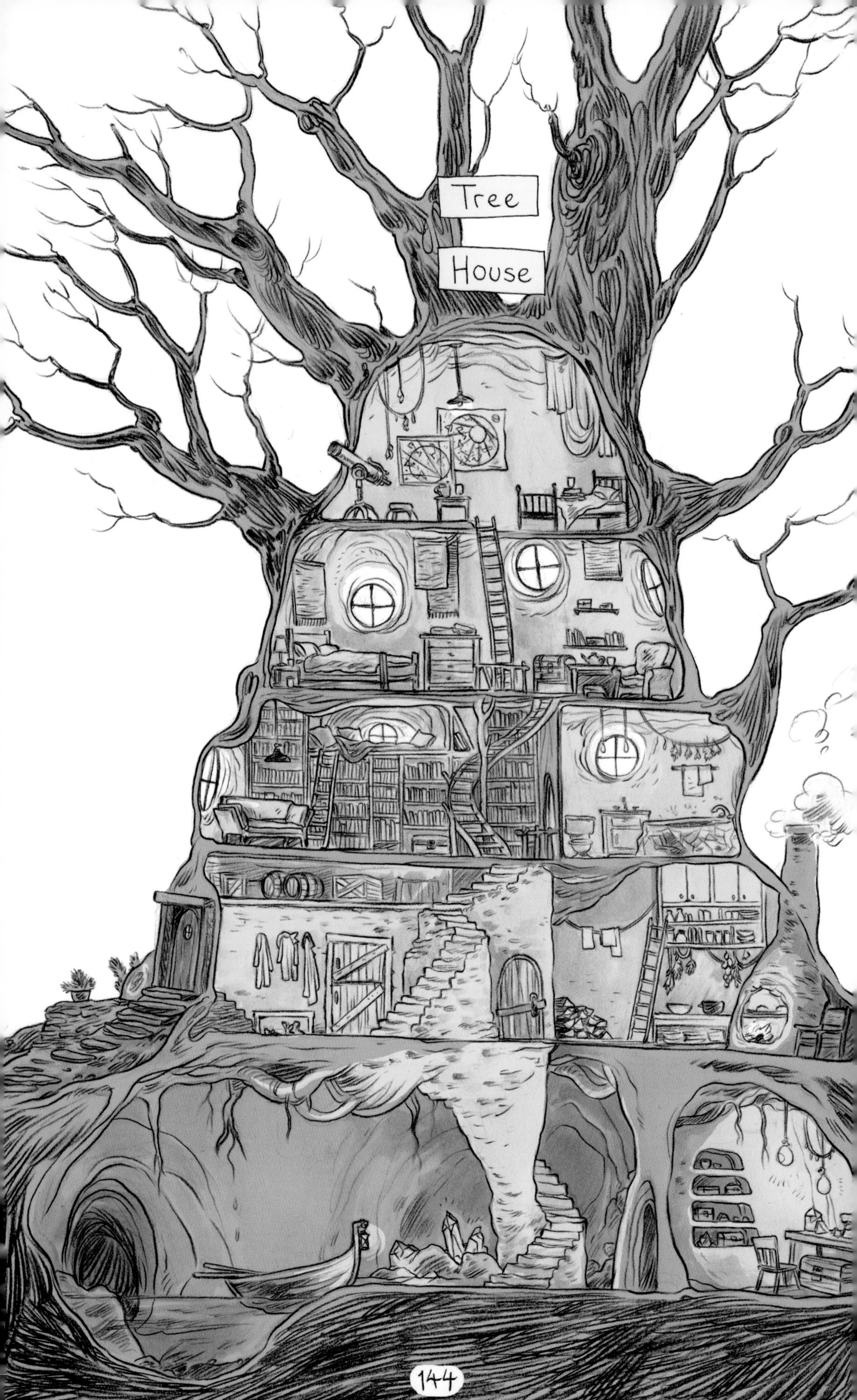
Tree
House

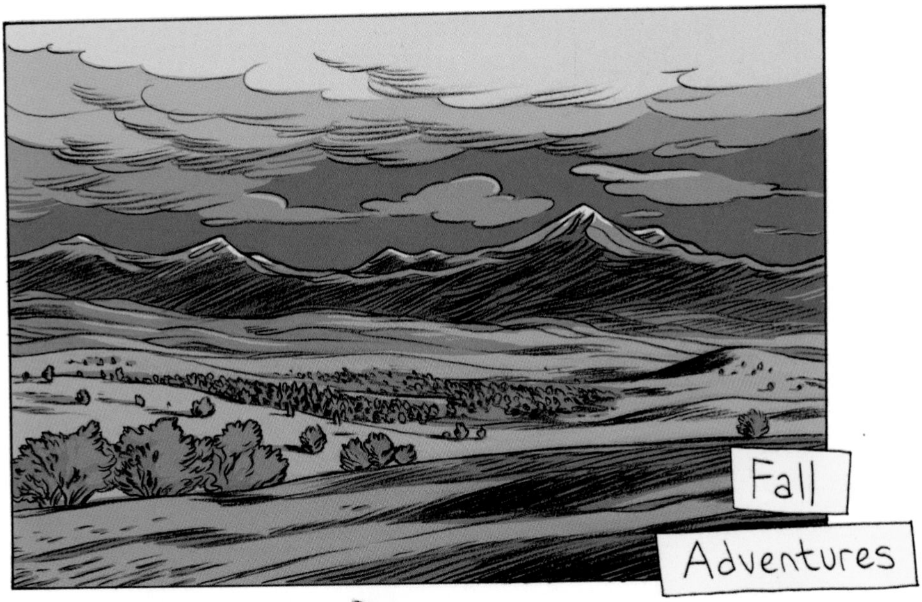
Fall
Adventures

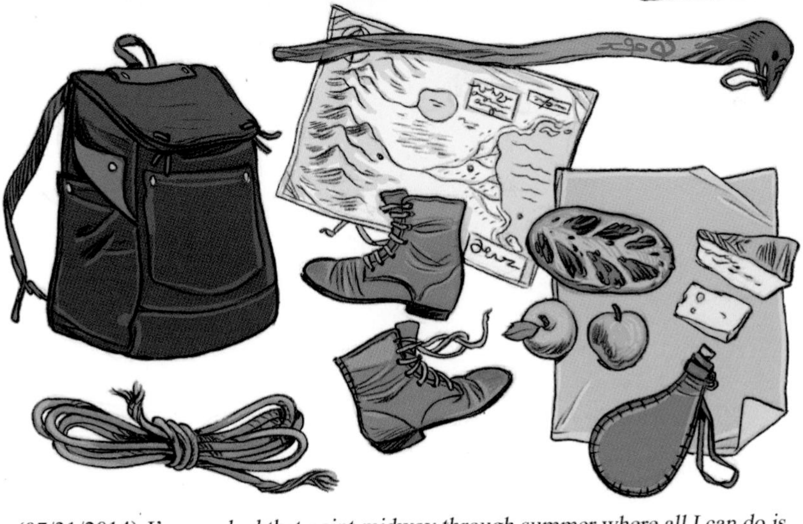

(07/31/2014) *I've reached that point midway through summer where all I can do is flop about from one petulant heap to another and whine (whiiiiine!) about how the never-ending sunshine is melting my flesh. I can't openly complain about it as much as I'd like, or my friends and family (and the fair folk of Middle Earth) will shun me, so I'm trying to find distractions that will pull me through until September. Yesterday I unlaced and cleaned my leather shoes and boots—regardless of whether they needed it or not (what most of them need are new soles). Then I systematically tried on and admired my wool jackets and my overcoat.*

Today I'm doing this fall adventures post.

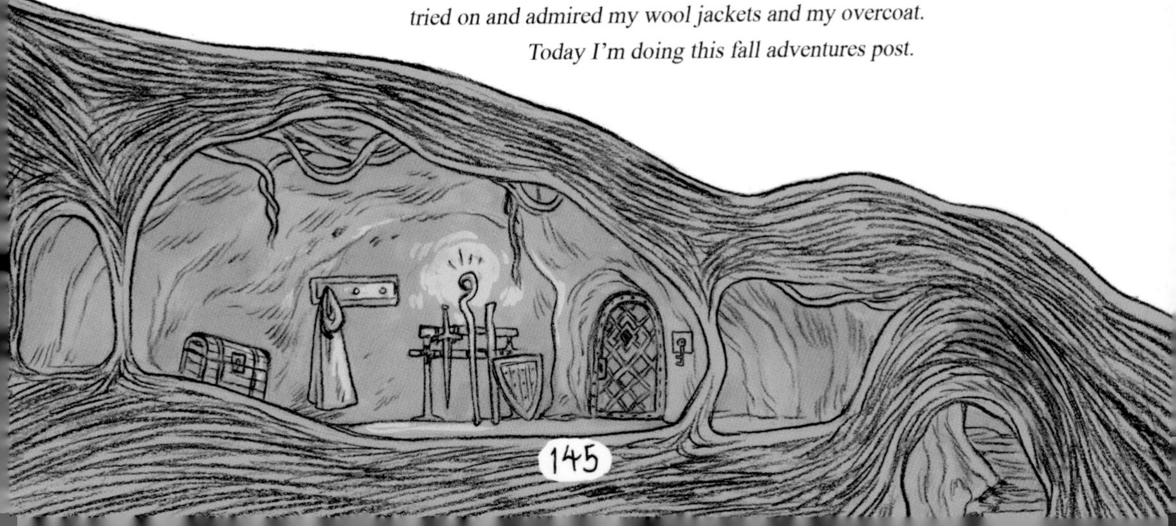

Vancouver

Cafés and Bakeries

Beyond Bread – 3686 West 4th Ave / (604) 733-3931
If I had to choose quickly in a hostage situation, I'd say this was the best bread bakery in town.

Fife Bakery – 64 East 3rd Ave / (604) 336-0652
And if there's a contender for the title, this is it. Currently my top choice.

Bâtard Bakery – 3958 Fraser Street / (604) 506-3958
Everything is great, here. I love the seasonal fruit flan, and their multigrain loaf is the seedy elven forest bread of all my lifelong hopes and dreams.

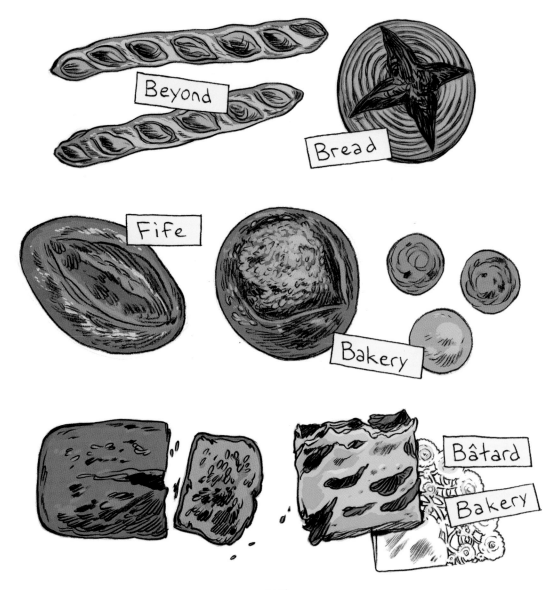

Beyond

Bread

Fife

Bakery

Bâtard

Bakery

Beaucoup Bakery – 2150 Fir Street / (604) 732-4222

These are some of the finest croissants (and croissant-brethren) to be found in Vancouver.

Butter – 4907 MacKenzie Street / (604) 221-4333

The best pies to be bought, that I know of. And probably the best cookies, too.

Sweet Obsession – 2611 W 16th Ave / (604) 739-0555 ext 2

A large selection of formal desserts, and cookies and pastries and whatnot. They've been around a long time, now, and they know what they're about.

Coco et Olive – 3707 Main Street / (604) 568-7447

This place meets all the criteria for a good drawing/working café: roomy tables, lots of natural light, and relative quiet. Plus, the coffee is good, and they have excellent pastries.

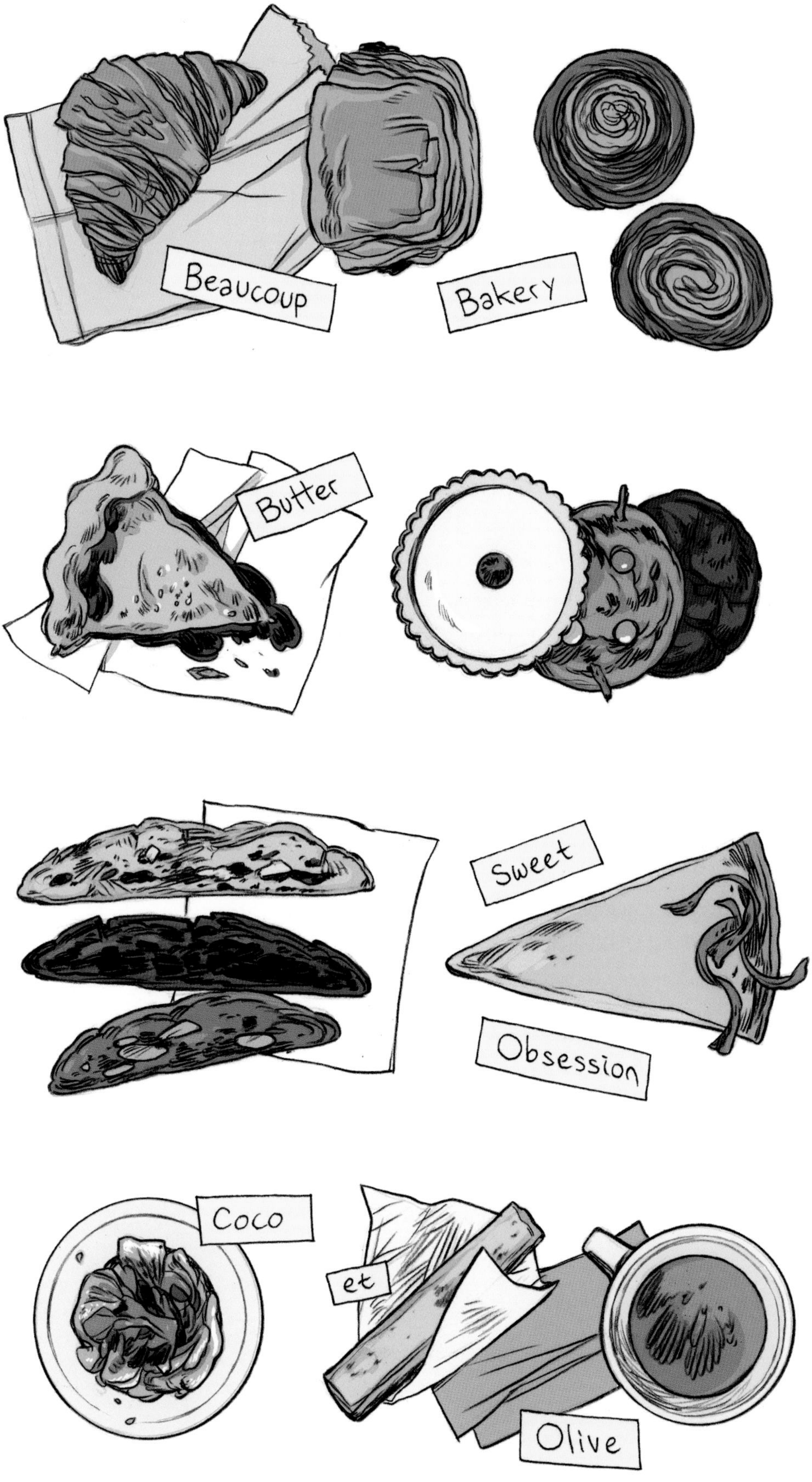
Beaucoup
Bakery
Butter
Sweet
Obsession
Coco
et
Olive

Elysian Coffee – 590 West Broadway / (604) 874-5909
This place does really nice coffee, and has a pleasing selection of baked things. They also have the best tucked away outdoor seating, for days when you want to sit under the burning daystar and draw.

Lucky's Doughnuts – 2902 Main Street / (604) 872-4901
I didn't think I liked donuts that much, but apparently I was wrong. I'm mostly into the simpler ones—plain glazed, and whatever fruit jelly they have in season—but I make an exception for the peanut butter and jelly, which is incredible.

Lemonade Gluten Free Bakery – 3385 Cambie Street / (604) 873-9993
I would never lead you to a gluten free bakery unless it was significantly better than most normal bakeries. You all know how seriously I take my pastries. I particularly like the cookies, but you'd be safe with anything.

Terra Breads – multiple locations
This is the local Old Reliable of fancy bread products. My favourites are the fruit and nut loaf, and the walnut bread, and I'll add a shoutout for my sister's number one, the green olive.

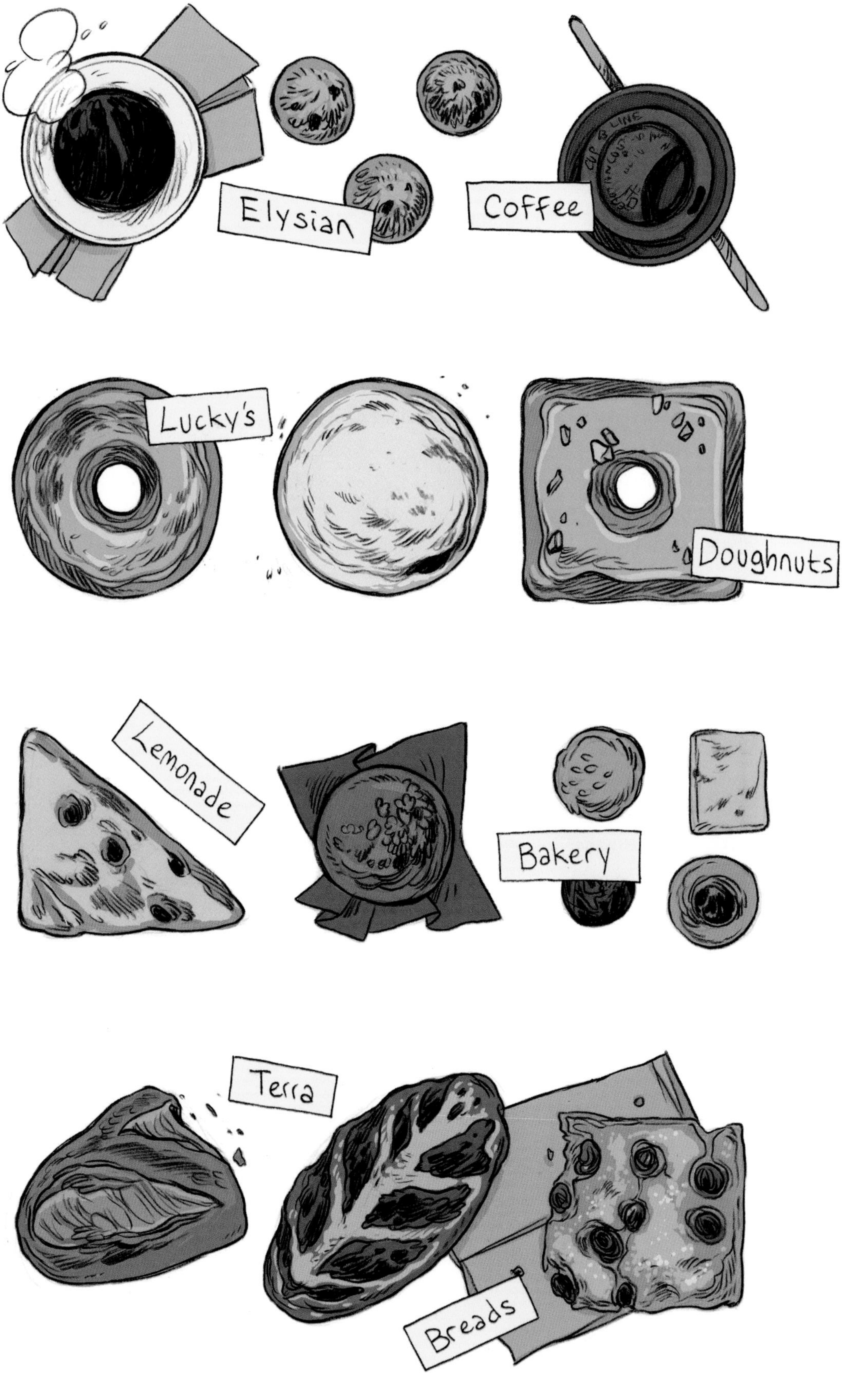
Elysian
Coffee
Lucky's
Doughnuts
Lemonade
Bakery
Terra
Breads

Lunch and Dinner

Shiro – 3096 Cambie Street / (604) 874-0027
Number one in my heart for fifteen years and counting. My favourite thing is the beni don (which is no longer on the menu, but worth immortalizing here).

Via Tevere Pizzeria – 1190 Victoria Drive / (604) 336-1803
My favourite sit-down pizza place. Best birthday dinner of my life.

Don't Argue! Pizzeria – 3240 Main Street / (604) 876-5408
Alternately, my favourite pick-up-and-take-home place. I almost always get the pesto ricotta.

Marutama Ra-men – 780 Bidwell Street / (604) 688-8837
I love chicken broth ramen, and this one is so creamy and so good. Also, perfect egg.

The Ramen Butcher – 223 E Georgia Street / (604) 806-4646
So rich! So delicious! I would kill to have a bowl of the spicy red ramen in front of me right now.

Hokkaido Ramen Santouka – 558 West Broadway / (604) 565-1770
I was overjoyed when this chain opened a store within walking distance of my apartment. Reliably tasty.

Five Guys – 635 Robson St / (604) 685-1585
I like a fast-food style burger better than the stiffer, less squashable restaurant version. Five Guys does it just right, plus you get a free little punnet of peanuts.

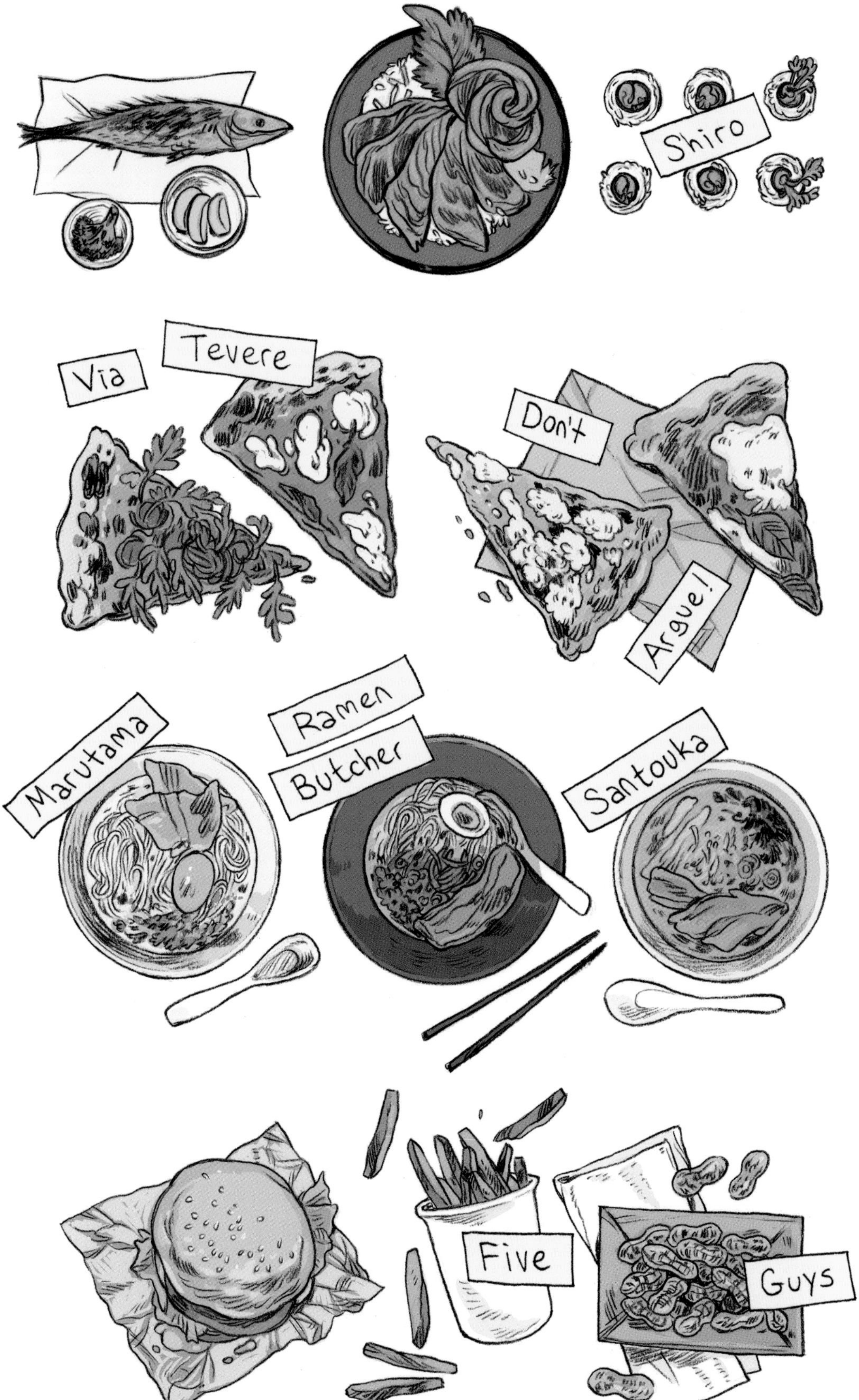
Shiro
Via Tevere
Don't Argue!
Marutama
Ramen Butcher
Santouka
Five Guys

Bai Bua – 1-2443 E Hastings Street / (778) 379-9699

I'm throwing this one in having tested it less extensively than the rest, but I feel confident. It's great: above and beyond tasty. Delicious coconut rice and curries.

Sal y Limon – Unit #5, 701 Kingsway Street / (604) 677-4247

I would perform dangerous trials of courage for these tacos—especially the lamb and cilantro.

Markets and Miscellaneous

Marché St. George – 4393 St George Street / (604) 565-5107

Lots of pleasing things to stock your larder with. They also do amazing lunches and pastries, if you feel like sitting down, and they make a fine, fine coffee. Altogether, it's one of the nicest spots in town.

Oyama Sausage – Granville Island Public Market / (604) 327-7407

I'm not much of a carnivore, but you can't make a fully rounded fantasy meal without fine rustic meats, and this is the spot for them. They have stuff like elk pepperoni and wild boar bacon that will make you feel like a dusty adventurer.

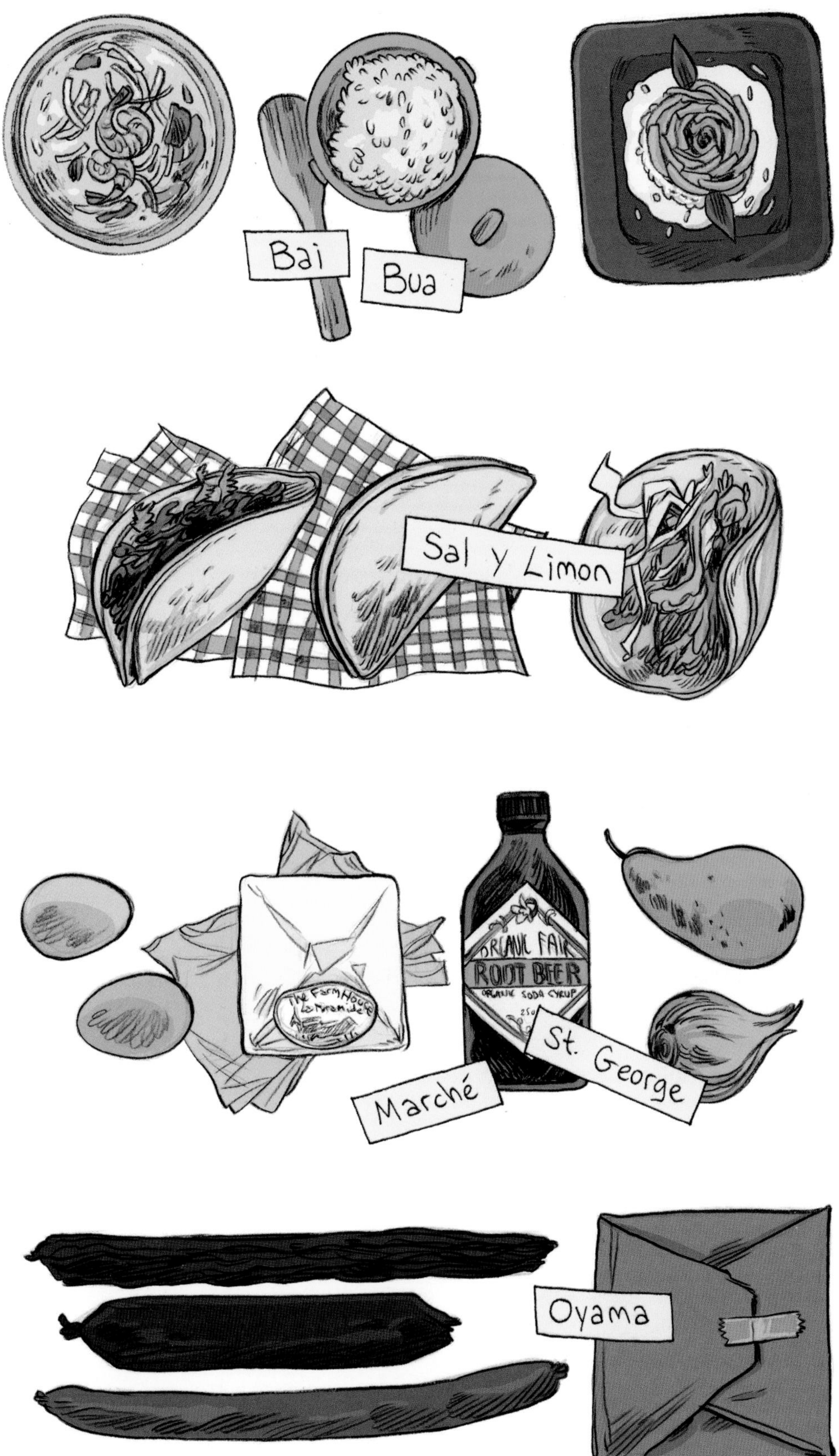
Bai
Bua
Sal y Limon
ROOT BEER
St. George
Marché
Oyama

Chilliwack River Valley Honey – Granville Island Public Market / (604) 823-7400
Vancouver has some really nice local honeys, but this company is my very
favourite. I particularly love the mountain, fireweed and thistle varieties. You can
find their stuff in fancy grocery stores, but they have the best selection at their
Granville Island nook.

Shinies and Choccy

Thomas Haas – 2539 West Broadway / (604) 736-1848
Reliably excellent chocolate, plus a full range of cakes and pastries and fancy
confections. I like the pâte de fruit. As an aside, every time I walk in here, I can't
help whispering, "can haas cheezburger?" Don't be like me.

Beta5 Chocolates – 413 Industrial Avenue / (604) 669-3336
I really debated with myself as to whether I'd include this place, because it's pricey
and I don't go there often. But then I rationalized it like this: if I was flush with cash
and really wanted to wow somebody with a show of affection, I'd buy them
chocolate from Beta5. So in it goes.

Amethyst Creations – 2746 West 4th Ave / (604) 736-7015
This is the platonic ideal of shiny store. It has the most appealing mixture of
impressive displays and tucked away boxes which you can rifle through for treasure.

The Crystal Ark – 1496 Cartwright St (Granville Island) / (604) 681-8900
If you happen to be at Granville Island, drop in to ogle the giant display crystals.

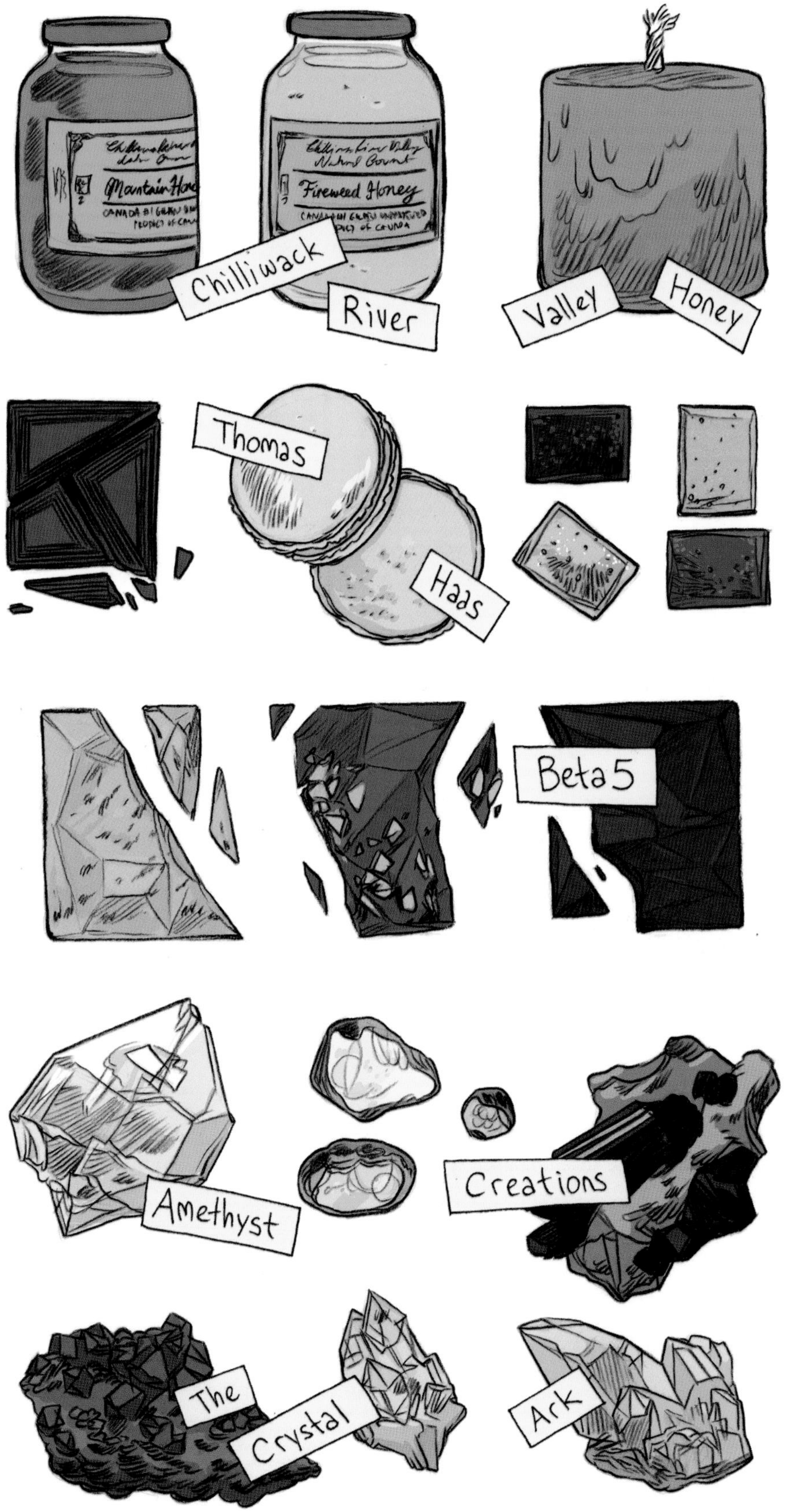
Fireweed Honey
Chilliwack
River
Valley
Honey
Thomas
Haas
Beta 5
Amethyst
Creations
The
Crystal
Ark

Acknowledgements

I was inspired by many designers while working on Hchom. Here is a list of those I've referenced explicitly.

Clothing and Jewellery

Acne Studios
67, 74, 90, 107

Anna de Courcey
40, 115

Barbour x Tokito
53

Borne
43, 68

Callisto Jewellery
103

Dries Van Noten
76, 104, 109, 115

Engineered Garments
60, 66, 90, 93, 103

Erin Templeton
73, back cover

Fortnight
72

Kika N.Y.
114

Lewis Leathers
45

Luxirare
46

N.D.C.
84, 86

Peppercotton
97

Roxanne Assoulin
40, 81, 115

S.N.S. Herning
85, 141

Southern Field Industries
72, 145

Valentino
111

Yoshi Kondo
54

Zeha Berlin
88, 90, 97, 145

Misc.

Dickie's Ginger Ale
29

Earnest Ice Cream
30

Finnska Licorice
89

Free and Easy Magazine
89

Opinel
86, 91

Raincoast Crisps
31

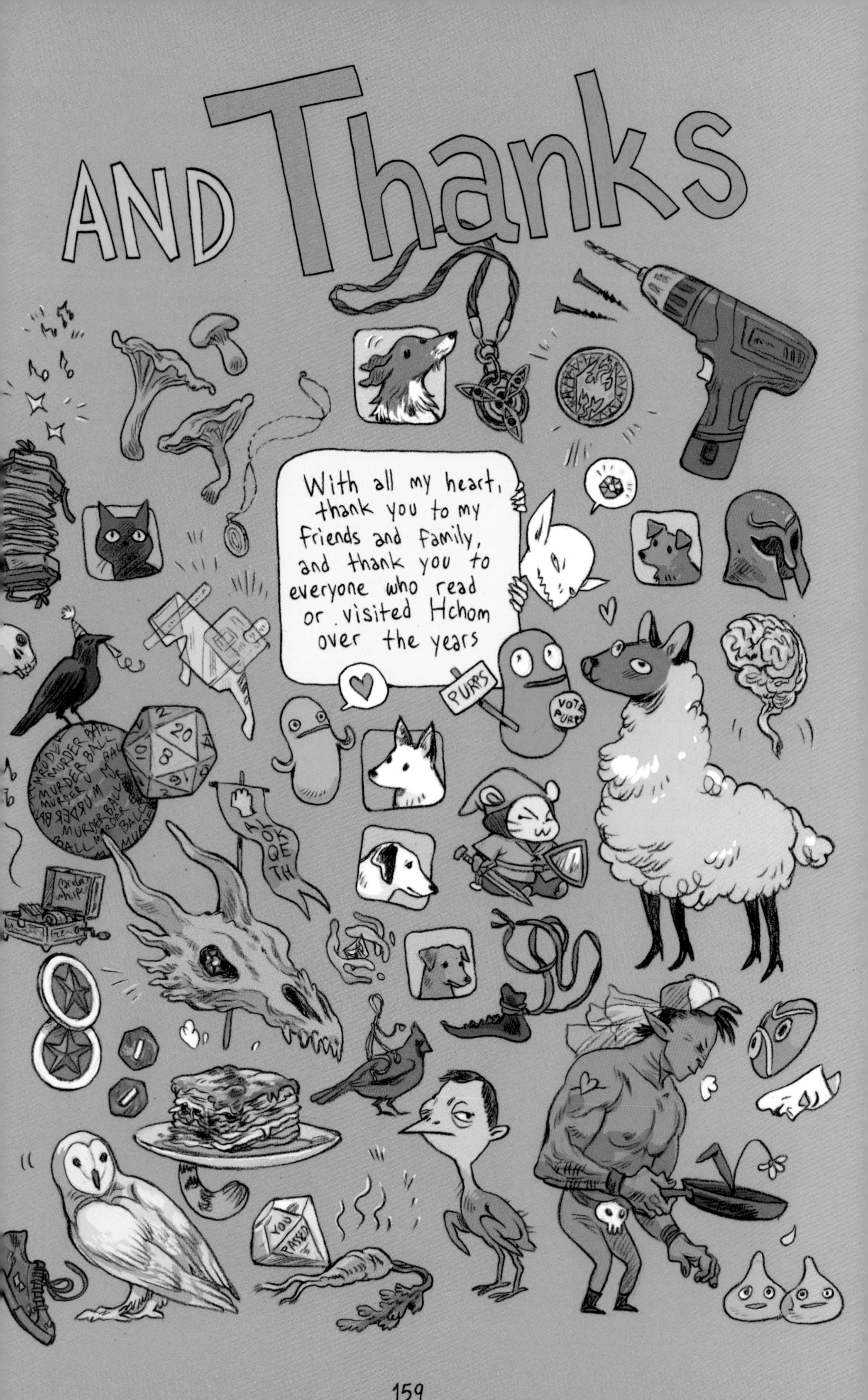
AND Thanks
With all my heart, thank you to my friends and family, and thank you to everyone who read or visited Hchom over the years
PURPS
VOTE PURPS
MURDER BALL
20
8
YOU PASSED

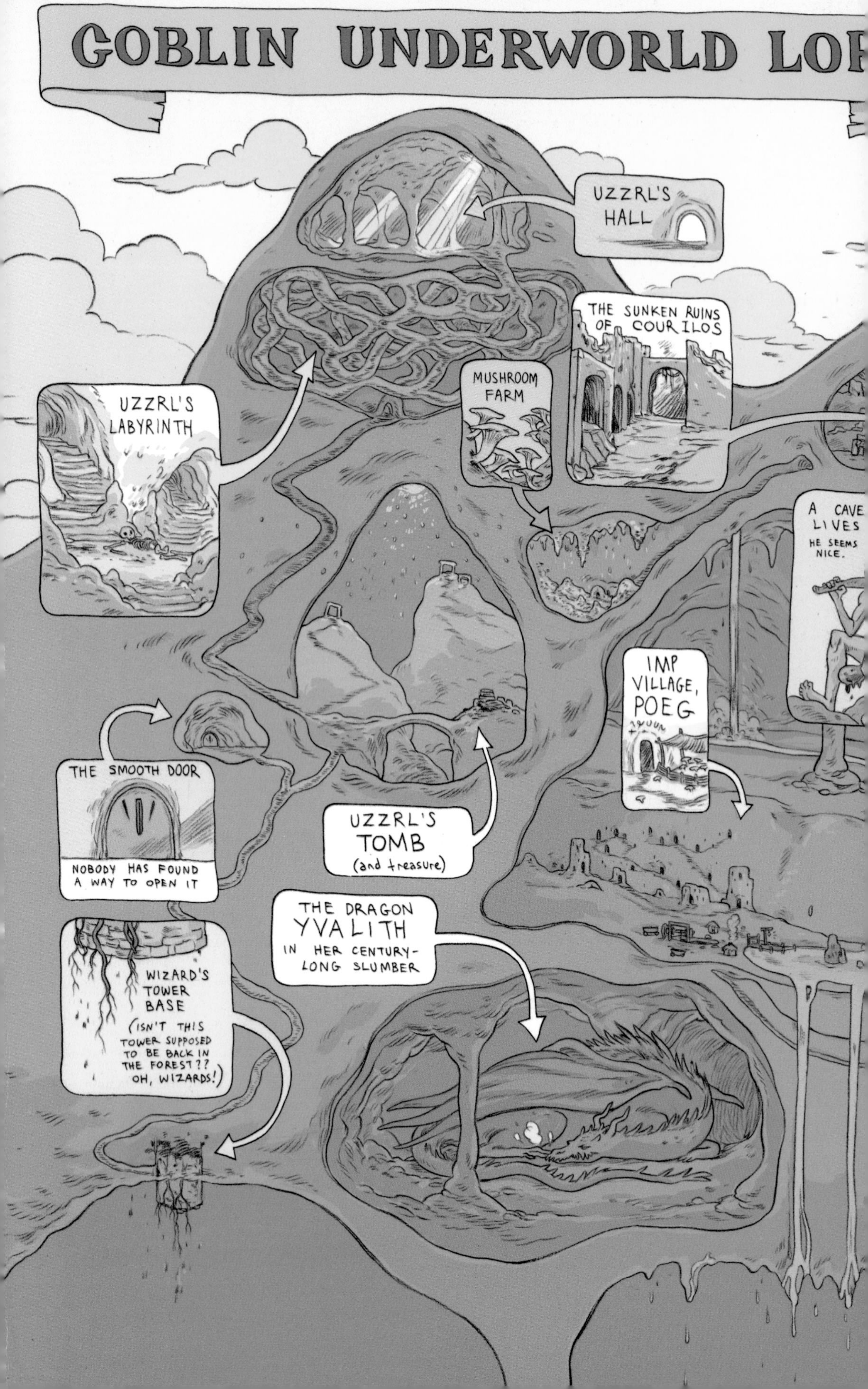
GOBLIN UNDERWORLD LO
UZZRL'S HALL
THE SUNKEN RUINS OF COURILOS
MUSHROOM FARM
UZZRL'S LABYRINTH
A CAVE LIVES
HE SEEMS NICE.
IMP VILLAGE, POEG
THE SMOOTH DOOR
NOBODY HAS FOUND A WAY TO OPEN IT
UZZRL'S TOMB (and treasure)
THE DRAGON YVALITH IN HER CENTURY-LONG SLUMBER
WIZARD'S TOWER BASE (ISN'T THIS TOWER SUPPOSED TO BE BACK IN THE FOREST?? OH, WIZARDS!)